Glittering parties
passionat

Regency

High-Society
Affairs

They're the talk of the Ton!

The Unruly Chaperon
by Elizabeth Rolls

&

Colonel Ancroft's Love
by Sylvia Andrew

The Regency

HIGH-SOCIETY AFFAIRS

Regency

HIGH-SOCIETY
AFFAIRS

Elizabeth Rolls &
Sylvia Andrew

*M&B™ and M&B™ with the Rose Device
are trademarks of the publisher.
Harlequin Mills & Boon Limited, Eton House,
18-24 Paradise Road, Richmond, Surrey TW9 1SR*

First published in Great Britain in 2003

REGENCY HIGH-SOCIETY AFFAIRS
© Harlequin Books S.A. 2009

The publisher acknowledges the copyright holders of the
individual works as follows:

The Unruly Chaperon © Elizabeth Rolls 2003
Colonel Ancroft's Love © Sylvia Andrew 2003

ISBN: 978 0 263 87555 3

052-0809

*Printed and bound in Spain
by Litografía Rosés S.A., Barcelona*

The Unruly Chaperon
by
Elizabeth Rolls

Award-winning author **Elizabeth Rolls** lives in the Adelaide Hills of South Australia in an old stone farmhouse surrounded by apple, pear and cherry orchards, with her husband, two smallish sons, three dogs and two cats. She also has four alpacas and three incredibly fat sheep, all gainfully employed as environmentally sustainable lawnmowers. The kids are convinced that writing is a perfectly normal profession, and she's working on her husband. Elizabeth has what most people would consider far too many books, and her tea and coffee habit is legendary. She enjoys reading, walking, cooking, and her husband's gardening. Elizabeth loves to hear from readers, and invites you to contact her via e-mail at books@ elizabethrolls.com

Chapter One

'Uncle Roger, let me be quite certain I have understood you correctly.' Lady Winter stood in the drawing room of her uncle's house, Broughton Place, carefully drawing off her York tan gloves, having dutifully kissed Lord Pemberton on the cheek.

'Aunt Pemberton wrote to me, asking me to come and stay with her during her approaching confinement, but now you tell me she wishes me to act as chaperon to Milly. At some house party.' Lady Winter's tone did not suggest that she viewed this disposal of her time at all charitably.

Tall and elegant in her rich brown, twill carriage dress, nothing in her dignified air or posture called to mind the rather gawky and shy Miss Matilda Arnold who had married Viscount Winter some seven years earlier. Her uncle, however, saw no difference.

'Now, see here, Miss—' Lord Pemberton began to bluster.

Lady Winter broke in. 'Surely Aunt Casterfield was chaperoning Milly this past Season? What has become of her? I should have thought that you would regard her as far more suitable than my poor self.'

The unarguable truth of this last remark did little to placate Lord Pemberton. He swelled dangerously. 'Now, see here…'

'Some fearsome scandal has made her unwillingly, or unfit, to continue her duties, perchance?' mused Lady Winter hopefully. 'Or have Milly's suitors shocked her so much that she must retire from the lists?'

'Her mother-in-law!' snapped Lord Pemberton, plainly goaded beyond endurance.

Lady Winter raised incredulous eyebrows. '*Old* Lady Casterfield has caused a scandal? Goodness me! How very shocking. Do you know, at eighty-eight, I should have thought she would be more up to snuff.'

'She's dying!' Lord Pemberton ground out.

Lady Winter affected surprise. 'Dying? There's nothing scandalous in that.'

Lord Pemberton practically had a seizure. 'My sister,' he snarled, 'very properly feels that, in such a situation, her mother-in-law's claim rates more highly than Milly's.'

Lady Winter gave this due consideration, and finally pronounced, 'Very proper indeed. But I still don't see quite where I come into your calculations. And, if I do, why I was not even consulted.'

Teeth audibly grinding, Lord Pemberton began. 'Your aunts and I do not see that it makes the least difference to *you*, where you are—'

His undutiful niece interrupted in tones of calm indifference, 'Very likely not, sir. But I am not to blame for your lack of percipience. You tell me that you have committed me to attend a house party, as Milly's chaperon, without even the courtesy of asking me?'

Lord Pemberton glared at her and attempted to assert his authority. 'You're our niece and ward, miss, and you'll do your duty!'

Lady Winter smiled sweetly. 'I fear you are mistaken sir. I'm no longer your ward, but rather Jonathan's widow. And my *duty* is to our daughter. Furthermore I am five and twenty and my own mistress. While naturally I have every sympathy for Aunt Casterfield's dilemma, so far as I am concerned the decision as to whether or not I attend this house party is entirely mine. And at the moment I am not at all inclined to do so.' She smiled even more sweetly. 'No doubt you will inform me of the venue, the hostess, and what arrangements have been made for my daughter, in your own good time so that I may make a final decision. Now I am weary and should like to retire for a rest before dinner. You may tell me all about it later.'

She dropped her uncle a slight curtsy and glided from the room, leaving a stunned and furious peer behind her. Lord Pemberton had seen little of his niece in the years since her marriage. Lady Pemberton had seen even less. Very much occupied with her own lyings-in, she took little notice of a niece that she actively disliked, and had not even attended on Lady Winter when her only child, Anthea, was born.

Having presented her husband with a son first, Lady Pemberton had safely dismissed the birth of the Honourable Anthea Cavendish as a matter of little consequence.

'How like that undutiful girl to have a daughter first,' had been her comment when the news arrived and she gave it no more thought, beyond directing her eldest daughter, Miss Amelia, to write to her cousin and say as little as was proper.

Lord Pemberton fumed and fulminated on his misfortune in having been forced to house such a girl as he poured himself a generous tot of brandy. Here was Amelia set to make the catch of the year—of the decade! And Miss Matilda—humph, *Lady Winter*—thought she could overset all their plans. Not a doubt but what widowhood had gone to her head. So she thought she could ride roughshod over them all, did she? Not while he had breath in his body!

He paced back and forth in front of the fireplace, recalling all the means he had used in the past to enforce his intransigent niece's obedience. Grimly he pondered. He'd even brought her to heel over her marriage to Viscount Winter. The same methods should work now.

Lady Winter, holding on to the rags of her dignity and temper with difficulty, ascended the main staircase of her ancestral home and headed straight for the best spare bed-chamber. Not unsurprisingly she discovered it to be inno-cent of her own baggage and that of her daughter. She smiled, consideringly, and tugged at the bell pull imperi-ously.

Five minutes later the startled housekeeper came in. 'What in the…oh! It's *you*, Miss Tilda!'

Lady Winter nodded and said, 'That's right, Mrs Penny. Has my luggage not yet been brought up?' Bright interest sheathed this artless question.

Mrs Penny blinked. 'Well, of course it has, Miss Tilda!' She encountered a haughty gaze and amended, 'My…my lady. The mistress gave orders that it was to be put in Miss Amelia's room, like always.'

Feigning innocence, Lady Winter stared in well-simulated astonishment, a mobile brow rising in haughty inquiry. 'And what use do you imagine Miss Amelia has for my belongings? Have them brought here, if you please. And precisely where is Miss Anthea?'

Floored by this defiance from one who had never said so much as boo to a goose, let alone defied her aunt, Mrs Penny opened and closed her mouth several times. 'Miss Anthea is in the nursery…with…with the other children.'

Lady Winter seemed to consider that. 'Oh. Visiting her cousins. Very well. But she may sleep here in the dressing room. Please see to all that, Mrs Penny. And I should very much like a cup of tea. Thank you.'

Somehow Mrs Penny found herself outside the door without quite knowing how she had got there. She shook her head in amazement. Marriage had certainly changed Miss Tilda, that it had!

As soon as the door shut behind Mrs Penny, Lady Winter, *née* Matilda Arnold, sank into a chair and breathed a sigh of relief. Really, this business of being assertive and sticking up for herself was exhausting. It *was* fun, though. Never had she imagined just how put out her uncle would be. Let alone poor Penny! Still, it wasn't over. She had yet to encounter her aunt.

She set her jaw mulishly. She was damned if she was going to run in their harness ever again. Certainly not for any plot to catch Amelia a rich husband. No, she would stay to assist her aunt, or if, as seemed likely, that affecting plea for support had been merely a ploy to lure her into their net, she could always leave for Leicestershire tomorrow. Well, maybe the day after, since the horses needed resting.

Her luggage and Anthea's arrived within fifteen minutes along with her maid, Sarah.

Barely had the door closed behind the footman who had brought the trunks than Sarah shot an amused glance at her mistress. 'I take it ye're set on puttin' 'em all on end, milady?'

Tilda simply grinned and said, 'Why not? Being polite and submissive never worked, so...'

The door opened again and a slender child of five, clutching a doll, came in.

'Mama, am I to sleep in the nursery? Great-Aunt Pemberton says that I must be there at all times and that I must sleep with Cousin Maria.' Worried hazel-brown eyes pleaded for a stay of execution.

Tilda laughed and held out her arms. 'You will need to be in the nursery with the other children when I cannot be with you, but you are to sleep in the dressing room here.'

A relieved sigh broke from Anthea. She flew across the

room and hugged her mother. 'Oh, good. Cousin Maria wanted to have Susan in *her* bed!'

'And what did you say to that?' asked Tilda, dropping a kiss on the brown curls so like her own. She cast a warning glance at Sarah.

Later. She didn't want Anthea caught up in the bitterness between herself and the Pembertons.

'I said she couldn't, and came to find you,' said Anthea, snuggling closer.

'Good girl,' said Tilda. 'Let's unpack and get everything sorted out, then we can have a story before you go back to the nursery for supper. I'll come up and put you to bed between courses.'

By the time she went down to dinner, Tilda had her plan of action worked out. It was simple, guaranteed to be effective, and, most importantly, would infuriate her family. She smiled into the looking glass and observed the stranger there with relief.

She *had* changed. Beyond colouring, there was little resemblance between the gangling, dowdy girl of seven years ago and the elegant matron who gazed back at her. Of course she was still far too tall, but at least she no longer tripped over her own shadow. Instead of the very plain scraped-back styles her aunt had insisted on for her, glossy brown curls were piled high on her head and confident golden brown eyes stared from under delicately arched brows.

She might not be a beauty, but she had improved. She had filled out for one thing, so the gown of deep green satin clung and shifted against her generous, yet slender curves in a most satisfactory way. It was cut quite discreetly over her bosom, but she could not think it at all a suitable gown for the chaperon of a young girl.

A fact which Lady Pemberton was at pains to point out the moment she set foot in the drawing room.

Resplendent in puce satin, she stared in outrage at the elegant creation swathing her niece's graceful figure. 'Good heavens, girl! That's not the sort of gown a chaperon wears!'

Tilda stepped back mentally to make way for Lady Winter, who raised one eyebrow, the same one that had annihilated Mrs Penny, and said languidly, 'No, it's not. How clever of you to notice. Good evening, ma'am. I trust you are well. My uncle said you were resting when I arrived so I didn't disturb you.'

Ignoring this greeting, Lady Pemberton said, 'And I understand you've set yourself up in the best spare bedchamber. Well, you may stay there for the night, but in the morning you must move back to your cousin's chamber. The guest chamber is for our guests!'

Lady Winter disposed herself gracefully in a *bergère*. 'Really? I had no idea that you were planning to entertain so close to your confinement, ma'am.' She cast a surprised glance at her aunt's very swollen belly. And smiled gently. 'You know, I cannot think that Amelia will welcome both her cousins in her room.'

Lady Pemberton frowned. 'What is this nonsense? Your daughter, Matilda, may stay in the nursery where she belongs. I'll have no spoiling.'

More than a hint of steel crept into Lady Winter's voice. 'I beg your pardon, ma'am, but I will order Anthea's life as *I* see fit. Naturally she will be with the other children during the day, but she is used to being within call of me at night.'

At this inopportune moment his lordship came in. Lady Pemberton enlisted his support at once.

'My lord! I must insist! Here is your niece, quite the grand lady! She has the insolence to insist on the best spare chamber!'

Her spouse immediately bent a threatening glare upon his niece and unleashed a hectoring tirade that would have reduced Miss Matilda Arnold to tearful obedience seven years earlier. He raged at her impudence, her undutiful behaviour, her ingratitude and finally said, 'You'll go the same way as your mother! Mark my words!'

Lady Winter sat back and listened with no more than bright-eyed interest. Even his final taunt failed to bring a blush to her cheeks. She commented merely, 'In that case, I'm stunned that you consider me a suitable chaperon for Amelia. If you've thought better of it, I'll remove my polluting presence from Broughton Place as soon as my horses are rested.' A faint smile curved her lips. 'In the meantime, I shall remain where I am.'

Lord Pemberton pulled up short and stared in disbelief. He was prevented from any further explosions by the entrance of his eldest daughter, Amelia, and his eldest son, Thomas.

A glance was enough to inform anyone that the pair were brother and sister. Both had dark curly hair and the bright blue eyes that in Lady Pemberton had faded somewhat. But whereas Amelia had inherited her mother's petite daintiness, Tom had favoured his father's height.

Turning to greet her cousins, Tilda thought that the years had not reneged on the early promise of beauty Amelia had shown. The rippling dark curls and vivid blue eyes were as startling as ever. Her figure was perfection. Small, yet beautifully proportioned, with just that hint of fragility that so many gentlemen seemed to appreciate.

For an instant she felt a gangling, awkward girl again, constantly being compared unfavourably with her far prettier cousin. But the stunned look of admiration on Tom's face as he surged forward to greet her swept all her nerves aside.

'Tilda!' He took her in a bear hug. 'I swear I wouldn't have recognised you!' He held her away at arm's length. 'You look famously. That green suits you. They'd better not send *you* to chaperon Milly. His Grace might decide he prefers you!'

A delighted chuckle broke from her. One that very few besides her daughter and eldest cousin had ever heard. 'Oh, Tom! What a Banbury story! As though anyone would prefer me to Milly.' She turned to Amelia and said sincerely, 'You look lovely, Milly. I need not ask how *you* go on!'

Amelia sniffed and said, 'I really prefer to be called Amelia now that I am out and grown up. Milly sounds so childish!'

'Oh stubble it, Milly,' recommended Tom with brotherly candour. 'Why, here's Tilda, looking as fine as five pence, a Viscountess to boot, and she don't fuss about her name!'

He turned back to his cousin. 'Tell me. Are those capital bays in the stables yours? And the grey mare?'

Tilda nodded, a faint twinkle in her eyes. 'Oh, yes. But I fear Frosty won't be quite up to your weight!'

Tom sighed. 'More's the pity, but those bays! Complete to a shade!'

The boyish longing in his tones made her smile. 'If you wish and my uncle permits, they may be harnessed to a phaeton or curricle tomorrow and you may try their paces.' She paused and added meaningfully, 'Once I am persuaded that you can handle them!'

Tom blushed and grinned self-deprecatingly, but his father stared. 'And pray tell, who is to make the decision as to whether Tom is able to handle this pair?'

Calm hazel eyes met his glare. 'I thought I made that clear, sir. I will.'

'Not in any carriage of mine, you won't!' pronounced Lord Pemberton awfully. 'Damned if I'll have a chit of a girl overturning my sporting carriages! You'll let Tom try those horses and there's an end of it.'

Tom flushed scarlet and shot an apologetic look at Tilda as though expecting to see her wilting under his father's fire.

She raised her brows and said bluntly, 'I'm afraid not, sir. They are my horses, and, since I've had no opportunity to see Tom drive since he overturned me in a mere gig eight years ago, I must decline to allow him to drive them alone until I am sure he is able to handle them.'

'Good God!' Lady Pemberton was scandalised. 'Do you set yourself up to know better than your uncle?'

'No, ma'am,' responded Tilda. 'But I certainly know my own horses better than he does. I will risk neither their knees nor Tom's neck. And do tell me, what does one have to do to be offered a drink?'

Tom laughed and said, 'You've done it, Tilda. What can I offer you? Ratafia?'

She shuddered artistically. 'No, I thank you. Jonathan was very particular in educating me. I would prefer Madeira.'

Pemberton's frown was darkling. 'In *my* day, a young woman—'

Mocking hazel eyes tilted up at him. 'Dear sir, don't say that. Why, anyone would imagine you were old enough… to…well, to be my husband!'

A stunned silence greeted this pointed reference to the fact that the late Lord Winter had been some thirty-five years his eighteen-year-old bride's senior. It was broken by Lady Pemberton.

She bridled and said, 'You were lucky to receive *that* offer!'

'I'm sure I was,' agreed Lady Winter pensively. 'Now, tell me all about Amelia's season. Your second season, is it not, Amelia? My! And not yet betrothed? Why, I was snapped up after merely *half* a season. Was I not, ma'am? Dear Jonathan positively beating a track to the door. Ah, thank you, Tom.' She directed a charming smile at her cousin and sipped the Madeira thoughtfully.

Amelia drew an angry breath. 'I see how it is. You're

jealous because I'm prettier. Because I have received more offers than you—'

She was gently interrupted. 'Not at all, Amelia. You are to be felicitated. And how many offers have you received?'

Before Lady Pemberton could frown her into silence, Amelia blurted out, 'Four! Five if you count his Grace!'

'Four!' Lady Winter smiled. 'You are indeed fortunate to have your choice. And here was I, thinking that the men in London must be blind that you are still unwed. You see, I thought it was imperative to accept the *first* offer in order that money might be hoarded for the next girl's come-out.'

'Oh, but that was Lord Walmisley!' protested Amelia. 'He is far too old. Why, he must be forty if he's a day!'

'Forty!' marvelled Lady Winter. 'That *is* quite an age. Dear me, I'm surprised poor Jonathan managed the walk back down the aisle.' She paused thoughtfully. 'Let alone the wedding night.'

Shrieking silence followed this, to be broken by Lady Winter who appeared to have lunched on shrapnel.

'And may one know which Duke Amelia has on a string?' inquired Lady Winter in dulcet tones. 'I collect it *is* a Duke that she has in her sights, and not a widowed Archbishop. You did say *his Grace*, did you not, Tom?'

Her dazed cousin nodded. 'Er, yes. St Ormond.'

There was an infinitesimal pause. 'Dear me,' said Lady Winter brightly. 'That *is* quite a conquest. Well worth passing over poor old Walmisley for. And just think; his Grace cannot be a day over six and thirty.'

At this point Providence took pity on Lord and Lady Pemberton by permitting their butler to announce dinner.

Dinner was not a success. Lord Pemberton's attempts to bring his niece to a sense of her iniquities were thoroughly hampered by the presence of the servants, while Lady Winter's barbed tongue appeared to run on wheels. She said nothing indiscreet, but it was plain that she was taking the greatest pleasure in mercilessly baiting her uncle and aunt.

By the time the ladies withdrew, Lady Pemberton was stiff with fury. Barely had the drawing room door closed behind them than she launched into a comprehensive condemnation of Tilda's manners and style.

Lady Winter sat back and listened with seeming attention. Only at the end, when Lady Pemberton paused to gauge the effect of her attack, did she speak. And then rather absent-mindedly.

'I do beg your pardon, ma'am. My mind was wandering. Could you repeat that? Oh, not all of it,' as Lady Pemberton gasped in disbelief. 'Perish the thought! Just the last little bit. You know, the bit about my not being fit to chaperon anyone. That *did* command my attention.'

Milly's gasp of amazement at her cousin's temerity was interrupted by the timely entrance of her father and brother.

His lordship came straight to the point. Directing a threatening frown at his niece, he said, 'I hope you have come to your senses and realise that your place is to do as you are told and abide by our judgement.'

'But of course, sir,' said Lady Winter with a mocking smile. 'My aunt has just informed me that I am unfit to chaperon anyone. I am more than happy to abide by that judgement.'

For a moment it seemed likely that Pemberton would fall victim to an apoplectic fit. His eyes bulged and his face went an unbecoming shade of purple.

Lady Winter took advantage of his momentary incapacity to press her advantage. She spoke in a soft, but deadly, tone. 'You see, my lord, I am no longer a chit of a girl, dependent upon you for anything. Frankly, I neither desire nor need your goodwill. Unbeknownst to yourselves, you set me free by forcing my marriage to Jonathan. I am an independently wealthy woman and I can do as *I* damn well please.'

She paused for breath and continued in a chilly voice, 'I came, not because you ordered it, but because I felt that the request made for my assistance during my aunt's lying-in was perfectly reasonable, and that I ought not, as a woman, refuse... And—' her voice shook slightly '—because I thought that you might at long last have discovered some slight affection for me. But I will not submit to being bullied or manipulated. If that is how you mean to go on, then Anthea and I will be leaving almost immediately.'

Lord Pemberton gave a scornful bark of laughter. 'Wealthy! You may choose to think your jointure wealth, but I can assure you that it will not go far if you continue to waste the ready on your back the way you must be.' His eyes raked the green satin gown, the expensive reticule and dainty satin slippers.

Lady Winter stared back incredulously. 'You really didn't know? You paid so little attention to the man you married me to, that you knew nothing of his capacity to support me?'

Her uncle shrugged. 'Everyone knew that Winter's estates were well enough. But you can't tell me that after providing for his daughter, he was able to leave you much. And tied up against your *possible* remarriage, no doubt.' His tone suggested that he saw such an eventuality as exceedingly remote.

Genuine amusement crept into Lady Winter's mocking smile, which deepened as she spoke. 'You really shouldn't let appearances blind you, sir. Despite the lack of ostentatious display to impress people whose opinion he couldn't have cared less about, Jonathan was extremely wealthy. That little jaunt to India in his youth was rather profitable, apparently, and quite independent of the title and estate, of course. He left half of it to me, whether or not I remarry.'

Tom was the first to recover his breath. 'Is this true, Tilda? You're not bamming us?' His voice held sincere, unalloyed delight.

She nodded.

'You're a wealthy widow?'

She nodded again, still with that faintly mocking smile lifting the corner of her delicately cut mouth. 'Shockingly wealthy, Tom.'

Savagely, Lord Pemberton broke in. 'No doubt you'll run through it in no time!'

She shook her head. 'Oh, no. Jonathan made quite sure I learnt how to manage my investments. And, until I am thirty-five, his heir is my principal trustee. He considered it…likely, shall we say…that he would predecease me. He always took his responsibilities very seriously. I am entirely capable of looking after myself.'

Her next shot was deadly. 'So, you see, asking me to chaperon Amelia is not at all a good idea. After all, even had my looks not improved slightly in seven years, I am now wealthy enough to give the most exacting of men a case of…selective blindness…to go with their…er… selective deafness, you know.'

Lady Pemberton gritted her teeth. Audibly. 'Then you intend to remarry?'

Lady Winter put her head on one side. A considering look crept into the golden eyes. 'I suppose I might. But really, I don't see the need.' One dark brow lifted suggestively. 'After all, the possibilities as a widow are *far* more appealing!'

'Why, you little *slut*!' exploded Lady Pemberton.

Milly blinked.

That dark brow arched even further. 'My dear ma'am, whatever can you mean? After all, there is not the slightest need for me to tie myself up in matrimony, depriving some poor girl of a husband. Besides, I like being my *own* mistress.' She smiled cheerfully, apparently impervious to the atmosphere of scandalised resentment. 'Anyway, enough of all this. I am a trifle fagged and will go up now. Goodnight.'

She left the field littered with dead and dying. Four pairs of eyes watched her go—two full of furious resentment, one of dazed wonder…and one laden with confusion.

Oddly enough, her signal victory over her family did not occupy Tilda's thoughts for long. She checked on Anthea, soundly asleep in the dressing room, Susan clutched possessively to her breast. After bestowing a tender kiss on each, she wandered back to her bedchamber, stripped off her gown and slipped into a silken nightgown and peignoir. She wriggled her shoulders appreciatively against the soft material. After years of wearing sensible, warm nightgowns of voluminous and unattractive aspect to appease her husband's fear of her contracting a chill, it was enormous fun to wear something frivolous and daring. Something that made her feel like a seductive hussy. Even if there was no one else to appreciate it. A state of affairs that she fully intended to maintain.

She tugged the bell and waited. Some ten minutes later Sarah came in.

'Here y'are, m'lady,' Sarah frowned. 'Lor', if I haven't told ye over an' over! I'm supposed to help you undress!' Bustling forward, she swept up the discarded gown and shook it out lovingly.

'Oh, stop that, Sarah!' said Tilda. 'For heaven's sake, you know I can manage for myself. Just tell me what they're saying in the servants' hall.'

Sarah sat down uninvited on the daybed, the gown cradled in her lap. 'All of a flutter at the difference in you, for starters. Most of 'em reckon it's a good thing.' Mildly, she commented, 'Must be quite a difference. Not havin' known you afore your marriage, I did just wonder.' Faint curiosity tinged her voice.

Tilda grimaced. 'I was the most browbeaten, pathetic excuse for a female that can be imagined. Not to mention the most gawky of Long Megs. I was used to trip over every-

thing and everyone.' She chuckled wryly. 'I daresay *Lady
Winter* is quite a shock to them all. Amazing what a difference clothes can make. Good. Now, what about this
Duke? St Ormond, I'm led to believe.' She said the name
lightly enough, but was conscious of the very slightest
tightening in her throat.

Sarah grinned. 'Seems to me the announcement ought to
've been in the papers already, the way they're talkin'. Miss
Pemberton's invited to a house party given by the Dowager
Duchess. Word is that it's a chance for his Grace to get to
know her before makin' an offer. They reckon as how he
was courtin' her in town. Dancin' at the balls, walkin' in
the park. Even came to see your uncle.'

Tilda considered. 'Very well. They want me to chaperon
her at this house party. Naturally my aunt cannot do so.
And had they asked me, rather than trying to bully me into
it, then I just might have consented. As it is, I rather think
we will be going home in a few days. Thank you, Sarah.
Go to bed. I'll ring for you in the morning.'

Sarah heaved herself to her feet and favoured her mistress with a grim smile. 'A Long Meg, eh? Don't sit up too
late!' After placing the silken gown tenderly in a closet,
she was gone, leaving Tilda to her thoughts.

Restlessly she paced up and down, the silken skirts of
her nightgown whispering around her ankles. St Ormond.
The name blazed in her mind. Seven years, and the name
could still conjure up that churning feeling of affronted
hurt, of anger and wounded pride. Seven years, and the very
name still had the same power over her, to enthral and
captivate.

Damn it! She was Lady Winter now! A wealthy and
passably attractive widow. Not the clumsy and painfully
shy débutante she had been. So why did the memory of a
childish fancy still affect her so deeply? A fantastical dream
that she had never taken seriously, even in her wildest
maiden fancies. It had not needed his Grace's unwitting

cruelty for her to realise that her path and his would not lie together, that he would never accord her a second glance. And that his first and only glance had left him unimpressed.

And she was not going to this beastly house party anyway, she thought, as she sat down on the chaise and curled her legs up under her night gown. So why was she shaking so much? Almost against her will, her memory drifted back to that dreadful night at the Seftons' ball... His Grace, as elegant as ever, in a superbly cut coat of blue superfine...she could still see the bright gold of its buttons...the diamond pin nestling in his elegantly tied cravat...powerful thighs encased in immaculate inexpressibles. Well over six foot, he towered over every man in the room, one of the very few she wouldn't have to stoop to dance with. His chestnut locks glowed with bronze lights and wicked green eyes narrowed as he laughed with a friend, the embodiment of a lonely and friendless maiden's dreams. The *parfait et gentil chevalier* of her imaginings.

She looked back at her younger self with gentle mockery, remembering how she had watched him from afar throughout the first weeks of her season, seeing him sought after, courted, flattered. Once he had reached down a book for her at Hatchard's; three nights before that he had actually stood up with her...

His intended partner, the lovely and graceful Lady Diana Kempsey, had been overcome by faintness at the start of their dance. He had returned her to her mama, and Tilda, with her usual half-full dance card, had been standing nearby with her aunt.

With his customary charm he turned and begged her to indulge him with a dance. 'Not the most flattering invitation you will ever receive, Miss Arnold, but I do beg you will accept!'

Accept? She smiled wryly as she remembered how she floated out to dance. He even knew her name! Speechlessly she placed her hand in his and felt the long fingers clasp hers. Unbelievably, it was a waltz. The scandalous dance had recently gained the approval of Almack's haughty patronesses, but due to her height, all five foot eleven of it, she was rarely solicited for the honour.

When she was, it became a species of musical torture. She could not fit her stride, her exuberant joy in the music, to the rather sedate young men with whom she danced. Invariably she stumbled, trod on their toes, bumped their shins, and her embarrassment made matters worse. So terrified was she that she could not even converse rationally.

With St Ormond she found her perfect partner. She felt it the moment his arms closed about her; a sense of rightness, of inevitability. His height suited her to perfection; she glided and twirled effortlessly in his embrace. And it went beyond physical comfort. She could even chat to him, responding to his banter and questions happily. She actually found herself telling him about her pet cat, Toby, raised by her from extreme infancy. St Ormond seemed to find her caustic description of raising an orphaned kitten in her bed hilarious, and had countered with a tale of raising an orphaned foal, now his favourite mare.

'Not that I raised her in my bed, of course. Mama would not hear of that. But I did spend a great many nights bedded down in her stall!'

All too soon the dance ended and his Grace returned her to Lady Pemberton, with a laughing injunction to be mentioned to Toby. And she responded in kind, asking him to give Sirene a carrot for her.

Lady Pemberton frowned mightily upon this exchange, calling her to order in a vicious undertone, telling her what a cake she was making of herself. That, in setting her cap at St Ormond, merely because he was too polite to snub her, she was shaming her family.

Tilda tripped over her next partner's feet and had to be taken home with a bloodied nose.

Three nights later Lady Pemberton relented from her

avowal never to take Tilda to another ball. Her lord's saner counsel had prevailed. How the devil were they to get the chit off their hands if she wasn't seen? And old Lady Pemberton was insisting that the girl be given a season—to silence the gossips. So she consented to take Tilda to the Seftons' ball.

His Grace of St Ormond was there, of course, but Tilda came nowhere near him until after supper, when she managed to withdraw to the retiring room for a few minutes to recover from a particularly gruesome dance with Lord Winter who was several inches shorter than she, and who had been painfully gracious about her assault on his toes.

Emerging from the retiring room when it filled with giggling young ladies, she slipped back to the ballroom and took refuge behind a potted palm. St Ormond had strolled by with his brother-in-law, Lord Hastings.

Their cheerful conversation still burnt in her memory.

'Really, Cris, here you have every charming débutante just itching to retrieve your handkerchief, and you tell me that not *one*, not even *one*, takes your fancy! You are becoming entirely too picky, my boy!' Lord Hastings twitted his friend with gentle sarcasm.

St Ormond shrugged and said, 'Take a closer look, James. There's really very little there. In most of them, anyway. Most of 'em aren't even interesting to dance with! All far too young! Now, take Miss Arnold for example! There's a chit who shouldn't have even been let loose in London...' The pair had moved away and the rest of his Grace's remarks were lost.

Thankfully lost. Seven years later she could still flush with humiliation for the naïve dreamer the eighteen-year-old girl had been, still remember the hurt. She'd come out from behind the palm, so white and shaking that even Lady Jersey, avidly gossiping nearby, noticed and took her to Lady Pemberton immediately. Somehow Tilda had made it through the rest of the evening, forcing herself to honour the few gentlemen on her dance card, forcing herself to respond to Lord Winter's kindly gallantry. Telling herself that St Ormond's thoughtless cruelty did not matter, that she had always known her dreams were insubstantial.

But it did matter, she found, when she finally buried her face in her pillow that night. In the cold light of his brutal assessment she could no longer indulge in the comfort of her daydreams, no longer lose herself in the fantasy where they wandered hand in hand in Arcadian delight. Instead of going to sleep dreaming of him, she cried herself to sleep, her dreams shattered into pathetic fragments. It might have been a hopeless dream, but at least it had been a comfort.

The next day her uncle had informed her that Lord Winter, a man thirty-five years her senior, had offered for her and that she was to marry him in three weeks, just as fast as the banns could be called. She had tried to rebel, terrified, revolted by the thought of marriage to a man she scarcely knew, a man slightly older than her uncle. Despairingly she saw herself trapped into a life even worse than the one she knew. Her uncle's tyranny replaced by the far more intimate tyranny of a husband.

Her rebellion had been doomed from the start. Unlike her mother, she had no one to take her side and, short of refusing to make her vows at the very altar, she could see no avenue of escape. Several beatings for impertinence had resolved her that, regardless of what the marriage bed involved, Lord Winter could be no worse than Lord and Lady Pemberton.

So she had married. And discovered that Jonathan Cavendish, Viscount Winter, was as kindly a man as ever lived. He treated his terrified bride with consideration and if her marital duties were initially extremely painful, at least with time they became merely boring.

Lord Winter was indulgent and, above all, treated her

with affectionate respect. She came in return to have a very real affection for him.

He had died some fifteen months ago, leaving her a very wealthy widow, with an equally wealthy four-year-old daughter. The estate and title had gone to his cousin, who had made it quite clear that he was only too delighted to have the Dowager Lady Winter quartered at the Dower House.

'Really, Tilda! Of course you must stay!' Max had expostulated when she had suggested that he and his wife might prefer her elsewhere once the period of her strict mourning was over. 'Jon practically ordered me to keep an eye on you, and Cassie and I would miss you dreadfully!'

She could not doubt the insincerity of their affection and so followed her own inclinations and stayed. At Winter Chase she was happy and protected. The people knew her and respected her. She had enough money to live in comfort, in luxury if she chose. And she had not the least use for society, or most of her family. Tom, the only one of her cousins to whom she had ever been close, was up at Oxford and spent the vacations with various friends. So the half-hearted commands to return to the bosom of her family were treated with the contempt they deserved. She strongly suspected that they had every intention of turning her into a drudge and very carefully kept the truth about her financial circumstances to herself.

That her marriage had turned out a blessing was due to no care of theirs. Indeed, in her more cynical moments the Dowager Lady Winter was inclined to wonder if they would have countenanced her marriage had they known the truth about the reclusive Lord Winter's wealth.

With a sigh she returned to the present. Nothing had changed. When the letter had come, requesting her to assist with the household during her aunt's tenth lying-in, she had felt it her duty to agree. She had been through one childbed herself and, despite her dislike for her aunt, could feel only sympathy for any woman facing her tenth.

Besides now that her period of strict mourning was over, she was beginning to find herself pestered by any number of men who plainly thought a generously dowered widow was just the thing to boost their sagging fortunes. And Tilda had absolutely no intention of ever marrying again.

The only problem was that she felt restless, confined— as though her safe, comfortable life was slowly choking her. Oh, she had Anthea and her independence—riches enough for any woman, even without the fortune Jonathan had left her. But what should she do with her independence? What use was it if she didn't use it?

So she had come, vowing that the confidence she had learnt over the years of her marriage should not desert her, that she would not become again the cowed and crippled creature she had been.

She had almost persuaded herself that this was a chance to heal the rift. To soften the loathing engendered by her mother's elopement with a young man of great charm and no fortune rather than marry a wealthy man twice her age. Since she had still been underage at the time, her marriage was only two months old when her baby was born. Her family had cast her off in disgrace and it had been with great reluctance that Lord Pemberton had received the orphaned five-year-old Matilda into his home. Indeed he had only done so because several of his sister's old friends, influential hostesses all, had kept on enquiring after the child.

Now, faced with the inescapable conclusion that she was to be manipulated and bullied into submission, Tilda had decided to hurl down the gauntlet. As far as she could see, Lady Winter was in an unassailable position. Even without the wealth Jonathan had left her, she was independent and did not need her family. Max and Cassie Winter considered her one of their closest friends. She was as happy as a grig.

So why on earth was she feeling so shaken up at the idea that she had been invited, however vicariously, to a house party hosted by his Grace the Duke of St Ormond?

A soft scratching at the door interrupted her singularly unavailing attempt to find an answer to this perplexing question.

Chapter Two

'Come in.' A puzzled glance at the clock on the chimneypiece confirmed that it was well after midnight. Who
on earth would want to speak to her now? Unless, of
course, her uncle wished to utter some specific threats…

Amelia's face, appearing hesitantly around the door, put
this unpleasant thought to flight.

'Milly! I…I mean, Amelia…what…?'

'Oh, don't call me that!' begged her cousin, coming fully
into the room. 'I still hate it, but Mama is so insistent that
I must be *Amelia* now. Tilda, is what you said true? That
they forced you to have only half a season to save the
money for me?'

Tilda flushed. She should not have said that in front of
Milly. There was no vice in the chit, she was merely
spoiled.

'No, Milly,' she said quietly. 'They didn't do it because
of that.'

'But they did cut your season short? As soon as Lord
Winter offered?' Milly's upset was evident.

'Yes.'

'But, why?'

Grimly Tilda faced the truth—the real reason her season
had been curtailed. Oh, Lord and Lady Pemberton had said

openly that they did not wish to waste money on a clumsy Long Meg, who had miraculously secured a respectable offer, money that could be better put aside for little Amelia and the other girls. So she had lashed out, hiding her grief at the truth. But the real reason was far more painful than that. A reason that had eaten at her heart for years before her season. One that she had dimly realised but had never put into words. Until the day her uncle told her that, whether she accepted Lord Winter or not, her season was over.

Incredulously she had stared at them. 'You hate me, don't you? All the discipline and...scoldings...it's not because you want to make sure I don't behave like Mama! It's because you hate me! Isn't it? *Isn't it?*' Rage at the injustice had flamed through her.

'Really, Matilda! Such intemperate language, such excessive emotion is to be deplored in a lady!' Her aunt's chilly rebuke had seared deep into her very soul. They had not even bothered to deny it.

At that moment she had made up her mind to marry Lord Winter. At least she would escape her family. He seemed kind enough. Nothing could be worse than this. And, besides, Lord Winter was over fifty. At untouched eighteen that ranked as extreme old age. The chances were that she would be a widow very soon and free to live her own life within the bounds set by society.

And so she had married, with widowhood as her aim.

She couldn't tell Milly all that. She knew that Lady Pemberton was genuinely fond of her children; that, despite Milly's irritation, she loved her mama. Tilda was not prepared to hurt by that means. It would be despicable.

'They don't like me, Milly,' she said gently. 'Because of my mother. They have always been afraid that I would take after her, disgrace them. So when Jonathan offered for me they...they insisted I accept...to...ensure nothing went wrong.'

'You didn't love him, did you?' It wasn't really a question.

'Not as you mean,' said Tilda. 'I did come to…care for him, in a friendly sort of way. He was very kind and considerate, you know.' She repressed a shudder at the memory of her wedding night, the awkwardness, her embarrassment, her revulsion at what was expected of her. No good could come of telling Milly any of that. With a younger man she was attracted to, or even in love with, things would doubtless be very different.

'Now, tell me all about St Ormond.' Somehow she forced her voice to remain light. 'I danced a waltz with him once, you know!'

'Did you?' asked Milly. 'Dancing the waltz with him is ghastly. He's so tall that I just can't keep up. And if he shortens his stride he treads on my toes!'

Tilda blinked. 'Poor man,' she said. It had never occurred to her that someone as elegant as St Ormond might be afflicted by his height in the same way she was. Milly *was* very small!

Her stare suggested that she thought Tilda had lost her mind. 'What about my toes?'

'They'll recover,' said Tilda with a faint grin. 'Try thinking about *his* mortification. How would you feel if your positions were reversed? If you were always feeling like a clumsy oaf with him?'

'Oh,' said Milly. Patently she had never exercised her imagination in this way before. 'I suppose you're right. Which brings me to what I came to say, to ask you. I have been speaking to Tom, and he said I must. Please, Tilda, will you come to this house party with me? Tom says you will know just how I should go on. That if I don't behave like a spoiled brat, you might agree.'

Tilda was aghast. 'Milly—'

'Please? I'm terrified. Apart from St Ormond, his mama, the Dowager, will be there and lots of other grand people.'

As Tilda shook her head, Milly bit her lip. 'Tom said Mama and Papa had set your back up so that you were liable to go straight home.'

'They did,' said her cousin drily. But that wasn't the real reason she quaked at the thought of attending this house party.

'Well, I'm apologising for them,' said Milly. 'And for being a brat at times,' she added generously. 'Please come with me.'

Tilda swore mentally. Aloud she asked, 'Do you like St Ormond?'

Milly flushed. 'Oh, yes. He's charming. And so handsome! He's the biggest catch of the season.'

'And how does he make you feel? When you're chatting? When he...touches you...?' Tilda had no idea if St Ormond would have attempted to kiss Milly yet, so she kept her questions general.

Milly blushed. 'He...he did try to kiss me once. I...I didn't like it at all. He scared me. I don't think he meant to, but he's so big!'

Tilda raged inwardly, *Oh, hell and the devil!*

Milly continued. 'And when we talk, well, I don't always quite catch his meaning, when he jokes. So I feel very uncomfortable. But he's very nice about it.'

Tilda nearly groaned aloud. *Worse and worse. At least I was never scared of Jonathan precisely. And I always understood him. In fact, he told me that was why he liked me. Oh, drat it! I'll have to go to this beastly party. Blast them all for landing Milly in this mess. And double blast St Ormond!*

Crispin Anthony Malvern, Duke of St Ormond, was pacing the Great Hall of Ormsby Park, his principal country residence, in a very unducal manner. His restlessness was due not so much to impatience at the tardiness of his intended bride, but to a powerful desire to be somewhere, anywhere, else. Hanging around the house on a bright summer's day was not his notion of fun. And he had been caught here all day as guests arrived.

True, they were family and did not expect him to do the pretty. Most of them had given him a cheery greeting and wandered off about their own pursuits, quite happy to make themselves at home. The Dowager, however, had insisted that he should be about all day to greet them. To his utter disgust, the carriage that must be bearing Miss Pemberton and her aunt had been spotted far down the avenue just after he handed his own Aunt Seraphina out of her antiquated and distinctly lopsided travelling coach.

'Damned thing's got a lean like a drunken sailor!' sniffed Lady Hollow. 'Have one of your people see to it, m'boy.' She had stalked up the shallow front steps, mightily resenting his supportive hand under her elbow. 'Not in m'grave yet!'

Crispin gritted his teeth, reminding himself that, had he not done so, she would have waxed lyrical over the omission, and decided that he'd done the right thing. After all, if the old girl took a tumble down the stairs she'd be quartered there for weeks. Politely he assured his aunt that her carriage would be seen to as a matter of urgency.

And now Miss Pemberton's carriage had been seen, rendering it useless to head back to the billiard room where his younger cousin Guy and his brother-in-law Hastings awaited him. He groaned as he paced up and down. Miss Pemberton was well enough, but her Aunt Casterfield was worse than Aunt Seraphina. At least the latter had a sense of humour.

Lady Casterfield, who had chaperoned her niece's second season, had very nearly put him off the whole idea of offering for Miss Pemberton. She was a holy terror, without the least leavening of humour in the lump. And she had made it perfectly plain that she did not consider his high degree or vast wealth in any way atoned for the scandalous reputation as a rake he had acquired over the years.

No doubt she would be playing her role of chaperon to the hilt. Making it impossible for him to have any opportunity to become better acquainted with Miss Pemberton. Just as she had all season in London. Damn it—he was intending to offer for the girl, had actually spoken to her father; and still he thought of the chit as *Miss Pemberton*! Surely it was about time he called her Amelia and she called him Crispin. Though doubtless Lady Casterfield would encourage her to use his title in bed. He shuddered to think of the likely result if she explained the duties of the marriage bed to her niece.

He could hear the carriage drawing up at the steps. Steeling himself to his fate, he went out under the portico to greet his guests of honour. His gaze narrowed, focused fully on the pair of sweating bays harnessed to the equipage. They were a far cry from the usual showy peacocks Lord Casterfield favoured. And they certainly weren't job horses. Blinking slightly, he switched his attention to the elegant grey mare hitched behind the chaise and the little grey Welsh gelding beside her. Good God! Surely Miss Pemberton—dash it all! *Amelia*—knew he could mount her perfectly satisfactorily? And what was the pony for? A dog-cart? He probably even had one of those collecting dust and spiders somewhere.

As his footman let down the steps of the chaise, Crispin affixed a welcoming smile to his face and waited for Lady Casterfield to descend.

To his utter stupefaction a small girl with a wealth of dark brown curls scrambled out and smiled sunnily up at the equally startled footman.

'Thank you,' piped the child. About five or so. Crispin assessed her dazedly. He'd seen enough of his sister's brood to hazard a reasonably accurate guess.

She was followed by a goddess. Or at least a very tall,

elegantly dressed woman, no doubt her mama, since there
was a striking resemblance between them. Dark brows
arched delicately over huge liquid golden eyes in a serenely
lovely face framed with silken brown curls. Her figure, ad-
mirably displayed by the well-cut carriage dress, was an
elegant combination of graceful lines and voluptuous
curves. All in all, she looked nothing like Lady Casterfield.
A fact that he assimilated with great approbation.

Just as he was thanking whatever gods had taken mercy
on him, the likely truth of the matter dawned on Crispin.
They must have the wrong house. Possibly, as his mind ran
over which of his neighbours might be expecting visitors,
the wrong county.

The descent from the chaise of Miss Amelia Pemberton
disabused him of this misapprehension.

She stared at him in obvious surprise. 'Oh! Your...your
Grace. I didn't expect *you* to be here!'

Crispin managed to choke back a moan of despair at this
singularly witless remark and said merely, 'I live here. Remember?'

He encountered a glare from the goddess that rocked him
to his toes. Wildly, he tried to remember which of the
Greek deities had been able to slay with a look. Whichever
one it was, she had been reincarnated right here on his
doorstep.

'What my cousin means is that she did not expect to find
your Grace adorning the front steps.' Her voice was divine
too; warm and husky, but with a hint of hauteur. And a
hint of familiarity—surely he'd heard it before?

'Oh...er...ah....' Crispin floundered. 'I was just greeting
my aunt. We saw your carriage so I...er...waited. No point
going back to the billiard room.'

He was stunned to hear himself sounding so totally at
sea.

The goddess, however, judging by the faint smile,

deigned to be amused at his expense. Her next words confirmed it.

'How romantically eager. So charming, your Grace.' The curve of her lips deepened. And his Grace wondered what they tasted like. Peaches, he'd bet, or possibly strawberries…something sweet, anyway…and probably hot.

Shocked at the direction of his thoughts, Crispin pulled himself together. Who in Hades was this woman?

'Perhaps you would be so good as to introduce your companion, Amelia,' he suggested as he accompanied them up the steps. 'While naturally delighted to welcome you both, I was expecting Lady Casterfield.' Encountering an indignant glance from his youngest guest, awaiting her elders with every indication of impatience at the top of the steps, he amended, 'I beg your pardon. I am delighted to welcome *all* of you.'

Amelia blinked up at him, patently surprised. 'This…this is my cousin, of course, your Grace. Mama wrote to you!'

'I beg to differ, Amelia,' he said very politely. 'Lady Pemberton wrote to *my* mother. Don't assume that I have been enlightened. All Mama saw fit to tell me was that you would arrive today.'

'Oh.' Amelia looked thoroughly flustered. 'Well, this is Tilda, I…I mean Lady Winter. She's my cousin.'

Crispin was conscious again of an odd feeling of recognition as he turned to Lady Winter. Somewhere, bone deep, he was sure he had met her before. That she had made an impression on him. The hazel eyes teased at his memory—beckoning…tugging… He shook his head slightly to clear it. He *couldn't* have met her before. The impression she was making on him now was not one he was likely to forget. Ever.

She was watching him, he realised. Calmly, but with a definite challenge in her bright eyes.

'The *Dowager* Lady Winter,' she added helpfully. It didn't help in the least. Because all his speculations about the taste of her lips suddenly stopped being academic. Given that this was almost entirely a family party, he'd been wondering just how he was to entertain his admittedly baser instincts. An unrelated widow had distinct possibilities…especially one this alluring.

Good God! Had his wits gone begging? Was he seriously contemplating the seduction of Amelia's *chaperon*? Imagining what it would be like to have her writhing under him, their limbs entwined, hearing her soft moans as he made love to her? He shook his head again, frantic to get some sense into it.

He forced himself to speak normally. 'And this, I take it, Lady Winter, is your daughter?' He smiled encouragingly at the child.

She smiled back. 'I'm Anthea,' she offered. 'And that—' indicating the pony behind the chaise '—is Henry. He's mine.' All the pride of ownership rang in her voice.

Crispin, who could remember the joy of his own first pony, responded promptly. Turning, he subjected the little grey to a searching appraisal, before saying, 'He's a beauty. Just the right stamp for a lady. Can he jump?'

Anthea looked a bit self-conscious. 'Well, *he* can, but Mama says I'm too little yet. But I'm getting bigger!'

Obviously a contentious issue, thought Crispin. He adopted guileful tact. Usually a safe bet with the ladies. 'I'm sure your mama will be the first to notice when you *are* big enough. In the meantime, come indoors. Henry will be well cared for, I assure you.'

Reeling from shock, he bowed them over the threshold, wondering just what else his mother might have concealed from him. He distinctly recalled making a number of pithy observances about Lady Casterfield only this morning. So why on earth had Mama neglected to mention the change of chaperon? On further reflection the reason was fairly plain. *His* Dowager had a streak of mischief a mile wide.

He was only surprised she hadn't managed to be on hand to witness his shock.

'Ah! We're all here, then. How simply lovely.'

Crispin bit his lip to hold back a laugh. The Dowager Duchess of St Ormond stood just inside the front door, a lilting smile on her face.

'Amelia, how pretty you look! And, Lady Winter, I'm delighted to see you and your daughter. You look so much like poor Sylvia! I knew your mama very well.'

The goddess turned to marble. 'Did you, ma'am? I'm afraid you have the advantage of me then.' Shards of ice formed on her voice—the hint of hauteur deepened. 'I scarcely remember her.'

Coolly she turned to Crispin. 'Perhaps, your Grace, we might be shown to our rooms.'

Rigid with anger, Crispin beckoned to his butler, hovering close by. 'Bebbington. Have Lady Winter, Miss Pemberton and Miss…Miss Anthea, shown to their rooms, please. No doubt they will wish to refresh themselves.'

Jaw clenched, he watched them go. Let Lady Winter try that with his mother again and she'd learn a lesson she'd never forget! His jaw set like granite, he watched with narrowed eyes as Lady Winter mounted the stairs, hips swaying provocatively, the luscious curves of her bottom lovingly outlined by the elegantly cut carriage dress. Heat roared through him as he imagined those curves filling his hands, heating, squirming against him as he… Damn it! She needed lessons in civility—not bed sports!

A light hand on his sleeve recalled him. Glancing down, he saw his mother twinkling up at him.

'Dear Cris! Don't go tilting at windmills on my account.' She seemed quite unperturbed.

He stared at her. 'Mama, she was atrociously rude! Scarcely a suitable chaperon, I'd have thought!'

She chuckled. 'Would you prefer Lady Casterfield? You

leave Lady Winter to me, Cris. I was, after all, appallingly tactless.'

Crispin drew a deep breath and counted to ten—slowly. 'I don't suppose you'd care to elaborate on that?' he asked.

She smiled and shook her head. 'No, dear. Not at the moment.' Five sweet chimes rang out. 'Great heavens! It's nearly dinnertime. I must change.'

A flurry of silken skirts and the Dowager was gone, flitting up the stairs with a lithe grace that thoroughly belied her fifty-six summers.

Crispin narrowed his eyes. He was damned if he could see how it was tactless to tell a woman you remembered her mother. His mother's calm acceptance of Lady Winter's rudeness notwithstanding, he fully intended to try a tilt with her ladyship. And when he was finished, she'd know that it didn't pay to cross swords with St Ormond! He'd teach her a lesson in civility; if he managed to teach her a few other things along the way, then that would suit him down to the ground.

Chapter Three

By the time she reached her room, Tilda fully regretted her instinctive reaction to Lady St Ormond's remark that she had known Sylvia Pemberton. Too often, during her first and only season, had matrons to whom she was presented remarked that they had known her mama. Such references had always been edged with disdain, a supercilious curling of lips. An all-but-explicit intimation that as the daughter of such a woman, she was herself suspect.

In denying that she remembered her mother she had lied. She remembered her sad and lovely mother extremely well. It was not a memory she had ever shared with anyone. There had never been anyone to share it with. Even Jonathan, kind as he had been, had found the subject of her mother's disgrace excessively embarrassing.

She had discovered that when, in an unavailing attempt to persuade him to withdraw his offer, she suggested that she might prove as headstrong. He had been scandalised, but the kindly way he took her to task for cheapening herself had helped reconcile her to the match.

Now she had been monumentally rude to Milly's prospective mother-in-law and mortally offended his Grace. So she would have to apologise—to the Dowager, anyway, for Milly's sake. With this in mind she rushed through her toilette in a fashion that made Sarah shake her head in disapproval.

Still, the result, when she examined it in a looking glass, would pass. Her gown of old gold silk suited her tall, grace-ful figure, its colour a perfect match for her hazel eyes. The narrow cut of the skirts gave her a willowy elegance and the neckline, while discreet, was cut to follow the contours of her bosom with tantalising faithfulness. She might not have Milly's beauty, but at least she put the ghost of Miss Arnold to rest.

'Humph,' was all Sarah would say when Tilda grinned at her mischievously in the glass.

'Humph yourself, Sarah!' said Tilda. 'Now, don't wait up for me, for heaven's sake. I should much rather you stayed by Miss Anthea.'

Sarah nodded reluctantly. 'Oh, aye. I'll do that. Not but what she's as happy as a grig. Would you believe that his Grace sent up a message to her that Henry was settling in and had eaten all his dinner?'

Tilda stared. '*Did* he? Whatever for?'

Sarah shrugged. 'I dare say he was hungry. Long run he had today.'

'His *Grace*! Not Henry!'

'Oh.' Sarah considered. 'No idea. Still, he did seem to take a liking to Miss Anthea. Maybe he just likes children.'

Tilda gave this her consideration as she went downstairs. It seemed odd to her. More likely he was trying to turn her up sweet, she thought cynically. As Milly's chaperon she had, she realised belatedly, a certain amount of power. The thought was a novel one. Naturally one would not abuse it, but it could do no harm to enjoy its existence, meditate upon its possibilities.

She had been uncomfortably conscious upon seeing him again that St Ormond was just as lethally handsome, just as disgustingly attractive as ever. Even more annoying was the fact that her stomach still turned over at the sight of him. And he hadn't even recognised her!

She was not entirely sure if that was a compliment or otherwise.

Sternly, she vowed that he should never realise the peculiar power he wielded over her. No doubt most women reacted like this to him. Instead, she would make him aware of her power. If she wasn't convinced it would be a happy marriage for Milly, then she would stop it if she could.

She entered the Blue Salon a good ten minutes early and, to her relief, found it empty. Good. With a little bit of luck the next person down should be the Dowager and she could get her embarrassing apology over and done with.

Sure enough, five minutes later the door opened and in sailed Lady St Ormond, regal in midnight blue, the famed St Ormond diamonds ablaze at her throat and ears. She stopped dead on the threshold.

'Goodness! Am I late? I'm so sorry, my dear. Did you ring for Bebbington? Should you care for a glass of ratafia? Or Madeira?'

Tilda blushed scarlet. Here she had come down early to make sure of finding Lady St Ormond alone in order to offer her an apology and the tables were reversed! A thought struck her. What if she had misinterpreted Lady St Ormond's remark?

Plunging in, she said desperately, 'Ma'am, I came down early to find you. To…to apologise for my rudeness—'

'Oh, no!' Lady St Ormond interrupted her at once. 'I should not have been so tactless. You could not have possibly known how fond I was of Sylvia. You have her eyes, you know. Just for a moment…I thought…well…it was foolish of me. And you were so small, it is little wonder you have no memory of her. Or of me.' Her lovely smile deepened as Tilda's eyes widened in consternation.

'That's right, my dear. I remember you as a little girl. Sylvia always brought you when she called on me. She loved you very much and she was so proud of you. You used to sit in the corner and play with my cat.'

Memory stirred. An image of a very large formal room came to Tilda. A very patient tabby cat and a lady who had always had some special toy ready for her to play with. But the woman's face was lost to her—it must have been Lady St Ormond. Very few had received her disgraced mother. And she had snubbed one of the few who had.

'I…I beg your pardon…I don't really remember…not properly.' Tilda blushed scarlet. 'I…I do remember Mama, but sometimes people…' Her voice trailed off. What excuse could she offer for rudeness?

'No, no, my dear!' Lady St Ormond was patently horrified. 'I told you only to explain my seeming tactlessness. You must not apologise. I dare say there have been many who have not scrupled to throw Sylvia's misfortunes up in your face. Now—' she smiled brightly '—where is Milly?'

Tilda's jaw dropped in ludicrous dismay. She had completely forgotten to escort Milly downstairs. And she was meant to be chaperoning the girl. Horrorstruck, she gazed at her hostess and wondered just how much worse this visit could get.

The Dowager simply collapsed laughing. When she could, she spluttered, 'You poor girl! Don't give it a moment's thought! She can't come to much harm here, you know. All the guests are family, so unless she gets lost she is perfectly safe.'

The door opened again to admit a tall young man whose attire proclaimed him a budding dandy. His intricately tied cravat was enormous, his shirt points dizzying and his cherry-striped waistcoat blinding. Tilda blinked at all this sartorial magnificence, but the Dowager merely raised her brows.

'Dear me, Guy, poor Crispin will feel quite put in the shade. Lady Winter, may I present my nephew, Guy Malvern. Dear boy, be an angel and go up to the pink guest chamber and escort Miss Pemberton down. Here is poor Lady Winter, so unused to the role of chaperon she has forgot her charge.'

The elegant Mr Malvern grinned engagingly. 'I should think you might, ma'am. You don't look like any chaperon *I've* ever been cursed by. Regular fusty mugs, most of 'em! Very well, Aunt Marianne, I'll fetch her down. As long as *you* explain to m'father why I'm down late!'

As he left, Lady St Ormond turned to Tilda again and said, 'You will find us all quite informal, but I dare say you are used to that. As I recall, Jonathan had never much taste for pomp.'

'Did you know my husband?' Tilda asked without thinking. Belatedly she thought that Lady St Ormond was probably not much younger than Lord Winter would have been if he were still alive.

'Yes, indeed I did,' said Lady St Ormond. 'He was friendly with my elder brother and often spent holidays with us as children. Now do tell me, is your little girl comfortable in her rooms? I put her in the old nursery because all Cris and Georgiana's toys are still there. But if you would be happier with her nearer to you, then we can shift her tomorrow. And you must not be thinking that she cannot join in with some of our entertainments. I know Cris wishes to have a riding picnic in a day or so if the weather holds fine. I will probably come in the gig so she could come with me, you know. Unfortunately Georgie has left her younger brood with her sister-in-law. A pity, but I am sure we can find plenty for the child to do.'

A rush of emotion flooded Tilda. She had been in terror that Lady St Ormond would resent Anthea's presence but she had not been able to face leaving the child with the Pembertons or sending her home alone. This kindness, this acceptance of Anthea's presence as perfectly natural, was quite unlooked for.

Her tangled thanks were lost in a gust of conversation as the door opened and several more people trooped in.

'Marianne!' A tall, military-looking man with iron-grey hair came forward and bussed the Dowager heartily. 'And who's this?' He cast an appreciative glance at Tilda.

'Lady Winter, may I present my brother-in-law, Lord John Malvern?'

Tilda curtsied gracefully as they exchanged greetings. So this was St Ormond's uncle. She could see a resemblance.

He glanced about him and frowned. 'Where the devil's that cub of mine? Boy ought to be down by now! Dare say he's still fussing over his cravat! In my day—'

'Dear John,' the Dowager broke in on what promised to be a scathing condemnation of modern youth, 'Guy is very kindly undertaking an errand for me. So helpful!'

She winked at Tilda, who choked back a laugh.

Lord John looked very slightly mollified. 'And so he should be!'

The next few moments passed in a whirl of introduction, under cover of which Milly slipped into the room with her escort.

She came at once to Tilda, who said, 'I'm dreadfully sorry, Milly. I should have come to your room to collect you.'

Milly smiled radiantly. 'It doesn't matter. Mr Malvern came for me. And he knows all about the house and has promised to show me around.'

Tilda felt it encumbent upon her to remind Milly of why she was here. 'Perhaps St Ormond would like to show you his home himself.'

Milly's crestfallen face suggested that this idea did not have anything like the cachet of Mr Malvern's offer to do the honours. Tilda couldn't blame her, but it would be the outside of enough for her to countenance Milly being shown the house by her prospective husband's young cousin.

'He might be too busy,' said Milly hopefully.

At this juncture Mr Malvern himself came up with a pretty young girl, whose height and chestnut locks proclaimed her a Malvern connection at once.

'Lady Winter, may I presume on Aunt Marianne's hasty introduction and present my cousin, Miss Hastings? Louisa, this is Lady Winter and her cousin, Miss Pemberton.'

Miss Hastings curtsied and said, 'I'm so glad you're here. Usually at these family parties, I'm the only girl. It will be nice to have company.'

Rapidly Tilda worked out that this was the eldest daughter of St Ormond's sister, Georgiana, Lady Hastings. Listening to her chatter with Amelia, it transpired that Louisa would be presented the following year, since she had only just turned seventeen.

'I'm out for family parties, but nothing else,' said Miss Hastings. 'Which makes no difference here, since Aunt Marianne always let us younger ones join in a bit. Why, Uncle Cris taught me to dance when I was ten!'

From which Tilda gathered that informal family fun was very much a way of life for the Malverns. It contrasted sharply with the rigid formality of the Pembertons' household where children were on occasion seen but most certainly not heard.

The door opened again to admit St Ormond. Tilda, in her position directly opposite, had a perfect view as he entered. To her great delight her stomach remained completely unmoved by the vision of understated elegance he presented. Plainly he studied to follow the dictates of Mr Brummel. His coat was a marvel of discreet black moulded to shoulders that filled the doorway, his cravat a monument to skilful patience. Unlike his younger cousin, who sported several fobs and rings, the only jewellery he wore was a single pearl in his cravat and a heavy signet ring.

Not a single flutter, she thought proudly. No doubt it was

just the shock of seeing him again for the first time in so long. Then she realised that he was making straight for her.

To her immense disgust, her stomach did a great deal more than flutter at his fluid, lethally graceful approach. Despite his height and powerful build, he moved with all the elegance and purpose of a large cat. Which would have been fine, she loved cats. But not when she felt like the mouse.

'Good evening Lady Winter, Amelia.' He bowed gracefully and his voice was positively arctic. 'I do hope my people are looking after you.'

Lady Winter smiled graciously. 'Everything is very comfortable, thank you, your Grace.' She couldn't blame him for the chill. After all, she felt just as savage towards those who sneered at *her* mother.

He nodded and turned to his niece. 'Hullo, Louisa. They tell me you're out now!'

Louisa nodded gleefully. 'Yes, Mama says I may be seen at family gatherings now. And she will take me to Bath this winter, so that I shall know how to go on next year in London.'

'God help us all!' said St Ormond in heartfelt accents. 'I shall have to go to ground for the season. Oh Lord, there's Great-Aunt Seraphina glaring at me. Excuse me, Lady Winter, *you* may have no complaints, but I can assure you, Lady Hollow will have several!'

Tilda viewed his departure with some relief. His ease of manner and fondness for his niece were disarming, but she was *not* going to succumb to the folly of permitting a childish fancy for a handsome face to cut up her peace!

Finding herself seated next to St Ormond at dinner annoyed her considerably. Someone, she thought crossly, had it in for her. Naturally she acquitted St Ormond of fell intent. On reflection, since she was the highest-ranking lady present after the Dowager, it would have been the height of rudeness to place her anywhere else but on his right. At least for tonight. But as far as she could tell, with the exceptions of herself and Amelia, all the guests were family. Surely in those circumstances they would not be starchily formal about rank and precedence?

'Lady Winter?'

Belatedly she realised that his Grace had addressed several remarks to her and was awaiting a response. With no idea of what he had said, she stared at him helplessly.

'I…I beg your pardon, your Grace…I didn't quite follow.' He would think her witless, but that was better than thinking her rude.

'I merely wondered if you would care for some wine.' His cool tone told her clearly that he was perfectly aware she had been wool-gathering—and that he was not used to being ignored by anyone and probably considered it a further example of bad manners.

Despite herself, she flushed miserably. Heavens! She might not have wanted to be a chaperon, but she had agreed to do it. Surely she could do better than this.

'I…no thank you, your Grace.' She lifted her chin defiantly and met his faintly mocking gaze. 'My wits are scrambled enough after our journey. I dare say a glass of wine would have me asleep at the table, not merely daydreaming.' If he disliked her, then it would be all the easier to keep her dangerous attraction to him under strict control.

His brows lifted sceptically. 'A tiresome journey, Lady Winter? But Broughton Place is no more than fifty miles, I believe.' Even as he spoke he reached for a jug. 'Water only, Lady Winter.' He filled her glass.

She snorted. 'I suggest you try travelling fifty miles with a five-year-old who has to be rested every hour, lest she succumb to carriage sickness! Not to mention regulating your speed to allow her pony to keep up with the chaise!'

Sipping his wine, his Grace thought about that. 'Hmm. You should have sent the pony over in advance, of course.

Or written to me, rather than to my very absent-minded mother! I would have been delighted to mount Miss Anthea. As for her travel sickness: use a coach with a driver, not postilions. Then she may travel on the box.'

Stunned at his response, Tilda stared open-mouthed. 'Travel on the box?'

He nodded. 'It worked with me as a child. In fact, that's how I learnt to drive. You cannot conceive of my father's horror when he discovered that he had been driven halfway to London one year by, as he put it, a scrubby school boy of eight.'

The vision thus conjured up, of an apoplectic Duke and his unrepentant heir, drew an unwilling smile from her. Somehow she gained the distinct impression that the present Duke's father had not been at all unsympathetic to his heir's infirmity. She grimaced inwardly as she recalled the journeys of *her* childhood. Any vestige of travel sickness had been treated as a premeditated crime and punished accordingly. Certainly no one had ever suggested that she travel on the box.

Without thinking she said, 'You are fortunate, your Grace.'

He blinked. 'What? In having suffered travel sickness as a child?'

'No. In that your parents were sympathetic towards it.' She kept her tone light, but it was laced with bitterness.

A forkful of beef stopped halfway to his lips. His expression was arrested. 'I think rather, Lady Winter, that you have been *un*fortunate.'

At the mere hint of sympathy in his voice, she froze. Pity was not acceptable! Angrily she lashed herself for allowing anything of her feelings to show.

To her vast relief he turned his attention to Lady Hastings at his left and she finished her duckling and green peas in relative peace.

'Should you care for some lobster?'

She turned and smiled at Guy Malvern, seated to her right. 'Thank you. I would love some.'

He provided her with a generous portion, based, she suspected, on his own abilities as a trencherman rather than any knowledge of hers. Rather daunted, she gazed at the massive helping, smothered in a cheese sauce.

'Aunt Marianne orders them from Bristol. No need to hold back,' he assured her cheerfully. 'There's plenty!'

There was indeed. On her plate!

Lady Hastings, seated directly opposite, caught her eye. Unmistakably she winked, before turning to respond to Sir Richard Benton, a local magistrate who had plainly been invited to entertain old Lady Hollow.

Much encouraged, Tilda embarked upon the lobster.

'I'm Cris's cousin, you know,' explained Guy. 'I must say, I was surprised to find you and Miss Pemberton here. Thought it was just a family party. Cris doesn't bother much about big house parties. He says he can think of much better ways to waste his blunt than entertaining a horde of hangers-on he doesn't like above half!'

Tilda murmured something about her mama having been a friend of Lady St Ormond. If his Grace had not seen fit to inform all his family of his intentions towards Milly, then it was certainly not her place to do so.

Guy did not seem to find her explanation at all unlikely. He nodded. 'Do you ride? Cris always has famous riding parties. Shooting too, later on.'

Her reply was lost as Sir Richard broke in. 'Shooting? Hah! There'll be precious little of that if St Ormond don't do something about these damned poachers! Not a bird left if the rascals have their way!'

St Ormond looked up from the head of the table. 'Poachers, Sir Richard? What do you imagine I can do about your poachers?' He did not seem at all shocked that Sir Richard was so informal as to have spoken across the table.

'You can stop encouraging them, that's what!' barked

Sir Richard. 'It's open knowledge that your keepers are lax about catching them! Should sack the lot, m'boy!'

One brow quirked and a flash of amusement lurked in his green eyes as St Ormond said mildly, 'Providing the country with yet another starving family and yet more poachers. Who would, of course, know my preserves so well that they'd strip them!'

Sir Richard glared at him. 'Do you tell me, St Ormond, that you are encouraging this menace? This…this criminal activity? Damn it all! If you don't do something I'll have to use the road when I dine with Whittlesea. One of the rascals will probably shoot me on that right of way of yours one night!'

'I trust not, Sir Richard.' St Ormond smiled. 'And I am not encouraging *criminal activity*. I am merely telling you that how I choose to manage my preserves is my concern. Frankly, times are hard. With the Corn Laws, the people are literally starving. I'd rather lose a few birds and a rabbit or two, than have my tenants turning to crime!'

'Poaching *is* a crime!' expostulated Sir Richard, quite patently shocked by this heresy.

St Ormond shrugged. 'Not if it's not bothering me it isn't,' he said calmly.

Sir Richard goggled. 'Just encouraging lawlessness,' he spluttered. 'These fellows should be laid by the heels and transported! Made an example of!'

'Leaving their children starving, turning to crime and ending on the gallows or being transported themselves?' St Ormond's voice suddenly lost its geniality. 'Tell me, Sir Richard, do you find the idea of a starving child of six or seven being condemned to the gallows for stealing his breakfast repugnant? Because I do! And I would far rather his father helped himself to a few of my rabbits!'

Tilda shuddered. A child of six! Anthea was nearly six…she felt ill at the very thought.

Sir Richard glanced at her. 'Here, I say, St Ormond!

Distressing the ladies! Can't expect them to listen to this over their dinner!'

Tilda's nausea disappeared in a blaze of anger at this well-meant, but ill-judged, gallantry. She was fully aware that the entire party had stilled, was listening to the exchange, but she weighed in regardless. 'I beg to differ, Sir Richard. Since you raised the subject, I must assume that you did consider it, with all its ramifications, a fit subject for discussion by all present. In what way is St Ormond, in tacitly permitting his tenants to have the occasional rabbit, doing anything wrong? Would it be wrong if he went out and shot a dozen rabbits a day to hand out to them? Why should they not catch their own dinners and save him the effort?'

'My dear Lady Winter,' he said patronisingly, 'your feelings do credit to your tender heart, but as a female, we cannot expect you to understand the legal implications of what you are saying!'

'So explain it,' she said dangerously. 'In simple layman's terms. If I don't understand, I'll ask a question. Or two.' Unconsciously her fist clenched on the table.

Plainly nettled by the challenge in her tone. Sir Richard responded bluntly. 'Put simply, Lady Winter, it is a criminal offence for anyone except a squire, or squire's eldest son, to kill game. Therefore St Ormond has no right to take such a lax attitude to the business. The law is the law, and must be obeyed by all.'

'Bravo!' St Ormond clapped lazily. 'Lady Winter, was that beyond your capacity to understand?'

She shot him a look that made him blink. 'Not at all, your Grace. But I do have a question.'

To her shock, he reached out and covered her clenched fist with his hand. A shiver ran through her, leaving her dizzy and breathless, scarcely able to concentrate on his next words. 'You will have to excuse her, Sir Richard. If I have learnt one thing about women in my thirty-six years,

it is that they always have a question. Or three.' He smiled
encouragingly at Tilda. 'Ask your question, Lady Winter.'

Desperately trying to ignore the light pressure of his fingers, she asked, 'Have you sons, Sir Richard?'

He frowned. 'Three. Though what that has to say to anything...'

Trying very hard to ignore the warmth stealing through
her whole body at the touch of St Ormond's hand, Tilda
asked sweetly, 'Then, can one assume that you forbid your
younger sons permission to shoot on your land? After all,
technically they are poaching, are they not? Guilty of a
criminal offence, in fact. Dear me! What a hotbed of crime
your average shooting party must be! Or does the host
make sure all his guests are legally permitted to accept his
invitation? I can tell you right now that my husband certainly never did anything of the sort!'

A stunned silence fell over the table at this. Tilda assumed that she had shocked the company with her outspo-
kenness. She couldn't have cared less, and waited with
flashing eyes for Sir Richard's reply.

Sir Richard turned an interesting shade of purple. 'Well,
naturally...of course...one cannot...' He floundered hope-
lessly.

'One cannot condemn, say, the youngest son of a duke?'
pressed Tilda. 'Then you are saying that the law is the law
and must be obeyed by some? While others may break it
at will, merely because of unearned aristocratic privilege?
Hardly justice, Sir Richard.'

'And that,' said St Ormond placidly, 'really does spell
the end of the subject. Even if Sir Richard could find a
decent argument to counter Lady Winter, he has, of course,
been brought up never to contradict a lady. Even one with
revoluntionary tendencies!' The note of authority in his
voice was not to be brooked. A babble of conversations
broke out, none of which mentioned anything to do with

poaching, crime or aristocratic privilege, unearned or otherwise.

Calmly, St Ormond reached for the claret jug and filled Tilda's glass.

'Your Grace…I…' Meeting his amused gaze, her voice trailed off.

'I don't think you're in any danger of falling asleep, Lady Winter,' he murmured, under cover of the general conversation that had sprung up. 'If anything, I should be plying you with wine just to blunt your blade.' He shot a glance at Sir Richard, fulminating to Lady Hollow. 'But you know, I can really fight my own battles.'

She glared at him. 'You may rest assured, your Grace, I did not speak out in your defence! It was…merely… that…you spoke of children…' Her voice faltered. She could not even frame the words. She had wanted babies so much…to hear of children being sent to their deaths in the name of justice… Her stomach clenched.

'Young children…going to the gallows?' His voice was hard.

She nodded.

'It happens, Lady Winter.' Hard and uncompromising, his voice bit into her.

'It should not,' was all she could manage.

'No, but what do you propose to do about it?'

Her eyes widened. Do about it? What on earth could she do about it? She could not stand for parliament and oppose the sentencing laws. She could not even vote. Most men did not have the right to vote. Yet his tone had not been mocking. Challenging, yes, but not mocking. Something deep within her responded.

'I have no idea, your Grace,' she said quietly and saw cynical amusement flicker in the green. Still more quietly she added, 'As yet.'

Surprise flared and a brow quirked. 'Lady Winter, your

blade is as keen as ever. I shudder to think what else you may be able to slip past a man's guard!'

The gentlemen did not linger over their port for long after the ladies withdrew. St Ormond, conscious that he really ought to make an effort to dance attendance on his prospective bride, brought the usual round of chat to a swift end. Sir Richard had not opened fire again, but was looking thoroughly disgruntled, not even responding to cheerful attempts by Lord John to engage him in conversation.

As they passed from the dining room, Lord Hastings drew his brother-in-law aside and murmured, 'Lady Winter dealt a knockout blow there, Cris!'

Crispin nodded. 'She did, didn't she?' He said no more. All his rock-hard certainties about Lady Winter had been shaken to their foundations. He had started the dinner determined to teach her a few lessons in the civility due to his mother. Now he was completely at sea. He'd thought her an arrogant, ill-mannered upstart, in serious need of a set-down. She'd shown herself, under the fashionable veneer, to have the tender heart of any decent mother, and the swift wits of a politician.

He frowned as he led the way to the drawing room. However much of an enigma Lady Winter might be, she had still been appallingly rude to the Dowager. And no matter what the Dowager might think, he was determined to put her ladyship right on that subject. Besides, it might take his mind off a few other things he'd like to teach her. On reflection, seducing his intended bride's chaperon would be in highly dubious taste.

Pondering how to put her in her place, he entered the drawing room.

To discover the subject of his thoughts chatting animatedly with his mother and sister. By all appearances the three of them were entirely happy with their company and scarcely glanced up as the gentlemen entered.

He glared. Damn the woman! She had an uncanny ability to wrong-foot him. He'd spent enough time on her anyway. A quick survey of the room revealed Amelia gossiping happily with Louisa. Suppressing a grimace at the girlish prattle he would have to endure, he made for them. It was time to become properly acquainted with Amelia.

On the surface she had every qualification he required in his duchess. Pretty, malleable, brought up in the right circles. She was young enough that he could mould her as he pleased. She would not be likely to cause him any worry whatsoever and he would be free to pursue his own life of untrammelled freedom while doing his duty in providing an heir in the direct line.

But as he sat down with his young niece and Amelia he was conscious of the effort he had to make to attune his conversation to their level. He frowned inwardly. He had never before felt chatting with Louisa to be onerous. He normally enjoyed her youthful enthusiasm, was happy to chat about female fashions, without ever betraying just how he happened to know so much. Suddenly, he knew that it was not something he would care to do all the time—that to forever have to guard his conversation, so that his wife was neither hurt nor shocked, would be a penance.

With a jolt he realised that if he sat discussing bonnets with Lady Winter, those bright eyes would widen, a dark brow would lift in unspoken, cynical understanding... He forced his mind back to the innocent talk of hats, and noted that while his niece was perfectly at ease with him, Amelia was not.

'I say, Miss Pemberton, your cousin's game, isn't she? Taking on old Benton like that!' Crispin looked up. Guy had joined them, a teacup in each hand. He grinned ingenuously at his cousin. 'Aunt Marianne asked me to hand the cups around. One for you, Cris?' He handed cups to Louisa and Amelia.

'Don't trouble yourself, Guy,' said Crispin lazily. 'Tea doesn't really thrill my soul at any hour.'

They chatted on. Amelia, Crispin noted, had relaxed substantially. Good. No doubt she was just feeling a bit shy, plunged into a family party, and not having seen him for some weeks. It was, after all, a very difficult situation for a young girl. Perhaps she felt herself to be on trial as it were.

He thought about that as he settled down in his very large bed later that night. He had not intended this party to be a trial for Amelia. Not really. Just a chance for her to see what she was taking on before he made a formal offer for her hand. He would have to reassure her that *his* mind was made up.

He wriggled his shoulders into the soft down. And turned over. Several times. After a few minutes he swore vigorously, sat up and relit the lamp beside his bed. He'd read for a bit. The bed was not really cold. He'd seen his valet, Stubbs, remove the copper warming pan. It was just his overactive, libidinous imagination creating that impression. Which, given that he was contemplating a permanent remedy for the problem, should not have worried him.

And it would not have, had the subject of his lurid imaginings been Miss Pemberton... As it was, her chaperon's lush curves threatened to inflict a sleepless night and headache on him. Not to mention an ache in an altogether different part of his anatomy.

In the next corridor Tilda tossed and turned. Why on earth should St Ormond have clasped her hand like that at dinner? It was as though he had thought they were in some sort of alliance! And why the devil should she worry about it? Why did her hand still burn at the memory of those powerful fingers? And why, oh why, did her body have to remember those same fingers lightly clasping her waist seven years ago? Why, when she closed her eyes, did she feel herself whirling down that wretched ballroom in his embrace?

Thoroughly frustrated in her attempts to sleep, Tilda sat up and hugged her knees. St Ormond's challenge haunted her. *What do you propose to do about it?*

Very well. What *could* she do about it? She was an independent lady of means. If she really wanted to do something to help, then she could. All she had to do was think of something. Something that she could help with in a practical way. Just giving money was too easy. She wanted to be involved.

She had always thought that with Anthea and her independence she could be content. Rapidly she was discovering that she could not. She had so much. And others had so little. At times the contrast made her feel guilty.

So, since she could not stand for parliament and join the reform movement, what could she do? The answer was probably to stop the children ever getting as far as having to steal their breakfasts. Which meant helping orphans, unmarried mothers and helping children old enough to find decent trades. She thought about that. It was plenty to be going on with and would do for now. Perhaps she should write to the Vicar at home. He would know what was needed.

She fell asleep still pondering the problem, but with a warm certainty that she had hit on the answer to St Ormond's challenge. Not that she was going to tell him, of course—but she sent a silent thanks winging his way. He'd forced her to think of something that would help others and lessen her guilty feeling of having far more than she deserved.

Chapter Four

A week later Crispin paced up and down his library in
considerable irritation. On the surface his house party was
perfectly successful. Everyone was having an agreeable
time with rides, picnics and boating on the lake. The
weather was superb from their point of view, although he
knew the farmers would welcome a little more rain. If it
didn't come now, it was bound to come just as they were
harvesting.

Unfortunately Lady Winter was proving as big a bugbear
as her predecessor Lady Casterfield. Worse, in fact. He'd
never been conscious of the least desire to creep into *her*
room at night, get into *her* bed and ravish *her*.

Furious at the well-travelled direction his thoughts were
taking, Crispin reined in his imagination and concentrated
on his legitimate complaint against Lady Winter, which was
that she was altogether too conscientious a chaperon. He'd
had scarcely a chance to see Amelia alone; the wretched
chit, despite his hint that he'd like to be on less ceremo-
nious terms with her, persisted in calling him *your Grace*.
And on the occasions that he had taken her arm she had
stiffened up like a poker!

Granted, she had never been more than accepting of his
suit, but now it was as though his addresses had actually

become distasteful to her. And he suspected that the reason was not far to seek—Lady Winter. The damned woman must be influencing Amelia against him. She had been content to receive his addresses before coming here and the only thing he could think likely to have changed her mind was her chaperon.

Lady Winter obviously disliked him. She had begun her visit by being very reserved and formal with everyone. Now she was on far easier terms with the entire party, including his Great-Aunt Seraphina. She was especially friendly with Guy. The pair of them had struck up a firm friendship and it irritated the hell out of him.

She liked everyone, in fact, except himself. With him she was completely reserved, addressing him only by his title—if she addressed him at all, and never, since that first evening, had she permitted him to see anything of her feelings.

It was plain to the meanest intelligence that Lady Winter disapproved of his suit. On what grounds, beyond her own dislike, he could not imagine. He was disgustingly wealthy, possessed of an old and proud title, loathed gambling so was unlikely to lose his fortune, kept his mistresses discreetly in the background and had every intention of indulging his wife. What her picky ladyship could cavil at in all *that* was beyond his comprehension!

What a coxcomb you sound like! He could almost hear Hastings saying it. He laughed. James had been thoroughly amused when he had confided his plans for Amelia. *If you intend tying yourself up in matrimony, at least let me be granted the blissful sight of you courting the girl! Good luck, and remember, the terms you offer a mistress won't do for a wife!*

So he'd invited Amelia down for the annual family gathering, thinking that it would give them a chance to see more of each other in a less formal setting, become acquainted. But Lady Winter had other ideas.

Feminine laughter rippled through the doors opening on to the terrace. He cocked his head... Louisa, by the sound of it...and...yes! Amelia! Excellent. It shouldn't be too hard to fob off Louisa.

He stepped out on to the terrace. 'Good morning, Louisa, Amelia.' He smiled approvingly. They really looked very pretty in those pale muslins. Just the thing for very young ladies.

'And where is Lady Winter this morning?' No point in getting rid of Louisa if her ladyship were about to appear and spike his guns yet again.

Amelia replied in all innocence, 'Oh, Tilda is teaching Anthea for an hour. She does so every morning just after breakfast and then takes her for a walk, you know.'

Crispin nearly choked. He certainly *hadn't* known that. Typical Lady Winter! She knew perfectly well that he handled estate matters for about two hours each morning, so she had timed her daughter's educational needs to suit. Of course, in all charity, it was the most convenient time for all concerned, but still!

'And what is Miss Anthea learning this morning?' he asked idly.

Amelia grimaced. 'French conversation.'

'An accomplished young lady, then!' said Crispin. 'Like her aunt.' He waited confidently for the self-conscious blush at his neat compliment.

Eventually Amelia looked up and found him watching her. 'Do you mean *me*? But I'm her cousin, really—even if Tilda and I were brought up together like sisters.' She pondered this. 'I don't feel *nearly* old enough to be an aunt or uncle.'

Very drily Crispin said, 'I can assure you at least that you will never attain the latter distinction.'

'Uncle Cris,' broke in Louisa. 'Have you any idea where Guy might be?'

He shook his head. 'No, but you put me in mind of the

fact that I need to speak to him. Would you mind very much finding him for me?' He knew a slight twinge of conscience. He'd spoken nothing but the truth when he denied knowledge of Guy's whereabouts, but he *had* seen him heading for the stables some time ago.

'Of course not,' said Louisa obligingly. 'Shall I send him to the library?'

'Or here on the terrace,' said Crispin. 'I shall keep Miss Pemberton company while you are gone.'

The look of dismay on Amelia's face was ludicrous, and, since Louisa was standing slightly behind her, seen only by Crispin.

Very naturally seeing no impropriety in leaving her friend unattended with her uncle, Louisa disappeared on her errand.

Crispin heaved an audible sigh of relief. He turned to Amelia and found her regarding him as she might an escaped lion. He smiled and said, 'Now we may be comfortable, my dear.'

'Oh, er…yes…of course, your Grace.' She didn't sound or look convinced. Her feet shifted nervously.

'Crispin,' he corrected her.

She stared.

'It's my name,' he reminded her.

Wordlessly she nodded. Then, 'Should we find Tilda, do you think? I…I mean…after all…'

Crispin sighed and gave up temporarily. 'Why don't we go and find my mama? No need to disturb Lady Winter.' Yet. But as soon as Miss Anthea Cavendish had done enough French conversation for the morning, he was going to have a long-overdue chat with her mama about the duties of a chaperon.

Tilda received his Grace's summons with outward composure. 'Thank you, Bebbington. Please assure his Grace that I will join him in the drawing room in about twenty minutes.' She certainly wasn't going to skimp on Anthea's education just to suit him.

Twenty minutes later, having sent Anthea off to change her shoes in readiness for their walk, she made her way to the drawing room. Her host was awaiting her, standing by the windows, a heavy frown upon his face.

Rapidly she searched her memory for any crime Anthea might have committed, but could think of none. 'Good morning, your Grace. Can I help you in some way?'

His Grace did not bother with any conventional greeting. He went straight to the point. 'You may clarify several things for me, Lady Winter. For a start, I should like very much to know what grounds you have for disapproving of my suit. And, secondly, I should like to know why, when her parents approve, you have taken it upon yourself to discourage Amelia from accepting!'

Tilda stood stock-still, blank amazement on her face. How on earth did *he* know that she disapproved? She hadn't said a thing! Certainly not to Milly!

Playing for time, she asked, 'What makes you think I disapprove?'

He snorted derisively. 'Oh, for heaven's sake, woman! Don't fence with me! It's moderately obvious that you dislike me. You make quite sure I never have a chance to converse with her privately. And, furthermore, it is evident that since I saw Amelia in town, she has become very nervous of me. *Someone* must have given her a reason!'

Sheer outrage took Tilda's breath away for a moment. A moment in which her fury crystallised. 'Are you suggesting, St Ormond, that *I* have traduced your character to my cousin?' Her voice dripped icy scorn.

Quite undeterred, he repeated his original question. 'I wish to know what you have against me as a suitor for Amelia. And what right you feel you have to influence her in this way. After all, you have benefited handsomely from marriage. Why discourage your cousin from making a good match?'

Had he punched her in the stomach she could not have been more shocked. He dared throw her marriage in her face!

'You arrogant beast!' she exploded. 'I should have thought my story would be enough to tell you exactly what my objection is! But since you have neither the wit nor sensitivity to think of it for yourself, I'll tell you! I think it iniquitous to force a young girl into marriage with a man she scarcely knows, well nigh old enough to be her father! You ought to be ashamed of yourself! Is it any wonder that Milly should feel nervous? Had she expressed the least desire to have time alone to come to know you, then I would have been the most compliant of chaperons!'

St Ormond was glaring back at her. 'You dare to suggest that *I* make Milly nervous? Then why the devil did she agree to receive my addresses? Why come to this house party specifically to meet my family, if she viewed my suit with distaste?' He paused for a moment. 'And I am not old enough to be her father!'

'She is eighteen!' Tilda pointed out. 'You, I believe, are thirty-six? I'm tolerably certain your Grace is just as capable of doing that piece of subtraction as I am. There are nearly twenty years between you. And since she has come here, she views you as the uncle of her friend Louisa! With respect and liking, but she cannot imagine you as her husband, her lover.'

'She has said all of this to you?' Cold and hard. The anger in his voice pierced through her.

'No! Of course not!' Tilda was indignant. 'I would never have blurted out something like that told me in confidence!'

'Then this is all your very vivid imagination, Lady Winter.' The vibrant anger has been replaced with scorn.

Hazel eyes flashing sparks, she riposted, 'Imagination has very little to do with it, St Ormond! Put it down to experience and cynicism having engendered a dislike of May and December marriages! But of one thing you may rest assured: I have said nothing to Milly, you are quite out there! I will do nothing to influence her one way or another. If she wishes to be with you at any time and ultimately to accept your offer, then I will wish her happy with all my heart! Now, if your Grace will excuse me, I will take my daughter for her walk. Good day!'

And she spun on her heel violently and marched from the room, her head held high, presenting Crispin with a thoroughly distracting view of her bottom shifting vigorously beneath her thin muslin morning gown.

The door shut with a snap on this enticing vision. It was not precisely a bang, but there was every indication that only severe restraint had prevented it from being one. What on earth had happened to the cool and cynically collected Lady Winter?

Crispin fumed impotently. The damned cheek of the woman! To infer that he was pressing an unwanted suit on a girl young enough to be his daughter! There were only eighteen years between them. Very well! His birthday was next month—nearly nineteen! But still!

He mulled over what she had said. She had let something slip about her own marriage. Had claimed to know what she was talking about when she explained Amelia's feelings. What on earth had she meant? Winter...Winter...the only Lord Winter he could remember had been a man somewhat younger than himself. A mild enough fellow, he'd died in some accident. And, oddly enough he still couldn't recall where he'd met Lady Winter before. Yet the feeling persisted that he had.

Who would know about her marriage that he could ask without making a complete fool of himself and setting tongues wagging?

The answer came to him almost immediately, but he

fought against it for several moments before humbling his pride and bowing to the inevitable.

'Mama? Are you too busy to answer a couple of questions?'

The Dowager looked up from her menus. 'No, dear. I think the green goose will round off the second course quite nicely, Simmy. And do ask Marcel if we might have that delicious tart again! The one with the pears and the almonds. Thank you, Simmy.' She smiled graciously at the housekeeper, who curtsied and gathered up her lists.

Crispin leapt to hold the door for her. 'You may add my pleas for the tart to her Grace's, Simmy. Good morning.'

Closing the door behind her, he turned back to his mother and said simply, 'Help!'

She burst out laughing. 'Whatever has happened? You look quite distracted.'

Crispin bit his tongue on the ready answer. No self-respecting rake admitted to his mother when he had been distracted by a lady's bottom.

Instead he asked, 'Mama, if I asked you for some very personal information about someone, and promised not to reveal it to a soul, would you give it me?'

Marianne St Ormond frowned. 'That would depend, dear, on the someone, what the information was, and whether or not I had been asked not to reveal it. And on why you wished to know.'

Crispin came to sit beside her on the chaise. 'Can you tell me about Lady Winter? Her marriage? Her husband? I think I have just planted my foot in my mouth.'

She blinked. 'But you were on the town when it happened. Indeed, you knew Lord Winter!'

Crispin shrugged. 'Only slightly, Mama. He was a few years younger than I, and I'm damned if I can recall anything about him that would make his widow so dead set against her cousin's marriage to me!'

'Oh.' The Dowager's tone suggested that she did. 'Tilda Arnold was not married to the man you recall. She married his heir.'

Arnold. The name stirred in his memory but he repressed it and said, 'Go on.'

Marianne sighed. 'To fully understand what happened…well, even I do not know the whole. After her mother's death, I believe Sir Roger only took the child in to still the gossip if he did not. It was plain enough, when Lady Pemberton brought Tilda out, that their only idea was to marry her off to the first man that offered, regardless of his character or fortune. Or his age.'

Sick understanding dawned. 'How old was he?'

His mother grimaced. 'Jonathan? He was fifty-three when he married Tilda.'

'*Fifty-three?* Mama, that is utterly appalling!'' He felt completely revolted. 'How old was she, for God's sake?'

'Just eighteen. It was seven years ago. The Pembertons ended Tilda's first and only season the minute Jonathan Cavendish offered for her. They were married four weeks later.'

Crispin was silent. A short engagement was not unusual. But he was perfectly capable of doing the arithmetic necessary to work out the age difference. Lord Pemberton had forced his niece to marry a man thirty-five years her senior. Eighteen! It was nothing short of criminal.

He reined in his disgust. 'You said Jonathan Cavendish. Wasn't he a friend of Uncle Ned's?'

'Yes, dear. He never expected to inherit the title, so when his first wife died he didn't remarry, but his nephew died out hunting and poor Jonathan had no idea who the next heir was after himself. So he decided it was his duty to marry. And to marry a girl young enough to give him several heirs.'

'Good God!' Crispin could hardly sit still. 'Then she was forced into this marriage?'

'I should imagine so,' said the Dowager soberly. 'But don't cast poor Jonathan as the villain of the piece. He was very kind and very understanding. He retired to Leicestershire with his bride after the marriage, so I saw nothing of them, but I have often wondered if he offered for Tilda partly to rescue her. Of course his choices were limited; not many parents will marry off their daughters to a man so much older. Especially since Jonathan went to some pains to keep his wealth hidden. He had made a fortune in India as a young man, but he lived very simply and only those of us who knew him well realised just how wealthy he was.'

Crispin absorbed this slowly. And realised he had still a few more questions. Why had Lady Winter needed rescuing from her own family? Why had Lord Pemberton disliked his niece? 'What happened to Tilda's mother? Can you tell me?'

'That's no secret,' she replied sadly. 'She was Lord Pemberton's younger sister and he, as her guardian, attempted to force her marriage to a man over twice her age.' She sighed. 'Sylvia was very lovely and very foolish. Instead of holding out until she came of age, she eloped with David Arnold to escape what she described as her brother's persecution. Tilda was born about two months after she married on her twenty-first birthday, Pemberton having refused his consent to the marriage. David Arnold was killed in a street accident a year or so later and Sylvia died when Tilda was about five.'

'So her uncle took her in…'

'To quell the inevitable gossip if he did not. Sylvia had been popular, you see. And although very few would receive her after her disgrace, when she died, opinion swung around. Your father and I felt sorry for her and I made it quite plain that she had my support, but you know what society can be like. It wasn't until she had died that other people began to say, openly, how stupidly Pemberton had behaved.' She sighed. 'I wrote and offered to have Tilda to stay several times when she was a child, but the answer was always that they believed it was of the first importance that she be brought up according to the strictest guidelines for her own safety.'

'For which read, they were determined that she should never have any joy or pleasure,' said Crispin savagely. 'Good God, Mama! I owe Lady Winter the most grovelling apology and how I am to make it without revealing what you have told me, I don't know.'

'None of it is a secret, dear,' she pointed out. 'Merely forgotten. Personally I should opt for openness with Tilda. She values that, you know.'

He smiled. 'You've become very fond of her, haven't you, Mama?'

Her nod was emphatic. 'Yes, Cris. I was fond of her as a tiny girl and somehow, despite what has happened to her, she is a very lovely person. A little cynical and wary perhaps, but a woman in her position needs a few defences.'

Her words haunted him as he went off to find out where Lady Winter might have gone. Just what sort of defences would a woman need after what his mother had described? An air of cool indifference? She had that right enough. Pride? That too was there. Courage? Determination? Both were present in large quantities. She had responded to his accusations with all the fury of a lioness.

And that puzzled him. Had it not been for her response to Sir Richard at dinner that first night, he would have said that Lady Winter did not indulge in emotions.

Anyway, emotions or not, he would now have to apologise. So where was she?

Bebbington gave him the clue. 'They went out the side door, your Grace. With a bag of bread. Miss Anthea was talking about the ducks.'

Crispin nodded. 'The lake, then. Thank you, Bebbington.'

* * *

Alone, it would have taken Tilda no more than fifteen minutes to reach the lake. With Anthea dashing aside to admire every flower and gaze enraptured at every deer or peacock in the park, it took close to half an hour to get within a hundred yards of it.

The prospect was lovely. The lake lay in a sheltered hollow, grassy slopes leading down to it. On the far side the ground looked marshy and yellow flag irises blazed among the reeds. Willow trees nodded gracefully to their shimmering reflections and water lilies spread over much of the surface near the edge. Between the lily pads, ducks paddled on the reflected clouds floating in the blue.

Tilda heaved a sigh of pleasure at such peaceful loveliness. It was just what she needed after her turn up with St Ormond. It would be beautifully cool under the willows too, a relief from the oppressive heat of the day. And she'd be able to think about the very enthusiastic response she had received from the Vicar at home. He'd sent her a six-page reply, franked by Cousin Max, detailing the number of orphans and unmarried mothers who would currently benefit by such a scheme in their parish. From what he said, it would barely make a dent in her very large income.

A letter from Cassie had accompanied it, full of her delight and determination to assist in the practical aspects of the plan.

Max is simply delighted. He has been thinking along these lines for some time and when the Vicar mentioned your idea, he was all for it...

A house would be needed, mused Tilda. And they would have to consider the sort of training to give the children and girls. And then people would need to be found to provide the training. Perhaps some of the local gentry would take extra staff to train—for those that wished to go into service eventually...

A faint shout behind them interrupted her thoughts. Calling to Anthea, now rushing ahead, to wait, she swung around. The tall figure striding towards her with such leonine grace was unmistakable.

St Ormond. Her eyes narrowed and her jaw hardened mulishly. What did he want now? An apology? When hell froze over!

She waited with her head held high and a defiant blaze in her eyes. When he came up she did not give him a chance to speak. 'If you have any more insults, your Grace, might I suggest that you air them privately, and not where my daughter will hear them. At the moment I am busy!'

He held up a cloth bag. 'More bread. I thought she might like to feed the carp in the lake as well as the ducks. They'll take it from her hands. There's a boat moored there under that nearest willow. If I push her off and tie the rope to a root she can feed them quite safely. Then I can apologise in peace. And you can tell me exactly what you think of me without fear of interruption.'

Stunned didn't begin to describe Tilda's reaction to his masterly speech. Every gun had been spiked. Every avenue of retreat sealed off. He'd completely rolled her up. All she could do was stare at him with her mouth open in disbelief.

Lightly, he placed a finger beneath her chin, pressing upwards. 'Don't look so shocked, my dear. I'm not really such an ogre as I've been making out.'

She stood helpless as those long fingers drifted along the line of her jaw, a light, compelling tracery on her soft skin. Eyes wide, she trembled, unable to break away. His feathery touch held her as surely as iron chains.

And his eyes. The friendly, teasing glance had blazed into a searing intensity that pierced her soul, sought out every secret she kept hidden. She knew the urge to step closer, closer into the heat she could feel pouring from him, feel that heat surround her, in his arms, his body, in the touch of his lips. She swayed, her weight shifted.

He stepped back abruptly, turning his head. 'Good morn-

ing, Anthea. I brought some extra bread for you to feed my
fish from the boat. Would you like that?'

*'Oui, Monsieur le Duc. Je voudrais bien manger votre
poisson! Merci beaucoup.'*

The twitching ducal lip suggested that Monsieur le Duc
had caught the slip, but would not dream of correcting it.

Tilda was made of sterner stuff. 'No, dear, *nourrir* not
manger! You would very much like to feed the fish, not
eat them!'

'Oh.' Anthea blushed.

'There's a line in the boat,' said Crispin with a grin. 'If
you can catch one, you can eat it. But I give you fair warning, a big carp will put up a big fight!'

'Ugh!' said Anthea. 'And they're so horridly slimy! But
feeding them would be fun.' She cast a glance at her
mother. 'Er…I mean…'

Tilda sighed. 'Never mind, pet. Let's declare today a
holiday. You may speak English.'

Five minutes later Anthea had been safely deposited in
the boat with all the bread, told very sternly by her host
that she was on no account to stand up, and pushed off.
Tilda watched St Ormond tie the end of the painter to an
exposed root with a very secure knot. She told herself that
she was merely checking that Anthea was safe, but in truth
she was utterly fascinated by the deft action of his fingers
as he made the line fast, and mesmerised by the ripple of
muscles under his coat as he shoved the little boat away
from the bank.

He straightened up and came back to her. 'I told her she
could push off further with the oar over the stern. She'll be
quite safe. If, God forbid, she does fall in, it's not deep. I
can just wade in and grab her.'

'Did you happen to tell her which bit is stern?' asked
Tilda, smiling faintly.

'Yes, my dear. I did!' He stood before her with a disarming grin and shrugged out of his coat.

The ripple of muscles under his shirt sleeves and waist-coat was even more riveting, Tilda discovered. Her lungs certainly thought so. Air was suddenly in very short supply.

He spread the coat on the grass. 'There you are. Sorry there's no seat, but that should save your gown.'

She started. 'Don't be silly! Your valet will have a fit!'

His voice took on a crisp tone of command. 'Sit, girl! I have an apology to make and I'm damned if I'll do it star-ing up at you. Sit!'

She had obeyed before she even realised, curling her legs and muslin gown under her to keep the delicate material off the grass. Resentfully she shot him a glare as he stretched out on the sward beside her. 'I am *not* one of your spaniel bitches, to be ordered around!'

He smiled. 'Put it on the list. I'll apologise for that too. Don't worry about my coat, I was taking it off anyway. It's far too hot.'

She swallowed. 'Really, your Grace...' If only he wasn't so appallingly handsome. And if only he wasn't reclining there beside her in this attitude of friendly intimacy under the protective willow. Just propped up on one elbow, long powerful legs in their immaculate leathers and boots stretched out before him.

'Crispin,' he said firmly. 'If you call me Crispin or even Cris, then Amelia might follow your lead.'

'But...' she tore her mind from the contemplation of his legs.

'Crispin, then,' he compromised.

'And how do you propose to address me?' she asked. She promptly wished she hadn't. He'd already called her *my dear* twice, and she'd rather liked it.

His smile left her breathless. 'Hmm. Matilda, isn't it? Pretty, but a trifle formal. I don't like Mattie, nothing in the least doormattish about you. Tillie? No. Rhymes with Milly. Not to mention filly. Too tempting to think up rude verses.' He quirked a brow at her uncontrollable laugh.

'Tilda. Very nice. And Mama calls you Tilda, I've discovered. As does Amelia, of course.'

'You wish to call me Tilda?' Why did her voice have to wobble like a blancmange, just because he wished to use her pet name? Or did that smile have something to do with it?

'Only if you will permit it,' he said with a twinkle.

She humphed. 'I'll save my breath for more important matters.'

'Excellent.' His direct green gaze held hers. 'Now that we have that settled; Tilda, I most sincerely beg your pardon for upsetting you, for imputing scheming motives to your actions and for being generally arrogant and overbearing...'

'Your Grace...' She met his challenging look. 'Oh, very well! *Crispin!* You need not abase yourself. I was not very civil either, so—'

'Civility was not deserved after the way I spoke to you and the interference I accused you of,' he said. 'It was unwarranted and unfair. Whatever your circumstances.' He drew an audible breath. 'And I have another crime to confess to you.'

Another crime? What was he talking about?

'You thought that I knew something of your past, your marriage. I did not. I had assumed you were the widow of a man I knew very slightly, a man some years younger than myself. My mother explained matters to me. I am afraid I have been prying into your personal affairs. But she told me nothing that had not once been common knowledge.'

Tilda felt a strange shiver pass through her. There would be very little that Lady St Ormond did not know. She had been intimate with her mama, she had known Jonathan. There was no point in blaming Crispin. She had assumed he knew her story, that even though he had said nothing, he remembered who she was, had been. She could not blame him for finding out.

'It doesn't matter,' she said at last. 'After all, it was a very long time ago.' She went on softly, 'I am free now, free to live as I please, make my own choices...'

'Free to choose your own husband, for example.' His voice was idle.

She gave vent to a cynical snort. 'What on earth for? Why would I saddle myself with a husband?'

Crispin blinked. 'There are a few advantages to us, aren't there?'

'Not that I can call to mind, no.' She smiled mockingly. 'It may be a universal truth, as Miss Austen would have it, that "...a single man in possession of a good fortune, must be in want of a wife..." but I can assure you that a single woman in possession of a good fortune would have to be a confirmed ninnyhammer to marry! I, for one, don't call it an advantage to lose all control of my fortune.' Certainly not now that she had thought of something worthwhile to do with it!

He grinned. 'Surely this is mere...er...*prejudice* on your part, my dear?' His choice of phrase and the twinkle in his eye told her that he'd recognised and appreciated the source of her cynical comment.

She glared at him. He'd said he wanted to call her *Tilda*. Just what was he about, using that infuriating endearment?

She continued smoothly, 'Not to mention losing the guardianship of my child. Neither do I call it an advantage to be the chattel of any man. I am my own mistress now and intend to stay that way. I can think of nothing a husband can offer me that I do not have already.' Except more babies and she'd dealt with that, albeit vicariously.

A wickedly lifted brow inferred that Crispin could think of at least one other thing, intimately connected with babies. And she doubted that there would be anything vicarious in his methods.

She blushed and suppressed a grimace of distaste. He *would* think of that. Didn't men ever think of anything else?

Upon reflection, probably not. Well, it certainly didn't interest her!

Lifting her head, she said defiantly, 'Even that. I am a widow, not a young innocent. If I choose to conduct a discreet liaison, no one will censure me. In fact, if you think about it, a mistress gets far better terms than a wife! She is not legally and morally bound to submit to his…desires. And she can give him his *congé* whenever she wishes.'

She viewed his startled gaze with relish. She sincerely hoped she'd shocked him witless.

Whatever Crispin might have said was lost.

'Mama! Your Grace! Look! They're eating out of my hands!'

Anthea was leaning perilously over the side of the boat, pandering to the shamelessly greedy appetites of half a dozen ducks, who quacked and squabbled over the largesse of the ducal kitchens.

'And the fish ate out of my hands too! One was *enormous*!' She spread her arms to an improbable stretch.

'That's Bede,' called Crispin. 'Be very polite. He's probably even older than I am!'

Anthea plunged back to the other side of the boat, searching for the venerable Bede.

The exchange reminded Tilda of one bit of incivility for which she certainly owed an apology. And a change of subject was definitely called for.

'I'm sorry I compared your affection for Milly to my own experience,' she said. 'My arithmetic is not that bad. There…there can be no comparison. And if you care for Milly…then…well, I came to be very…attached to Jonathan, so I dare say…' she tried to ignore the explicable sensation that the words were choking her.

He stared at her, an arrested look on his face, 'But I…' He stopped. 'Perhaps we should be reeling her in now. It must be nearly lunchtime. Getting hot too. There'll be a thunderstorm tonight.'

The walk back to the house was enlivened by Anthea's chatter about the fish, the ducks and the boat. Tilda was very quiet and tried to force her mind to concentrate on the letters she planned to write to her cousins and the Vicar. Her host, she noted, had a set, hard look to his jaw and appeared to be annoyed about something. Probably her outspoken remarks on the institution of marriage had disgusted him.

A fact which she assured herself bothered her not one little bit.

No doubt he found such attitudes highly convenient, but disliked hearing them voiced by a gently bred female. She grimaced. If he had inveigled her mother's story out of Lady St Ormond, he might not, in fact, consider her gently bred.

After lunch Crispin excused himself and retreated to his library, ostensibly to finish his correspondence. In reality he needed time to sort out the confusion of emotions surging through his blood with unbridled enthusiasm, before facing his family again. And Lady Winter…damn it! Tilda! He'd had to exercise the greatest self-discipline on the walk back to the house not to openly admire the lady's walk, the graceful swaying of her hips and the temptingly long legs… He stopped his train of thought right there.

In itself, admiring her would have been harmless enough. What infuriated him was the unpalatable knowledge that he might not be able to resist the temptation to sample one or all of those enticing curves. He was barely in control of his passions.

He glared ferociously at an inoffensive bust of Plato, which only survived the experience unscathed since it was already made of marble.

He had a sinking feeling that insisting on Christian names would prove a serious tactical error. Not that he feared *she* would develop encroaching habits and take advantage, but that *he* would! Naturally one knew that widows were fair game. Especially one with her family history.

Also, she was perfectly right in her assessment that, if she were discreet, no one would be censorious if she took a lover. Certainly no one would censure the man who took her as his mistress.

Except himself. The mere thought of another taking advantage of her situation and shocking views made his hackles rise.

Which was utterly outrageous, because he could think of nothing he would like more than to take shameless advantage of her. Several times. Right now. And make sure that fleeting expression of distaste never crossed her face again by proving that not all men were such liabilities in bed as her husband must have been.

Which led him to the unpleasant conclusion that he was behaving in a very ungentlemanly, dog-in-the-mangerish sort of way. He really couldn't attend to Lady Winter's education himself. Seducing his intended bride's cousin, let alone her chaperon, would not be at all acceptable. So why on earth should he cavil at her very logical appraisal of her situation? Why should the idea of another man attending to the matter make him feel like issuing challenges in advance?

And why, in the name of all that was holy, did her very accurate, if cynical, view of the respective merits of marriage versus whoredom shock him? He had, on occasion, uttered very similar sentiments himself, and certainly had no qualms about using such mores to his advantage. Maybe Amelia was right…he must be getting old.

Chapter Five

Given the oppressive heat of the day, most of the ladies, including Milly, cried off the afternoon's proposed riding party. Milly, indeed, succumbed to a headache after lunch and retired to her bedchamber at Tilda's behest.

'Oh, Tilda, I do feel so rude, going off like this,' she wailed as her cousin tucked her up on the chaise. 'Do you think anyone minded?'

'Why should they?' asked Tilda. 'It's a horridly hot day. You rest here and you'll feel much more the thing by this evening. And remember—there is the ball tomorrow night. You want to be fully recovered by then. I'll be about the house or in the shadiest part of the garden with Anthea. Go to sleep, love. Everyone gets a headache occasionally!'

She handed Milly a steaming cup of herbal tea. 'Drink this. I got it from Mrs Simms. Yarrow and feverfew. It should relieve your poor head.'

Milly took the cup and sipped obediently, pulling a wry face at the bitter concoction. 'I hope it works better than it tastes!' she said.

Tilda chuckled. Milly always complained about medicine. She was about to leave when Milly spoke.

'Er, Tilda? Do you like Mr Malvern?'

For a moment Tilda was at a loss. 'Mr...oh, you mean Guy. Yes, very much. Don't you?'

The telltale blush that spread over Milly's cheeks was answer enough. She liked him far more than a young lady should if she were contemplating matrimony with another.

'Oh, yes.' Milly looked away and said, 'He seems very much taken by you.'

'Guy?' Tilda thought rapidly. 'Is he?'

Milly met her eyes squarely. 'Yes. He flirts with you all the time. And you flirt with him.'

Tilda improvised. 'You know Milly, being a widow has certain advantages. Young men are much more inclined to flirt outrageously because there is not the same expectation of marriage attached to a widow. We have had our turn at the marriage stakes.'

'Oh.' Milly digested that.

Tilda waited a moment and went on, 'I might add that a sensible young man should always be awake to the benefits of buttering up the chaperon of any young lady in whom he is interested!'

Milly stared. 'But...but I have to marry St Ormond.' She didn't sound happy at the prospect.

'Says who?' asked Tilda. She thrust away the knowledge that her behaviour was shocking. No respectable chaperon gave her charge this sort of advice.

'Well, Mama. And Papa, of course,' answered Milly.

'You can always refuse,' Tilda pointed out. 'That's why it's called an offer of marriage, rather than an order.' She comforted herself with the thought that she had, after all, given her uncle and aunt plenty of indication that she was most unsuited to the task laid on her.

'*You* didn't.'

Tilda flushed. She could hardly tell Milly that she would have accepted an offer from the devil himself to escape Lord Pemberton. She swallowed convulsively as the memory of his visit to her chamber the night before her capitulation seared her.

'Tilda?'

Milly's voice called her back out of her pain.

'I had no other choice, Milly. You do. And your mama and papa are much fonder of you than they are of me. So drink up that revolting tisane and shut your eyes.'

Milly obeyed and Tilda tiptoed from the room, tolerably certain that her cousin would be asleep in minutes. She needed time to think. She had done exactly what St Ormond had accused her of doing. Oh, not exactly perhaps. She had not *traduced his character*. But she had given Milly every encouragement to refuse his offer.

She met Crispin on the stairs and blushed furiously.

'Is she better?' he asked. 'Should I send for a doctor?'

'Good heavens, no!' said Tilda, rather touched at his concern. It also racked her with guilt. None of this was his fault. 'It is just the heat. I have given her a tisane and left her to sleep. I am sure she will be better this evening.'

He nodded. 'Mama thought we might have a little musical entertainment. Louisa plays well, as does Georgie. Guy even has a tolerable voice. And then maybe a few round games. We can go out on the terrace for dinner. There will be a thunderstorm later, I'm sure, but not that early.'

Tilda nodded and excused herself. Since Milly did not need her, she would spend the afternoon with Anthea. And she'd borrow that little travelling writing desk from Lady St Ormond and write to the Vicar at home about her orphans. She smiled to herself. She'd taken to thinking of those as yet faceless and nameless unfortunates as very much hers.

And she had better think very carefully about how she intended to handle Milly and Guy Malvern. If he married her, good. But if he didn't and Milly had conceived a *tendre* for him and married his cousin…disaster. Tilda shuddered.

Had she been horribly irresponsible? Should she warn Milly of the dangerous path she trod?

The evening was stifling. Even on the terrace the air scarcely moved and although she was much recovered, Milly ate very little. The seating had been contrived to place her next to Crispin, who exerted himself to entertain her in as light a vein as possible.

From further down the table Tilda could see that Milly was more relaxed with him, less nervous. But the smiles in response to his jokes and witticisms were rather automatic, she thought. More as if Milly perceived from his tone that he had made a joke, than as if she had really understood it.

He was simply too sophisticated for Milly, Tilda realised as she sipped at her hock. His age was not the problem. It was the trend of his mind. Subtle, witty. He would be the wrong man for Milly even were he ten years younger.

She was still frowning over this as she went to bed, bed hangings, curtains and casements wide open. Sarah had left, muttering her disapproval and predicting all sorts of gruesome disorders attendant upon the noxious night vapours, but Tilda ignored her. She'd rather risk the night air than succumb to a thumping headache herself.

What to do about Milly and St Ormond?

Or Crispin, rather. So far Milly had not followed her cousin's lead. She had stared, shocked, when she heard Tilda tentatively use his Christian name. On the other hand she was on very easy terms with Guy Malvern, who had hovered about them after dinner, bringing cool drinks and keeping them both in a ripple of laughter with his inconsequent chatter.

Tilda grimaced as she sank back on her pillows. There was nothing automatic about the beaming smiles Milly accorded Guy. Oh, dear! Should she warn Milly that it would be very foolish to allow herself to form a *tendre* for her prospective husband's cousin?

She had not the least doubt that Lady Pemberton would roundly condemn the advice she had given Milly and would be furious if she ever found out what a dressing down her niece had given St Ormond. Tilda shuddered to think of her reaction should she ever find out her niece was on Christian name terms with him and had spent a peaceful and happy half-hour in his company under a willow.

Her own reaction to Crispin was more worrying. Far more so than her girlish fancy for him. Then she had merely seen him as a figure of fantasy, an improbable character in her daydreams. The flesh-and-blood man was far more lethal.

He constantly slipped past her guard; making her lose her temper, inducing her to say things that would have been much better left unsaid. To wit, her outrageous avowal that she would never remarry. That in itself was perfectly acceptable, but to have told him her reasons and declare that she would rather take a lover smacked of insanity. She could only wonder what maggot had got into her head to make her reveal such thoughts to anyone, let alone a man renowned for his amorous conquests.

Luckily he didn't find her attractive. Otherwise she'd be fending off his advances. At least she hoped that she'd fend them off. But he didn't seem to find her at all interesting in that way. Indeed, if he wanted Milly, then his preference was for small dainty women who could look up to him. Not great beanpoles who could nearly stare him in the eye! He'd almost said as much all those years ago. No doubt she hadn't changed that much.

Sighing, she blew out her candle and snuggled down. Tomorrow she would concentrate really hard on playing propriety. And she would see what she could do to encourage Milly. After all, if Crispin wanted her, he would make a charming husband…

* * *

She awoke with a start several hours later to a crash of thunder. Another one followed almost immediately and a flash of lightning lit the room. Sullen rumbles echoed on and the wind could be heard whining around the chimney pots.

Tilda flung back her covers and leapt out of bed. Swiftly, she lit a small lamp, grabbed the robe on the end of her bed and headed for the door. Anthea was terrified of thunderstorms and in a strange house... Sarah slept like the dead and Anthea would never call out for the maid who was in the old nurse's room... she was deeply ashamed of her fear.

Nearly running, Tilda made her way along the corridor to the gallery that led to the stairs up to the nurseries. She should have thought of this and moved Anthea down to her room for the night. Crispin had said a storm was likely... if only she hadn't been so taken up with his concerns and Milly!

She slipped into Anthea's room to find the child sitting bolt upright in bed, clutching Susan and telling the doll in a high voice that she mustn't be scared, Mama was coming very soon...

'I'm here, dearest,' said Tilda. She crossed the room swiftly and got on to the tiny bed, taking Anthea in her arms.

'G...good,' said Anthea. 'S...Susan was getting very scared...I...I couldn't...'

A crack of thunder drowned her voice and with a squeal she buried her face in Tilda's breast. Tilda held her and murmured words of comfort, drawn from her own childhood terrors. After her mother's death she had always been left to deal with them alone, whatever they were.

So she sat with Anthea huddled in her arms and whispered nonsense to her, making a story of the storm as she always did. Last time the angels had been playing battledore and shuttlecock. Tonight they were moving house.

'They are shifting all the furniture about, dearest... Listen! Wasn't that a big crash! What do you imagine it might be?'

'A…a big desk?' quavered Anthea. 'Like…like that one in the library at home.'

'Good idea,' said Tilda at once. 'I wonder what angels use a desk for.'

'Counting up all the good people,' suggested Anthea. 'Like Papa. Maybe they like to know who's coming so they have enough sets of wings.'

'Maybe they do,' agreed Tilda. Another crash rumbled.

'I…I know what that is!' said Anthea at once. 'It's God telling the angels that they are too noisy, they are keeping us awake!'

And so it went on until the thunder finally died away in the distance. By then Anthea was half-asleep and so was Tilda. Tired, she lay Anthea down in the bed and settled beside her. She might as well stay until she was sure the storm had completely gone. Rain was drumming down steadily now. She could hear it beating gustily against the window panes…a pattering rattle…constant, comforting.

She awoke, stiff and cramped in the grey dawn, the lamp long since gone out. Anthea was sleeping soundly, smiling faintly. Tilda felt her heart contract sharply as she gazed down at the small, flushed face. It seemed so recent, yet so long ago, that she had been a tiny, helpless baby, then a chubby little toddling thing…and now she was a little girl who could greet 'Monsieur le Duc' with perfect aplomb. All too soon she would be growing up, making her come-out…finding a husband…

'I should be glad,' Tilda whispered to herself. 'She will have her choice of husbands, not be forced into marriage with the first man to offer. She will be happy, I'll make sure of that…' Defiantly she thrust away the thought that she could only do so much to protect her child.

She shook her head to clear it of the crowding thoughts.

It was time to slip back to her own bed. Later today she'd speak to Lady St Ormond about having a truckle bed in her dressing room for Anthea in case of another storm. Somehow Tilda was sure that she would not see it as spoiling, that she would understand.

Yawning, she made her way back downstairs and along the gallery. She had not had a tinder box upstairs so she had left her unlit lamp behind and the gallery was very dim, since the curtains across the big windows at the end were drawn. To her absolute horror she felt something strike her elbow, wobble and fall.

To Tilda's shocked senses, the ensuing crash was worth all of the angels' best efforts overnight.

'Oh hell and the devil!' she muttered. It was that Grecian-looking marble pedestal with the little marble statue of Cupid and Psyche perched on top. From the muffled nature of the thuds, the wretched things had landed on carpet at least, but it still sounded deafening.

Cursing softly, she knelt down and tried to lift the pedestal. It was quite heavy and Tilda wondered crossly as she struggled, just how such a glancing blow could have toppled it. Of course it would be easier if she were using both hands and not modestly clutching her robe about her. After all, there was no one to view the shocking sight. She let go of the robe, grabbed the column with both hands and stood astride it. Ah! That was much better.

A faint click was followed by a flare of light.

'Just what do you think you are doing?' Crispin's voice held only mild curiosity, as if females astride Grecian pedestals, their robes revealing far too much, were an everyday part of his existence. He stood calmly watching by the light of a lamp, in a gorgeously embroidered silken robe that did nothing to disguise the blatantly masculine form it shrouded.

She dropped the pedestal with another resounding thud. It was followed by an equally resounding curse. 'Blast!'

said Tilda vigorously. She glared at him. 'What do you *think* I'm doing, St Ormond?'

He raised one eyebrow, set the lamp down on a console table by his door and strolled over with an almost offensively casual grace.

'All sorts of things come to mind,' he said pensively. 'But I feel sure that none of them are at all consistent with a virtuous widow.'

He bent down and started to pick up the pedestal effortlessly, one-handed.

Tilda, from her vantage point astride the pedestal, had a literally breathtaking view of a broad expanse of muscular hairy chest flexing powerfully as the pedestal was lifted. St Ormond, she realised dizzily, did not bother with a nightshirt on hot nights. At least, she rapidly reviewed the guests, she assumed that was the reason for his scandalous attire. Or lack thereof. She backed up hurriedly as he raised the pedestal, practically tripping in her rush to get out of the way.

Paying no attention to the flurry of silken skirts, he set the pedestal back closer to the wall than it had been. 'So inconsiderate of me to leave it lying around.' Bending down again, he rescued Cupid and Psyche from the floor and placed them on top. Then he turned to Tilda.

'Might I suggest, my dear, that next time you make, shall we say, different arrangements? Servants, not to mention hosts, are apt to come by all manner of strange notions when they find half-clad ladies flitting around the corridors at dawn.'

Far too dazed by the aesthetic treat she had been granted, Tilda really only made sense of the comment on her attire.

'Half-clad?!' she protested. 'You can talk! I mean…' Unfortunately this only served to focus her senses on his chest once again. She realised in shock that she was wondering what the hair on his chest would feel like under her hands…was it soft? Rough? Would it tickle her lips?

Her lips! Where had that thought come from?

Desperately she wrenched back control of her mind. Her knees were really not up to this sort of thing and neither were her lungs. He probably had a point. She'd have Anthea in her room if another storm threatened. 'Yes…well, next time I'll make other arrangements,' she said shortly.

His brows nearly disappeared into his hairline. 'Do, my sweet,' he said softly. 'You see, the servants will not so much as bat an eyelid if they see myself, or any other gentleman…er…flitting around the corridors.'

He paused and Tilda stared up at him in utter confusion. Where had that contemptuous, scathing note come from? Still silky soft, yet now his tones bit into her, like a velvet knife. And he was looking her up and down for all the world as though he were trying to gauge the capacity of a filly to bear his weight… Suddenly she felt a great deal *less* than half-clad, she was conscious of a scorching heat flaying her skin…of shivers racing up and down her spine… and the queerest melting sensation…

He went on. 'Neither, of course, will you have to contend with the attentions of other interested parties who may waylay you on your trip back to your chamber.'

The implications of what he was saying finally crashed in upon Tilda. He thought that she…that she…her mind lurched away from his implied accusation in, of all things, hurt. Not anger, she realised in shock. Hurt. Plain and simple. She was hurt that he could think that of her. Belatedly she remembered her avowal that she would rather take a lover than marry again…

And now what was he doing? She was completely paralysed as he advanced on her with all the sinuous grace of a large predator, stalking its prey. She should run, scream, anything rather than stand there like a rabbit hypnotised by a weasel!

For a moment he stood looking down at her, a fierce blaze in the green eyes. The next instant she was in his arms, helpless as his mouth crashed down on hers, devouring, ravishing. At first shock reigned supreme. Jonathan had *never* kissed her like this! Always gentle and considerate, his embrace had been a colourless, temperate sort of thing. Not this hot, surging riot of blinding fire, incited by savagely plundering lips and steely arms. And she had never felt even remotely excited or even vulnerable in Jonathan's arms after the first time.

And not even then as she did now. Completely and utterly vulnerable. And terrified. Not because of what he was doing, but because of what she, her body, was doing. Namely, yielding, melting in a surge of answering desire that she had never imagined. Even as the stunning realisation smote her, even as she remembered that she ought to be struggling, attempting to push him away, it was too late.

Her body had softened in his arms, was instinctively moulding feminine curves to masculine hardness. Her hands had drifted up to cling, to sink into his shoulders. The powerful muscles shifted and flickered under the silk as his arms tightened. And her mouth had opened, flowered in obedience to the demanding surge of his tongue against her lips.

With a groan that seemed to tear itself from him, he took instant and shameless advantage, plunging his tongue deep into her mouth in total possession. But even as he did so and her world rocked, she felt the tenor of his kiss change. His mouth eased on hers, gentling to match her tentative response. The surges of his tongue became a tender exploration, a seductive tasting that drew forth her very soul. With a dazed whimper of passion she realised that her own tongue was shyly stroking his, revelling in the taste and texture of his mouth.

His arms, though still locked, steel hard, around her, now cradled rather than confined as heat poured from his body through two thin layers of silk into hers, melting it bone deep until she would have fallen had he not held her up.

Molten liquid heat thrummed through her veins in time with her pounding heart, in time with the languid, tantalising surge of his tongue.

Then she felt one hand drop to her hip and slide caressingly over the smooth curve, over her rounded bottom, kneading, possessing. She sighed her pleasure into his mouth and felt the increased tension in his body, in his hand on her bottom, an instant before he jerked her closer, pressing her against the heated, rampant power of his loins. At the same moment his other hand shifted to close about one swollen breast.

She gasped as knowing fingers stroked and teased her nipple. He swallowed the sound as he thrust his arousal against the yielding softness of her belly in a slow evocative rhythm, matched by his surging tongue. Wild longing erupted within her, scalding hot. Her nipple hardened to a burning little bud of exquisite sensation. Then she felt him moving her backwards, gently but inexorably.

The small part of her brain still capable of rational thought screamed a warning. She cracked open heavy-lidded eyes to discover that she was being steadily pushed back towards his bedchamber. Her body said yes, but somehow, with her last remaining shred of sense, she baulked. Tearing her mouth from his, she forced her hands to his chest and pushed.

For a split second she felt his arms harden, saw the desire in his eyes and his mouth descending again. And she knew fear. Real fear. Because if he kissed her again, she would surrender willingly. Because she wanted him with every fibre of her enflamed body. It was only one tiny part of her brain that shrieked denial.

He released her and stepped back. Bereft of his support she staggered, her limbs still molten, unable to support her. Lightning swift, his hand shot out and gripped her wrist. Held her up. Slowly, her wide eyes never leaving his face, her breathing steadied slightly. Very slightly. She tugged at her wrist. His fingers felt like a brand encircling it.

Breathing raggedly, he let her go, saying with peculiar emphasis, 'Next time, my little wanton, I suggest you *start* with me. I think I can guarantee that you won't feel the need of anyone else's embrace once I've finished with you. And, after all, this is a family party. No matter how generous *I* may be about my preserves, I fear my sister will not be nearly so accommodating.'

She stared at him, beyond speech, conflicting emotions— desire, fright and rage—battering at her senses. And fled.

Crispin watched her disappear around the corner of the gallery, her robe fluttering behind her. His jaw was set and grim, his fists clenched with frustration. He was fully and unbelievably aroused; to the point of pain. He wanted the delectable widow in his bed. Now. At once. Five minutes ago. And there was not a damn thing he could do about it! Except go and wait for it to be a decent hour to ring his bell and request a cold bath.

With a groan he turned and went back to his chamber, slamming the door behind him and leaning back on the panels. Gradually, as his heartbeat returned to something approaching normal and his urge to follow her eased, he managed to ask himself what the hell he had thought he was doing. He had practically assaulted her. In anger, for God's sake! Only when he had felt the wondering innocence of her response, the answering fire on her lips, had he instinctively eased into seductive tenderness.

He shook inwardly at her remembered response, at the wild sweetness of her kisses, at the tangible surprise as he had plundered her mouth.

Groaning, he wondered if she would tell Guy what had happened. For of course, it must be Guy who had bedded her. He was the only other guest with a bedchamber in this direction for a start. Besides, knowing the devotion between Hastings and Georgie, and his uncle's starched-up notions, he dismissed the idea that she could possibly have been warming the beds of either of those gentlemen.

Lucky Guy! thought Crispin acidly, as he stalked back to his now chilly bed. Anger surged again, and with an almost physical shock he discovered that nearly all his anger was directed at Guy. Why couldn't the wretched boy have gone to Tilda's room? That was the accepted way to do things. Rule number one in conducting a discreet affair: don't shock the servants. They wouldn't think twice about Guy wandering about.

He discarded the dressing gown and slid between the sheets, wrapping his arms around the pillow for want of anything more responsive. What was Guy about to expose Tilda to such a risk? He was tempted to remind Guy of his obligation to protect the lady's name if he embarked upon an *affaire*.

The briefest of reflections served to convince him that this would not be well received. Guy was twenty-seven and his own master. Besides, if he mentioned the subject to Guy, he just might find himself strangling his cousin while informing him that if he couldn't do a better job of satisfying a lady, then he had no business seducing her in the first place. He should, in fact, leave it to his more experienced cousin.

Which brought him to the real problem. He was jealous. Pure and simple. His fury at Tilda had been borne of his jealous rage with Guy for having her, when he wanted her himself. And couldn't have her. Certainly not now. He could not possible poach on Guy's preserves!

And in all probability she was furious with him. Although what the damned woman expected if she was going to wander around a rake's residence in the dawn, clad in only her night rail and robe, he couldn't think. If she cared nothing for her own reputation, then she might at least consider her duty as a chaperon.

Still, he shouldn't have insulted her, let alone assaulted

her. The sensible thing to do would have been to say nothing. Well, nothing much anyway. There might have been some hope for him then. As it was… with a disgusted curse at himself and the whole situation, he resigned himself to watching helplessly as Guy furthered his liaison with Lady Winter.

The name didn't suit her at all, he thought. The reserved, icy goddess had been all clinging, melting nymph. The thought of all that unavailable, wanton delight was enough to drive a man demented! She had felt so right in his arms, so familiar, as though he had held her before…that odd niggling sensation deepened.

He had to be wrong. He couldn't have forgotten something like that, could he? And besides, where would he have met her? According to his mother she had been married off at eighteen and had lived on her husband's estate ever since. *Arnold.* Still the name nagged at him, tugging at some long-buried memory…

He punched the pillow. With a bit of luck she would not appear for breakfast this morning. He needed ample time if he were to preserve a dignified front with her, because he had made two appalling mistakes. He'd overestimated his own powers of control and seriously underestimated the lure of her body. Which was a combination guaranteed to cut up his peace.

It did. Much to his disgust he found Tilda before him at the breakfast table, chatting quietly to his mother. She accorded him her most charming, chilly smile and turned back to Lady St Ormond.

He blinked. He hadn't thought she'd be quite so brazen. Couldn't she even manage a token blush? And why on earth was *he* flushing? She was the one who'd been prancing around the corridors at dawn!

He greeted with relief the intelligence that his bailiff was in the estate room and would like a word with him. He finished his breakfast quickly and beat a hasty retreat, just as Guy entered to be greeted with Lady Winter's most spontaneous, *un*chilly smile.

Suppressing the urge to snarl, he stalked out. She was a shameless hussy, and the less he thought about her, the happier he'd be.

Rigby was waiting for him in the estate office.

'Good morning, your Grace,' he said apologetically.

Despite his annoyance Crispin smiled. 'It's all right. I had finished my breakfast.'

Rigby grinned. 'Glad to hear it. It ain't that urgent.'

'Good,' said Crispin. 'What is it?'

'You know as how your Grace told Marlowe and me as we wasn't to worry too much over the odd snare and rabbits and suchlike disappearing?'

'Yes.' Crispin nodded encouragingly. Marlowe was his head gamekeeper. He'd found the notion of turning a blind eye to poaching rather hard to swallow at first, but he'd come around when Crispin had put his arguments.

'Marlowe was saying yesterday as how there's been a lot more snares in the past week or so,' said Rigby. 'He thought as how some of the labourers might be taking advantage, so to speak, of your Grace's generosity.'

Crispin frowned. 'How do you mean, taking advantage?'

'Well, Marlowe thinks more is going than before. More than can be accounted for by a few labourers having rabbit stew once a week or so. He wondered if someone might be selling game.'

'They'd better not be!' said Crispin. 'I've already got Sir Richard breathing down my neck for flouting the game laws! If he manages to catch anyone selling game, he'll transport them. Or have them hanged!'

Rigby shuddered. It was a very moot point as to which was the worse fate. 'Yes, your Grace. Marlowe's been sniffing about quiet like, trying to find out who it is. Just to give 'em a friendly warning, as you might say.'

'Good,' said Crispin briefly. 'Tell him to come up and see me at his convenience. He can tell me what he's discovered and we'll have a think about what to do.'

He cursed fluently. This was the last thing he needed to really set up Sir Richard's back.

'When you see Marlowe, tell him to keep it quiet,' he said abruptly. 'I don't want this getting back to Sir Richard. We don't need him taking too close an interest in any local poaching. I'd rather settle it without proceeding to extremes.'

Rigby nodded. 'Surely, your Grace.'

Chapter Six

Tilda was vastly relieved at St Ormond's early departure from the breakfast parlour. It was only with the exercise of extreme self-discipline that she could maintain her calm in front of him. Only by reciting lists of irregular French verbs could she keep her mind off his hands and mouth and the hard seductive strength of his body. She needed time to get her emotions back on an even keel.

By the time she dressed for dinner, she found that she was able to think rationally about what had occurred. About some aspects of it, anyway. For a start, she could scarcely blame St Ormond for thinking the worst: that she had gone to some gentleman's room. It was, after all, the obvious reason for her presence. And she supposed that she could hardly blame him for dallying—she choked on that slightly; it was an understatement, but she didn't feel capable of *that* much clear-sightedness—dallying with her himself if he thought her available…a loose woman, a widow enjoying the benefits of her independence.

Slipping a fine linen chemise over her head, she flushed as she thought about just what Lady St Ormond might have told him. No doubt he believed that her mother's history made it all the more likely. What was bred in the bone would out in the flesh. At least he had released her when she resisted. She forced away the memory of that dreadful moment when she had thought he was about to ignore her struggles.

Full well did she know that her resistance would have been of short duration. She resented that mightily. A frown creased her brow as Sarah passed her the elegant gown of green silk of which Lady Pemberton had so strongly disapproved. How dare he force such a shameful response from her! For he had used force initially. It was only when he felt her willingness, had thought she would not fight him, that he had been gentle with her. Hah! Well, he had learnt his mistake! She would not be seduced by him or anyone…no matter how much she wanted it.

And that definitely surprised her. Her experience of marriage had given her no hint at all of the passion St Ormond had unleashed in her. She had always wondered what on earth possessed women to take lovers. She had never understood why they would submit to something that was at best boring and at worst painful, when they didn't have to.

Now she knew. Or at least had some idea. Her whole body had responded to his touch, had melted in anticipation. And she knew what it had been anticipating. If he had pressed her, she would have surrendered totally to his passion. Just as his kisses had had nothing in common with Jonathan's beyond the bare fact of being kisses, she did not doubt that his possession of her body would be something quite different. Never before had she literally ached with empty yearning. She could feel it now, just thinking about him…maybe she should…*after all*, whispered an insidious little voice, *you're a widow now. The propriety demanded of a young girl doesn't apply to you, nor the loyalty of a wife. You could find out for yourself…*

No! She shook her head angrily. It was not possible. On several counts. For a start he was courting her cousin. She could not so betray Milly or lower herself. Or, she realised, permit him to dishonour himself. The thought shook her.

Why the devil was she so concerned about *his* honour, for goodness' sake? He'd made it plain enough *he* held such things of small account!

And besides, he thought she'd bedded with Guy as it was. At least so she assumed. He was the only guest quartered near the gallery. She should probably disabuse St Ormond of that particular error...for several reasons. She frowned, thinking about it. But her whole being revolted at the thought of going to him and assuring him that he was mistaken. For any reason. No matter how she put it, he might well think she was making known her availability. To him. And she had very little confidence in her ability to hold him off.

She flushed scarlet at the knowledge that she was, after all, the wanton he had called her. If, on the other hand, he thought she was having an *affaire* with Guy anyway, that would probably be enough to keep him out of her bed. No matter what he might think of her, he was not the man to attempt to seduce a woman with whom he thought his younger cousin was involved.

A faint frown creased her brow. She didn't like it much, but better he thought that than seduced her himself. She did him the credit to believe that he would never tell a soul what he believed. No harm would be done. And it was probably the best way to protect herself. She had absolutely no intention of putting her more cynical views into actual practice.

Very well, they were to be entertained with a ball tonight, got up for the local gentry. It would be the perfect opportunity to demonstrate to St Ormond—she refused to indulge in the intimacy of his Christian name any more— that she was entangled with Guy.

Milly! What about Milly? She has already noticed that Guy and I are friends...

Tilda groaned. What if Milly were becoming attached to Guy? The poor girl would be devastated if she thought her own cousin could behave so shabbily. Frowning, Tilda thought about it. She had to admit that Milly's understanding was not superior and she was very innocent. It was in the highest degree unlikely that she would suspect an affair. But even Milly must notice a flirtation obvious enough to deflect St Ormond.

Telling Milly what she was up to was out of the question. She would be thoroughly shocked. And she was far too transparent to connive at such a deception.

Tilda nibbled at one finger. Transparent. That was it. If Milly felt upset about what was going on, it would be very obvious. Especially to someone who knew her well. If that happened, then Tilda would just have to convince her that she regarded Guy as a nice boy, just as she did her cousin, Milly's elder brother, Tom.

She went down to dinner and was delighted to find herself seated between Guy and St Ormond's brother-in-law, Lord Hastings. Fully aware of the occasional glances her host shot in her direction, she set herself to charm both these gentlemen, always remembering to save her sweetest smiles for Guy, who was seated between her and Milly—who sat beside St Ormond.

Quite a number of the local gentry had joined them for dinner. The fierce Sir Richard was there again. Plainly, despite his disapproval of St Ormond's attitude towards poaching, he was a close friend of the family. Tilda liked that; clearly the Duke was not the man to resent a little plain speaking. She frowned. It was not a good idea to think of him *too* charitably just at the moment. Rather, she should concentrate on all the things she knew to his discredit. Unfortunately all those things made her heart pound erratically and shortened her breath.

'I say, Lady Winter!' Guy's voice sounded horrified. 'Have I said something shocking?'

She blinked. What was he talking about? He'd been rattling on in the most unexceptionable way about sailing. She bestowed her most ravishing smile upon him. 'Of course not! And please, must you be so formal?'

His face brightened. 'May I call you Tilda? I should like that very much! You weren't glaring at me, then?'

In point of fact she had been glaring at St Ormond without even realising it. 'Goodness, no! Now tell me, which bit of a boat is the boom? And why did you have to dodge? It sounds thrilling! I should so much like to try it.' That headed him off neatly. Odd how men always liked to feel they knew so much more than a mere female.

When the next course was laid, St Ormond, who had been chatting to Milly, turned his attention to his Great-Aunt Seraphina. Guy, with an unblushing wink at Tilda, switched his attention to Milly.

Oh dear, thought Tilda, as she turned to Lord Hastings.

To find him gazing over her head with a speculative glint in his eye.

'Tell me, Lady Winter,' he said quietly, as he met her eyes, 'just how far settled are matters between...?' He gestured vaguely, but she could not mistake his meaning. He wanted to know if St Ormond had offered for Milly. And if he had, if he had been accepted.

She hesitated. It was not for her to discuss the matter with St Ormond's family. She raised her brows in what she hoped was an expression of quelling hauteur.

Lord Hastings smiled. 'Acquit me of vulgar curiosity, my dear. I merely wondered if Guy had any notion why you and Amelia were invited to what is, after all, a family party. Permit me to help you to some goose.'

She inclined her head graciously, wondering why her heart rate remained quite unaffected by Hastings calling her *my dear*. Couldn't the wretched organ work up the slightest flutter? After all, Hastings was just as handsome as St Ormond and equally as charming.

He went on. 'You may have noticed that the Malverns are, as a family, quite close. Naturally one would not care to see that disturbed. I was wondering if someone should just drop a hint in Guy's ear. Apart from Lord John, of course, which I cannot think would be at all consistent with Guy's dignity!'

Tilda stiffened. 'You think that *I* should do so, my lord?'

'Perhaps you might answer my first question,' he said gently.

She gave her attention to her dinner for a few moments, thinking hard. Finally she said, 'His Grace has spoken to my uncle, and been approved. He has not, so far as I am aware, spoken formally to Milly. They have been getting to know one another. She is, of course, aware of his intent.'

Beyond that she would not go. She could say nothing of what she believed to be Milly's doubts about the proposed match, let alone what Tilda suspected to be her growing affection for Guy Malvern.

Lord Hastings looked pensive. 'Hmm. I perceive, of course, that you are awkwardly placed. Very well. I had best take my wife's very blunt advice and keep my nose out of Crispin's affairs.' He smiled down at her. 'Do not be thinking, my dear, that we are criticising the way you are handling this business. I merely thought we should be informed so that we can be of some support to you, in the shocking event that Guy cuts Crispin out!' He grinned. 'After all, a dukedom is a mere accident of birth! It confers no common sense on the holder whatsoever. If Guy can open Crispin's eyes a trifle, so much the better!'

She could not keep her eyes from widening and he hastened to reassure her. 'I think, Lady Winter, that you want your cousin's happiness above all.'

Speechless, she nodded.

'Do you seriously think that she would be happier with St Ormond, than Guy, or someone like him?'

Without hesitation she shook her head.

He nodded. 'Precisely. She's a charming girl, Lady Winter. Well brought up, well bred. A virtuous young lady.

Everything St Ormond's bride should be. But...' he hesitated.

'But?' she prompted him.

He cocked his head on one side. 'Well, to be perfectly frank and thoroughly vulgar, Lady Winter—she ain't up to Crispin's weight!'

With which candid, if crude assessment, Tilda could only mutely agree.

Tilda had been vehemently ousted from her role as chaperon that evening by no less a person than Lady St Ormond. 'Certainly not, my dear! You'll have fun like everyone else and leave chaperoning Milly to Seraphina and myself. I dare say you'll have just as many offers to dance as she will!'

Tilda had blushed and disclaimed. But by the time she had been besieged for the first dance and had been persuaded on to the floor by one of St Ormond's neighbours, a very serious and worthy man in his early thirties, she had to admit the accuracy of the Dowager's prediction.

It was a country dance. Her partner performed it very correctly, chatting to her about the local scenery, asking her where she hailed from.

He seemed quite disappointed when she told him she lived in Leicestershire.

'Oh. Perhaps I may see you in town then,' said Mr Barnes hopefully.

She gave him to understand that she never went to town, with a smile to soften the blow. He reminded her slightly of Jonathan. So earnest, so kind...so safe.

The next dance was a waltz. Lord Hastings claimed her hand for this. Out of the corner of her eye she could see Guy leading Milly out. St Ormond was doing his duty by Lady Markfield.

'Don't give it a thought,' said Hastings, following her gaze. 'After all, the chit must dance with someone. Give rise to all sorts of gossip otherwise.' He swept her into the dance.

He was just as tall as St Ormond and Tilda had no difficulty in fitting her steps to his. Her mind swept back to that dance with St Ormond seven years ago. The dance he had totally forgotten. Perhaps it had just been the novelty of dancing with a man taller than herself, of feeling physically comfortable during a waltz, that had given rise to her fantasies...

She was enjoying this dance enormously. Hastings was delightful; charming and engaging, without once going beyond the line. And she felt comfortable. That was all. Comfortable. No doubt if she were to dance with St Ormond again she would discover that her memories were just that—memories, gilded by time and a young girl's dreams.

As they whirled around she caught a glimpse of Milly waltzing with Guy. Despite the fact that he was nearly as tall as his cousin, Milly was not having the least difficulty. Judging by the animated way she was chatting to him, she was not having to concentrate upon her steps much... perhaps she had gained some extra confidence...

The next waltz put paid to that notion. While Guy claimed Tilda's hand, she was fully aware of St Ormond, pointedly ignoring her, while he solicited Milly's hand. She bestowed it with a shy blush and seeming willingness. Tilda breathed what she assured herself was a sigh of relief and gave her attention to Guy.

He danced well and flirted with her outrageously, keeping her in a ripple of laughter. She thought that if this was how he'd been with Milly, she could well understand the sparkle in her cousin's smile as she danced with him. She said as much.

He looked startled. 'Flirt? With Milly? Oh, I wouldn't dream of such a thing!' A frown crossed his face. 'She told me she was hopeless at waltzing with tall men. So I told her what a dreadful little liar she is...but maybe she has a point...'

As he swung her about in the dance, Tilda could see precisely what he meant. Her young cousin was finding it absolutely impossible to waltz with St Ormond. It was very hard to tell who was having the more painful time. Neither looked to be enjoying the dance.

They turned again and Tilda lost sight of them.

'Tilda?' He paused.

She looked questioningly at him and waited.

'Please be honest with me. Am I making a cake of myself?' He sounded thoroughly downcast.

'Over what?' she asked, a trifle breathlessly.

He flushed. 'Milly. Is she really...? Well, I couldn't believe it. She's not at all like his usual...well, mum for that. He's never considered marriage before, but...'

'Who said...?' She couldn't believe that Lord Hastings or Georgie had said anything. He had as good as said that they would mind their own business.

He laughed ruefully. 'Who else? Great-Aunt Seraphina, of course. Mind you,' he continued with a faint grin, 'I did think she was exaggerating slightly when she informed me that in *her* day, a man like Cris would have called me out for making up to his betrothed!'

'She was definitely exaggerating!'' said Tilda firmly.

'But not by much?' suggested Guy. When she didn't respond, he smiled bitterly. 'I take your meaning. He has not yet been accepted, but I would be an arrant fool to think that my suit could stand against his.'

Tilda bit her lip. He was probably right, but she did not have the heart to say so.

They finished the dance without another word on the subject. Guy resumed his good-natured flirting, and, if it lacked his earlier spontaneity, few others would have divined the difference.

* * *

Few besides Crispin, that was. He had been far more assiduous in keeping Tilda in sight than she had in watching him. He had known Guy since the cradle and he could tell at once that something had upset him. He stepped on Milly's toes for the umpteenth time and forced a smile down at his scarlet partner.

'I beg your pardon, Amelia.' What ailed the girl? She had danced easily enough with Guy, for heaven's sake! Unbidden and definitely unwanted, Lady Winter's suggestion that he unwittingly intimidated Amelia reared itself.

'I hope I'm not upsetting you, Amelia.' He strove to infuse his voice with kindly encouragement.

Her disclaimer was immediate. 'Oh, no, your Grace! I'm sure you don't…I mean…of course not!'

Revealing too, he thought, as she nearly tripped over. He tightened his grip to support her, drawing her closer. And felt her stiffen in shock as her breasts grazed his coat. She gasped and pulled away. He eased his hold and gritted his teeth. Never had he longed so devoutly for the end of a dance.

Chatting lightly, he escorted her back to the Dowager and met Tilda coming back with Guy. He eyed them narrowly. They seemed perfectly at ease together, but he could not rid himself of the notion that something had upset Guy. Tilda, as usual, revealed nothing except calm, good humour.

Until her gaze lit on him, that was. He had to admit, he certainly had a talent for provoking her, one way or another. Her golden eyes glittered dangerously and when she spoke it was as though an icicle had uttered speech.

'Ah, St Ormond! I hope you enjoyed your dance. Such a delightful occasion.'

He returned her glare with interest. How dare she needle him like this!

'So glad it meets your approval, Lady Winter,' he returned, hoping no one would realise he had avoided commenting on the first part of her remark.

Lady Winter's smile suggested that she had noticed. 'Oh, I am not excessively difficult to please, St Ormond,' she said sweetly.

He bowed. 'Indeed, my lady, I should have said that you were excessively easy…to please.'

The pause was just long enough for *her* to stiffen, but not long enough to be readily noticeable to anyone else. His lips curved in a triumphant smile as she lifted her chin, but then, just for a moment, he thought he saw something flicker under the ice…hurt…shame? His brows snapped together, involuntarily his hand went out.

But she recovered in a flash, if there had ever been anything there beyond chagrin.

'I shall bow to your Grace's wider knowledge,' she said, dropping him a curtsy.

'Er…Tilda?' Guy interrupted tactfully. 'Should you care for a glass of champagne? And, Milly…ratafia for you?'

Tilda turned to him with a relieved smile. 'That would be lovely, Guy. We shall come with you. Good evening, St Ormond!'

Milly smiled up at him politely. 'Thank you so much for the dance, your Grace. I'm dreadfully sorry about your toes.'

He disclaimed gallantly and heard Lady Winter say, as they went off, 'Really, Milly, you must be careful. Sometimes older gentlemen suffer from gout!'

Not for one moment did he doubt that she'd intended it for his ears. He'd declared war and she'd struck back at once. But the thought that he had actually hurt her bothered him. Crossly he shrugged it off. She was a brazen little hussy and deserved everything she got. Gout, indeed!

He was promised to Sir Richard's granddaughter for the next waltz, but when he came up to claim her, he found her sitting beside her mama looking extremely wan.

'I am so sorry, your Grace,' said Mrs Benton. 'Jane is feeling the heat rather badly. I am just about to take her to the withdrawing room.' She smiled up at him kindly. 'Perhaps you might dance with someone else.'

He shook his head gallantly. 'Certainly not. Perhaps you and Miss Benton would care to stroll on the terrace? I shall be quite happy to sit out with her.'

'Oh, no!' said Miss Benton, patently shocked at the idea of so august a personage as St Ormond sitting out with her. 'It is very kind of you, but you should dance with someone else…' She hesitated and then brightened. 'Why, here is Lady Winter with the water she offered to fetch.' She smiled up at Crispin. 'You could dance with her, could you not?'

Crispin turned to find Tilda at his elbow, her face a study in frozen civility. The urge to strip the mask from her was overwhelming. Along with more tangible items. And if he was going to be denied the pleasure of her in his arms under any other circumstances, he might as well take this opportunity.

Gracefully he removed the glass from Tilda's unresisting hand and presented it to Miss Benton with a deep bow. 'Miss Jane, I am your servant to command. I will do myself the honour of dancing with you another time.

'If Lady Winter will treat my infirmities with kindness…' His smile just short of mocking triumph, he offered his arm to Tilda, as the music started. Staring up at him wordlessly, she extended her hand and permitted him to lead her out. To his shock her hand was trembling slightly and she stumbled slightly as he swept her into the dance. He tightened his arm and drew her back into the rhythm, prepared to adjust his steps to hers. And then, to his utter amazement, her stride found his and they whirled together effortlessly. She felt so right in his arms, as though she belonged there…

And then it happened. So few women he danced with

could match his long strides easily that his memory inevitably slipped back—to another dancer whose steps had fitted his...golden eyes smiling up at him shyly. A girl he had invited to dance because...because his partner had felt faint, and she had been near by. The years fell away and he suddenly recognised the shy and awkward débutante in the gracefully mature woman.

'Tilda...' he began, not quite believing what his senses were telling him.

Bright eyes blazed. 'I should infinitely prefer that you ceased your familiarities, your Grace! Including that one!' Her chin lifted in an attitude of defiance, revealing the slender column of her throat, the soft hollow at its base.

He went on, regardless of this unintentional distraction. 'This is not the first time we have danced, my dear, is it?' He smiled down at her. 'Now I know why you have been pricking at my memory. When was it? Seven years ago? Your first and only season?'

Her gaze flashed up, surprise clearly etched in her face. She nodded.

'I remember now,' he said. 'My partner was unwell, so I asked you to dance. I doubt I ever realised your connection to the Pembertons. And you have changed so much I didn't properly recognise you again.' *Until I held you in my arms this morning...until I danced with you...*

'You flatter me, your Grace,' was the cool reply.

He winced. This was Lady Winter, chilly ramparts fully guarded. Where was Tilda? The vibrant, passionate woman he had kissed in the dim gallery? Where was the awkward débutante who had so amazingly turned into a swan in his arms? He had never really forgotten it. He had noticed the girl stumbling through her infrequent dances; he had vaguely been aware of her name and made a mental note to avoid her. Then, when he had been put in the position of having to dance with her or hurt her feelings, he had discovered that, with him, she was graceful, that their steps matched effortlessly. Just as they were doing now. Circling the floor with ease. She had felt absolutely right in his embrace…

And they had talked. He remembered that; of what, he had long forgotten. But he remembered that he had enjoyed the dance because his accidental partner had unexpectedly charmed him. That he had looked for her in vain over the next few weeks. No doubt that was when her uncle had forced her to accept Lord Winter's offer.

She had changed so much! Oh, she had filled out in all the right places, so that her tall frame was now elegant rather than gawky. She had grown into herself. But it went deeper than that. She had been a shy, yet oddly open girl. Now she was shuttered, reserved. Her social charm was delightful; but it was like a suit of armour, he thought. And she used her wit like a rapier! To protect what?

Even now as she circled with seeming ease in his arms, he was aware of the barriers she had set about herself. Her body might flow with his in the dance but some vital spark was missing. Something he knew was there, because it had fanned into a blaze when he kissed her.

'Would you accept my apology?' he heard himself ask gently. And couldn't quite believe it. Why the hell was he offering an apology to her? Surely not for forgetting a single dance…what? Seven years ago? She was the one who'd been scampering around his corridors half-clad in the early hours of the morning! She was the one who'd spent her night in bed with his cousin!

You wouldn't have been insulting if she'd spent the night in your bed. His conscience pointed that out with a certain sarcasm. *This is jealousy, not a sudden and uncharacteristic attack of morality. Let's be quite clear about that. You hurt her; that's why you should apologise.*

The lashes fluttered down, veiling her eyes. 'Why…why should you apologise?' Her voice shook slightly. 'You cannot be expected to remember every dance partner.' *Even if they remember you.*

They whirled through a turn. He answered very quietly. 'I owe you an apology because I had no right to treat you as I did. It is no concern of mine if you have an affair with my cousin.' He felt her flinch but continued firmly, 'I do suggest, however, that *you* should not be wandering the corridors. That will give rise to gossip, which you would not desire.'

The soft curve of her mouth twisted. 'The eleventh commandment, in fact,' she said bitterly.

He raised his brows questioningly.

Her laugh was brittle. '*Thou shalt not be found out.* Society's golden rule of hypocrisy.'

He nodded. 'For your own protection you should play the game according to the rules.' He was aware of a foul taste in his mouth as he gave this piece of worldly advice, a constriction in his throat... Suddenly it seemed wrong, ugly...

Tilda appeared to agree. Her eyes flashed fire. 'Your Grace labours under a misapprehension...' An infinitesimal pause. And then, 'When I play games, your Grace, I will play them by *my* rules. I have played by the rules of others for quite long enough.'

Sheer horror at the revenge society would exact if she flouted its rules made him protest. 'Tilda...think...your mother...'

She froze in his arms. 'You are not free to take liberties with my name!' Her gaze speared him. 'Or with my person, your Grace. As a widow I have the right to choose with whom I share my...affection.'

His arms tightened reflexively. 'And you have chosen?'

She inclined her head. 'I have chosen.'

The dance came to an end and she stepped back. For a split second he held her, unable to release her. Conscious of nothing but the desire to sweep her back into his arms and kiss the vibrant, glowing nymph of the dawn back into existence, right here in front of all his guests.

And in doing so you would have compromised her so badly, you'd have to offer for her!

The scales fell from his eyes with a resounding clang, just as she pulled back from his hold. His eyes cleared of the glorious vision that had blinded him, and he faced reality. Lady Winter...Tilda...stepping away from him... politely thanking him for a delightful dance. Instinctively he moved with her, escorting her back to her seat amongst the older ladies, exchanging smiles and greetings with his guests. And all the while his brain reeled at the revelation, and he wondered how the hell he had missed seeing the truth—that he loved her.

By the time he had bowed over her hand and headed for the refreshments, all the impossibilities of his situation had crashed around him. Firstly, he had been on the point of offering for her cousin, whom she was chaperoning! That circumstance would be enough to set society's tabbies purring with sly innuendo and malice—the claws would be out—and all aimed at Tilda.

Secondly, if she were having an affair with Guy, it was entirely possible that *he* intended marriage. She was a wealthy widow after all. It would not be odd if his cousin had jumped the gun a trifle! In fact, it would be perfectly understandable, thought Crispin savagely.

The last and most pertinent obstacle was simply that he had given Tilda every reason to dislike and distrust him. He swore under his breath. He could see now, apart from his physical frustration, just why she had bothered him so much...why he had not been able to place her properly. It had not been merely that nagging feeling that he already knew her; he had been falling in love with the wretched female without even knowing it!

And she had chosen someone else. Namely his own cousin.

He smiled automatically at Sir Richard Benton and gave at least part of his mind to the older man's hectoring attempt to bring him to a sense of his obligations to his order. He nodded and smiled and occasionally shook his head. All the while pondering on just *why* he had fallen in love with Tilda.

At least he assumed it was love. From all he had ever heard, love was a confoundedly uncomfortable, not to say dashed inconvenient, emotion. He could understand that now, after years of pooh-poohing the whole idea. He was now prey to two diametrically opposed urges, the one as powerful as the other. In the one breath he was conscious of the urge to go to her and, sweeping all her objections aside, ravish her, make her realise that she was his; and at the same time he wanted to protect her, even from himself.

So what the hell was he supposed to do? Marry Amelia in the sure knowledge that such a marriage would entail seeing Tilda far too often for his own comfort? And what if Guy offered for Tilda?

'So you agree with me, St Ormond?' Sir Richard's mollified tones brought him speedily back to reality. 'And you'll do something to lay these criminals by the heels?'

Good God! What had he been agreeing to? 'I'll think about it, Sir Richard,' he said diplomatically. That was true enough. He'd have to do something about the vastly increased trapping that Marlowe had reported. He was seeing the man in the morning.

Sir Richard humphed, but Crispin smiled charmingly. 'I'm always prepared to *listen*, Sir Richard. But I still have to think about it.'

'Precious little to think about,' the old man growled. 'Hah! Think I haven't heard you're losing more game than ever? These things get about, m'boy! And I tell you this! If I catch any of your rascals selling game, I'll have them ticketed for Botany Bay, before you can blink!'

Crispin grinned. 'As long as you haven't been shot for visiting Sir Matthew, of course. How is he?'

'Whittlesea?' barked Sir Richard. 'Gouty. That's how. Not here tonight, I notice. I'll get over to him in a day or so. Still likes a rubber of piquet.'

Crispin was getting into bed before it occurred to him to wonder just how Sir Richard had come by his information. He'd asked Rigby and Marlowe to keep quiet about the business. He paid his servants generously and demanded discretion in return. And if anyone going beyond the tacitly accepted limits was talking, it betokened a stupidity he could not quite comprehend. The penalties for poaching and selling game were well known and there would be nothing even he could do to protect a man taken for such an offence.

He blew out his candle and frowned into the darkness. Hopefully Marlowe would have something to report this morning. Best to scotch the affair quickly and quietly. The last thing he wanted was to see one of his men decorating a gibbet, or facing seven years' transportation, which would probably prove a death sentence anyway. He rolled over and settled down ready for sleep.

Unfortunately, blowing out the candle only served to focus his mind more clearly on Tilda. Just what was it about her that had caught him after so many years? She was, in point of fact, no lovelier than many women he had taken under his protection over the years. So he could acquit himself of falling in love with a pretty face and lovely figure. Yet he had never wanted a woman as much. Certainly he had never lost sleep over one—or not until he'd got her into his bed at all events.

He liked her intelligence, her quick wit—oddly enough, he even liked her cool reserve—now that he knew the fiery passion simmering beneath. The calm exterior was no more than skin deep, a cloak for wilder passions. He bit back a groan as he imagined just how that silken skin would heat and burn at his caress, how she'd feel beneath him—all soft and hot—wanton.

He swore—that was lust, not love. It kept sidetracking him. He was used to lust. Usually he could control it. This time it was controlling him, confusing him, preventing him from seeing clearly.

As Tilda herself did, he suddenly realised. She gave the impression of a cool, watchful cynicism. Anyone who got too close was deflected with her wit and occasionally barbed tongue. With two glaring exceptions—her daughter and his mother. Everyone else she held at arm's length, so skillfully they didn't even realise she was doing it.

That was why she had fascinated him from the start, he thought, thumping his pillow savagely. Why she continued to fascinate him—because he'd seen past her camouflage. Because he wanted to know the real Tilda. Intimately.

Chapter Seven

Despite the late night he was up unseasonably early and conferring with Marlowe and Rigby over tankards of ale in the estate room by nine. The news was not good.

'Found ten more traps yesterday, your Grace,' reported Marlowe. 'Mainly wire snares, but two of the steel-jawed traps I'd use for foxes and badgers. If your Grace let me use 'em, that is!'

Crispin frowned. 'It doesn't make sense. Surely most poachers don't use those sort of traps! Damn it all, they're not exactly cheap and they're not useful for most game. And where on earth would they get the blasted things? We don't have any on the estate, do we?'

'No, your Grace,' confirmed Marlowe. 'I used 'em in your father's time. Him being more interested in shooting than what your Grace is, we kept the vermin down more. But when your Grace said just to leave the animals to theirselves...' Marlowe shrugged. 'I gave a lot of the stuff away to keepers on other estates.'

Crispin nodded. He had no argument with that. He knew that he was unusual in leaving his fields and coverts very much to take care of themselves, but although he enjoyed taking a gun out alone or with one or two friends for an afternoon's sport, he had no taste for the sort of ritualised mass slaughter indulged in by many landowners with their big shooting parties.

So he could see little point in trapping vermin. If they didn't keep the pheasants, rabbits and hares in check, his farmers would be cursing. Besides, having found one of his pet dogs in a steel trap years ago, he loathed the things with a passion. He could still remember the mangled leg, the terror in the brown eyes, the screaming agony of Jasper before he managed to free him. Jasper had limped for the rest of his days, and Crispin had sworn that he would never permit traps like that to be set on his land.

Still, other landowners used them, and that was their business.

'It suggests to me,' he said slowly, 'that a professional gang has moved in on us. Do either of you have any clue that some of our men are involved?'

Rigby shook his head. 'No, your Grace. I did happen to mention to one or two that you'd be main angry about the use of steel traps…' He shook his head in reluctant amusement. 'Well, if Hardy and Jem Beckett had aught to do with it, then your Grace might as well send 'em up to London and recommend 'em at Drury Lane! Right shocked they was. Beckett reckons one of the best things about working here is that he don't have to worry about one of his kids steppin' in a trap, and Hardy agreed.'

A reluctant smile curved Crispin's lips. Jem Beckett and Bill Hardy were two men who regularly supplemented their families' diets with a little poached game. They were highly unlikely to rock the boat.

'Very well. We can probably count them out. But at least they are warned. They'll pass the word around. I particularly want tenants with children warned.'

Marlowe nodded in agreement. 'Aye, your Grace. Rigby's got the right of it. An' if someone on the estate were up to summat like that, that pair would be on it immediate. There's just one thing though…' he hesitated '…I'm not so sure about a professional gang…'

Crispin raised his brows. 'Why not? Where else would the money for those steel traps come from?'

Marlowe scratched his chin. 'They're old ones, your Grace. Could have come from anywhere. But it's the *way* the traps are being set. Lordy! I could do better meself!'

The note of affront in his voice brought a crack of laughter from his noble employer. 'I dare say you could! You must know at least as much as any poacher.'

Marlowe grinned self-consciously. 'You could say that, your Grace. No, these traps was set by a rank beginner. The two steel traps wasn't dug in proper. I reckon a rabbit could have dragged one of 'em! An' the snares was set too high an' in the wrong spots. I tell you, I barely had to step off the main paths to spot 'em. Too obvious by half they are. You know as well as I do that you set traps in the little runs and trails the beasts make in the undergrowth. Not right beside a main path! Whoever it is must be a right lazy beggar. Stupid, too. Why, the number of people who use that path at all hours!'

Despite never having really given it any thought, Crispin knew precisely what he meant. Game didn't commonly hang about on the woodland paths used by humans. They had their own hidden trails and paths. A good poacher would know all about them; where the pheasants were nesting and were likely to fly; the exact position of a form, and which way the hare would leave it. He certainly wouldn't use a well-known right of way where he might be seen by anyone from the local magistrate down.

'So we have a very unskilled poacher,' he mused.

'Aye,' said Rigby. He added, with no trace of sarcasm, 'Which lets out all the usual suspects.'

'Hmm,' said Crispin. 'Very well. Leave the snares. But I want a close eye kept for any steel traps. Don't remove them, but check them daily and spring them. And I hate to say it, but you'll need to keep an eye on some of those snares you find. The ones you think aren't being set by one of our regulars. Whoever it is will have to come to check his traps. Obviously he doesn't share your expert knowledge, Marlowe. He'll be expecting to find something!'

Marlowe looked pleased. 'Aye, I'll fix 'un!'

Crispin levelled a straight glance at him. 'Like hell you will!'

Outraged, Marlowe protested. 'Master Crispin…your Grace! Lettin' a few tenants have a meal be one thing. You can't be lettin' someone get away with this!'

'Hardly!' said Crispin. 'But if you think I want some criminal taking a pot shot at you, you're vastly mistaken. Watch, see who comes to the traps. Don't let yourself be seen, and when you have identified the beggar you can come and tell me who it is.' He grinned boyishly. 'Believe me, if I see fit, I'll take all due measures. But I want to know who it is first. And I certainly don't want to be looking for a new keeper!'

Marlowe flushed and disclaimed, 'Pshaw! Plenty of keepers, your Grace! 'Tis me job—'

'Maybe,' cut in Crispin ruthlessly. 'But it took me long enough to convince you to leave the foxes alone and turn a blind eye to the odd snare. I'm damned if I want to go through that again with a stranger!'

Having breakfasted late, Tilda and Milly occupied themselves with a stroll in the shrubbery with Anthea after breakfast. French conversation was again the order of the day and, having discussed the scent of the roses on their way through the formal parterres and gardens, they were now engaged upon a discussion about how to spend the rest of the day. Anthea was firmly of the opinion that *'une promenade dans les bois'* would be just the thing to *'évoquer les esprits!'*

She giggled furiously when it was suggested that a walk

in the woods might well raise their spirits, but raising ghosts would have quite the opposite effect.

A cheerful hail from behind them heralded the appearance of Guy. Tilda noted with mixed feelings that Milly was plainly delighted, and that although Guy made no effort to single her out, it was plain that she was the main reason for his joining them. There was something about his eyes when they rested on Milly, a gentleness in his voice when he spoke to her. It was quite different from the funning banter and flirting manner he used with herself, she reflected. And it would drive her mad. She'd had quite enough of being treated like porcelain for one lifetime.

They strolled together for some time before Guy managed to draw not Milly, but Tilda apart.

He chatted on indifferent matters for a few moments but the tension investing him suggested to Tilda that he had something on his mind.

At last he came up to scratch.

'Tilda, will you tell me something?' He didn't wait for an answer to this very rhetorical question, but ploughed straight on. 'In your opinion, is Milly attached to Crispin or vice versa?'

After a moment's silence, in which her thoughts whirled and half a dozen polite disclaimers to knowledge jostled with several biting set-downs, she raised her eyes to his face and found him watching her with an expression of embarrassed sincerity on his face.

She sighed. 'Why do you ask? How will knowing the answer influence you?'

He shrugged. 'If Cris is deeply in love with Milly, or she with him, then I have my answer. I will leave as soon as may be and stay out of the way until they reach a decision.'

'That might be the best thing to do anyway,' said Tilda gently.

He shook his head. 'No. If I left now, who is to say that

Milly might not accept Cris, merely because she feels she has no other choice?'

'I cannot answer for your cousin,' said Tilda stiffly. Her body throbbed with the memory of his caresses two nights previously. How that could possibly equate with being in love with Milly, she didn't know. Unless of course he was suffering from frustration. But gentlemen were well known to have odd urges of the flesh, unconnected with any serious attachment they might feel. And she could hardly cite St Ormond's attempted seduction of herself as evidence that he was not in love with Milly!

But what to say about Milly? 'I do not think,' she said carefully, 'that Milly feels the degree of attachment to St Ormond that you are suggesting. He has charm, wealth and a title; he is exactly the sort of man she has been brought up to marry...' She paused. 'I do not know if her affection for another would be sufficient to make her defy her parents, or indeed to fly in the face of what she has been taught.'

'She's not comfortable with Crispin, is she?' said Guy bluntly.

Tilda flushed. 'I really should not say any more, Guy. You are just as observant as I. But I will say this: I think Milly and your cousin are not ideally suited. But that does not mean that they will not be tolerably happy together. Especially if Milly is given no cause to regret her choice.'

She dared not speak more directly but he caught her meaning at once. 'You may rest easy there, Tilda. I would do nothing to cause her unhappiness. Very well. I will bide my time. I suppose I should approach her father, but—'

'No!' Tilda was vehement. 'You would be forbidden to approach her. My uncle will never countenance her marriage to you while St Ormond's offer is still on the table. If he offers and she refuses...'

Guy snorted. 'And just how much pressure do you think will be brought to bear on her to accept?'

Tilda felt the blood drain from her face as she recalled
the rage that her own intransigence had provoked; the abuse
she had been showered with, the actual beatings. But Milly
was their daughter, and they were fond of her, had always
indulged her... Shaken, she replied. 'You may rest assured
that she will not be unsupported if she does make a stand.
And if they disown her, then she will have a home with
me.'

He grasped her hand and raised it to his lips. 'You are
the best of women!' he exclaimed fervently.

She smiled. 'Second best, perhaps. Now do stop trying
to flummery me! I haven't said I'll do anything for you.'

Still holding her hand, he replied, 'You will support
Milly. That is a very great deal. It is the devil of a coil.
Cris has always been very good to me, my mentor, not just
the head of the family. And he is the best of good fellows.
To find myself with a *tendre* for his intended bride...well,
it doesn't bear thinking about!'

Tilda could see his point. But she wished bitterly that
she did not feel so confused about her role in all of this.
She definitely did not think it was a good idea for Milly to
marry St Ormond. But why? Was it merely because she
was convinced Milly was not in love with him? Or he with
her, for that matter! Or were her motives far less pure?

Was she influenced by her own tangled feelings for St
Ormond? And what were those feelings? Did she merely
desire to put a rub in his way by disrupting his courtship
of Milly? There was one other possible motive; and it was
one which she did not dare examine too closely.

Only one thing was certain. She would have to try to
ascertain St Ormond's motive for courting Milly. Only by
knowing that could she help Milly, by making her look at
what she wanted in her marriage. And she could only see
one way of finding out what St Ormond thought on the
subject.

She'd have to ask him.

* * *

She ran her host to ground in his library. She hesitated at the door. Faced with that imposing barrier of solid oak, her plan to ask St Ormond, not merely to make clear his intentions, but his reasons for them, seemed ludicrous. Drawing a deep breath, she screwed up her courage and knocked. After a brief pause, her gentle tap was answered by a rather muffled, 'Come in.'

Nervously she swung the enormous door open, marvelling that anything so large could move so silently. Peering around the door she discovered that the library, which she had not previously entered, was just as enormous as its door implied. And just as imposing.

It quite took her breath away. The room was a classic double cube in its proportions and it was flooded with light. In the centre of the long outer wall, a huge bay of windows, tastefully draped, looked out over the gardens and woods, and more light poured through the windowed dome high above in the centre of the heavily ornate ceiling, fracturing in the chandelier that hung directly below. A gallery ran around the wall and the sunlight glowed on the leather-bound spines of thousands of books.

At first Tilda nearly froze with fright. Then something about the room reassured her. For all its grave decorum, it was still a room for people. Comfortable sofas and chairs were arranged here and there, tables for chess and so on. The room had been designed as a place for the whole family to gather.

So caught up was she in the atmosphere of peaceful harmony, that she nearly forgot what had brought her there. Until her host's deep voice drew her back.

'Lady Winter. This is a pleasant surprise.'

She winced inwardly at the note of irony in his tones, and swung towards his voice. Just for a moment she could not locate him, but then she saw him, standing between a large leather-topped *bureau plat*, and the window, the light blazing behind him.

'Is there something I can do for you, Lady Winter?' The bored, indifferent voice rattled her momentarily.

She braced herself. In a moment he wasn't going to sound bored. He was probably going to sound thoroughly offended.

'There is something that I wish to discuss with you, your Grace.' Determinedly she forced her voice to a semblance of cool detachment, refusing to acknowledge the fluttering of myriad butterflies in her stomach. Crossly she told herself that anyone would be nervous who had come to ask what she was going to ask. That it had nothing, *absolutely nothing*, to do with the broad shoulders and generally magnificent physique of the man coming towards her.

'Perhaps you would care to be seated at my desk, Lady Winter.' He gestured towards the desk and she saw that there were a couple of chairs set in front of it.

She shook her head firmly. That would smack too much of an interview. 'I should prefer to remain standing,' she said. 'This is not a business matter.'

He lifted one brow. 'A sofa, then.' He led the way to one of them and inexorably handed her into it. She desperately tried to quell the trembling of her hand at the light touch of his long fingers. Her prepared, succinct and direct speech had vanished into the ether. She groped for it wildly, insanely aware not only of her host, smiling down at her in a distinctly cynical manner, but also the array of classical busts that stood around the walls directly beneath the gallery. In the face of all these supposedly wise and logical minds, her own fluttered like a trapped bird.

Sitting down had definitely been a mistake. St Ormond was looming over her in a very ducal sort of way... If only the wretched man would sit down! For a moment she considered the possibility of thinking of something else to say to him. And then, with an outraged mental shake at her own timidity, she plunged in.

'What I wish to ask you should not take long, but I

should perhaps warn you that it is of rather a personal, not to say intimate, nature.' She hesitated. 'I...I should not like you to think me presumptuous, but in this situation I can see no other way forward...'

One brow lifted. 'How very, shall I say, gratifying, Lady Winter.'

She blinked up at him. What on earth was he talking about? And why was he smiling in just that predatory and cynical way? And why in God's name was he sitting down...and sliding along the sofa towards her? Tilda decided that she had been seriously mistaken in wishing him to sit down. He had been far less threatening standing up!

She shut her eyes for a moment to drag her thoughts together.

Only to find that her breath, as well as her mind, seized completely as she felt a hard, masculine thigh press against hers. A powerful arm encircled her. She opened her eyes to find that he was surrounding her, with his heat, his body, his penetrating green gaze.

'I think I can guarantee, Lady Winter, that I will be only too delighted to satisfy all your...curiosity.' His lips curved enticingly as he leaned closer. 'And I promise you that I shall not think you presumptuous! No matter how...er... intimate you choose to be!'

Dazed, she stared back at him. And wondered if his face was a blur because she was dizzy or because he was getting closer and her eyes had forgotten to focus. The latter, she realised, as his lips brushed hers, gently, featherlight, melting her effortlessly. His arms closed around her, drawing her close, fitting her to his body. Instinctively her hands lifted to his shoulders, sliding over the moulded muscles that tightened under her touch...it felt so right, so wonderful...except it wasn't what she had come for...

Grasping wildly at the last shreds of her rapidly departing wits, she dragged in a sharp breath.

'Milly!' she gasped. And pushed hard on the rock-solid

wall of his chest, shoving him away and scrambling out of his reach along the sofa.

For one crazy, heartstopping moment Crispin thought she was calling *him* Milly. His heart was pounding, his blood was afire and he was again aroused to the point of pain. What the hell was she talking about Milly for?

'Why Milly?' she was saying. It didn't make sense. All he could think about was *her*! So soft and vulnerable in his arms. Her lips, about to part under his... He wanted her with a desire that rocked him to his foundations. Dear God! One kiss and he was in agony. What she'd do to him in bed didn't bear thinking about.

She repeated the question with a painful intensity in her voice.

'Why Milly?'

'Why Milly what?' His voice grated harshly even on his own ears. He saw her flinch and knew a savage twinge of satisfaction. Good! He felt rage with himself that he should want her so much, even to the point of wishing it was possible to marry her, despite knowing that she was engaged in an affair with Guy. And now she had come to offer herself to him! Doubtless she thought he had more to offer one way or another.

'What has Milly to do with what you are offering, my dear?' His voice was silky smooth and his eyes never left her face. So he saw the shock and anger that surged across it. And something else that flared momentarily in her eyes.

Then they blazed at him. 'I wish to know why you desire to marry my cousin!' she said angrily. 'Somehow I doubt, given your propensity for molesting *me*, that love enters into your calculations!'

'I should have thought, my lady,' he said bitingly, 'that such a question should be best left to her father!'

She snorted in disgust. 'All my uncle is concerned with is your wealth and title! I want to know *why* you want

Milly. Why her, and not some other attractive, well-bred virgin?'

His eyes narrowed. Just at that moment he didn't care the snap of his fingers for attractive, well-bred virgins. What *he* wanted was a statuesque, outrageous, not to mention outraged, widow! And he wanted her now! A fact that made his answer less than politic.

'Why Milly?' he mused. 'Why indeed. You have provided the answer yourself, Lady Winter. She is attractive, well bred and, perhaps I might add, biddable. Her youth is certainly an asset in that regard! And, of course, the indispensable qualification...her virginity. I need have no fear that my heir will be sired by another.' He spoke with a chilly brutality, born of the knowledge that he didn't give a damn about any of the above. That all he desired was one intransigent widow! A widow who was glaring at him as though all *she* desired was a blade with which to run him through. He wasn't entirely sure her eyes weren't going to do just that.

'Why, you arrogant, conceited *coxcomb*!' she exploded into incandescent rage, her golden eyes flaming in a flushed face. 'Why don't you just go out and buy yourself a nice little brood mare? Or an obedient little spaniel? Yes, that's more like it! A fawning, malleable puppy to roll over on her back for you!' Venom spat from her eyes. 'You don't want a woman to wife! And you certainly don't want Milly! Not even in the most basic way!'

All Crispin could do was wonder just how he could be supposed to want Milly, when all his mind and body was taken up with wanting *her*!

She continued in tones of contemptuous loathing as she sprang up from the sofa and paced furiously, every graceful, swaying line infused with quivering anger. 'Does it mean nothing to you that your bride will submit to you, give herself to you, in complete trust? May even care for you? And what have you to give in return? Your wealth and title have already bought her breeding and virginity! What have you to offer for her affection and trust? Or don't they matter to you?'

Pain shivered through her voice, pierced him. 'How will you make her happy? Do you even care about what will make a woman happy?'

He was beyond rational thought by now. There was just enough truth in her savage flaying of his motives and character to enrage him. And his well-nigh unbearable arousal combined with his anger to make a volatile mix of emotions.

She had ceased pacing and stood before him, her gaze challenging, awaiting his response.

He met her challenge with one of his own. 'And just what makes you, of all women, think that I cannot please your cousin, Lady Winter? Do you not think that I can persuade my bride to give herself willingly?'

She stiffened. 'Not if she knew what a beast you are!' she flashed.

Green glinted dangerously. 'As you do, Lady Winter?' His voice held a purring menace.

Golden sparks flew. 'Forewarned is forearmed,' she countered.

'There is that, of course,' he admitted. 'But even if armed, one must sometimes surrender to…er…superior firepower.'

Her gaze narrowed. 'I think not, St Ormond.' Cold as ice, the chilly dismissal proved the final spur to his temper.

Rising slowly to his feet he approached her. 'We shall see, shall we?'

Defiance flamed in her eyes, her stance. He could see the effort she made to hold steady against his advance, yet she stood fast, refusing to yield an inch.

She would yield a great deal more than that, he thought savagely, as he reached for her. His hands closed on her slim shoulders and he drew her closer, into the circle of his arms. She came stiffly, unwillingly. For a split second he wondered why she wasn't struggling. Then he understood. She intended to prove that whatever he did to her, she would remain unyielding.

She was about to realise her mistake.

He closed his arms around her stiff form and then slowly raised one hand to her throat. Long fingers grazed over it, teasing, tantalising. Her jaw clenched and with an inward smile, he traced it, lingering beneath her chin, his thumb rubbing over the soft lower lip. She was still rigid in his arms, but he could feel the tension, the desperate resolve her defiance was based on.

Still caressing her lip he feathered his lips over her jaw, found her ear and breathed warmly, sensuously. His reward was a definite shudder, a wildly indrawn breath. Lightly, delicately, he circled the shell-like curves of her ear with his tongue, breathing softly. And felt her gasp, felt her body ease against his.

Holding his scorching passion in check, he pressed warm kisses back along her jaw until he came to the corner of her mouth. She was still trying to hold out against him, but her eyes fluttered shut as he covered her lips with his own and ran his tongue along their soft curves. He teased and probed, requesting, demanding entrance. Still she resisted.

His lips curved in a smile even as he continued to kiss her. She was shaking in her effort to remain unmoved. Her eventual surrender would be all the greater...all the sweeter. Unhurriedly he shifted the hand on her waist to cup the gentle swell of one breast. Under the fine muslin the nipple surged and hardened in his palm. He trapped the bud between thumb and forefinger and massaged it. Mercilessly. And felt the despairing moan that rippled through her as her besieged mouth surrendered, as her lips softened and parted.

He took possession at once. Deeply and thoroughly. Claiming her, branding her. His tongue stroked hers with sensuous abandon, exploring the hot sweetness of her mouth with slow, thrusting expertise. With surges that echoed the fire in his loins, the burning need that coursed through his flesh.

Inexorably he drew her back to the sofa, drew her down on to it. When he felt her hands flutter like a protesting dove at his chest he deepened the kiss still further, distracting her while his fingers worked swiftly at the buttons securing her bodice.

It gaped before him and without breaking their kiss, he slipped his hand inside to find the ribbons of her chemise. Gently, almost reverently, he felt the silken, heated skin of her breast under his searching fingers, found the hardened peak and tortured it.

His mouth absorbed the sobs of pleasure that shook her. They mingled with harsh groans that he barely heard. His mind was awash with pleasure, aflame with the desire to taste more of her sweetness. Her head was resting, leaning back against his arm. Her body flowed like molten silk in his embrace. Completely unresisting, completely helpless to fight the spell of desire his hands and mouth were weaving.

Giddy with delight, he laid her back on the sofa, pressed her down beneath him and allowed his mouth to travel down over the soft throat. He paused to lave and suckle gently at the fluttering pulse below her ear and felt her writhe beneath him, felt her hips soften and flex against him.

A surge of triumph roared through him as he shifted his mouth to her breast and heard her whimper in shock, jerk under him as he teased and circled the tempting bud. And then to his joy he felt her hands frame his face, stroking, caressing, urging him to take her breast as he had taken her mouth.

Slowly he took the rosy tip into his mouth, grazing it with his teeth, licking and finally, as she arched and sobbed under him, suckling it, until she cried out softly and clutched at him, her hands gripping his scalp with frantic urgency.

Almost without knowing it his hand was sliding under her skirt and petticoat, following the graceful curve of her calf, her thigh, so warm and soft. Higher, to clasp her hip possessively and at last to tangle searching fingers in soft damp curls.

She tensed and he immediately suckled harder on the breast imprisoned in his mouth, flaying it with pleasure, distracting her, until he felt the muscles in her thighs soften, felt them part to yield their treasure to his wickedly knowing fingers. And for a moment he knew delight unimagined as she yielded those secrets, as she writhed and sobbed in wanton abandon while he stroked and teased.

And then he heard one coherent and devastating word. 'No.' And then two more. 'No more.' And on a fractured sob, 'Please.' Her hands were pushing at his shoulders. Hard.

He hesitated. It would be so easy to ignore her plea, to overwhelm her with pleasure, until she begged him to take her...he couldn't do it.

Even as temptation licked hotly at him, he was releasing her, lifting his weight from her trembling body, smoothing down her rumpled skirts. He tried to help her sit up, but she flinched away from him. His hand dropped and he got up from the sofa. Tried not to watch as she fumbled with the drawstring of her chemise, as her unsteady fingers struggled with the buttons of her bodice. Tried to ignore the painful intensity of his arousal, the primitive instinct which urged him to take and possess her.

Civilisation won. Just.

He searched for words of apology. There were none. Because he wished he hadn't had to stop.

Finally she stood up. Her voice was low and shaking. 'Very well, your Grace. We have established that you can please a woman. And how do you think she will feel afterwards, knowing that your *expertise*—' she laced the word with bitter scorn '—can compel not only her bodily surrender, but her heart and soul as well? How do you think she will feel to know that these commodities are of not the slightest use to you? And that the only use you have for her body is as relief for your own urges and as a vessel for your seed? That the only joy you feel in her surrendered virtue and innocence is the assurance of your paternity?'

She paused and passed a trembling hand across her face. A face which had become a pallid frame for suddenly over-bright eyes. 'I doubt happiness is what she will feel, St Ormond. And frankly, I don't give a fig for what you will feel!'

She turned away sharply. But not before he saw the bright eyes flood, spill over.

'Tilda...' His voice was ragged, compounded of passion and searing shame.

She wasn't listening. Blindly, clumsily, she was heading for the door.

Instinct spurred him on. He strode after her and caught her, swinging her to face him. The shamed fury in her eyes scorched him. Then he saw her eyes narrow with intent. An intent he'd never seen in a woman's eyes before.

Then he felt his head snap back as a tooth-rattling right hook crashed into his jaw.

'Let me go!' she raged at him. 'I have no desire to be insulted by you any longer!' Her voice shook with emotion.

'Then stay here,' he said roughly. 'I'll go. God knows who you'll meet if you leave now. And you're not in a fit state to be seen by anyone!'

He strode past her and left the library, barely able to navigate for the conflicting emotions racking him.

Dazed and trembling Tilda stared at the closed door. He had gone. Leaving her confused and...furious. Furious with him and with herself. What on earth had she been about to permit him to touch her like that? With a sob of despair she turned away from the door and found a chair by the fireplace. Sinking into it, she wondered if she had in fact completely lost her mind.

Surely only a bedlamite would have allowed—no, challenged a gazetted rake like St Ormond to attempt to seduce her. Which was what her behaviour had amounted to. She had offered a challenge. He'd accepted. She supposed that she ought to be grateful that he had drawn back when she begged him to stop.

Her body burned at the thought of what he'd been doing, that she hadn't stopped him earlier. But, in truth, she'd been so startled and enthralled by his caresses that she hadn't wanted to stop him. Jonathan had never touched her thighs like that, so that she felt all aching and melting. He certainly hadn't…hadn't caressed her…intimately…like that; hadn't made her feel all hot and wet. Empty. No, he'd just stroked her thighs a little, then pressed them apart and…

She shuddered at the realisation that Crispin hadn't had to press them apart. She'd opened them willingly. And she'd have opened them further if he'd pressed his advantage. If what she had experienced so far was anything to judge by, his possession of her body would be very different from anything she had known in her marriage. She'd *wanted* to feel him inside her, taking her… Which was why she'd reacted with such fury afterwards.

With a stab of percipience, she knew that if Crispin once possessed her body, he would have her soul as well. And she had told him that she would rather be mistress than wife…

She hadn't really meant it. When he'd challenged her assertion that the male sex had absolutely nothing to offer a woman in her circumstances, she'd had no idea of the magic his mouth and hands could invoke. She hadn't, in fact, known what she was talking about. So she'd said the first thing that came to mind, fully intending to shock him.

Now she did know what she was talking about. Or at least had an inkling, which terrified her, because she wanted to know more. And despite her scornful cynicism about the respective merits of being mistress rather than wife she had no intention of becoming a notorious widow. She very much doubted that that would give her any more pleasure than marriage in the long run. And deep down at the very bottom of her bruised heart she knew that was not what she wanted.

She did not dare to look closely at what she wanted for the simple reason that she would never have it. A tear trickled down her cheek as she stared into the empty grate. At least on the next cold day some kindly soul would come and light a fire in it.

She shook her head to clear it. That particular fire would leave her colder than ever when it finally went out. Scorched and burnt and chilled to the marrow, it would destroy her because she would be nothing to him but a casual conquest. The insidious little voice she'd heard before whispered cajolingly. *Why not take what he offers? Who will be harmed? You're being fanciful...as long as you are discreet, who would care?*

No. She'd had enough of being a toy, a pawn in a man's hands. She'd prefer to live her life on her terms. And she very much doubted that if she surrendered to St Ormond, she would be able to do that. Men had a way of enforcing their terms on a woman, even when they didn't mean to.

Chapter Eight

Crispin's headlong flight from the library was summarily halted by a familiar voice. 'Ah, Crispin dear?'

Dazed, he stopped dead in his tracks to face his mother, standing halfway up the main stairs. 'Yes, Mama?'

'I was looking for you, dear. Are you dreadfully busy? Or could you spare me a moment?' she asked, giving no sign that the less than pristine state of his cravat and his generally distracted manner had registered.

Dear God! What if she had strolled into the library seeking him? Dragging in a deep breath, he assented. 'As many moments as you like, Mama.' It might even help him to get his emotions and urges back where they belonged, under his control. At the moment they were rioting about completely unchecked in a way that was making him slightly dizzy. Never before had he been in anything less than total control where a woman was concerned.

'Where shall we talk?' he asked as he joined her on the stairs.

'Well, I did think my sitting room,' she mused. 'No one will disturb us there.'

Which meant she had something important to say.

Part of his brain wondered just what was on her mind as he escorted her upstairs. But by far the greater part was taken up with his unprecedented loss of sangfroid. Desire was an open book to him. He'd read it from cover to cover. Frequently. But although he'd known what it was to want a woman, never before had he found himself acting against his better judgement, let alone against the dictates of his honour.

For that was what he had been doing. In trying to shame Tilda, he had shamed himself. Vaguely he realised that his mother had been speaking to him.

With a mental shake, he summoned up a smile for her and held the sitting room door open. He followed her in and said ruefully. 'I'm sorry, Mama. My mind is wandering.'

'I noticed,' she said drily. 'Do you want to tell me what is bothering you?'

'No,' he said baldly. 'I value your good opinion far too much. You tell me what is bothering you.' Hopefully he could do something about that.

Lady St Ormond sat down on a canopied sofa. 'I hope you won't think that I'm interfering,' she said slowly, and then looked up with a self-deprecating twinkle. 'Which should be enough to warn you that I'm about to be atrociously interfering!'

He smiled wanly. 'Interfere away, Mama.'

'Very well,' she said. 'It is simply this. I was wondering why you are contemplating marriage with Milly Pemberton.'

Without thinking he asked sharply, 'Has Lady Winter discussed this with you?'

She looked amused. 'No, dear. But I dare say our concerns have much in common, despite the difference in perspective. Naturally she is primarily concerned for Milly's happiness and I am concerned for yours.'

'I see,' said Crispin. 'And you think I wouldn't be.' Tilda had made it moderately plain that she held doubts for

Milly's happiness, but he didn't feel it necessary to share that with his mother.

A faint frown creased her brow. 'I think you might become a trifle bored.' She elaborated hurriedly. 'Milly is a dear, Cris. She is a good affectionate girl. Well brought up, attractive…but I wonder if she is the girl to hold your affections or give you the companionship you need. Naturally if your affections are engaged, then there is no more to be said…but they're not, are they?' A quizzical lift of her delicate brows stripped the question of all possible offence.

Ruefully he shook his head. There was no point in trying to hoax Mama. She knew him too well.

'No. They're not,' he admitted.

'So why Milly?' she pressed gently.

He shrugged. 'Why any girl? I ought to marry. For an heir if nothing else. And you yourself said that Milly is attractive, well brought up, affectionate…they seemed to me to be admirable qualities in a wife.'

'They are, of course,' concurred Lady St Ormond. 'But has she the maturity to be a companion to you?'

Crispin winced. 'You think she's too young? That I'm too old for her?'

Gently she said, 'It is not a matter of years, Cris. I think Milly will always be too young for anyone like you. Think about it, dear. I suspect it would make little difference if she were as old as Tilda. She is simply unsuited to you. And I think, you know, that she is aware of it.'

He stared.

'Oh, yes.' She nodded wisely. 'She is not really comfortable with you. But I doubt that she is fully aware of why. Just that you make her a little nervous…'

'You think I have frightened her?'

'Good God, no!' she protested. 'The last thing you, of all men, would do is frighten a woman.'

Sudden, scorching heat suffused his cheeks. Was Tilda

still in the library...still upset...still burning with shame? His shame.

He forced himself to concentrate on what the Dowager was saying.

'If you marry Milly, then I think you may become bored very rapidly. That your marriage will simply become a fashionable union, a marriage of convenience. If that is what you desire, then I have no more to say. Such marriages can, of course, prosper. Except that I think you would be better advised to wed a woman with the maturity to understand what is expected of her. Or at least capable of developing that maturity, which is probably why Tilda is concerned.'

Unable to help himself, he asked harshly, 'And did Lady Winter possess that maturity?'

She gave no hint that the question surprised her, but frowned consideringly. 'No, dear. I shouldn't think that she did. At first. But she possessed the capacity to develop that maturity. And I suspect that Jonathan was very fond of her, in a fatherly way.' She paused and then added with uncharacteristic tartness, 'Which would at least have had the charm of novelty for the poor child!'

She cast a glance at the glass-domed gilt clock on the chimney piece. 'Good gracious! Is that the time? We shall be late for lunch! Thank heavens it's only the family!'

Crispin escorted her down to the small parlour where a small, very informal luncheon was set out on a sideboard, to discover that they were indeed late and that Lady Winter appeared to be her usual calm and reserved self. Until Guy came in, apologising profusely for his tardiness and made a beeline for the empty chair beside her at the round table as soon as he had piled his plate with food. She brightened considerably as he sat down beside her and they resumed what, to Crispin's ears, sounded like a well-established flirtation.

He looked at Milly, sitting happily beside Lord John. She

did not so much as glance his way, giving him ample time to observe her. His mother had a point, he realised. She was never this relaxed with him, and it was not as though he had ever subjected *her* to any violent lovemaking. A few chaste kisses were all he'd ever pressed on her. To which she had submitted dutifully, but not at all as though she liked them.

Absently carving a second plateful of ham at the sideboard, he considered that. Along with the fact that she never really joined in a conversation with him. She had little to say beyond yes and no. And just listen to her now. Positively prattling away to Lord John about fashions! Who looked as though he didn't mind in the least. It would drive him insane!

'Here!' Guy's voice broke in on his thoughts. 'I know you're the host and all that, Cris. But you've got half the pig on your plate already.'

Startled, he looked down at the mountainous pile of ham he'd carved. 'Oh, it's not all for me!' he prevaricated wildly. 'Help yourself. And I...I thought Lady Winter might like some!'

Guy looked dubious as he speared half a dozen slices. 'You could try, but she's not very hungry. Still...' he grinned '...she might be prepared to do you a favour and help you with it! You sit beside her. I need to have a word with Hastings.'

Hell! thought Crispin. That was what came of speaking without thinking. Now he would have to go over to that vacant seat beside Tilda, when no doubt he was the last person she wanted within arm's length of her. Or even in the same room.

Steeling himself, he took the laden plate and went to her side. The only sign she gave that his presence was unwelcome was a stiffening. She went completely and utterly still. Glancing sideways at her, Crispin saw that her face was very pale, her eyes slightly reddened. Her calm was a façade. He couldn't quite believe how calm she appeared. What brand of courage did it take for a woman to appear so unmoved in this situation? Whatever it was, he could only admire it. He could think of few other women who would have put in an appearance at lunch in these circumstances.

How to apologise, without anyone else realising what he was about? 'Should you care for some ham, Lady Winter?' he asked gently. 'I do not wish to press anything on you, but I have carved far too much for myself.' He saw her eyes flash up, a guarded, shuttered expression in them. 'In fact, Lady Winter, I have bitten off more than I can chew, and I look to your generosity to assist me.'

Warily she said, 'What gives you to think that I am generous, your Grace?'

Steadily he met her gaze. Tried not to think about the way she had responded to him, surrendered to him, which was the very essence of generosity. Softly he said, 'Guy has not yet called me out.'

Burning colour flooded her cheeks. 'He has no reason to do so.'

Piling ham on her plate, he said, 'That you can say so is further proof of your generosity.' Did she value herself so cheaply? He was shocked to think so. Indeed, he was horrified to realise that his own behaviour suggested that he held her cheap. Gradually the colour receded from her face. Sad, resigned eyes lifted to his. 'Perhaps then, your Grace, you might pass me the mustard.'

He did so, desperately searching for some way to change the subject, before he said a great deal that ought to remain unsaid. She had accepted his apology. That was enough. For now.

Inspiration dawned. 'By the by, Lady Winter, if you are taking Anthea out for any more walks, keep to the paths if you enter the woods.'

She looked up, an oddly grateful expression on her face.

'I try to do that anyway. Otherwise my mending pile is vastly increased. But is there a particular reason? Will she upset your birds?'

'I don't care if she does,' he said frankly. 'But some fool has been setting steel traps on my land,' he continued. 'I don't allow them, but my keeper has reported a couple. It seems my poaching problem is getting a little out of hand and I should not like Anthea to fall foul of one.'

Surprise coloured her tone. 'If you don't permit steel traps, how on earth do you protect your game from vermin?'

Rather conscious that what he was about to say rated as heresy for most of his contemporaries, he shrugged. 'I don't. Big shooting parties bore me to death and, quite frankly I saw enough slaughter with the army on the Peninsula in the two years that I was out there before my father's death.' He said this with a bitter twist to his mouth and then continued lightly, 'I enjoy taking a gun out with a friend or two for an afternoon's sport, but I can see little need to trap foxes and badgers just to preserve a few extra grouse to ruin the crops!'

'And your hens?'

He smiled. 'Ask Mama. She deals with the hen woman. But I believe, when the necessity arises, that my keeper has been known to lie in wait for any overly bold fox with a shotgun!'

This reached the Dowager's ears. 'What's that about foxes and the hen yard? They're not really a problem. There's so much game in the woods that they rarely bother the hens.'

'Humph!' Lord John sounded disgruntled. 'In your father's day the vermin would have been properly trapped and shot! Not left to feast on grouse and pheasant to their heart's content!'

Crispin hid a smile. 'It's you then, sir! You're the rogue

setting traps and snares! Trying to make me see the error of my ways!'

'What's that?' Lord John was shocked. 'Someone setting traps? On your land? Country's going to pot!'

Mildly Crispin said, 'I thought you said I *ought* to be having traps set.'

'*You*, yes!' asserted Lord John. 'Not some other fool!'

'Thank you for that vote of confidence, Uncle John,' said Crispin drily.

'Someone has to tell you, Cris,' said Lady Hastings with sisterly candour. 'Apart from me, of course!'

Lord John snorted. 'You know what I mean, boy! Your land, your rules. I may not agree with you, but that's neither here nor there! What about your farmers? Could they be trying to rid themselves of vermin?'

'Shouldn't think so,' said Crispin. 'They know they are welcome to shoot any fox bothering their lambs or hens. And since the foxes keep the game down, they don't have grouse and pheasant destroying their crops. It's a mystery. Marlowe and Rigby are convinced that, despite my tacit acceptance of a bit of poaching to supplement several families' diets, it's not my tenants.'

Lord John looked sceptical. 'Don't know about that, m'boy. Give 'em an inch and they'll take ells, some of 'em! Still, your grandfather did the same and nothing came of it, so I dare say you're in the right of it.'

'*Did* he?' Crispin was stunned. 'I never knew that!'

The Dowager laughed. 'It nearly drove Sir Richard's father mad!' she reminisced. 'He used to harangue your grandfather without ceasing every time he dined here.'

'My, my, my!' murmured Tilda. 'How some things do run in families.'

Glancing down at her, Crispin was relieved to see that she had recovered some of her usual even good humour, lightly spiced with irony. 'I beg to differ, Lady Winter. I recall my grandfather as being a curmudgeonly old man who argued with every improvement my father suggested for the estate and was damnably hot at hand!'

'That was the gout, dear,' said Lady St Ormond. 'He was quite a rake, too, in his time,' she added, with a perfectly straight face.

Tilda met her eyes with an equally bland expression. 'Naturally, ma'am, one should only wear a cap if it fits.'

Lady St Ormond's eyes danced suddenly. 'Naturally, my dear.'

Lord Hastings smothered a laugh very unsuccessfully.

'I thought we were talking about poachers,' said Milly in some bewilderment.

Crispin groaned mentally. Mama definitely had a point. She obviously hadn't followed the thread at all, whereas Tilda had slipped her foil straight past his guard with the greatest of ease.

Guy, on the other hand, didn't seem at all put out. He smiled and patted Milly on the hand. 'Don't give it a second's thought, Milly,' he said kindly. 'Poachers are not at all the sort of thing a young girl needs to concern herself with.'

Good God! thought Crispin. He devoutly hoped his wife *would* take some interest in the things that concerned him! Otherwise, what on earth were they going to have to say to one another? While he could be frivolous quite happily, at some stage one did need to think about the basics of life! And Milly showed no sign of having the least interest in the running of large estates. Tilda had been chatting to Lord John quite happily the other night about the principles of crop rotation, even disagreeing mildly on occasion.

Grimly he thought that, apart from dutifully admiring the latest opera, the latest popular novel and the most admired paintings at the Royal Academy, he had never heard Milly utter an opinion on anything. Granted most men did not desire a wife who would argue and disagree. He had always found arguing intelligently with someone else helped him to formulate his own thoughts.

Tilda, in sharp contrast, had strongly formed ideas. He had heard her arguing during dinner with Hastings one evening on the rival merits of Sir Walter Scott and Miss Austen. And she was a staunch admirer of Beethoven, despite his admiration for Napoleon. He wondered what she thought of the marble of Cupid and Psyche that she had knocked over, it was a fine piece after all...and found that his thoughts had naturally progressed to what it would be like to wake up and find her leaning over him...naked...all warm and flushed...with his lovemaking...with the anticipation of more.

'Cris!' He jolted back to reality. Georgie was glaring at him from across the table. 'Pass the mustard, for heaven's sake! You've got plenty!'

He looked down. And wondered just how he had managed to get so much mustard on to his plate without noticing.

The following morning, instead of their usual walk, Tilda took Anthea for a ride with Georgie, Milly, Louisa, Hastings and Guy. St Ormond had excused himself on grounds of some work to do.

It was a bright, clear day and they enjoyed their ride immensely. Guy and Hastings took Anthea in hand and introduced her to the delights of jumping logs.

'Regular stitcher, that one,' commented Georgie, as Anthea sailed over a six-inch log with a gleeful whoop. 'Don't worry, Tilda. Guy and James taught all mine to ride. Along with Cris, of course. We've had a few broken bones, but nothing serious.'

Tilda grimaced. 'Am I being over-protective?'

Georgie laughed. 'Of course. We all are, but when you have several you start to get used to it. She's your only child. It would be incredible if you *didn't* worry about her.'

While the others went on for a longer ride, Tilda and Anthea turned for home after an hour. Tilda mulled over Lady Hastings's words. Georgie was right; she did fuss about Anthea too much. The last thing she wanted was to smother the child. She'd have to be careful. More children were no longer an option.

Upon their return to the stables they found St Ormond in a lively discussion with his head groom. His Grace was seated in a very unducal manner on a bale of straw, his long legs stretched out in front of him.

Without seeming to rush, he reached her mare long before any of the grooms who rushed from every corner of the stables to lift her down.

'My lady.' He inclined his head. 'May I have the honour?'

She glared down at him. It was the essence of the rhetorical question. Unless she wished to offer him a direct snub in front of a dozen servants, she had no choice.

'Thank you, your Grace,' she said sweetly. 'I would be most obliged.'

She steeled herself for the touch of his hands on her waist, telling herself that, as a widow of twenty-five, she ought to be indifferent to such things. Men lifted women down from horses every day without the sky falling in, so...

His hands closed gently on her waist, spanning it effortlessly. She was a tall woman, of Junoesque proportions, yet he made her feel little, protected, and completely and utterly vulnerable, as though he could break or seduce her with equal ease. His very gentleness only heightened the impression she had of something hot and dangerous leashed. The easy strength with which he lifted her and set her down made her swallow convulsively.

And then he had released her and was turning to Anthea. 'Good morning, Miss Cavendish. I trust Henry has no complaints about my best oats?' He ran a knowledgeable eye over the little Welsh grey. 'I must say he looks to be in rude health. And very well groomed. Did you do that yourself?'

He swung Anthea off and spun her around before setting her down.

Tilda blinked. She kept forgetting that St Ormond was an experienced uncle, entirely used to his sister's children, and from all she had observed, fond of them.

Anthea was responding happily. 'Do you mean, groom him myself? Could I?' Plainly the idea of getting thoroughly dirty and smelly in the stables appealed to her enormously. She turned to Tilda. 'Mama, please may I stay and help to groom him? Please?'

Tilda frowned. 'The men have work to do, dear. You will be very much in their way.'

Farnham, the head groom, demurred. 'Nay. She'll not be a trouble, me lady. I taught Lady George to manage her own pony. I'll keep an eye on her.'

Hesitantly Tilda said, 'You're very kind, but...'

All at once, she remembered the pony she had learnt to ride on. He had been the pony who pulled the mower— Tipsy, a very elderly, worn-out excuse for a nag, who had narrowly missed out on a trip to the hunt kennels. She had adored him and would have happily spent hours grooming and fussing over him, but had never been allowed to do so. And hadn't she just been vowing to cosset Anthea less?

She hesitated fatally and St Ormond settled the matter. 'If Farnham and his predecessor survived Lady Hastings and myself haunting the stables, he'll hardly be put out by Anthea. She'll be perfectly safe, Lady Winter. Farnham has a genius for letting a child get kicked just hard enough to learn a lesson! Perhaps you could consider it an exercise in independence.'

'Very well.' Tilda knew when she was outgunned. 'An hour, Anthea. And then you must come back up to the house. I shall be...' She paused as she considered where she should wait.

'In the library,' supplied St Ormond helpfully, offering his arm.

Belatedly she realised that, in agreeing to Anthea remaining, she had effectively robbed herself of her chaperon, that she had allowed herself to be outflanked as well as outgunned. And she had the shrubbery to get through unscathed! Unscrupulous beast! She was all the more infuriated to realise that her heart was pounding at the thought. Sheer fright, she told herself very unconvincingly. On his previous record, she'd be lucky to make it back with her honour intact! And he was still holding out his arm.

She could either take it, or offer him the cut direct in front of his servants. Again, she had no choice.

Outrage stiffening every line of her body, she laid her hand on his arm, trying not to let her fingers cling, trying to ignore the powerful muscles and taut sinews beneath the fine material. She might have succeeded had he not brought his free hand across to anchor her fingers more firmly.

Heat flashed through her at his touch—melting, softening heat. The urge to nestle closer, to lean on his arm, was overwhelming as he escorted her out of the stable yard.

Instead she glared up at him, to find his eyes on her face, a rueful smile curving his lips.

He shook his head. 'On my honour as a gentleman,' he said quietly.

She snorted. 'I was under the impression that you were merely a nobleman. With distinctly feudal tendencies.'

The rueful smile deepened. 'That, too,' he admitted. 'But I swear I'll keep all my *droit de seigneur* instincts under control.'

'For how long?' Mentally she cursed her unruly tongue and the waspish tone that suggested she also disbelieved in flying pigs. Although it *was* helping to hide her feelings.

'For as long as you wish,' he responded blandly. 'At

least, I promise to give you a few seconds' warning before they get out of control again.'

She bit her lip. He'd given plenty of warning yesterday. And she hadn't availed herself of it. After all, she had known perfectly well that he intended to kiss her, even if the other liberties he had taken had been a complete shock.

And if, as she kept trying to convince herself, she really hadn't wanted him to kiss her; why on earth hadn't she grabbed the *pot pourri* bowl on the wine table and cracked him over the head with it? Or just said *no*? He had stopped the minute she protested, so why hadn't she protested sooner? As for the episode outside his bedchamber—he'd had her halfway to his door before she'd realised and made her escape.

The answer made her even angrier. With her free hand she lifted her skirts clear of the wet grass as they walked through the shrubbery in silence. He led her into the formal part of the garden and along a box-edged path to a side door.

She risked a sideways glance at her host as he held the door open for her. He appeared perfectly calm, if a trifle distant. His face gave not the least clue to his thoughts. Clearly he was not having the least trouble with his instincts at the moment. Which was just as well, since she was having a great deal of trouble with hers. And it didn't help in the least that they had never troubled her before and were taking shameless advantage of her inexperience to run riot over her orderly, cynical detachment.

'Why do you wish me to come to the library?' she asked.

'I wanted your advice,' he replied.

She blinked. 'My advice? What on earth can you possibly want my advice on?'

He looked down at her, his gaze shuttered. 'Your cousin. You had a great deal to say yesterday. I am afraid I did not do you the courtesy of listening. I am inviting you to have your say without fear of interruption…or…other interference.'

Tilda's stomach lurched. 'I…I…no.'

'No?'

'No.'

'Why not?' His tone was cool, uncompromising.

She dragged in a deep breath. And wondered where the air had ended up. She took another breath. 'I was angry yesterday. And upset.'

He nodded. 'You had reason to be. But does that mean that you meant none of what you said?'

She didn't answer, but walked beside him to the library with an awful feeling of impending doom. This time she permitted him to escort her to one of the chairs in front of his desk. She didn't care how much like an interview it seemed. At least with that great desk between them, she was safe from any chance caresses or kisses. And any not-so-chance responses on her part. Because there was one thing that she was certainly going to take the opportunity of saying.

'There is something that I would like to make plain, your Grace,' she said as he gracefully lowered his frame into his chair.

He raised a brow and she ploughed on. 'No matter what my behaviour and my…my remarks may have led you to believe, I am not in the least interested in becoming your mistress!' She blushed as she said it, but held his suddenly arrested gaze gallantly.

'I see,' he said calmly. 'How very disappointing. But I feel I should point out that I have not asked you to do so.'

Somehow she managed to blush even more deeply, conscious of having made a complete fool of herself. Why on earth had she thought St Ormond would want a great, gangling creature like her for more than a casual tumble? She might have improved slightly, but she hadn't changed that much since the night of the Seftons' ball so long ago, when she'd heard him ridicule her to Hastings. No doubt he had far prettier and daintier women falling over their feet to receive his favours. Not to mention his intended bride, Milly.

She swallowed, and managed to say coldly, 'Good. As to our conversation yesterday—'

He interrupted her. 'Conversation?'

The amused tone flicked her lightly. 'Conversation,' she reiterated firmly. 'I may have expressed myself very badly, but...'

'Not badly,' he assured her, with a faint smile.

'Very well! Rudely!' she grated.

'That's more like it,' he said approvingly. 'You needn't waste any tact on me, you know, my dear. We had an argument. Quite a lively one.'

'Would you kindly stop interrupting?' said Tilda crossly. She was insanely aware of the urge to laugh, and she had yet to explain to him why she had spoken as she had.

He inclined his head and she drew a deep breath.

'It is not that I dislike you or think you a monster of depravity or anything of that nature...'

'Generous of you, under the circumstances,' murmured Crispin. 'That or your definition of depravity is more liberal than most.' The twinkle in his eye robbed the remark of any hurtfulness. A tremor ran through her at the note of gentleness in his voice.

'I meant to apologise properly, by the way,' he added.

She stared, completely losing the thread of her thought. 'You did?'

'Mmm. One of my rare, gentlemanly impulses,' he said. 'Don't count on me having another in the foreseeable future.'

'I won't,' she assured him. 'Well, I...I mean, I shan't mind it then. 'I...I won't give it a moment's thought. I dare say it won't happen again?' She could have kicked herself for sounding so damned uncertain. So unsure of whether that was a good thing. Of course it was a good thing!

One brow rose ironically. 'You misunderstand me. I wasn't apologising for kissing you.' A slight pause in which her eyes widened. 'Or for anything else I did, for that matter.'

'Then just what the devil *are* you apologising for?' she demanded. 'You haven't left very much!'

'Just my appalling lack of tact and the insulting excuse I used.'

'Excuse?' What on earth was he talking about? Excuse for what?

He sighed. 'Never mind. I hurt you and insulted you, for which I am deeply sorry. I'm not sorry I kissed you, because I enjoyed it. A lot. And so did you. Now, since you don't think me Blue Beard incarnate, why do you object to my marriage to Milly?'

She had to fight to clear her head enough to recall what she had been saying. He'd enjoyed kissing her. The intense light in his eyes was blinding her to all else. And her voice had deserted her.

At last she managed to say, 'It is just that I don't think that Milly would be terribly happy in the sort of marriage you envisage…that you…described to me yesterday. She doesn't have the…she wouldn't understand…she is very soft hearted…' Her voice trailed off.

'Unlike her cousin?' He was silent for a moment. 'Tell me, Lady Winter, how did you develop the necessary hardness of heart to manage in a marriage of convenience? Or did you have it already?'

Her face whitened, shocking Crispin. For a moment she did not answer and then she rose to her feet.

The soft curves of her mouth were trembling, her eyes overbright. She spoke as though the words were dragged from her. 'Whatever I developed, it is not something I would wish on any other woman. Certainly not Milly.' And left the room.

She left his Grace staring after her in remorse. For all she hadn't intended to answer his question, he'd seen the truth in her suddenly vulnerable eyes. She'd never developed that particular defence. However she'd managed, it hadn't involved hardening her heart. All her cynicism and cool façade were no more substantial than wreathing mist to sheathe her and protect the woman underneath from being seen. They were not really part of her. They would not even deflect as armour would. Her defences, her armour, were pure illusion.

Somewhere under the confident, yet reserved, Lady Winter, the shyly confiding girl was hidden. And she could still be hurt—all the more badly because very few would know she was there.

Setting his jaw, he forced himself to hope that Guy had seen through the façade to the truth. That Guy wouldn't hurt her even more than he had done.

Chapter Nine

A week went by peacefully enough in riding parties, boating on the lake, walks in the park and enjoyable evenings during which the Malverns argued about everything under the sun with the greatest good humour. St Ormond paid no more attention to Tilda than to any of his other guests and she gradually relaxed, convinced that he had no real interest in her. A state of affairs that should have relieved her mind exceedingly.

Unfortunately, it merely gave her the opportunity to observe him without the distraction of wondering when he was going to pounce on her next. She was free to make all sorts of unhelpful observations about his person and character. Such as the regard in which he held his family. It gradually became plain to Tilda that St Ormond was head of his family in the best possible sense.

Far from being overbearing or telling anyone how to run their life, he was simply there to give advice. When requested. Overhearing part of a conversation between his Grace and Miss Hastings one evening, Tilda could not doubt this.

She did not wish to listen, but such was Louisa's youthful indignation at her parents' seeming callousness, that she had little choice since she was pinned to her seat by Lady

Hollow, who was regaling her with a great deal of forth-right advice on the rearing of daughters.

He listened to everything that Louisa had to say about the young neighbour who was showing signs of being thoroughly smitten by her. Much to Tilda's surprise, when she asked his opinion, instead of simply telling her what to do, he commented that she was behaving very sensibly in considering her options and then asked her what she thought should be done. Did she wish for a London Season before making her choice? Or did she wish to bestow her hand and heart on the young man and retire to what he dubiously referred to as domestic bliss, without having a bit of fun first?

Not labouring the point, he immediately changed the subject—to the delights of the next year's London Season and how much he looked forward to standing up with her at Almack's.

'It will convey such an aura of respectability on me,' he said with a twinkle. 'I shall be able to make the acquaintance of dozens of charming girls without anyone raising so much as an eyebrow!'

Louisa giggled and Tilda silently congratulated his Grace on a tricky situation well-handled.

He caught her eye and gracefully excused himself from Louisa's side to approach her and offer to take his aunt's teacup.

Lady Hollow snorted. 'I can manage, St Ormond. Think I'll take myself off now. Not as young as I was. Goodnight, m'dear. Don't take what I said amiss. You're doing a fine job with the girl!' Heaving herself to her feet with the aid of her stick, she added, 'And if St Ormond can keep Louisa from making a cake of herself, he'll be doing as well!'

Crispin rolled his eyes at her departing back and, lowering his voice, said teasingly, 'No words of censure to counterbalance that, my dear?'

A tinge of colour washed into her cheeks. 'I assure you that we were not listening intentionally!'

He grinned. 'Children of that age never remember that others may be able to hear.'

She raised her brows. 'Do you consider Louisa a child then, your Grace? She is nearly eighteen, after all.'

It was his turn to colour, a faint flush staining the high cheekbones. *'Touché,'* he acknowledged. 'Your blade is as keen, and your aim as unerring, as ever.'

Guy came up at that moment to be greeted with a friendly smile from Tilda that drove Crispin away with a distinctly ungracious mutter He refused to acknowledge Guy's startled gaze and stalked off stiffly, fully aware that his conduct was atrocious. The knowledge did not help his mood in the least. Lady Winter had made it as clear as possible where her choice lay.

He watched them together out of the corner of his eye as he chatted to Georgie. They looked so easy together. Tilda seemed so relaxed. Grimly he realised that they were much of an age. After her experience of a much older husband that probably counted for a great deal.

Milly joined her cousin and Guy, and Crispin forced himself to turn away.

The next morning, having finished his estate business, Crispin emerged from the library to be hailed by Guy and Hastings.

'There you are, Cris! Come and pot a few balls. Papa's waiting for us in the billiard room,' urged Guy.

Crispin hesitated. He felt so utterly confused about his attitude to Guy just at the moment, that he would liefer do anything else. And that bothered him greatly. Despite the ten-year gap in their ages, they were good friends. It was very disturbing to feel like taking his insouciant cousin by the scruff of the neck and shaking him, merely because Guy was having an affair with a woman *he* wanted to marry! A perfectly willing, widowed woman; who had stated un-equivocally that she would prefer to take a lover than ever enter the lists of Hymen again. Just because he was suffer-ing from an unprecedented attack of chivalry and…very well, damn it! Love!…was no reason to call Guy out, or even harbour the urge to do so!

'You can't *still* have work to do!' protested Hastings.

Crispin noticed that Guy looked suddenly uncomfortable.

'Never mind,' he said. 'We'll manage.'

That brought Crispin to his senses. The last thing he wanted was to cause a coldness between himself and Guy. And last night Guy had looked thoroughly hurt by his be-haviour.

'No. Of course I'll come,' said Crispin grinning. 'I've been meaning to take my revenge for our last match!'

'Oho!' chuckled Hastings. 'Beat you, did he?'

'Just!' averred Crispin loftily.

'Several times!' struck in Guy.

'I was off my game,' said Crispin with an inward grin.

'Hah! We'll see about that!' Guy rose to the bait at once and the three of them repaired to the billiard room where they found Lord John knocking the balls about.

The match had not progressed very far when the door opened unceremoniously and Rigby came in hurriedly.

'Your Grace! Thank Gawd I've found you!'

Crispin, having just missed a shot, handed his cue to Guy and looked at the bailiff questioningly. 'Something urgent?'

'Aye.' Rigby flashed an apologetic glance at the others. 'Sorry to interrupt but, your Grace, Farmer Willis's sheep were attacked last night. Five, with their throats ripped out afore Shepherd could call his dogs to drive it off. And one of the dogs in a bad way too. Just one dog it was, but a damn big one, mastiff, Shepherd Hughes thought.'

'Hell!' said Crispin. 'That's all we need. Anything else?'

Rigby nodded. 'He reckoned it was fair torn about by his dogs, since they had blood all around their mouths when they came back after chasing it off. Thing is, it came this way. And Marlowe came in just now and told me he'd found a rabbit ripped to pieces in a snare early this morning. In the woods. He thought from the tracks that it was a dog.'

A horrified exclamation from Hastings brought Crispin's head around.

'James?'

Hastings was white. 'Lady Winter took her daughter for a walk about an hour ago. They were going to go through the woods to the village.'

Something very strange happened to Crispin's stomach. It lurched and contracted in a spasm of sheer unadulterated terror. The thought of Tilda and Anthea meeting a badly injured and savage mastiff chilled him to the marrow. He felt sick and unashamedly downright terrified.

'Which way did they go?' He rapped out the question in a harsh voice that shook very slightly.

'Around the lake, I think,' said Hastings slowly. 'Yes. Anthea was going to feed the ducks on the way.'

'Come on, Cris!' said Guy. 'They might still be there if we hurry.'

Cris stared at him. Why was Guy...? He remembered. Tilda was not his. Guy had every right to take charge... He turned to his brother-in-law. 'James, make sure the entire household is warned. Rigby, I want the grooms to warn every household on the estate.'

'Already left, your Grace,' said Rigby. 'I told Farnham when I left my horse at the stables. Three boys have gone.'

'That's it, then,' said Crispin grimly. 'Come on, Guy. We'd better hurry. We'll need guns.'

It was a lovely morning with the promise of heat to come. Anthea ran out of bread very quickly owing to the greediness of the ducal ducks. Heaving a sigh of resignation, she left them and followed Tilda on around the lake and into the shady woodland path.

Mindful of the warning St Ormond had given her a week ago about traps, Tilda kept Anthea close by, constantly pointing things out and challenging her to spot various birds and flowers.

The air was full of birdsong and the drifting scent of wildflowers and, walking slowly, they saw a willow warbler feeding three fat babies on a branch. Anthea watched entranced.

'I'm glad you didn't feed me worms, when I was a baby,' she whispered, as they moved on.

'Who says I didn't?' asked Tilda, her eyes twinkling.

'Ugh!' said Anthea. 'You didn't!' Then she caught the twinkle and swung vigorously on Tilda's hand. 'You're just teasing!'

They continued on along the twisting path until an odd sound came to their ears, a strange mixture of snarl and whimper. Instantly Tilda froze. It sounded like an injured animal, she thought. A fox, perhaps, or a badger.

'Stay beside me, Anthea,' she said very quietly and moved forward.

The source of the sound was just around the next bend, by the side of the path. A very large, yellow-brown dog with one hind leg ripped by a steel trap. It was worrying savagely at the limb, snarling and whining in a mixture of fear and rage.

Tilda stopped dead, prepared to back away. But Anthea, who had never seen an injured creature in her life, had no idea of the danger and rushed forward.

'Oh, the poor thing!'

'Anthea! *No!*' Tilda shrieked and flung herself forward instinctively, just as the dog looked up and hurled itself forward with a savage bark. Horrified, she realised that the trap was not dug in, that the brute had been able to drag it. That it was going to reach Anthea!

Frantically she caught Anthea and swung her away from the dog one-handed with a strength born of desperation, fending off the huge animal with her other arm.

'Run, Anthea!' she screamed as she felt teeth sink into her arm, ripping effortlessly through her light spencer. She staggered back under the force of the attack, but struck at the dog with her free hand, aiming for his eyes.

'Mama!'

She could hear Anthea screaming.

'Run!' she shrieked. She knew she would not be able to hold the dog off for long. It was too big and it was insane with fear and hurt. She staggered back, stumbling over a tree root. As she hit the ground she had no idea whether Anthea had obeyed or not. The dog landed on top of her, savagely biting and worrying at the upflung arm.

Crispin and Guy had no idea just how close they were behind Tilda and Anthea until they heard Tilda scream, heard the dog's bark. Exchanging a horrified look they broke into a run, and practically fell across Anthea, running for help.

'Mama,' she gasped. 'Oh, quickly, please!'

'Stay here!' ordered Crispin. They sprinted on.

And came upon a scene of horror.

Tilda was struggling weakly on the ground, desperately trying to fend the dog off, but it was snapping and snarling, trying to get past her torn and bloodstained shielding arms to her throat.

Guy instinctively raised the gun he carried to his shoulder but Crispin knocked it up as he ran forward, yelling a challenge with his gun reversed.

The dog looked up and, recognising a greater threat, sprang clumsily. Much bigger than Tilda and armed with the gun, Crispin clubbed it aside easily enough, sidestepping so that he was between it and Tilda.

For a fatal moment the dog hesitated. Crispin brought

the barrel of the gun to bear and fired at point blank range just as the brute gathered itself to spring. Full in the chest the charge struck it, and it sank to the ground, the life slowly ebbing out of it.

Crispin didn't even bother to look at the dying dog. He had spun around and dropped to his knees beside Tilda. She lay horribly still, blood pouring from the innumerable gashes in her arms. With a shudder of relief he realised that the dog had not reached her throat. Even so, she was losing too much blood.

With a stab of horror he saw the red pulsing and beating in time with her heart at one wrist. He swore savagely. The brute had torn an artery. He'd seen men die because bleeding like this was not stopped fast enough. He was aware of Guy at his side as he ripped off his cravat.

'I'll need yours too,' he said grimly. 'Give it to me and find Anthea. Don't let her come back—'

'Mama? *Mama!*' A small figure stood stricken beside them. 'She's not…?'

Crispin glanced up from his rapid bandaging. 'No, sweetheart. Just fainted. She'll be fine. Don't worry. I'll look after her.' It had to be the most stupid piece of reassurance in history, he thought, but it seemed to work. Although still obviously shaken, the wild terror left Anthea's eyes. And the effort of reassuring her seemed to steady him slightly. Steadied the frantic beating of his heart. Calmed the waves of panic washing over him.

'Cravat, Guy,' he said shortly. It was in his hand as he spoke. 'We'll need more,' he said as he wound it tightly around Tilda's mauled arm.

'My…my petticoat…' Anthea was hitching up her skirts even as she spoke.

'Good girl,' he said approvingly.

Tilda moaned as he worked at ripping up the petticoat into strips. 'Anthea…Anthea…' Her eyes fluttered open and her confused gaze fell on Crispin.

'Crispin?' Her voice was weak. She tried to struggle up but he dropped the petticoat and held her down.

'Anthea is fine. She came and found us,' he reassured her quickly. 'Look. Here she is.' He gestured Anthea to where Tilda could see her. 'See. She's quite well, sweetheart. Just let us look after you.'

'The…the dog…it attacked…'

'Dead,' he said shortly. 'Don't think about it. Just stay quiet and breathe deeply. Calm down. You're both perfectly safe with us.' He kept his voice soothing, low. The more frightened she was, the faster her heart would beat and the more blood she'd lose.

'About the only thing that you have to fuss about is the fact that your daughter just ripped off her petticoat in front of us,' he continued. 'Obviously she's going to be a complete hussy! You worry about that.' As he spoke he was tying a strip of the said petticoat loosely around her upper arm to use as a tourniquet.

'Find a…' Even as he spoke Guy handed him a short stout stick. 'Ah. Thanks.' He slipped it between the strip and her arm and twisted it. 'Excellent.'

Breathing hard, he looked at Guy. 'I'll carry her as far as the edge of the woods while you keep that arm elevated and keep the stick tight. Then you can run back and bring some sort of carriage. The gig, anything. I'll keep the tourniquet tight. Send one of the grooms for the doctor and a message up to the house.' He held the stick twisted tightly in the tourniquet.

Guy nodded. 'Let's go! Should I take Anthea with me?'

Crispin hesitated. It would be better for the child to go, but taking her would slow Guy down. He shook his head. 'She'll stay with me. You'll be quicker alone.' He glanced down at the child. 'You can talk to your mama and cheer her up. That arm must be hurting, don't you think?'

'Very well,' said Guy. He bent down and grasped the

injured arm and stick. 'We'll have you safe home in a trice, Tilda,' he said quietly.

Crispin pulled his watch out of his waistcoat pocket, un-clipped the chain and gave it to Anthea. 'Can you tell the time, pet?'

She nodded.

'Good. Tell Guy when twenty minutes have gone by. Then it will be time to loosen the stick. Will you do that?'

'Yes, your Grace.'

'Why don't you just call me Uncle Cris, like my nieces and nephews?' he suggested. Hearing a five-year-old call him *your Grace*, made him feel beyond elderly.

He glanced at Guy. 'Ready?'

At Guy's affirmative nod, he swung Tilda up into his arms and began walking.

To his immense relief, by the time they reached the edge of the woods, Guy reported that the bleeding had stopped. He sounded jubilant.

'You'll be fine now, Tilda. Cris's tourniquet has stopped the bleeding. Just you stay here and I'll be back in a trice with the carriage!'

She barely responded. Just a faint smile, then her eyelids fluttered shut, as if she were too exhausted to speak.

Crispin noted worriedly that the sky had clouded over considerably and to his experienced eye it looked as though rain was on the way. And lots of it. He bit back a curse and settled down under a large oak, telling Anthea to strip his jacket off.

Casting a glance at the sky, Guy shrugged out of his and tossed it to him, saying, 'You may as well have this too.' Then he was off, sprinting for the house.

The first drops of rain fell before Guy was out of sight over the rise towards the lake. Mentally cursing, Crispin ordered Anthea into Guy's jacket and wrapped his own around Tilda. Despite the seriousness of the situation, with Tilda in his lap and Anthea snuggled against his side, he felt oddly complete. As though everything was right with his world.

Pure illusion, he told himself bitterly. And given that Guy had cheerfully allowed him to assume command and stay with Tilda, it looked as though their affair was no more to him than a transient pleasure to while away the time.

Crispin found himself desperately hoping that the woman in his arms felt the same way, that he had been wrong in thinking her cynicism was only skin deep. Because if it wasn't, the hurt Guy would deal her would bite deeper than the injuries to her arms.

Within fifteen minutes the rain was blinding, and despite the shelter of the oak, they were all drenched to the skin in half an hour. Crispin tried to protect Tilda from the worst of it, gathering her into his arms like a baby, shielding her with his body. He bent his head over the soft, damp curls, resting his cheek on them as he tried to persuade himself that he was only keeping the rain off.

He concentrated on Anthea. She had nestled against him, pretending that the thunder wasn't bothering her at all. But the way she flinched at every crash alerted Crispin to the truth.

'You're very brave, Anthea,' he said encouragingly. 'My sister Georgie, Lady Hastings, was terrified of thunder when she was your age.' Which was an outright lie, but he had his reward in Anthea's response.

'I...I don't really like it,' she said. 'But with you and Mama here...'

'If you don't like it, then that's extra brave,' he said seriously. 'Being brave means doing something you're scared of.'

'Like Mama stopping the dog attacking me?' asked Anthea with a sniff, pressing a little closer at a particularly loud crash.

'Is that what happened?' asked Crispin. A shiver, that had nothing to do with the icy water trickling down his spine, racked him as he imagined what the result might have been had the dog reached Anthea. She might well have been killed, judging by the state of Tilda's arms. On Anthea the attack would have come straight at face and throat.

He didn't have to use his imagination to know how Tilda had reacted. Sheer protective instinct would have taken over; just as it had for him. He doubted that she had even had time to feel afraid for herself; or that it would have slowed her if she had. Her fear for the child must have been overwhelming. And now, when she must be in the most appalling pain, she lay quiescent in his arms, her lower lip gripped between her teeth, only an occasional sob escaping to testify to her pain.

His arms tightened around her as he said to Anthea. 'You're a very lucky girl to have your mama. Just as lucky as she is to have you.'

Unthinkingly he turned his head and pressed a gentle kiss on Tilda's hair, breathing the soft fragrance in, enjoying the tickle of damp tendrils. A rush of tenderness shook him as he felt her sigh and snuggle closer. He wished he could hold her like this for ever. But reality, far chillier than the rain, told him he only had until the carriage arrived. And he knew deep down that the sooner it arrived, the better. Before she caught a chill. Before the sensation of soft, womanly curves impressed themselves indelibly on his heart. Before he couldn't let her go.

The carriage arrived in what had to be record time, driven by Farnham in a manner that bordered on the reckless. The pair of greys harnessed to it were steaming.

The lad who leapt down from the box said breathlessly, 'Mr Guy took Apollo and rode for the doctor, your Grace.'

Crispin nodded as he lifted Tilda into the carriage. Trust Guy, he thought. He'd done the sensible thing, taken the fastest horses available and gone himself.

There were several horse blankets in the carriage and

Crispin wrapped the nearly unconscious Tilda in them tenderly. She needed to stay warm. He could feel the chill creeping through her body. Shock, he thought, and loss of blood as well as the rain.

By the time they reached the house a warm bed was ready for Tilda. The Dowager met them in the hall. 'Take her straight up, Cris. Milly and her maid are there waiting. I'll take Anthea. A hot bath is ready for her.'

She held out her hand to the child who hesitated, glancing up at her mother, cradled in Crispin's arms.

Tilda raised her head slightly and said weakly, 'Go with her Grace, Anthea. I don't want you taking a chill. Your Uncle Cris will look after me.'

Guy arrived back with the doctor within half an hour and brought him straight up to Tilda's room. She was in bed by then. Milly and Sarah had chased Crispin out with about as much ceremony as they would have accorded a bedbug, while they changed her into a nightgown and got her between the sheets.

But the moment he knew she was safe in bed, he came back and not all Milly's polite murmurs nor Sarah's outraged protests could shift him from his position at the side of her bed. He sat there, gently holding her hand, his face strangely still, a cold, hard mask for the scorching passions beneath.

Something in the set of her jaw suggested that she was not unconscious, that she was hanging on to her self-control by a hair's-breadth. Her courage took his breath away. She hung on to her control with all the grim determination of some of the wounded soldiers he had seen in his years of war service.

When he arrived, the doctor did not appear to see anything out of the way in his presence by the bed, but nodded to him briefly before unwinding the makeshift bandages.

He swore when he saw the damage. 'Damnation! Begging your pardon, ladies, but what the devil possessed her to get in the way of the brute?'

'It attacked her five-year-old daughter,' said Crispin shortly.

The doctor nodded 'I see. Inevitable, then. Thank God she was there. This would have killed a child. Very well. The right arm is especially bad. I'll need to stitch most of that. Are you awake, Lady Winter?'

Slowly Tilda's eyes opened. Crispin felt his heart contract. There was no hint in the pain-soaked hazel that she was anywhere near unconscious. He had been right. She was in full possession of her senses but had barely made a sound.

The doctor was speaking again. 'I'm going to give you a little laudanum, Lady Winter. Just to deaden the pain a trifle while I stitch up the worst of your injuries.' He turned to Crispin. 'Even with the laudanum, I'll need someone to hold her. And someone to hold her arm as I stitch.'

Shakily Milly spoke up. 'I...I could hold her...I'm her cousin.'

Stephenson shook his head as he prepared his instruments. 'Being her cousin won't give you the strength to hold her steady, young lady.' He glanced at Crispin.

Crispin nodded. Without looking up he said, 'Milly, find Guy. We'll need him to help. She knows him and trust him.' He only hoped she extended him the same trust.

'But...'

'Milly. Find him.' The note of absolute authority in his voice sent Milly running from the room.

She was back within moments with Guy.

He came across to the bed and said, 'Isn't this a bit...?'

'We'll have to hold her down,' said Crispin. He drew a deep breath and said, 'If you would prefer, I can hold her arm, while you...' He left the sentence hanging. He couldn't bring himself to actually finish it. He knew how he would feel were their positions reversed. Savage, primitive, ready to murder the man holding her. Exactly as he did now at the mere thought of Guy holding her.

Guy was staring at him in disbelief, his jaw slack.

'For God's sake, Guy!' said Crispin. 'Take her!'

Guy shook his head numbly. 'You hold her. I...I don't think I could. I'll hold her arm.'

Crispin couldn't quite believe what he was hearing. Belatedly he remembered that Guy had never been on a battlefield, had never seen the appalling injuries inflicted by war. Nodding, he turned to the bed and lifted Tilda back into his arms. She opened her eyes again and gazed up at him, her underlip caught in her teeth.

He smiled at her tenderly. 'It's all right, I've got you.'

'I know,' she whispered and leaned her head on his chest. His heart tightened. So trusting, so helpless.

'Drink this, Lady Winter. It will ease the pain.' Stephenson held the tumbler of laudanum to her lips. Obediently she drank and very soon the bright hazel clouded over.

When she was quite limp in Crispin's arms, Stephenson turned to Guy. 'Very well, Mr Malvern. Hold her arm steady. Like so. Keep it absolutely still. The laudanum won't deaden all the pain, but it will take the edge off it and weaken her struggles. Ready, your Grace?'

Crispin nodded, suppressing a shudder. He had wrapped Tilda in his arms, holding her tightly against his body, one hand gripping her head to rest on his shoulder, the other anchored to her waist.

He knew when the doctor began work. He felt her body jerk in his arms, felt the whimpering intake of breath. Instinctively he tightened his hold. Not just to restrain—but to comfort and protect. To reassure. 'Hold on to me,' he murmured. 'It won't take long. Just breathe deeply.' He kept talking, gently, slowly. Talking nonsense, telling her how brave she was. Anything. To his amazement she didn't struggle, just clung to him desperately with her free arm, her face buried in the curve of his shoulder, muffling her cries. Sweat beaded on her brow.

He could hear soft-spoken instructions and requests from the doctor. At last he felt her slump against him and realised from the sounds that her arm was being bandaged. *Thank God.* Her trembling seared his body. He shuddered to think of how much it must have hurt. He looked around wildly and his eye lit on a damp cloth being held out by Milly.

'Good girl.' He took it and wiped the sweat from Tilda's face with a featherlight touch.

'Right. Change sides, your Grace.' Stephenson's quiet command brought a soft moan from Tilda.

Regardless of Guy's presence, Crispin dropped a gentle kiss on her hair. 'Hold tight, sweetheart. It won't be long now.'

'I've done the worst, Lady Winter,' said the doctor. 'You're a very brave woman.'

Carefully Crispin shifted across her, freeing her left arm and wrapping her bandaged right arm around him. Settling her back in his arms, he held her tightly as the torture began again. Every jolt of her body, every stifled sob tearing through him as though it was his flesh that had been lacerated. Sweat sprang out on her brow again. He could feel the tension in her jaw as whimpers of pain struggled for release. And he felt her body pressed against his in complete trust. It nearly killed him to remember that she wasn't his.

At last Stephenson was finished and Crispin lay her back on the pillows, his mouth tightening, his whole body struggling to resist the urge to lean over and kiss the soft, trembling mouth, stroke the damp curls back from her brow and caress the blanched cheek.

Grimly he forced himself to stand up and turn to face Guy. Fully expecting to meet a blazing challenge.

Guy had moved away and was standing by the end of

the bed, looking as though he were about to be sick. He met Crispin's eyes.

'I need a drink,' he stated in shaken tones.

The doctor looked up with a grim smile. 'Take him out, your Grace. Before he faints on us. She'll do well enough. When I'm finished here I'll see the child. Make sure she's not too shocked.'

Unable to think of a single excuse to stay, Crispin nodded and followed Guy who was already heading for the door. They found the Dowager right outside.

'How is she?' Lady St Ormond gripped Crispin's arm.

'Stephenson says she'll be quite all right,' said Crispin, patting her hand.

She heaved a sigh of relief. 'Thank God for that. Georgie and Louisa are looking after Anthea. They're in the drawing room. For heaven's sake go and tell the child. She's in a terrible state. I'll go in now and arrange with Milly and the maid about sitting up with Tilda tonight.'

Casting an experienced glance at her white-faced nephew and son, she added, 'And have a drink, both of you. Several, in fact. You look as though Stephenson stitched up your arms.' So saying, she opened the door and disappeared.

Guy shuddered. 'Come on, Cris. I don't know how anyone could do that for a living. I felt ill just watching.' As they walked slowly down the hallway he went on, 'Was she unconscious, do you think? I could hear her, but she barely moved at all while he was working. And it must have hurt like hell.'

Crispin knew from bitter experience just how much it had hurt. 'No. She was at least partly conscious,' he said shortly. He could still feel her clinging to him. Trusting him.

'Pluck to the backbone,' said Guy admiringly. 'Lord! I'd have been yelling blue murder.'

* * *

The rest of the day passed very quietly. Once Anthea had been reassured as to her mother's safety, been examined by the doctor and taken up, clinging to Crispin's hand, to see Tilda sleeping soundly, she was packed off to bed with a very light sleeping draught.

'Just to make sure she sleeps,' said the doctor. 'Should be with her mama, but that's not possible tonight. Keep her close tomorrow, your Grace. She'll be shaky and out of sorts for a few days. As for Lady Winter, keep her in bed for a couple of days. I'll call tomorrow to see how she goes on. I've left instructions with her Grace, Miss Pemberton and the maid. They'll manage. Good day, your Grace.'

'Good day, sir,' said Crispin. 'I'm more grateful than I can say.'

Stephenson snorted. 'Thank yourself! Mr Guy told me how fast you stopped the bleeding. I'll tell you to your head: you saved her life. Just as surely as she saved the child's life.' With a brusque nod he was gone.

Crispin was left in the great hall with his thoughts. Most of them unwelcome. Although it was obvious that Guy was upset by the incident, Crispin could detect no sign that he was more upset than he would have been by an accident to any other woman he considered a friend. Certainly he was not moping around, snapping off the head of anyone foolish enough to speak to him. He betrayed no signs that he wished to be at Tilda's bedside in case she woke and needed him.

Which suggested that he was not in love at all.

This left Crispin in an unenviable dilemma; whether he should shout a paean of joy to the skies, or wring Guy's stupid, ungrateful neck. Or very possibly do both at one and the same time.

In the event he settled for moping around and snapping everyone's head off, so that by the time the tea tray was brought in after a very subdued dinner and he announced that he was going to bed early, everyone heaved a collective sigh of relief.

On her way to bed an hour or so later, Lady Hastings was moved to observe to her husband, 'Got it very badly, wouldn't you say, James?'

Hastings laughed. Never thought I'd see the day.' He scratched his head. 'Can't imagine what's holding him up though.'

Georgie snorted. 'I can. Easily. Male scruples. Silly clunch! I think it's time to bend the rules a trifle.'

Hastings eyed her dubiously. 'You're not going to interfere, are you?'

Her response was a wicked chuckle. 'You know I don't interfere. But a little nudge won't hurt matters. Trust me.'

He groaned. 'Georgie, do you have the slightest idea how much it scares me when you say that?'

'Naturally,' she purred. 'Why else would I say it?'

Chapter Ten

The thunder, which had rumbled around in the distance for most of the evening, broke overhead in another fully fledged storm just after midnight. Crispin, who had been sleeping restlessly, his dreams haunted by enormous dogs savaging everyone he loved, jerked back to full and welcome consciousness.

He listened for a moment, wondering why the storm had disturbed him. He'd weathered so many appalling storms in the Peninsula during the two years he'd served there that he rarely awakened for mere thunder.

And then he remembered. Anthea was scared of thunder. He was out of bed in a flash, reaching for the tinder box to light a lamp, then rummaging in his chest of drawers for a nightshirt. Swiftly he dragged it on over his head and looked round for his dressing gown.

Still fumbling with the sash one-handed, he took the stairs that led to the nursery suite two at a time. Which room would she be in? He paused for a moment and then heard a high scared voice reassuring someone else. Georgie's old room, of course, with all the dolls. Gently he tapped on the door.

'Who...who is it?'

'Me,' he said, opening the door. 'Uncle Cris. Are you all right?'

She was sitting up in bed, clutching a doll, her eyes wide with fright but a familiar set about the jaw. A set he had become only too familiar with the previous day.

'I'm...I'm very well...but Susan is scared,' she said. 'Did the storm wake you, too?'

'Mmm.' He smiled at her. 'Would you like me to stay for a while? Maybe I could tell Susan a story.' Should he sit on the bed with her? Hold her? What would Tilda do?

Thunder crashed directly overhead and Anthea gasped as she clung to Susan, her face white. Crispin didn't stop to think. He was seated on the very small bed and had the child in his arms before the rumbles had died away. He could feel the small body shaking as she burrowed against him. Instinctively he cradled her closer.

'It's all right...I'm here...you're quite safe.' His hands soothed and petted, stroking the tangled curls. Gradually he felt her relax. A story, he thought. Something to distract her...

'Did Mama ever tell you the story of Cinderella?' he asked. It had been Georgie's favourite as a child. He couldn't begin to count the number of times he'd heard his mother read it. Personally, he'd preferred 'Jack the Giant Killer', but no doubt 'Cinderella' would be more to Anthea's taste.

She was nodding. 'Yes. Do...do you know it?'

'Yes. Shall I tell it to you?'

She snuggled closer. 'Yes, please. Susan likes it too.'

'That is a consideration,' he said gravely. 'Very well— once upon a time, long, long ago, there lived a beautiful little girl with golden brown eyes and bright brown curls...'

'She had blue eyes and golden hair,' corrected Anthea.

Crispin looked down at her, amused. 'Who's telling this

tale, Miss Cavendish? She was the loveliest little girl in the world and her hair and eyes were exactly as I have described them.'

'Oh,' said Anthea. 'Did she look like Mama, then?'

'That's right,' said Crispin. 'Shall I go on?'

'Uh huh.'

'She lived in a beautiful house with her mother and father who loved her very much…'

When the Dowager came softly up the stairs twenty minutes later, to her immense surprise she heard a very familiar voice, a very deep voice, using a tone she had never heard before.

'…and the fairy waved her magic wand and Cinderella turned back into the lovely princess and the prince kissed her and begged her to marry him and they lived happily ever after.'

'Do you think he knew her before she turned back into the princess?' Anthea's voice sounded very sleepy.

'I'm sure he did,' came Crispin's voice again. 'He was just so delighted and relieved to have found her at last that his voice wouldn't work at first. You always recognise people when you love them. Even if you don't know it at first.' His voice had softened and slowed, trailing off.

Stepping softly to the door and peeping in, Lady St Ormond blinked back sudden tears. In the glowing lamplight she could see her son propped up on Anthea's bed by several pillows, with Anthea and her doll held securely in his arms, his cheek resting on the soft brown curls.

She scarcely dared move lest she disturb them. Praying that he would not notice the flickering light of her candle, she backed away very quietly.

The deep, tender voice drifted after her. 'Sleep now, sweetheart. I'll stay with you…'

Holding her breath, Lady St Ormond crept away. Crispin, she thought mistily, was going to be a wonderful father.

* * *

Later that morning the Dowager came to find Crispin.

He looked up at once when she entered the library. 'How is she, Mama?'

'Improving. Still in a great deal of pain, of course, and she was very worried about Anthea last night. I'd forgotten that the poor child is afraid of storms...'

He smiled at the memory of Anthea sound asleep in his arms. 'It's all right, Mama. I knew. I went up.'

'Yes, dear.'

He stared at her and she went on, 'Tilda begged me to go up to her. You were already there. She was rather surprised when I told her.'

'Oh.' Crispin was conscious of a faint heat along his cheek bones. What the devil was his mother thinking? She had the smuggest, most devious smile that he'd ever seen on her face.

'Tilda asked me to thank you. For everything. Not just that.'

Suddenly his cravat felt far too tight. He suppressed the urge to loosen it with one finger. When he spoke it was rather sharply. 'It was nothing...no one could have left the child alone. I should have thought earlier. Put her in Louisa's room for the night. And as for the rest...I could hardly let Tilda bleed to death in front of me!'

Encountering his mother's raised brows, he groaned. 'Oh, damn it, Mama. I'm sorry. I didn't mean to snap! It's just...just...' *Just that I want to marry her and I don't know what Guy's intentions are or even if she cares for me...and what to do about Milly...*

'Just that you had a very nasty shock yourself and need some peace and quiet?' suggested his mother.

He looked at her gratefully. 'That will do to be going on with,' he said with a half-smile. 'Can she have visitors?'

'Later, perhaps,' said the Dowager. 'She's asleep again now. Have you found out where the dog came from?'

Crispin frowned. 'Not yet. Rigby and Marlowe reported

in earlier. They're making enquiries around the neighbourhood, but you'd have thought one of us would have noticed
a dog like that. Shepherd Hughes identified it as the one
that killed the sheep the night before. Whoever owned the
brute is going to wish he'd never been born!'

At this moment Bebbington came in. 'Sir Richard is here,
your Grace. Shall I ask him to wait?'

'No. Ask him to come in.' There was nothing to be
gained in making Sir Richard wait. No doubt the old man
wished to harangue him about the poaching again and if
that damned dog had belonged to a poacher, he'd gladly
see the scoundrel in Botany Bay for the term of his natural
life!

Sir Richard came in with a queer set look on his face.
'St Ormond. Met your bailiff, Rigby, out riding. He...he
says Lady Winter and her daughter were bitten by a dog.
And that you shot it. Is that true?'

Slightly surprised, Crispin nodded.

Sir Richard's groan shocked him. 'Dear God. What sort
of dog?'

'A mastiff,' said Crispin puzzled. 'Why? Do you know
who owned it?'

Numb-faced, Sir Richard nodded. 'Bull.'

'I beg your pardon.' Crispin didn't know anyone of that
name.

'Bull.' Sir Richard groaned again. 'Dear God what have
I done? He was mine. Did you...did you have to shoot
him? He wasn't really savage...'

If it hadn't been for the Dowager's hand on her son's
sleeve, Sir Richard might have found himself the recipient
of a leveller. As it was, Crispin had a breathing space in
which to recall all the impropriety attached to assaulting a
man nearly twice his age.

He drew a deep breath and spoke in tones of icy rage.
'Your dog, Sir Richard, attacked so viciously that when Dr
Stephenson saw the injuries to Lady Winter, he gave it as
his opinion that Anthea would have been killed had her

mother not faced the attack.' He felt sick as he remembered the blood pulsing from Tilda's wrist, her white face. And the terrified screams that had alerted him to her danger—screams that had nearly stopped his heart, that he would never forget.

'But—'

Crispin interrupted. 'The dog had been caught in a steel trap that some fool set on my land. He'd dragged the trap and was ready to attack anything and anyone. I had no choice but to shoot.'

'A trap? But—'

'Did Rigby mention the sheep?' Crispin's rage was boundless, surging through him in torrents. 'The night before last, five of one of my tenant's sheep had their throats ripped out by your dog. The shepherd has identified your dog as the one responsible! So I would have been perfectly within my rights to shoot him anyway!'

Clearly dazed, Sir Richard sat down. 'I…I beg your pardon, St Ormond. Is Lady Winter…is she badly hurt?'

Crispin scarcely trusted himself to answer. 'Badly enough,' he said savagely. 'She needed a great many stitches to her arms and one artery was torn. Had my cousin and I not been close at hand she might well have bled to death!'

He noted with grim satisfaction that Sir Richard looked sick. As sick as he felt. 'Might I suggest that you keep—'

'Enough, Crispin.' His mother's voice was quiet, but for all that it stopped him. 'Go and find Anthea. She should go out for some fresh air. Just a turn around the gardens, but she will feel safer with you.'

Shaken by the sheer force of his emotions, shocked at the force of the fury surging through him, he obeyed. Nodding brusquely to Sir Richard, he left the library. His mother was right. A turn around the gardens with Anthea would calm him down a trifle.

* * *

When the Dowager found them half an hour later in the rose garden, he was recounting the story of how he had raised Sirene and Anthea was trying to persuade him to take her down to the stable to see her pony.

'My mama said a turn around the garden,' he said basely. 'I'll take you down after lunch if she says I may.'

'Do you still have to do as your mama says?' asked Anthea, very much surprised.

'He most certainly does,' said Lady St Ormond with a perfectly straight face. 'And right now she is telling him to take you up to see your mama. She is awake and would like to see both of you.'

Anthea squealed with pleasure and raced off towards the house.

Crispin and the Dowager followed slowly.

'I shouldn't have lost my temper, Mama,' said Crispin ruefully.

She shook her head. 'No, but never mind. He quite understood that you were upset, you know. He hadn't had the dog very long and it got away the other night when he took it out for exercise.'

'Oh.' Crispin felt the last of his fury drain from him, leaving him oddly empty. 'Does Tilda really wish to see me?'

'She wishes to thank you,' said his mother. 'You did save her life, after all. One does like to thank people who do us these little favours.'

He smiled. 'I dare say. Guy did help me, you know.'

'So Milly keeps pointing out to her,' said Lady St Ormond drily. 'But it doesn't seem to be sinking in. And Guy himself just says that you knew exactly what to do and took complete command. That all he did was follow orders.'

Crispin grunted.

He kept his visit to Tilda brief. Her pallor made his heart clench and her eyes told him clearly that she was still in pain. And he didn't trust himself not to take her in his arms, to reassure himself that she was all in one piece.

Tilda knew a singing joy in her heart as she saw who had brought Anthea to her. She owed him her life. Of that she had not the least doubt. But he looked so grim, so forbidding. She stammered her way through her thanks. 'And...and you went to Anthea last night...'

She still couldn't quite believe it, but then, as she saw the sudden, tender softening of his face, she could. He was kind. He had always been kind. He would never knowingly hurt anyone. Certainly not a clumsy, gawky débutante blinded by an impossible dream. Had he known that she had overheard his remarks he would have been mortified.

He had held her and protected her yesterday, held her while the doctor stitched her arm, comforting her terror. She knew that she could never have borne the pain and fright without him. Somehow, being in his arms had given her the courage to endure, not to struggle. He had been a very haven of safety. She had known that the moment she had heard his voice as she tried to fend off the dog. From that very instant she had known that she was safe, that he would protect her.

Anthea was speaking. 'He came up just like you did the other night, Mama. Except he told me "Cinderella". And his Cinderella had brown eyes and hair, just like you.'

Aware of his suddenly arrested gaze, Tilda glanced up. He was staring at her with the queerest look in his eyes. She couldn't place it until he spoke.

'That night you knocked over the statue, you'd been with Anthea.' It wasn't a question. She nodded. And flinched at the pain in his eyes. The sudden guilt and shame.

'I'm sorry.' He spoke very quietly.

She felt her cheeks burn as she realised why he was apologising. He was apologising for making an assumption in which she had encouraged him. Not only that, an assumption that her behaviour and comments had made possible. It was not his fault.

'There...there is nothing to apologise for, your Grace,' she said very sadly. She had herself given credence to his belief. She had accepted it and used it to deflect what she had mistakenly seen as his interest in her. And all because she had known that she couldn't depend on her treacherous, yearning body not to betray her.

Almost to herself she murmured, 'If the cap fits...what a fool I've been.'

She was the wanton he had called her, in thought, if not in deed, ever since her dreams had been haunted by what might have been had she not fled in the chilly dawn. Visions of what could have been, had she let him take her to his room and make love to her, teased her. She'd had her chance and she'd been too scared to take it. It might have been the sensible thing to do, but she was reasonably sure that she was going to regret it to the end of her days.

His voice, so gentle and resigned, broke in on her thoughts. 'I should be going now. You look tired. Sleep. I'll send Guy up later.' She nodded. Milly would be delighted to see him. And he might cheer her up slightly. Momentarily anyway. She didn't feel as though she would ever be truly cheerful again.

Crispin left with Anthea just as Milly came back into the room.

She smiled at him and said, 'Come back later. Tilda should have a sleep now.'

'I'll send Guy up with Anthea,' he said shortly.

Milly stared. 'Guy?'

'That would be better, I think,' he said gently. 'Look after her, Milly.'

He took Anthea down to his mother and went out for a walk, prey to bitter and gloomy thoughts. She had not been to Guy's bed that night after all. She had spent the night, or part of it, comforting Anthea.

And he... He groaned as he recalled how he had attempted to seduce her. How for a moment he had thought she was going to surrender, come to his bed. The heady, surging pleasure he'd felt. The scorching desire and the tempering awareness of her relative inexperience. Doubtless that was why she'd allowed him to get her so close to his chamber—quite possibly she hadn't realised at first what he was doing, what he wanted.

But she'd said no apology was needed. She was generous. What had she whispered? *If the cap fits...* She must feel that, since she had been to Guy's room at other times, his assumptions were well founded, if untimely. It didn't excuse his actions. And he would never be able to find the words to apologise properly without telling her how much he cared about her. How deeply he loved her.

He was rather surprised to find that he had reached the lake. That he was in the cool green shade of the very willow tree where he had first offered an apology to Tilda. The boat Anthea had sat in nodded to its own reflection as the waters rippled in response to a caressing breeze. He stripped off his coat and sat down on it.

He would have to attempt to sort out the muddle he had created and make it clear that he would not offer for Milly. That would be atrociously unfair to Milly and would bring him into contact with Tilda far too often.

If Guy married Tilda, then he would have to bear it. But he certainly wasn't going to make the situation any more fraught. The Pembertons would be furious, but he couldn't help that. And he was quite sure that if their anger was directed at Milly, that Tilda could be counted on to protect her cousin.

You could, of course, just go to Tilda. Tell her you love her and beg her to marry you. He could, of course. But she had told him point blank that she didn't want marriage. And if she were reconsidering, then it was Guy she was thinking of. He knew beyond all doubt that Tilda would never give herself lightly, despite that outward cynicism. So if she had been in Guy's bed, then it was because she loved him. After all, she had had no difficulty repulsing his own amorous advances.

He didn't want to hear her pitying refusal. He didn't want her pity. He wanted her, all of her, soft and warm and loving, in his life in his bed. She was already in his heart.

He went back up to the house much later, gloomily resigned to his fate. Bebbington greeted him and explained that nearly everyone had gone out for a ride, including the Dowager and Miss Anthea.

'Lady Hollow is resting in her bedchamber, Miss Pemberton is with Lady Winter and I believe Master Guy is in the billiard room.'

Crispin nodded. Perhaps he should go and find Guy. Subtly try to encourage him to offer for Tilda. It would nearly kill him, but he wanted her to be happy—whatever the cost to himself. It was the right thing to do, he told himself firmly.

So the sight that greeted his eyes as he quietly opened the door of the billiard room was guaranteed to send the blood surging through his veins in primitive fury.

Quite oblivious to the fact that they were no longer alone, Guy and Milly stood locked in each other's embrace, kissing passionately.

Even through his rage, a small, cynical part of Crispin's rakish mind assimilated the fact that Guy was going to develop a crick in the neck very rapidly if he didn't find something for Milly to stand on. And he noted wryly that Milly, who had been terrified at the chaste kisses he had bestowed upon her, showed nothing but enthusiasm for the far from chaste kisses Guy was pressing upon her.

The prudent course would have been a quiet retreat, but Crispin was too angry to think clearly.

'Just what the *hell* do you think you are doing, Guy?'

The pair broke apart and spun around. Milly gave a startled squeak.

Crispin had to credit Guy with the fact that, beyond simple surprise, he didn't react at all nervously. He drew Milly into the protective circle of his arm and spoke calmly.

'Kissing my betrothed, Crispin. I'm sorry if this is a shock to you, but—'

Crispin broke in, his tones biting. 'It doesn't occur to you that there may be another, with a greater claim to—?'

'No.' Guy spoke coldly. 'Milly assured me that you have never offered for her and never spoken of love to her. I will be writing to her father tonight.'

Crispin blinked slightly.

'No!' Milly clutched at Guy's arm. 'You musn't!'

Guy stared down at her. 'But, my love…'

Crispin gave a mental snort. Guy was doubtless about to discover the true meaning of the difference in their estates! The lure a title and wealth could be… He could almost feel sorry for him.

'Papa will be furious,' said Milly urgently. 'With Tilda! He'll blame her for not chaperoning me better. And she's not well enough to argue with him. You can't write yet. Tom told me what happened when Lord Winter offered for her!'

'What happened?' Crispin rapped out.

Milly flushed. 'I shouldn't have said that. Tilda doesn't even know he told me.'

'Get on with it, Milly,' said Guy. 'What did Tom tell you?'

Milly bit her lip. 'Mama and Papa aren't very fond of Tilda, because of her mama. You…you know about that?'

Crispin nodded grimly and she went on. 'Tom said that when Lord Winter offered, Tilda refused at first. So they shut her in her room and said she should stay there until she agreed. Tom says that he saw Papa come out of her room with his riding crop one night and that the next morning Tilda agreed to marry Lord Winter.' She paused. 'So you see, even though he couldn't possibly do that to her again, he might upset her. Please, Guy, wait till she's better.'

Guy looked sick. 'What do you think, Cris? Lord knows I don't want to cause trouble for Tilda…'

What Crispin was actually thinking, about Lord Pemberton, Guy and anyone else who might reasonably have been expected to protect Tilda, did not bear repeating. He dragged his wits together and said, 'Do as she says. Even knowing that Pemberton is likely to descend upon us will upset Tilda. Wait until she is recovered. And accept my congratulations.' He turned to Milly. 'You have my sincere best wishes for your future happiness, my dear. Perhaps you might excuse me now. I will speak to you later, Guy. I fancy you will need my support with Pemberton.'

He forced a smile and left the room. Before he could break Guy's neck. Retreating to his library, he flung himself into the chair behind his desk and felt it shudder at the impact.

Blast Guy to hell and back! Had it even occurred to him that Tilda might be expecting an offer? That even if she wasn't, his betrothal to her cousin would hurt her appallingly? Had his affair with Tilda been nothing more than a cover for his pursuit of Milly? And why hadn't *he* realised sooner just how well suited Guy and Milly were?

A thought struck him. Had Tilda realised the truth? Was that why she had tried to find out if *he* cared for Milly? He groaned. It was all so damned complicated.

The only certainty in the whole mess was that Lord and Lady Pemberton were going to think Guy, quite literally, a very poor substitute for himself. If they were to pull the thing off, he would need to convince them that nothing was further from his mind than an alliance with their daughter. Before they realised that his target was their despised niece.

And if they had any idea of visiting their wrath on *her*

then they would discover that they had his Grace the Duke of Ormond with whom to deal. No wonder Tilda was so cynical about marriage if she had been physically forced into hers. He couldn't blame her for never wanting to put herself in anyone's power ever again. After that experience, her independence would be past price. His mother had assured him that Lord Winter had been a kindly man, but even so...she didn't want to marry again.

He swore softly as he realised that her hurt might well put her beyond his reach forever. Unless he could find a way to heal it.

Chapter Eleven

'Guy's offered for who?' The Dowager could hardly contain her disbelief at her daughter's news, that evening.

'Milly Pemberton,' repeated Georgie. 'You know, Mama. Small, pretty. Blue eyes. About as suitable for Cris as Louisa would be.'

The Dowager eyed her rather smug-looking daughter with something approaching awe. 'Whose idea was that?'

Georgie looked shocked. 'Guy's, of course! You must have noticed the way the pair of them were smelling of April and May.' She snorted. 'The wonder is that Cris didn't notice! But Guy was being so...so gentlemanly about it...you know, Crispin's intended bride...I'm not good enough for her...that sort of fustian, that I did give him a bit of a nudge.'

'A nudge?' repeated the Dowager, who had her own ideas as to why her usually observant son had been so uncharacteristically blind. 'And what constitutes a nudge?'

Georgie grinned. 'Commented to James in Guy's hearing that I didn't think Milly would be happy with Cris. And added something about how pushy Lord and Lady Pemberton could be and that it would be a pity if Milly felt she had to accept an offer from Cris just because nothing else offered!'

Lady St Ormond blinked. 'Well, if that's a nudge, I'd hate to see a shove!'

'It worked,' said Georgie with cheerful insouciance. 'And don't try and hoax me that you thought Milly suitable for Cris. She's a dear, but she'd bore him in a week.' She thought about that. 'Less.'

The Dowager sighed. 'Very true, my love. Well done. I was concerned, but you may trust me when I say that I very much doubt Cris would have offered for her.'

Encountering a questioning gaze from her daughter, she shook her head. 'No, dear. It's none of your business. And one other thing...' She paused for a moment and fixed Georgie with an uncharacteristically steely eye. 'Don't apply any of your *nudges* to any other interested parties. There are a few cliffs about that you aren't aware of.'

'Oh very well, Mama,' said Georgie. 'But you must admit, it worked beautifully.'

The Dowager nodded. 'It did. But leave Cris alone. I have a feeling that this *nudge* may be enough for him anyway!'

'He has asked you to marry him?!' Tilda was stunned.

Milly nodded, biting her lip. 'Yes, but...'

'Well...that's wonderful, isn't it?' said Tilda, puzzled at Milly's unhappy face.

'Yes, but—you don't understand,' said Milly miserably. 'He was so pleased when I said yes that he...it was me, too—it wasn't all Guy's fault...we...well, we were...'

'Kissing?' suggested Tilda. That, she thought, would tactfully cover a multitude of Malvern sins.

Milly nodded, blushing scarlet. 'He...he had his arms around me and...'

Tilda nodded. 'I get the idea.' If he'd still had his arms around her then things hadn't got too far out of hand. Not by Malvern standards, anyway. She went on reassuringly,

'It's all right, Milly. You are allowed to kiss him if you are betrothed. As long as you like it…?'

She allowed a faint note of query to creep in. After all, Milly had been less than enthusiastic about Crispin's kisses. Which to Tilda's mind ranked as insanity…

'Oh, it was wonderful,' Milly assured her, with a beaming smile. 'But you see, St Ormond came in and—well, he seemed very angry at first.'

Tilda whitened. How ghastly! What a truly dreadful way to find out that the girl you were about to offer for loved someone else. Even if St Ormond wasn't in love with Milly, the affront to his pride would be considerable. To be cut out by his younger cousin, especially after her scathing comments on May and December marriages, would be particularly galling.

'Oh, Milly! Was he very upset?'

'I think so,' said Milly guiltily. 'I felt awful. I never meant to hurt him. He never seemed to care that much for me—but he was always so polite and charming. I could never work out what he was thinking, but then—I thought he was angry for a moment and then he looked terribly sad. He congratulated Guy—as though he'd rather strangle him—and wished me happy…as…as though he meant it!'

'He probably does,' said Tilda wisely. 'If he cares for you, he will wish you to be happy and men are far more likely to feel rage with the man in these cases, I dare say.'

'But it was just as much my fault,' argued Milly.

'Yes, but you can hardly expect a man to take that logical view,' said Tilda, with a faint smile. 'They don't think that way.'

'Oh,' said Milly. 'Can I ask a question?'

In Tilda's experience people only prefaced a question like that when they had an absolute facer for one. She nodded and braced herself.

Milly blushed delicately. 'Are you allowed to tell me about the wedding right now?'

Oh, dear God! Aloud she said, 'I'm not the right person to ask, Milly.' And, seeing Milly's forming protest, went on doggedly, 'My experience of marriage was not the same as yours will be. You know I scarcely knew Lord Winter, that he was much older and that I did not love him... I know nothing of what it means to share the bed of the man who loves you and whom you love in return...'

She hesitated. That wasn't quite true. She knew to her bones that to share Crispin's bed would be wonderful, even if he didn't love her.

Slowly she continued. 'But if you enjoyed being kissed by Guy, then I think you will enjoy your wedding night. Being kissed by the man you love is wonderful.

Milly stared at her. 'Then there was someone you loved?'

Tilda nodded sadly. 'Yes. But don't waste any pity on me. I always knew it was nothing but a dream—he never even knew I cared...'

'Not...not Guy?'

Tilda looked up sharply. 'Guy?'

Milly met her eyes squarely. 'Yes. He flirts with you all the time. And you flirt with him.'

Damn, I thought I'd scotched that. Tilda improvised. 'Milly, while I think Guy is a dear and I applaud your choice, he is not at all the sort of man to appeal to me in that way. If you must have it, he reminds me rather of your brother, Tom.'

'*Tom?* But he's not at all like Tom!'

'Not to you, obviously,' said Tilda drily. 'Have you ever considered what a disaster it would be if we all fell in love with the same sort of man? What will do for you, Milly, would not do for me. And vice versa.'

'Oh, I see,' said Milly slowly, as if she actually did see. She brightened for a moment, then sobered again. 'But there was someone you cared about?'

Biting her lip, Tilda nodded. 'Don't mind it, Milly. It was a very long time go.'

'Are you still in love?'

'Yes.' Probably always. Tilda blinked away tears. 'But believe me, Milly, it is not Guy. Even if it were, it would make no difference. Guy loves you. Think about my fortune, dearest. Despite my wealth and Guy's affection for me, he has asked *you* to marry him. That speaks for itself.'

'Ohhh! I never thought of that,' said Milly, beaming with obvious relief. 'But you could tell me something, couldn't you? About the wedding night?'

Tilda shook her head. 'Nothing that you don't already know. Ask someone else. But don't believe anyone who tells you that a lady must not enjoy her husband's attentions.' She hesitated. If Milly asked her mother... She went on firmly, 'Ask Lady Hastings or Lady St Ormond. They both married for love, as you are doing.' She smiled ruefully. 'Would you mind very much if I had a sleep now, Milly? I'm a little tired.'

'Of course not.' Milly bent over to kiss her gently and went to the door. She turned back briefly. 'I persuaded Guy not to write to Papa until you are well again. He's going to be so angry that I thought it was better.' She smiled and left the room quietly.

Tilda heard the door shut and breathed a sigh of relief. Not having to explain herself to her uncle immediately was definitely a good thing. And Milly's questions had brought back all sorts of memories. The sort of memories that she needed to be alone with.

Her aunt's advice... *Only a whore, like your mother, would enjoy it. Your duty to your husband, as a lady, is to lie still and quiet. Otherwise you will disgust him...you must accept the pain without a murmur, it is your duty...* and so on.

By the wedding night she was terrified and Jonathan had known it. He'd been careful and after a while her duties became merely boring. At least, she had comforted herself, she was a lady. Surely that one gasp of pain didn't count...

Then she had heard other married ladies talking, giggling, over luncheon, over cups of tea. Gradually it was borne in on her that some married ladies, especially those in love with their husbands, did enjoy the marriage bed. A very great deal. And that this delighted their husbands.

So one night she'd tried to encourage Jonathan a bit, thinking it might help matters between them. He'd been scandalised at her sudden curiosity. At her suggestion that instead of merely raising the hem of her nightgown, he might like to take it right off as well as his own night rail.

After this fiasco she had concluded that she might as well accept boredom as her lot. She knew that many women would have looked for pleasure outside their marriage, but Jonathan was kind and cared for her. She could at least give him loyalty.

And always at the back of her mind was the knowledge that, despite her much improved looks, she was the...*chit who shouldn't have been let loose in London.* Why would anyone want her? She was plain, clumsy, and far too tall to please any man of discrimination. Jonathan had married her out of necessity and chivalry. He'd needed a wife and she'd needed a rescuer. He hadn't wanted her *per se.* And after he'd discovered that he had a perfectly acceptable heir in Max, he had said very kindly that there would be no further need for him to press his marital rights upon her.

She wriggled her fingers. Her injuries were abominably itchy, which no doubt meant they were healing. She only wished this other itch would go away as easily. This itch to find out, first-hand, just exactly what she had missed out on.

At the Dowager's insistence, Tilda spent two full days in bed, attended by Milly and Sarah.

For a seemingly gentle woman, the Dowager Lady St

Ormond could be positively dictatorial given due cause, reflected Tilda. All her protests about being a nuisance and having to chaperon Milly were swept aside.

'Nonsense!' Lady St Ormond had come up to sit with Tilda while Milly was out walking with Georgie and Guy. 'Seraphina, Georgie and I can chaperon Milly when she is not with you. And Cris is looking after Anthea. She may not be making much progress with her French but she is doing quite well with her riding, he tells me.'

Her smile was wicked. 'He seems to be very much taken with the idea of having a daughter one day. So far his thoughts have all been centred on sons and heirs.' Sobering slightly, she went on. 'Tell me, my dear, are your uncle and aunt going to be very much vexed by the way things have fallen out? Naturally Guy is not as wealthy as Crispin and has little chance of inheriting the title, but he is quite comfortably off and I suspect Milly will be far happier with him than with Cris.'

Tilda breathed a sigh of relief. 'You do not mind, then?'

'Good God, no,' laughed Lady St Ormond. 'Poor Milly would be quite out of her depth with Cris. He's far too old for her! Or she is too young for him. She would be too young if she were your age. Oh, not in years, but in maturity. She is the wrong woman for him. Even in a marriage of convenience, which he seems to think is what he wants.'

'Why should he want it?' asked Tilda, without thinking. She blushed. It was none of her business to be asking such a personal question.

Lady St Ormond did not take it at all amiss. She wrinkled her brow. 'Do you know? I am not sure. My marriage was a love match, of which he is perfectly well aware. But I suspect it is simply that, since he didn't meet the right girl years ago, he has become far too used to enjoying himself *out* of wedlock. His life is comfortable, hedonistic to say the least, and he thinks that a marriage which leaves him free to pursue that life will be easiest.' She considered that.

'Come to think of it, he may well be right. But easiest doesn't necessarily mean happiest.'

Tilda looked at her inquiringly.

And the Dowager elaborated. 'A happy marriage needs hard work. And compromise on both sides. And if either or both parties to it are in love, there needs to be an understanding of how dreadfully they can hurt each other.' She smiled. 'But enough of this solemnity. Tell me instead how you are feeling. Recovered? Up to coming down for dinner tonight? We miss you very much, you know!'

'Miss me?' No one, for as long as she could remember, had ever said they had missed her. On one occasion when she had come back downstairs after a bout of flu, her uncle had merely glanced at her and grunted, *Oh. It's you, is it?* Tears sprang to her eyes. Whatever was the matter with her that she should be feeling so weepy and depressed? It must be shock or something, turning her into a positive watering pot.

She had Sarah help her to dress in her very best gown of blue satin that evening. Her arms were still bandaged and she sighed as she realised that the effect of the gown was quite spoilt.

Correctly interpreting the sigh, Sarah said, 'Never you mind, milady. You still take the shine out of all of 'em.'

'Me?' Tilda laughed at her in the looking glass. 'With Milly there? Don't be silly, Sarah! Oh, I'm well enough, but who would give me a second glance with her there?'

She clasped a string of pearls about her neck and put on the matching earrings. Tilting her head to one side to view the effect, she smiled at the idea anyone would think her beautiful. Better than seven years ago, true enough—but all she saw was a too tall, admittedly slender woman, with plain brown hair and hazel eyes—with heavily bandaged arms. She frowned slightly, wishing that she could hide them.

Then inspiration dawned. Hunting through a drawer, she found a Wellington jacket in deep Turkey-red silk. Jonathan had always fussed tremendously when she came down to dinner in a light dress. She'd made this to appease him, so that he'd stop worrying about the inflammation of the lungs he was convinced she'd die of.

She had just slipped it on when there was a light tap on the door. Milly, she supposed and nodded to Sarah to open it.

'His Grace, milady,' said Sarah respectfully.

Tilda whirled and there was Crispin, waiting with an oddly shuttered look in his eyes. Every plane of his face was set and tense as though he held something under guard.

Her heart lurched. She thought she knew what that something was. He must have cared more for Milly than she had realised. Perhaps, she thought sadly, more than he had realised; until he lost her.

'Your Grace?' She felt as puzzled as she sounded. What on earth was he doing here? Shouldn't he be down in the drawing room?

'I came to escort you down to dinner.' The deep voice seemed to stroke up and down her spine in a warm caress.

He'd come to escort her down to dinner? Why? He hadn't even visited her again in the past three days while she kept to her room. Of course, had the other gentlemen in the party not come up to visit her each day, she might have put his omission down to a sense of propriety. Given, however, that Lord Hastings had come up with his wife and daughter, Lord John had visited briefly with Lady Hollow and Guy had come in with Milly, she had decided that his Grace was simply not interested.

In truth, the answer was very straightforward. His Grace had simply not dared. He had been far too afraid of his likely reaction if he found himself, by some unforeseen circumstance, left alone in a bedchamber with Tilda. He wanted her as he had never wanted any other, and he definitely didn't trust himself.

Only now, when he knew her maid to be with her, and when his visit would necessarily be of the briefest, did he dare cross that threshold. When he couldn't keep away any longer.

Tightening his grip on the reins of his self-control, he said quietly, 'You look lovely, my dear.' He noted the amazed lift of her brows. The softly parted lips and the delicate blush, like a girl receiving her first compliment.

A grunt from Sarah caught his attention. 'Humph! And so I tell her. But does she ever believe a soul? Not her!'

Tilda's blush deepened as Crispin looked back at her. Something stirred in his memory. The shy, rather plain débutante she had been, awkward and clumsy, until she'd danced with him. He was startled at how clearly he remembered that girl now, how he'd thought she needed time to bloom, like his sister, Georgie. She too had been a tall, potentially clumsy girl who had blossomed late—*It took me years to realise that I'd actually stopped being gawky and filled out in a few of the right places! And I only believed it because James kept telling me…* Georgie's laughing voice echoed in his memory.

Had Tilda never had anyone to tell her how lovely she had become? Had no one ever complimented her, loved her with words? The question leapt to his mind: loved her at all? He knew from his mother that she had received little enough love from her aunt and uncle—but how had her husband viewed her?

His mother's voice drifted through his mind: *I suspect Jonathan was very fond of her, in a fatherly sort of way…*

Slowly he said, 'Lady Winter may believe me that she is very lovely…' *And lovable, desirable and that I need her like I need to keep breathing!* He saw Tilda's eyes widen and fasten on his in startled query, knew that his own eyes were blazing and immediately added, as lightly as he could, 'And as a self-respecting rake, I never offer Spanish coin!'

With relief he saw the odd tension ease from Tilda. She raised a brow, 'May one ask, why not?'

He grinned and offered his arm. 'Far too dangerous, my dear. Besides, if I did that, the women I really wished to compliment would never believe me.'

She glared up at him as she came out and placed her hand on his arm. 'You, sir, are a cynic!'

'The pot is speaking to the kettle,' he said, closing the door behind them and trying to ignore the blaze that leapt up in him at her touch. He shuddered to imagine the effect her touch would have upon his senses were it not muted by his shirt and coat. Devastating was the only possible word. It was bad enough just thinking about it.

Tilda flushed again. No doubt he was joking, but still... 'I'm not really quite as cynical as you might have thought,' she said quietly.

He glanced down at her and she met his eyes gallantly. He looked so sad, she thought. Had he really cared for Milly? Had he pretended not to care just to guard against this sort of hurt? She wished desperately that there was something, anything, she could do to ease what must amount to a sense of betrayal.

'I know.' Crispin was conscious again of the urge to wring Guy's neck. If *he* had seen through her bright armour, surely Guy could have done so! And to offer for Milly the moment Tilda was out of the way—injured, perhaps needing his care and reassurance. She must feel betrayed. If she hadn't been cynical about men before, she certainly would be now. He longed to ease her pain, assure her that he at least truly loved her, for herself, as a woman.

'Tell me. Why do you disbelieve the evidence of your mirror?'

His question took her so much by surprise that she was startled into the truth.

A surge of bitter hurt welled up. 'And as for Miss Arnold, there's a chit who should never have been let loose in London!' Her voice flared with anger.

Patently shocked, Crispin asked, 'Who the devil said that?'

'You don't even remember, do you? Any more than you remembered me,' she said softly. 'You said it, your Grace. To Lord Hastings at a ball some days after our one and only dance.'

Memory flared. He *had* said something to James about Miss Arnold. What had he said? Strangely, he remembered the occasion. His mother had been worried that he'd shown no sign of settling down and he'd agreed to give the season's débutantes a look. He'd been grumbling about how boring they were and their unsubtle pursuit of his fortune and title. But Tilda, Miss Arnold, had been different. Clumsy and shy with everyone else, she had flowered in his arms—what on earth could he have said to James?

'Tilda, whatever I said to James was not meant to hurt you,' he began. 'And I didn't forget you. You had changed so much that I didn't properly recognise you. Yet I was sure I'd met you before. It drove me insane.' That and the raging desire that seared him whenever he laid eyes on her.

He laughed harshly. 'If you want proof that you have become a beauty, you have it there. In the fact that I did not recognise you again when I met you.' With the words, the gist of what he had said to James came floating back. 'I think you cannot have heard all of what I said to James. As far as I recall, it was along the lines that you should not have been brought out until you had a chance to blossom a little, gain a bit of confidence.' An eyebrow quirked. 'I was right.'

As simple as that, she thought. She'd overheard only part of what he'd said. And in her insecurity she had allowed it to fester—nursing it bitterly, instead of putting it aside. Because she'd loved him even then.

He made sure his voice was perfectly indifferent before he spoke again. 'Guy has written to your uncle and wishes to send it if you are feeling well enough. Milly insisted that he wait until you recovered.'

Her sigh, soft though it was, tore at him. 'Better sooner rather than later. If he ever suspects he was not told at once…it will make Guy's case worse than ever. Lord Pemberton will not be happy with any of us.'

'I had thought, under the circumstances, a little subterfuge might be acceptable,' said Crispin thoughtfully.

Tilda blinked. 'How do you define subterfuge?'

'Any deception that doesn't involve an outright lie,' replied Crispin promptly. 'Lord Pemberton has been told in the letter that you were badly bitten by a dog, and while you were in bed Guy offered for Milly. He'll think you didn't even know until you recovered, so he won't believe it was your fault.'

A sceptical snort greeted this. 'He might reasonably expect that I should have noticed something earlier and put a stop to it. Reminded Milly that she was supposed to have bigger game in her sights!' She forbore to tell him that Lord Pemberton would not require any excuse to rip up at her.

A warm husky chuckle broke from him. 'True, but you could always say that it never occurred to you that Guy was so lost to all propriety that he would do anything so outrageous as to consider proposing to any girl without her father's consent, let alone one his cousin was supposedly courting.' He hesitated and then went on, 'After all, I didn't notice. I have formed the intention of enclosing a letter with Guy's assuring Lord Pemberton that as head of the Malvern family, the match has my full support and that I merely thought the three younger members of the party, namely Miss Pemberton and my niece and cousin were gravitating together—with a bit of luck he'll assume you thought the same.'

Tilda thought her heart must break at this proposal. 'You

are…very generous.' What must it have cost him to do this? she wondered. To actively promote a match which, whatever his heart's involvement, must make him look a complete fool. She had seen enough of London society to know that his interest in Milly, and their subsequent presence at this house party, would not have escaped remark.

His shrug was indifferent. 'What else can one do? Shall we send the letters tomorrow? Are you sure you are up to it?'

They had reached the drawing room door and he held back from opening it to hear her response.

She looked up at him searchingly, but could read nothing in his eyes and the hard planes of his face. That told its own tale, she thought. She could not offer comfort—he would not want to be pitied, but she must say something, acknowledge his decency. Her heart would burst if she did not.

' "If 'twere done, 'twere best done quickly." ' She smiled tremulously. 'Delay will only worsen the pain.' She would have seized the door handle and gone ahead of him, but a strong hand grasped her wrist and gently drew her back.

Before she could think, she found herself enclosed in a tender embrace, warm and safe. He held her in a grip as gentle as it was unbreakable. Featherlight, a finger caressed her cheek, drifted down the silken line of her throat to firm under her chin, lifting it to meet a kiss that melted her heart in its aching sweetness.

Instinctively she leaned into the kiss, into the hard strength of his body, softening still more as she felt his arms tighten. His mouth moved lightly on hers, and then she felt the hesitant touch of his tongue, pleading, requesting entrance. Without conscious volition her lips parted as her soul flowered in love. She felt with joy his gentle, yet passionate possession of her mouth, the erotic stroke of his tongue against hers. And sighed her pleasure as she tentatively returned the caress. Invited him deeper.

For a moment he accepted the invitation, deepening the kiss, drowning in her response until his senses whirled and every leashed demon within clamoured for release. Until the very small part of his brain left functioning rationally reminded him what a bounder he would be to take advantage of her hurt and pain in this way. She wanted comfort, not seduction.

Somehow he raised his head, breaking the kiss, shocked to find his breathing ragged and his arousal complete. And he had a drawing room full of people to face—most of them family who knew him too well for any dissembling. Added to which, the fashionable, skin-tight cut of his breeches was of no help at all. He swore mentally and met Tilda's clouded golden eyes.

'Go in. I'll…I'll join you all in a moment.' He turned away abruptly, hoping that she hadn't noticed his state, the tension in his body screaming for release. Screaming for her.

She stared after his rapidly retreating form in considerable confusion. Her fingers touched her lips in dazed awe. This kiss had been nothing like their earlier encounters. It had deepened to passion quickly but it had started so tenderly, as if he were wooing her, as if…her mind reeled at what her heart was saying…it had started as if…as if he loved…

No! It wasn't possible! She had offered comfort and he had accepted that offer. Comfort—that was all he had wanted. But his was a passionate nature and, if he were to be believed, he found her reasonably attractive. No doubt it was only natural that he should kiss her passionately. Perhaps, she found herself trembling at the idea, there was an element of frustration in his loss of Milly. She was no innocent schoolroom miss. His arousal had been immediately and thrillingly apparent to her.

She shook her head to clear it. To think about it all now was impossible. She had to face his family, who must not be allowed to guess that anything untoward had occurred. Lady Winter's bright armour must be burnished up to deflect all the kindly, prying eyes that might penetrate the shields to espy her secret.

So she summoned up a smile and opened the door, forcing her lips to curve more deeply at the babble of sincerely delighted greetings that broke out. And steeling herself to answer the Dowager's startled query as to what the devil had happened to Crispin. She had quite thought he must be escorting Tilda down to dinner.

Somehow Tilda got through the pre-dinner gathering. When Crispin appeared he seemed perfectly collected, if a trifle preoccupied. To her immense relief she was not seated by him at dinner. Her partners were the kindly, if irascible, Lord John and Lord Hastings, both of whom seemed to be delighted to have her with them again.

The chat was general, full of laughter and banter. Everyone seemed to be in a festive mood. Tilda found herself comparing it with the polite formality that had always prevailed at the Pembertons' board. When relatives had descended upon the Pembertons *en masse* like this, it had been viewed as a duty, something to be endured. The moment the unwelcome hordes had left Lady Pemberton would be complaining about the tedium of the visit and the expense.

Tilda had not the least doubt that Lady St Ormond's only regret would be her family's departure. She'd be missing them and planning the next visit almost before they cleared the carriage drive. Even the acid-tongued Lady Hollow was embraced wholeheartedly, if carefully.

Casting a surreptitious glance towards Crispin, chatting quietly to his Aunt Seraphina at the end of the table, she thought that he at least would not look back on this visit happily—but from all she had observed and heard, he was normally delighted to welcome his family and looked upon it as a pleasure, not a duty.

At the end of the second course Lady St Ormond broke into the hub-bub by tapping gently on her wine glass. Gradually silence fell and heads turned her way.

Once she had everyone's attention, she stood up.

Georgie protested. 'Mama, it's much too early for us to leave! Isn't there another course?'

'I was intending,' said Lady St Ormond mildly, 'to propose a toast.'

Crispin looked up sharply. Tilda saw the suddenly hard set of his jaw. Please, she thought, don't propose a toast to Guy and Milly. He'll be too hurt... She looked away quickly, not wishing him to think he had betrayed himself to her yet again.

Lady St Ormond raised her glass and said simply, 'To Tilda. And her recovery.'

Before anyone could respond, Crispin rose to his feet. He'd seen Tilda's swift, anguished glance, and the gallant way she'd tried to hide her pain. She must have thought a toast to Guy and Milly was in the offing. He could think of nothing else to explain her reaction. And she was so sad, so quiet. Even the cool, witty façade of Lady Winter would have been better. She must have been even more attached to Guy than he had thought.

'I'll add to that,' he said very quietly. 'To Lady Winter. The bravest woman I have ever met.' And raised his glass in salute amid a chorus of approval. As Tilda turned crimson, everyone around the table stood and drank the toast.

Completely tongue-tied, she said as they all sat down, 'Thank you. But it wasn't brave...I didn't even think...I...I just...'

'Rubbish!' asserted Hastings. 'You'd have done it even if you had thought. No matter how damn scared you were! If we say you're brave, then you are. And there's an end of it!'

'Hear, hear,' said Lord John firmly. 'Crispin's in the right of it, m'dear. Now drink up. This is something my brother laid down. Rather nice drop of burgundy.' He turned towards the end of the table and said, 'By the by, Cris. Any notion yet about these traps?'

Slowly Crispin nodded. 'I have, as a matter of fact. But my idea is so outrageous that I haven't even mentioned it to Rigby and Marlowe. So if you don't mind, Uncle John, I think I'll hold my tongue.'

'In *my* day,' intoned Lady Hollow, 'they was strung up and there was an end of 'em!'

'Yes, well,' said her undutiful nephew, 'in your day, Aunt—which, I might add, seems to be far from over—they did all sorts of things that would bring a blush to our cheeks.'

'Humph!' was the response to this. 'At least we did something!'

Chapter Twelve

With Tilda's return downstairs the letters were sent off the following day. When no response came in the post on the third day following, Tilda and Milly prepared themselves for the worst.

'He'll be here tonight,' said Tilda. 'Now remember, Milly, let St Ormond and myself deal with it. No point in you setting his back up. He'll be furious with me anyway, so stay out of it as much as possible.'

They were strolling through the shrubbery while Anthea skipped ahead of them.

Milly swallowed hard. 'It's going to be dreadful.'

Tilda glanced at her and said, 'Probably not as bad as you think.'

Wide blue eyes stared in shock.

Tilda allowed herself a smug smile. 'You haven't considered, Milly. Instead of simply writing and ordering me to bring you home, he is coming himself. You know how conventional your paper is about matters of rank and precedence. How much would you care to wager that once he gets here and is confronted with St Ormond in his top-loftiest mood, he will find it nigh on impossible to refuse Guy's suit?' Her smile deepened. 'If he had given the matter a moment's thought, he'd have written and ordered you home. Now he will have to tell St Ormond to his face, that his cousin—and let's face it, to all intents and purposes, heir presumptive—is not good enough. And if you can see him doing *that*, then I would suggest that you have been reading too many rubbishy novels!'

The blue eyes widened even more as Milly absorbed the truth of this summing up. When at last she spoke it was in tones of awe. 'I never thought of that. Oh, Tilda! You're so clever!' Abruptly she frowned. 'But he'll still be cross with you. And surely, if he has to rein himself in with St Ormond and agree to the match, he'll be even angrier.'

Tilda shrugged. '*Plus ça change*. Nothing new in that. After all, he can only roar at me. So stop worrying about me and start thinking about your brideclothes!' So saying, she neatly diverted Milly's thoughts away from a highly unwelcome subject.

While she was confident that Lord Pemberton had manoeuvred himself into a position in which he would be completely outgunned and outflanked, she was not so sanguine about his likely rage with herself. *He can only roar at me...* Lady Winter could deal with that. She did not think he would dare to hurt her physically. But still the memories of her childhood reared before her, the pain of knowing herself unloved, unwanted, a blot on the family. And in her present mood she knew that keeping her bright shield in place would be very hard.

They strolled on, Tilda giving half an ear to Milly's musings on the merits of different carriage dresses for her going-away outfit.

She was on the fret when the hour arrived to dress for dinner, yet nothing had been heard from Lord Pemberton. Was he after all going to write in a day or so and demand Milly's return home? Would he try to stop her marriage to Guy? And how would Crispin respond to that?

* * *

'Lord Pemberton has arrived, your Grace.' Bebbington made this announcement as the party gathered for dinner.

Crispin felt a surge of triumph sweep through him. Sharply he swung around to look at Tilda. She looked completely unsurprised—even faintly smug. He snorted mentally. Her wits were rapier sharp. No doubt she had assessed the advantages of Pemberton arriving in person to retrieve his daughter. She would have interpreted the lack of a written response the same way he had.

He watched in awe as her reserve grew deeper, as the expression on her face reverted to the cool, watchful cynicism with which she had arrived. So gradually had her barriers disintegrated with his family, that he had scarcely noticed the process. Until now, when she retreated behind impenetrable calm and became again the untouchable goddess he'd first seen on the front steps.

Her chin lifted, the expression grew haughty, her lips, which had been curved in laughter at some sally of Georgie's, set in a smile that lowered the temperature considerably.

'Show Lord Pemberton in, Bebbington,' he instructed. 'Please assure him that we are *en famille*. He need not scruple to join us in his travelling dress.'

Accordingly Lord Pemberton was ushered in respectfully a moment later, to be greeted with a perfectly balanced blend of deference and easy informality by his host.

'My lord.' Crispin strolled forward to greet him. 'I do hope you haven't dined. We are just about to go in. Will you join us?'

Without awaiting a response he turned his head to the butler. 'Another place if you please, for my lord.' The impassive stare he received told him the place was either being laid or had just been laid. And that Bebbington had been butler at Ormsby Park since he, Crispin, was in short coats and certainly didn't need to be told to set an extra place for an unexpected guest.

Lord Pemberton glared. 'I'm in my travelling dress…'

'But of course you are,' said Crispin. 'No need to change. It's just the family tonight. Pray don't give it another thought!'

'Slovenly!' snapped Pemberton, evidently determined to make his presence felt.

Crispin raised a brow. 'My dear sir! I should not dream of describing a gentleman thus.' His smile verged on the dangerous, a faint hint of hauteur crept into his voice, giving Pemberton ample warning that his intransigent attitude would win no support.

He shepherded Lord Pemberton further in. It was vital that Pemberton sat down to eat with them and was forced to do the pretty. He would find it all the harder to retreat later. Especially if he were treated to a display of ducal magnificence in the meantime.

'Now, I am sure you are acquainted with everyone here, my lord,' said Crispin.

Gruffly Lord Pemberton admitted that he was. And glared around until his fulminating eye lit on Tilda.

Crispin felt the older man stiffen and followed his gaze. For an instant all his protective instincts surged. He had to restrain himself forcibly from stepping between Tilda and her uncle.

'My lord, how delightful to see you,' said Tilda. 'Do you know, I quite expected you would merely write. How nice of you to come in person. And how is my aunt?'

The best defence is a good offence, reflected Crispin. He smothered wry amusement as Tilda, in one classic move, opened hostilities and pointed out to her uncle the fatal flaw in his strategy—far too late for him to retreat and regroup. Judging by the arrested look on Pemberton's face, he had realised his error and was totally thrown by it.

'A daughter,' he growled. His tone did not suggest that he viewed this outcome with any expectation of future joy.

'Oh, how lovely,' said Tilda. 'Girls are such a comfort in one's old age! I know Jonathan thought so.'

Crispin nearly choked with suppressed laughter as he caught Hasting's eye. Little vixen! It was the first time he had heard Tilda's full battery turned on anyone but himself. Not being on the receiving end gave him a far greater appreciation of her technique. Dig a hole and let the victim trap himself. Nevertheless, he intervened firmly before the effort Lord Pemberton was making at self-control proved fatal.

'Do have a drink, my lord,' he urged. 'I'm sure it would prove restorative!'

As Lord Pemberton meditated on the excellence of the Madeira, Crispin drew Lord John forward with a lift of one brow. Better to let the two older gentlemen grumble together about the foolishness of the younger generation. He was quite sure that his uncle would do so out of ingrained habit and then cheerfully turn around and tell Pemberton, as though it were a *fait accompli*, how delighted he was that his son had chosen Milly.

If Pemberton had the bottom to buck then, they were in trouble. Otherwise the outcome was a foregone conclusion. Especially if they could puff off the betrothal before Pemberton got home to his lady!

He turned his attention to Lord John's conversation just in time. 'Humph! All of a piece with this generation. Only good thing about it is that he's chosen so well. Charming girl. Ought to be proud of her! Milly! Come here, m'girl. You too, Guy!'

Crispin swore mentally. He hadn't expected on this quite so early. He cast a worried glance at his erstwhile intended, but she had herself well in hand. As did Guy. Calm and self-assured. He had to wonder if Tilda had been giving lessons.

'Good evening, Papa. I'm so pleased to see you. Is Mama

quite well? We feel so dreadfully, dragging you away from her at such a time.'

Guy agreed. 'Indeed, yes. How do you do, my lord. It is quite some time since we met at White's. Papa has been insisting that I learn my way around managing the estates.'

Bravo! thought Crispin. Just the gentlest of reminders that the Malverns are wealthy enough to endow their younger sons very generously.

Breathing a sigh of relief, he moved away. Better to leave himself right out of it. The very last thing he wanted was to give the impression that he was eager to foist Milly on to Guy. Far more effective if he appeared indifferent. His letter to Lord Pemberton had merely been in his capacity as head of the family, to assure the Pembertons that the match had his approval.

And he was reasonably certain that the forthcoming display of ducal splendour would quite flatten any rearguard action Lord Pemberton might consider mounting.

Somewhat to Tilda's surprise when Bebbington announced dinner, her host came to her side and murmured, 'Follow my lead, my lady.'

He conducted her, all the others behind them, to the State Dining Room. She had peeped in with Anthea one rainy afternoon and been suitably stunned at the size and style of the apartment. And that had been with the room under Holland covers. Not even on the night of the ball had this room been used.

Now with the table revealed, twenty feet of highly polished mahogany supporting an array of silver and crystal calculated to make one blink in the blaze of light from innumerable wall sconces and candelabra, not to mention a chandelier that verged on the ostentatious, she realised that his Grace must also have expected her uncle to arrive.

Lord Pemberton, she reflected, was being given no chance to exercise a father's rights. He had been placed at the Dowager's right hand with Lady Hollow to his right.

Two influential ladies he would not dare to offend. And his conversation would be confined to them. Something about the very formality of the setting precluded the general easy chat that had characterised their dinners up till now.

The talk was all very polite and serious, not a frivolity to be heard, let alone a heated disagreement.

'You planned this, didn't you?' she said very quietly to Crispin.

He inclined his head. 'But of course, my dear. I learnt from Wellington that one of the cardinal rules of warfare is never to expose yourself to the enemy unnecessarily. And if your opponent is cork brained enough to do so, take full and immediate advantage.' His green gaze speared her. 'A rule you appear to be well versed in. Can it be possible that you play chess? The same rules of strategy apply there, of course.'

'Do you often use this room as a chessboard and your guests as pawns?' she enquired sweetly.

His grin was disarming, oddly out of place with the splendid surroundings. 'You should have seen the maids and footmen getting the place ready,' he confided. 'And poor old Bebbington thought I'd run mad! We haven't used it since Georgie's betrothal ball!'

Tilda laughed. 'A good omen then for Guy and Milly!'

Again the green gaze lanced into her. 'You see it that way?' His voice was deep, gravelly, laced with something indefinable.

She bit her lip. So caught up had she been by their shared amusement, that she had forgotten his pain. That he probably thought she had, at least in part, caused it.

Gently, she said, 'That…that is how it must be seen. I will admit that I came here determined to stop Milly marrying you, but I believe, had she not met Guy, that you would have made her very happy…' She could not for the life of her imagine how any sane female could not be happy with him for her life's partner. Would not be overjoyed to know that she was in his care, would be cherished and protected. And loved? Ruefully she reflected that Milly might never have known the difference, had she not met Guy.

Falteringly she met his intent gaze. 'All I ever wanted for Milly was her happiness. And to make sure that she was not pushed into a marriage she did not want.'

'You have achieved that.' His tone held no emotion whatsoever.

'Yes,' she agreed softly. 'But at what cost?' She felt his anguish as a barb in her own heart. A heart that felt all too much just at the moment. A heart that was breaking and could instinctively recognise a fellow sufferer.

Their eyes met.

'Perhaps we might test your skill at chess one day soon,' suggested Crispin.

Tilda nodded, grateful to have the conversation back to a less emotional level. She had felt that she was drowning, unable to breathe, lapped in liquid heat that cocooned her in its warmth and safety.

By the time the covers were removed Lord Pemberton had been neatly backed into a corner by Lady Hollow. And Lady St Ormond's legendary charm had so distracted and bemused him that he wasn't even aware of having been manoeuvred. He had been well wined and dined, especially the former, and he was in no position to gainsay everyone's assumption that the match between Milly and Guy had his approval.

Lady St Ormond took the final trick effortlessly. 'We are so pleased to see you, my lord. Do you know, we had imagined that a stern, paternal letter demanding your daughter's return would be forthcoming! But here you are, come to set your seal of approval on the happy event!'

Her bright voice cut through the other conversation effortlessly. Every head turned.

Crispin, deep in conversation with Georgie, held his breath. If Lord Pemberton were to baulk, he had to do it now. Crispin waited a moment, counted to five, waited again and then stood.

'Perhaps if everyone has a full glass, we might drink a toast to them,' he suggested, flicking a glance at the footmen who sprang to life. He heard Tilda's sharp intake of breath, but he couldn't help it. The chance was too good to pass up. Another rule of warfare; be prepared to take any opportunity to deliver a knockout blow. And there were always casualties. His heart ached at the knowledge that he was consciously causing her pain, but he stood firm and waited while the footmen scurried about, filling glasses.

When everyone was ready, he raised his glass. 'To Milly and Guy. May their marriage be long and happy!' A murmur of assent greeted this and the toast was drunk. Crispin remained on his feet. 'And to Lord Pemberton's *youngest* daughter. May she grow to be as lovely and charming as her elder sister and cousin. Congratulations, my lord.'

Lord Pemberton hummed and hawed. As far as he could see, the birth of another daughter was nothing to be pleased about. Still, it was very pleasant to be toasted by a duke, no doubt about it.

He was still mulling over it when he realised that Lady St Ormond and the other ladies were rising. Hurriedly he scrambled up and his eye fell on his niece, standing at St Ormond's side. All of a sudden, his chagrin at the outcome surged to the fore.

Oh, they might all be putting a good face on it! They had cornered him into giving the match his blessing, and it was a perfectly acceptable one. Guy Malvern was an only son and would have a patrimony many a nobleman would envy, but in comparison to the position Milly would have had as the Duchess of St Ormond—it was a bagatelle! And no doubt all caused by Matilda ! Undutiful, scheming wench!

He'd wager an egg at Easter she'd had something to do with it. For a start, she couldn't have been much of a chaperon not to have noticed what was afoot! She'd probably encouraged it, just to cause trouble. Well, he'd have something to say to her later on. Something she wouldn't forget in a hurry.

Savagely he noted how St Ormond's eyes followed her from the room. His gaze narrowed. She'd as good as said she'd take a lover in preference to a husband. No doubt she'd snared St Ormond, distracting his attention from Milly. Perhaps she even thought a ducal husband might be rather more to her taste. Lord Pemberton took a vicious delight in reflecting that St Ormond was far too experienced to be caught by a soiled widow.

He had no opportunity to speak privately with Tilda in the drawing room when the gentlemen joined the ladies. She was surrounded by Malverns at all times. Lady Hastings appeared to have a great liking for her and Lady St Ormond was constantly summoning her. And St Ormond himself was hanging around her—that told its own story, he thought nastily. He could think of only one thing a man of the Duke's cut would want of Lady Winter.

Tilda knew quite well that Crispin was still upset. She could see it in the rather forced cheerfulness he assumed with Guy, in the way he spoke to Milly—as though she were his niece. Gently teasing her about her approaching nuptials, referring her to various London modistes whom he guaranteed to be of the first stare.

She had to bite her lip not to laugh at Milly's innocent acceptance of his first-hand knowledge of such feminine fripperies and their cost.

She nearly drew blood when Milly said ingenuously to Crispin, 'How nice for your mama to have you take such an interest in her wardrobe!'

It was not so much Milly's unworldliness that overset her, as St Ormond's startled face as he recalled that he

ought not to know of such things. And if he did, most
certainly ought not to betray such knowledge to a modest
maiden. With only the faintest of colour highlighting his
cheekbones he murmured something about trying to be a
good son, and left Milly's side as soon as he decently could.

The tea tray had just been brought in and he promptly
volunteered to hand the cups around for his mother.

Unable to resist teasing him a little, Tilda raised one
brow as she accepted her teacup. 'Doing it rather too
brown, aren't you? Even Milly will smell a rat if you push
the dutiful son image too far.'

A soft laugh escaped him. 'Trust the cynical Lady Winter
to be awake on all suits! Had you responded as she did, I
should have known I was being roasted. As it is...' His
wicked green eyes invited her to laugh with him and she
did so, even while her heart ached for the performance he
was putting up.

'Milk and no sugar, isn't it?' he said.

'You remembered.' She was rather surprised. He had
only passed her a teacup once before.

With a queer smile he said, 'I doubt I'll forget much
about you, my dear.' Bowing slightly, he left her and returned to his mother, to be given more cups to distribute.

Tilda trembled. No doubt he meant that he'd remember
her as the woman who destroyed his happiness. For a moment she felt ready to sink, but rescue came from an unexpected quarter.

'Starting to look like a ghost, that gel!' announced Lady
Hollow. 'Send her up, Marianne! No need to chaperon
Milly with all of us here, not to mention his lordship!'

Lady St Ormond, chatting to her son-in-law, cast a mea-
suring look at Tilda.

'She does look pale, doesn't she, James?' said Lady St
Ormond. 'Off you go, my dear. We will see you in the
morning.'

Tilda blinked, but before she could demur, Crispin appeared at her side. 'Mama is right. It is time you were abed. Everything is under control. Trust me.'

There was nothing she had liefer do. She'd trust him with her life. Forever. If she were given the chance.

Bowing to the inevitable—she reflected that she had been manoeuvred just as neatly as her uncle—she bid the company good night.

Giving Milly a hug, she whispered. 'It's in the bag, love. Sweet dreams.' Her own would doubtless be much as they had been for nights past—disturbing, bittersweet and frustratingly unresolved.

Putting her thoughts aside, she went to her uncle. Far too tired to indulge in waspish remarks and far too grateful that all had gone so well, she said simply, 'Good night, sir. I will look forward to seeing you in the morning.'

He grunted and turned away.

Tilda blinked back a sudden heat in her eyes and squared her shoulders. Nothing had changed. She doubted that it ever would. If nothing else, the Malverns had shown her what family life could, and should be like.

The party broke up relatively early and went up to bed. Crispin, who had rather been hoping that someone would indulge him with a game of billiards to take his mind off his gloom, retired to his chamber and rang for his valet.

After getting into his nightshirt and settling into the very large, and very empty, ducal bed, he reached for his book. Only to recall that he had finished it last night and returned it to the library. He'd been doing rather a lot of reading in bed. It was preferable to the alternatives: to wit, lying there in a state of complete frustration waiting for two things— one which never came and one which was increasingly tardy—respectively, Tilda and sleep. And when the latter did deign to shut his eyes, he dreamed in shocking and explicit detail of the former. He didn't know which was worse—thinking about her or dreaming about her.

Swearing, he got out of bed and grabbed his dressing gown. He'd have to go down and find a book. Or three. Something guaranteed to put him to sleep. Gibbon's *Decline and Fall* might do the trick, he mused. Or possibly a volume of sermons might be better. There was even an outside chance they might give his thoughts a more proper direction. A very outside chance.

It took him quite some time in the library to select a volume of sermons exhibiting the required level of solid theological virtue, but in the end he headed back upstairs, the volume under his arm. He thought wryly, that even if they didn't send him to sleep, the effort of holding the book up in bed would certainly exhaust him.

He had gained the corridor that would lead him past Tilda's room when suddenly he heard raised voices muffled by a door. Frowning he stopped. Surely that was Tilda. He listened hard but heard Lord Pemberton's voice.

'I might have known you'd do everything you could to spoil her chances! You little whore! You even managed to distract St Ormond long enough for young Malvern to snare Amelia!'

Crispin stiffened. What the hell was Pemberton insinuating?

Tilda's voice, low and furious. He couldn't make out what she was saying.

'Oh, spare me the twaddle, girl! I've but one thing to say to you!'

A scream rang out, followed swiftly by a very masculine yell of pain.

'Get out! Don't you dare come in here again or I'll ring to have you thrown out!' This time Tilda's voice, shaking with emotion, rang loud and clear.

Crispin drew back in the shadows of a large niche and prudently blew out his candle. All his protective instincts had surged to the fore, but it sounded as though Tilda were managing by herself thus far. If he charged in now—were even seen in the vicinity of her room in his night rail—the scandal might ruin her.

The door opened and Lord Pemberton emerged hurriedly, one hand clutching a candlestick, the other clutching his head. Neither of which concerned Crispin in the least. He was hearing Milly's worried voice: *Tom says he saw Papa come out of her room with a riding crop one night...* Pemberton was carrying a riding crop.

Chapter Thirteen

Fury blazed through Crispin's soul, igniting every nerve, scorching everything in its fiery path. It was all he could do to remain out of sight until Lord Pemberton had turned the corner into the gallery.

Except for the thump as the sermons hit the floor, he never remembered the last few strides to her door. Only opening it and seeing her whip around like lightning, as the violently opened door bounced back off the wall. Seeing the fear in her eyes, the fierce defiance, the heavy brass candlestick raised threateningly.

'Oh…I thought…'

He saw the convulsive movement of her throat, the quivering tension in every graceful line—and her eyes, clinging to his.

Slowly the tension drained from her body. He could see it as she set down the candlestick on her dressing table. She stood silent, clad only in a light silk nightgown gathered in beneath her breasts, her eyes on his face, huge and vulnerable in the soft light. And even in that light, the red welt on her bare upper arm screamed its accusation, bringing a curse to Crispin's lips.

'Damn his soul to hell,' he said in deadly quiet tones.

'I'm…I'm all right,' she managed. Her voice sounded

shaky. 'I hit back, you see…with the candlestick. It took him by surprise. I didn't do that last time, so he didn't expect it.'

Last time. Milly had been right.

He was across the room before he could consider the danger, the likely outcome of such a move. She was wrapped in his embrace, her warm, scented body pressed to his in complete surrender, her arms twining around his neck and her mouth lifting to his in blind supplication.

Crispin groaned and took her lips, her mouth, in a kiss of searing passion that incinerated the angry tension investing his body, only to replace it instantly with another sort of tension—urgent, hard-edged, scorching need. She was so soft, so deliciously wanton in her embrace, in the way her pliant thighs shifted against his, innocently caressing, inciting, responding to his hand, which kneaded and stroked her hip, pulling her against him.

For she was innocent, he thought wildly, as his fingers firmed around one swelling breast. She might not be a virgin, but her ardour was fresh and spontaneous, something that was an integral part of who she was under the bright armour. Something distinctly lacking in the rather jaded and world weary embrace of other widows he'd had.

On the thought, he knew where this was heading. Without even realising it, he was backing her to the bed. He tried to stop and discovered that, this time, the manoeuvre was mutual. Tilda was backing herself and taking him along with her.

His head whirling, his veins full of scalding desire and his loins ablaze, he somehow broke the kiss and stood firm. With some difficulty he removed the hand from her bottom. The one at her breast was a lost cause. Even as he rested his brow on hers and drew breath, his fingers continued to circle and adore the hardened rosy nipple peeping through the diaphanous silk.

'Tilda.' He could barely speak as he pressed kisses on

her brow, her eyes, her hair. He had to make sure she really wanted this. In fact, he should probably walk away right now, rather than take advantage of her hurt in this fashion. But there were limits to his self-control and he was nearly beyond them.

'Just kiss me,' she whispered, a shy finger stroking the corner of his mouth. The light touch nearly stopped his heart.

Raggedly, he said, 'Tilda, if I kiss you again, I won't be able to stop. Do you understand what I am saying? I'll have you on that bed, writhing under me...'

He shuddered at the image he had created.

Her next words were so soft that he barely heard them. 'I need you, Crispin. And I don't want you to stop.' Then, so softly he could not swear to it, he thought he heard her breathe, 'Ever.' She lifted her head and met his burning gaze, her golden eyes clouded with desire, her lips swollen from his kisses. Even as he watched, her tongue slipped out to sheen them.

He groaned and lowered his mouth to them, holding himself back to gently savour their trembling sweetness. One small hand trailed down his chest, his stomach, and lower to touch him with passionate curiosity. He nearly died. He would have if her tentative caress hadn't been muted by his nightshirt and dressing gown.

He was lost. Heart and soul. She needed him. Even if she only needed the comfort of his body. And now she was pressing against him in a way that told him clearly of her need.

His hand framed her jaw, cupping it, exerting subtle pressure to open her mouth, even as his tongue traced the outline of her lips in growing hunger. She flowered for him sweetly, her body softening even further as he took possession of her mouth with slow erotic surges that echoed the shift of his loins against her.

He felt the gentle tug at his shoulder and responded by

swinging her up into his arms. Effortlessly he carried her the few steps to the bed and stopped beside it. He lowered her on to the covers gently, but stopped her as she would have slipped beneath them.

'No.' His eyes were blazing. 'I've waited too long for this, my sweet. I want to see you. All of you.'

She stared up at him, dazed by the riot of sensation pouring through her body, the tingling skin, the aching nipples, the surging heat pooling in her loins. And the sheer mind numbing joy that he appeared to want her as much as she wanted him. That he was not shocked by her desire, by the fact that she had touched him intimately.

He was taking his dressing gown off. It fell unheeded to the floor and to her amazed delight he grasped the hem of his nightshirt and removed that as well. She felt a ripple of wild excitement as she gazed with unashamed curiosity. At the broad shoulders, with their smooth, muscled curves, powerful hair-dusted forearms. The wide chest covered in crisp curls, over the flat stomach to...

Her eyes widened. She'd just touched it, but only through his dressing gown...she hadn't realised. Her eyes flew to his and met them hot with desire, but with a tender understanding tempering the passion.

She swallowed. He was a much bigger man than Jonathan, after all...taller, more powerful. She risked another glance down. This time all she felt was anticipation, excitement.

'Good.' His voice was a growl of satisfaction. Belatedly she realised that her face must be revealing every thought. She blushed. And realised he was joining her on the bed.

She would have moved to make room for him, but he caught her mouth in a fierce kiss and braced himself over her, before lowering his weight on to her and rolling, with her locked gasping in his arms, to the middle of the bed. The feel of his body pressed to hers, the shifting weight, sent her senses spiralling.

They ended with Crispin half on top of her, his mouth locked to hers, one powerful thigh wedged demandingly between hers. Tilda surrendered completely. To his hands, to his mouth, to his hard, rampant flesh pressed against her hip. And to that thigh which shifted so provocatively, so enticingly, in its soft cradle.

She gave herself unreservedly to the joy of the moment, to the delight of knowing, just this once, the ecstasy of giving herself to the man she loved. Even if he had only come to comfort her and had stayed to accept the comfort of her body. She would give him everything she had. And in return she would have a night of passion that would warm her dreams in her lonely bed for the rest of her life. There would be no regrets. For this one night she would be his and count herself lucky to have had that much.

Never had he known such a total yielding to desire. Never had a woman surrendered to him so wholeheartedly. She held nothing back, there was no reserve, no barrier to her soul. He drank from her sweetness again and again, revelling in the taste and texture of her mouth as his fingers dealt expertly with the row of tiny buttons fastening her nightgown. At last her bodice was open. Lifting from her, he drew back to look, to worship his goddess. She lay beneath him, her eyes shut, face flushed, and lips rosy with his kisses.

As he watched her eyes fluttered open, passion dazed golden pools a man could drown in. Her hair, reflecting golden lights, spread in tumbled abandon on the pillow. Slowly, reverently, he drew his fingers through the soft waves, spreading them out, wondering at the silken texture, the heady fragrance of rosemary that drifted from them. He'd never forget this.

'Crispin?' Her voice wobbled.

'You're beautiful,' he murmured. Slowly he set his hand to the bodice of her gown and slid the two halves aside, one at a time, to reveal one by one her swollen, hard-peaked breasts. Scarcely able to breathe, he brushed the backs of his fingers over one rosy nipple and she arched against his caress like a cat, with a gasp that spoke eloquently of her state.

She wanted him as much as he wanted her.

He stroked her breast again, teasing the nipple with the pads of his fingers before turning his attention to its twin. Slowly, expertly, he fondled and caressed, while all the time she twisted and sobbed her pleasure with an unrestrained abandon that fired his own dangerously engaged passions.

Tilda had forgotten everything she had ever been told about the proper way a lady should behave. Dimly she was aware that the cries and gasps, the moans of delight, were hers. She couldn't believe that the body that was burning and dying under his ministrations was really hers. It had never felt anything approaching this before. Even their previous encounters had not prepared her for this. She had expected pleasure, not total ecstasy. Nothing could be better than this, surely.

And then she felt his mouth on her breast. Her body nearly exploded as he drew one nipple into the hot wetness of his mouth and suckled. She'd forgotten. Even so, their encounter in the library had been nothing compared to this. Then she'd known that she had to stop him. This time she wouldn't stop him if her life depended on it. She arched against him, her hands threaded through his hair, holding him to her.

One hand slid down over his shoulders, tracing the flexing muscles that held her so safely, adoring the broad planes of his back and around to his ridged abdomen, feeling it tense beneath her fingers. Exploring, caressing, she breathed in the musky, male scent of him. Gloried in his groans of delight, muffled against her soft breast. She sent her hand lower, to touch wonderingly, to stroke and, finally, to grasp. She marvelled at the contrasts, so hard, so hot, and yet so silken. Her body throbbed in yearning, aching emptiness.

Crispin had known from the start where she was headed. Had tried to steel himself. He was only partially successful. At least he hadn't simply lifted the hem of her gown and taken her. But he had to get the damn thing off or he'd be doing just that.

Lifting himself from her, he tugged the gown down over her shoulders and gathered it at her waist.

'Lift up,' he whispered harshly. And caught her startled gaze. The sudden tension in her body.

He stopped at once. 'Tilda?'

'What…what are you doing?' A siren's voice, husky, seductive. And innocent.

Shock tore through him. He drew a deep breath to steady himself. 'Your nightgown. You don't need it.' And he sure as hell didn't. 'I'll warm you.' All night if she'd let him.

'Oh!' A long breathed sigh of delight. Then, 'Jonathan never…we always…do you really want to take it off?'

Apart from the fact that her late husband, his undoubted kindness and chivalry aside, had been a conservative and undeserving clod, that innocent revelation ripped the scales from Crispin's eyes in another matter.

Reaching for control, he sat back. Even in his frantic state he knew he couldn't ask her point blank. But he needed to know just how careful he'd have to be. So he circled the issue, with all the skill he'd just lavished on her breasts.

'How long ago did your husband die?'

Tilda trembled. She'd given herself away completely. 'About sixteen months ago,' she said. Then, 'But he was ill for a year or so before that…' She left the sentence hanging, so that he could draw what conclusion he liked. Would he be angry about her deception? Nervously she avoided his eyes and wished he'd just start making love to her again.

A large gentle hand framed her jaw. She found herself meeting simmering emerald passion. 'And how long before that?'

Her blush mantled her breasts.

'Before...before Anthea was born.' She floundered on. 'You see, he located Max, his distant cousin and heir. Jonathan liked him and he...he didn't want to risk cutting him out...by...with an heir. And I...I think he'd been so much in love with his first wife that...he decided not to...have any more children, so...'

There was a moment's fraught silence while Crispin struggled to frame his next question.

'So you haven't...been...with a man in nearly six years?'

He didn't need to hear her soft assent. The truth was screaming from every dejected line of her body. He groaned mentally.

And took a deep breath. 'Then we'll take this slowly. Very slowly.' Suiting the action to the word he drew her back into his arms only to stop immediately as she wriggled to be free. Reluctantly he released her.

He stared in escalating desire as she sat up, whisked her nightgown over her head and flung it away. She knelt there, naked, her body softly flushed as he gazed at her.

Tilda felt that gaze as a heated caress, that scorched over her breasts, her slim arms, the curve of her waist and hip. And zeroed in on the curls at the base of her belly. Dizziness swept through her as the pent-up need surged through her blood.

Catching her breath, she said, 'I don't want to go slowly.' She wanted him to take her right now, ravish her, release the burning tension that sang and throbbed in her body.

His answering grin was devilish. 'Maybe not, my pet. But I can assure you, I do.' His gaze speared her and he said, 'I'm going to savour every single moment, every touch, every moan, thoroughly.' Her eyes widened as his

words sent a surge of heat through her. Her mouth opened
but nothing came out.

He nodded as if she'd spoken. And spoke even more
softly. 'And when I take you, I'll enjoy every sob of pleasure, every scream.' Then he reached for her and enveloped
her in a steely embrace, capturing her lips in a kiss that
was inexpressibly tender.

His hands were everywhere, kneading, caressing and
teasing, until she was a whirlpool of urgent need, pliant and
heated. Still kneeling, she felt one hand splayed over her
belly, felt the long fingers slide into the springy curls. And
reach further, pressing into soft, melting heat.

Instinctively she shifted slightly, opening herself to him,
inviting him to further intimacy. He accepted her invitation
and she cried out wildly against his mouth, whimpering as
he explored and loved her. Slowly, powerfully, tenderly.
Until her body was melting, aching with the need to feel
him inside her. Processing her, taking her.

And still he teased, stroked and caressed the sensitive
swollen folds. Unerringly he found a place she had never
even known existed. A place where the sensations speared
straight through her body in a melting agony of desire. She
gasped and arched, pressing herself against those wickedly
knowing fingers. Pleading wordlessly. One long finger slid
deep inside. She shuddered at the sensation, the shocking
intimacy of such an invasion. It wasn't enough—she
wanted him, all of him—now.

But his mouth was crushing hers—absorbing her cries
and sobs. His tongue surged and retreated, filling her
mouth, stroking sensuously, plundering her softness—and
yet his hand was so gentle—it was driving her wild.

Crispin's blood was an inferno. She was so soft, so hot,
so excruciatingly ready for him. And her voice—it was a
siren's song, urging him on. He had to have her now. Grit-
ting his teeth, he urged her back against the pillows, and
discovered that he wasn't merely pressing her down, she

was drawing him down. Opening her body to him, wildly eager, cradling him, lifting towards him as he let his weight settle on her, nudged her thighs wider. He felt her gasp of pleasure as he gently opened her with his fingers, probed and stroked the hot wetness until he heard a single coherent word.

'Please.'

And then another. 'Now.'

He had long ago lost track of who was taking whom. And it didn't matter. The taking was mutual. With that thought burning through him, he pressed against her, felt her hips tilt in wanton invitation.

He groaned. 'Lie still.' He didn't want to hurt her, and after so long, who knew. Somehow he would have to rein back the instinctive urge to ravish, to possess mercilessly. If he could. If she'd let him.

He tried. Eased inside her, slowly, carefully. Using every ounce of willpower he possessed to stay in control, he sank into her heated body, as she flowered and yielded, softening round him. Trusting him. That knowledge both humbled and elated him. It tempered the scorching passion with tenderness. A tenderness he had never known before—the urge to protect, controlling the urge to take.

Tilda lay still, stunned at the sensation that assailed her. Heat pooled in her belly as his masculine hardness slid inside her. His weight rested on her, holding her captive beneath him, yet all she felt was deliciously vulnerable. And safe. She felt safe, surrounded by his warmth, by his strength, by his tenderness.

She felt him shudder, felt the sudden tension as he drew back slightly. She cried out in protest and he took her mouth passionately, silencing her as he thrust deep, burying himself to the hilt in her body. Then a gentle hand stroked her cheek, so tenderly she felt a tear slip from under one eyelid. 'Are you all right?' Somehow she opened her eyes. He was watching her, his jaw rigid with tension, heavy-lidded eyes smouldering with passion. Then he lowered his head and kissed the tear from her cheek.

'Yes,' she breathed.

He brushed his lips across hers. 'Good. Then tilt your hips towards me a little and wrap your legs around my hips.'

She obeyed instantly and gasped as he sank even deeper. His groan of pleasure was unmistakable as he took her lips and mouth again. His tongue stroked hers in slow posessive surges and, frantic with need, she kissed him back wildly.

Slowly, almost teasingly he began to rock his hips back and forth, shifting inside her rhythmically, the crisp mat of hair on his chest rasping against aching, swollen nipples, using his whole body to love and worship her.

And she responded, catching his rhythm, tilting, lifting to meet each thrust, as he drove her steadily on, higher and higher, until she was nearly insane with need. His own body was screaming for release but he held tight to the reins of his desire as he revelled in the wanton fever he could feel within her, burning in her veins, heating her skin. All silken, heated passion, she shifted and burnt beneath him.

He watched her, enthralled, enslaved by her total surrender, her complete abandonment to the moment. All her defences, her shields were down. This was the real woman, who had revealed herself to no one else, had truly given herself to no one else. She was his; he'd never let her go now. The knowledge sent his passions blazing higher, almost beyond his breaking control. He shifted within her more urgently, deeper, harder, seeking to bind her to him, so that later, when he could finally tell her of his love, she might remember and accept the truth.

She felt the change and her senses seemed to expand, yet she was only aware of him, of his body possessing hers and being possessed in return and something else, that poured from him in waves of heat and found its match in her. Something that held her very soul spellbound.

Her body was enslaved, hungering for more. Writhing and sobbing beneath him, she cried out in protest as she felt his body lift away from hers. Frantically she clung to his shoulders as he braced himself over her. And fell back as he changed the tempo, surging into her yet more powerfully, far more deeply.

He looked down at her, spread beneath him, in thrall to his loving. The sight urged him on. Brown curls tumbled in wild abandon over the pillows, glowing with golden lights in the candle's gleam. Her face, flushed with passion and her eyes closed as she lifted to meet him, all reserve forgotten in the inferno that raged between them.

He groaned and reached for control. It was gone. She had incinerated it.

Tilda cracked open her eyes and gazed up into his face. At the passion in his eyes, etched in every line of his face. And heard his urgent whisper.

'Now. Let go. Come with me.' She felt his hand press beneath her hips, cradle her bottom and lift her to him, holding her against his loins as he thrust deeper and harder. Again and again.

And then she felt it. The coil of tension spiralling out of control, lifting her high on a crest of molten desire, hovering over the blinding abyss. He withdrew almost completely and drank in her frantic cry of need, felt her lift towards him in desperate entreaty, pleading for release. For a moment he held her there, poised on the very cusp of fulfilment. With one thrust, he sent her tumbling, flying over the edge. She screamed as she shattered beneath him, into shimmering fragments that scorched in fierce delight and then melted slowly into sated oblivion.

With a groan of delight, Crispin let his body have its way and went with her into the void of ecstasy. He gloried in a release more profound than anything he had ever known. And he gloried even more in the knowledge that her release had been as cataclysmic. He could feel it in the convulsions of her body, beneath him, around him. In the way she clung to him, sighed his name in a dazed, broken whisper.

Awash, drowning in the golden glow, he sank back down onto her and rolled, taking her with him still wrapped securely in his arms. Soothing her with tender murmurs and even more tender kisses, he settled her safely. Warm, relaxed curves snuggled against him, silken limbs entwined themselves about him.

He flicked a glance at the candle still burning on the bedside table. It was very low. It could gutter all by itself, he decided. For nothing less than an earthquake would he risk breaking the dreaming enchantment that held them. He held at bay the small part of his mind that warned him his joy was illusory, and would die as surely as the candle.

Tilda awoke in the depths of the night to find herself still wrapped safely in his embrace. He was lying half beside her, half on top of her, one powerful thigh lying between hers, as though to stake his claim. His arm, warm and heavy, encircled her, as though he couldn't bear to let her go. Rough hair rasped sensuously across the soft curve of her waist as she shifted against him.

A dream, she told herself. But dreams are to be enjoyed. Believed in while they lasted. So she snuggled even closer, pressing a kiss on his shoulder.

The dreams she'd had of what it would be like to surrender and be loved by him had disturbed her sleep night after night. They'd taunted, tantalised with their promise of delight. And they had faded to pale shadows in the blaze of the reality. Never had she imagined such exquisite ecstasy, such a burning of passion, such a complete giving.

Just as wonderful was the joy of lying here in his arms, held safely against his warm, relaxed body. Cocooned in safety. And it was real. The dream would never fade for her now. She knew that she would always hold it deep in her heart, that it would be a warmth and a comfort in the years ahead.

She nestled against him and pressed another gentle kiss on his shoulder. Only to feel his arm tighten, feel the hair-brushed thigh shift and caress her suggestively, demandingly.

Then a husky voice spoke into the velvet darkness. 'Once was never going to be enough. Not with you.' And knowing hands were drifting over her, teasing, stirring her body to urgent life. She heated under his touch and moaned as she felt him shift to take one aching nipple into his mouth.

She melted in an agony of love and surrender in the darkness as he loved and caressed her until she was crying out in her need. Until he covered her and took her again, possessing her, body and soul, so that her world began and ended with him.

The darkness heightened her senses so that she was exquisitely aware of every touch, every thrust. Aware of the sharp masculine scent of him. Aware of every small sound—groans of pleasure, the whisper of his hair roughened skin caressing her silken flesh, his murmurs of encouragement in her ear. And she was wildly aware of the taste of him, of his mouth as he sated her with languorous kisses, of his body as she pressed open-mouthed kisses over his chest and shoulders, even suckling at one of the hard, flat nipples.

Until the end came and they spilled out into the abyss locked together in the bliss of their fulfilment.

He loved her again as dawn crept into the room, bathing them in pale light. She had been dreaming and woke to find that her dream had become her reality. That he was deep within her, igniting her body, possessing her soul. She clung to him, urging him on, loving him in the only way she could. This would be the last time. When she awoke again, he would be gone. Then the memory locked in her heart would have to be enough.

Crispin finally forced himself from her bed in the sure and certain knowledge that if he didn't, one of the maids would see him leaving her room. That was the last thing he needed. For Tilda, when he offered for her, to have the least doubt of his motives.

He just hoped to God that the night he'd spent in her bed wasn't going to precipitate him into any rash action. That he'd be able to control his desperate need to possess and protect her. She needed time to come to terms with what had happened between them. She needed to accept Guy's marriage. And then she'd need time to accept his own love. He'd never rushed a woman in his life, and he had no intention of starting with her.

To his immense relief he managed to gain his own corridor before meeting one of the maids. Who merely bobbed a curtsy and wished him a good morning without batting an eyelid. She might have been a little suspicious had she been able to read the title of the massive book tucked under his arm. His Grace was not renowned for his interest in the sermons of Dr John Donne.

Crispin made it to his room and tossed the volume on to his bed with scant respect. The poetry of the youthful Jack Donne would have been far more to his taste at the moment, he thought.

Lord Pemberton had slept very badly. A rapidly burgeoning headache was not the least of his problems. He finally awakened as dawn crept through a chink in his curtains and fell on his eyes. He opened them with a groan. For the pain. And for the fact that he was going to have to explain the bruise and lump above his left eye.

Savagely meditating his revenge upon his niece, he dressed. Maybe some fresh air would help his head. He had just passed Tilda's door with a muttered malediction when he heard the soft click. Startled, he swung around. The door was opening.

Instinct took over, propelling him into a nearby embrasure, still cloaked in shadow. He pressed back, eyes widening in scandalised triumph, as his host appeared in his dressing gown and night rail, cast a swift glance around, picked up a large book lying on the floor, and set off down the corridor with a swinging stride.

Jaw dropped, Lord Pemberton savoured his victory. Fate had just dealt him an ace. If he played his cards carefully he might be able to block Amelia's marriage to young Guy and force St Ormond to wed her. Not even St Ormond would willingly face a scandal where he was accused of seducing his intended bride's chaperon and then foisting the unwanted bride on to his cousin!

As for Lady Winter; his eyes narrowed. A few discreet whispers to the servants as they'd be watching her like a hawk. It would only be a matter of time before one of them caught his Grace leaving. She was a doxy like her mother before her and he'd see her destroyed if he could.

Chapter Fourteen

'Ah. Good morning, your Grace!' Lord Pemberton was positively wreathed in smiles. His eyes glinted with such good humour that Crispin snapped out of his mood of relaxed calm instantly. He couldn't believe that a night's sleep would have fully reconciled Pemberton to Milly's betrothal. Or even that he'd had a good night's sleep with that bump on his head. He viewed it with savage satisfaction.

Senses at the stretch, he responded politely, 'Lord Pemberton. I trust you were comfortable. But what is this?' He indicated the bump. He certainly didn't wish Pemberton to suspect his prior knowledge.

To his intense pleasure, Lord Pemberton flushed. 'Oh! Ah, just a little altercation with a bedpost! But enough of me! I do hope your Grace spent a…*satisfactory* night.'

In the act of reaching for the door to the breakfast parlour, Crispin froze. There was something about Pemberton's voice, a note of vicious triumph. He turned, exerting every nerve to control the impulse to choke the grinning life from Lord Pemberton.

'Just so, your Grace. Perhaps we might have a brief word. About marriage settlements.'

'In my library.' Crispin swore mentally. He'd have to

tread carefully here. If Tilda ever suspected he'd offered because of her uncle's threats, he'd be sunk. The man had forced her into marriage once; she'd never submit to that again.

Seating himself in a comfortable chair, Lord Pemberton's first words disabused Crispin of his initial suspicions.

'I believe, your Grace, that in light of recent developments, we might like to review the eligibility of Amelia's proposed marriage.'

Crispin stared, dumbfounded.

Lord Pemberton permitted himself an oily smile. 'Even you cannot seduce your intended bride's chaperon and then expect your cousin to marry the unwanted bride, while you pursue an affair with her cousin. If such a tale were to leak out…' This time the smile was beatific. 'Ruin, your Grace.'

It would be ruin all right and tight, thought Crispin. For Tilda. A discreet affair would be condoned. But it was plain that Lord Pemberton had other ideas. A tremor of sheer revulsion ran through Crispin. This man could contemplate destroying his niece. Pemberton had destroyed his own sister in much the same way.

Icy rage took hold. Crispin's jaw hardened, every line of his body stiffened in barely leashed fury. His voice, when he finally spoke, cut like a burning knife.

'If, my lord, one word of this is breathed, you will find that society has nothing but condemnation for a man who treated a young girl under his care as you did, and that in protecting my betrothed wife, a widow of unblemished reputation, my actions will meet with no argument! I will have no hesitation in making quite sure, Lord Pemberton, that your place in society is forfeited. Do I make myself quite plain? Perhaps you might care to go to breakfast now, before I am tempted to make my position even clearer.'

Observing that his Grace's fists were clenched, Lord Pemberton didn't even stop to apologise. His Grace's voice halted him by the door.

'Miss Pemberton's marriage to my cousin will take place as soon as the banns can be called. As will mine to Lady Winter. Any attempt by you to upset these arrangements would be most unwise!'

As the door closed hurriedly Crispin cursed vehemently. He'd have to offer for Tilda immediately. Somehow he had to persuade her to marriage without her thinking he offered under duress and without mentioning the word love. She was honest to the core. If she thought he offered his heart and she could not return his affection, she would refuse him.

There was something else—her clearly stated avowal that marriage had nothing to offer her, that she had her independence, both personally and financially, and did not care to lose either in matrimony. He would have to reassure her that she would lose neither in marrying him.

And as for her belief that marriage had nothing else to offer that was not freely available without interference of clergy! He thought, with a tender smile, that when she had said that, she had spoken in all innocence. Now she knew better. And that was the only trump in his hand as far as he could see. He would have to play that card very skilfully. He would have to convince her that as far as he was concerned, the only way she would get a repeat performance was in the marriage bed. After which he'd have to try and keep out of her bed until the wedding night.

Grimly he strode from the library. He had to get to Tilda before Lord Pemberton could announce the betrothal.

He ran across Bebbington in the hall and greeted him with relief.

'Is Lady Winter down yet, Bebbington?' The steadiness of his voice was rather a surprise to him. Inwardly he was shaking.

'Her ladyship is, I believe, breakfasting privately in her room. Shall I send a message up, your Grace?'

'No,' said Crispin and headed for the stairs. He turned

on the second step. 'And if anyone is asking for me, you haven't seen me.'

'Your Grace wishes me to lie?'

'Through your teeth,' his Grace affirmed.

Tilda had awoken just in time to hear her door shut gently. He was gone. And her body still glowed with the aftermath of their final loving, still throbbed to the rhythm of his possession. If she closed her eyes and dreamed she could still feel the weight of his body on hers, feel the strength of warm muscles surrounding her, feel him buried deep inside her.

Slowly she came to terms with what had happened. She had seduced, and been seduced by, Crispin Malvern. Deliberately. At least on her part. She had taken the pleasure, the ecstasy that was offered. In return she had given herself without reserve.

And now he was gone. When she saw him later in the day she would have to meet him as though nothing had happened. As though he had not spent the night in her bed. As though she had not spent the night writhing and sobbing in his arms like a wanton as he made love to her. Not once, but three times.

She snuggled back under her tumbled bedding. God only knows what the maids would think when they saw it, she thought sleepily. Sarah would probably be fussing after her all day, thinking she'd had a bad night when quite the opposite was the case. She fell asleep, still smiling.

Tilda had finished her breakfast—rather startled to find herself with an enormous appetite—and was handing the tray to Sarah, when there was a peremptory knock at the door.

Sarah cocked her head and glanced at her mistress.

Tilda nodded. No doubt it was Milly, come to see if she was up yet.

She was shocked to hear Crispin's deep voice requesting entrance.

Then he was in, looking impossibly handsome and rested. For a moment she wondered if she had merely dreamed that he had spent the whole night making love to her, until she saw the flare in his eyes as they rested on the tumbled bed. Saw the thoroughly wicked and knowing smile that curved his lips.

She blushed, clutching her robe tightly around her. And saw that smile deepen…with unmistakable satisfaction.

Her attention was briefly diverted by a strangled sound from Sarah. Eyes wide, Sarah was glancing from this very improper visitor to the muddle of bedding. Somehow Tilda managed to meet her gaze and saw Sarah's jaw drop. Then, to Tilda's outrage, a smile every bit as wicked and satisfied as St Ormond's lit her maid's face.

'Hmm. Well, I'd best be getting along,' she said. 'I'll leave you to it. Good morning, your Grace. Milady.' She picked up the tray and headed for the door.

Tilda was rather touched to see Crispin leap for the door and open it. How very kind of him, she thought. She rapidly revised her estimate of his chivalrous intent as she heard the lock click home.

She gulped. No matter what she'd done last night—and she'd done plenty—this surely couldn't be a good idea. One was supposed to be discreet. Wasn't one?

'Good morning, your Grace.' She managed to sound as though dukes wearing suggestive smiles visited her like this every morning. And encountered a raised brow.

'Good morning…Tilda.' His tone suggested that formality was the last thing on his mind. He had a point—it was probably a little late for that now.

'Is there…is there something I can do for you?'

The unholy grin that split his face had her wishing she hadn't phrased her question in quite that way.

His features straightened with what was obviously an effort. 'Later,' he said gravely.

She blushed hotly. Even more so since he knew just how heated that flush was making her skin, just how far it extended—and just how to make it go even further, burn even hotter. He'd demonstrated that last night.

'Tilda,' he began. 'About last night...'

She rushed into speech. 'Please, your...Crispin...there is no need. I...know you did not intend... I am just as much to blame... You need not say anything...' She nearly choked on the hard lump that rose in her throat. 'I promise I will not regard it. It was just last night...I...I quite understand that you meant only to comfort me.'

'You think I didn't mean to make love to you?' There was a queer, tight note in his voice.

She flinched. It had felt like he'd meant every burning touch, every tender caress—but if he'd truly wanted her, he'd have come before. Wouldn't he?

'I think you did not intend to make love to me before you came to my room, no,' she said shakily.

'You would wish to leave it there?' His voice was very quiet and deep.

Her eyes flashed to his. 'Is that not what you wish?'

'No.' Very short and hard. 'I can't.'

A shudder ran through her. Then he wanted a liaison. Wanted her to be his mistress. She closed her eyes to hide the pain. She had brought it on herself. He had every reason to think that she would welcome and enjoy such an arrangement. She forced her eyes to open and meet his.

He took a deep breath. 'I told you last night; once was never going to be enough with you. Nor, it seems, will one night be enough. Tilda, please, I am asking you, no, begging you to be...'

'Please, no.' She couldn't bear to hear him say it. 'You do not need to beg me. I...I accept your...offer.' She couldn't think what else to call it. Her experience did not extend that far. To her relief he seemed to accept her reply. Indeed, the joy and relief that surged into his face stunned her.

'You will?' It reverberated in his deep voice.

Desperately she forced herself to concentrate. Best find out now what he envisaged. For how long. Where. Bitterly she realised that this was the end of the joyous dream she had created with him last night. One night of passion could be cherished tenderly in the memory. But a relationship such as he now asked for would inevitably be soured by a parting. Kindly and generous on his part, no doubt. And with outward smiles to protect the broken heart on hers. Yet she could not find it in her to refuse. Her own need she might have managed to deny, but she loved him too deeply to deny his.

'What…what terms did you envisage?'

He blinked slightly. 'Well, the usual ones, I suppose.'

That didn't tell her a dratted thing. She had no idea, in specific terms, what gentlemen offered to their paramours. But she could see one overriding problem. Her home was in Leicestershire. His was here.

Perhaps he intended to remove to London where it would be possible for her to rent a house and he could visit her privately.

'Where do you wish me to live?'

He stared. 'Ah, here, of course…'

'Here?' Tilda felt the shock as a physical jolt. *'Here?'* It was unheard of. Even she knew that much after her mother's experience. Gentlemen did not live openly with their mistresses. No matter if all society knew the truth, one still played the game. The game society called discretion; the one she called hypocrisy. She gulped—obviously Crispin shared her views.

'But, naturally.' He seemed thoroughly puzzled. 'It's my home. You seem to like it here. And Guy and Milly won't be far away. So you can visit and…'

Tilda stared. He thought that she could live openly as his mistress and still visit her cousin? Surely not! Not even the Malvern arrogance could extend that far.

Another objection occurred to her. 'But your mama, Lady St Ormond—she won't be very pleased...she lives here...we can't...'

A very wicked chuckle interrupted her. 'My dearest goose! When Mama hears the news, she'll probably have my greys poled up and be straight down to the Rector to have the banns called immediately. She's been waiting for my marriage for so long that she'll positively fall on your neck!'

Only two words in this speech actually penetrated Tilda's suddenly numbed brain. *Banns,* and *marriage*.

The truth burst on her like a bombshell. He was asking her to marry him! She corrected herself sharply. No, he'd already asked her. And she'd accepted. At least, he thought she'd accepted. But how was she to explain what she'd thought? What she'd intended to accept.

Because she didn't want to marry him! At least, she did. Of course she did! But not without love on both sides. She didn't dare.

Somehow she forced her lips to frame the words. 'Crispin, why do you wish to marry me? After all...this...' she gestured wildly '...you won't feel this way forever...' Her voice trailed off. She couldn't go on. His pain would be gone one day and then he would find himself tied to her. Tied to a wife he didn't really want. She'd rather be his mistress and have him leave when he tired of her than see him trapped.

He was speaking again. 'You think not?'

To her shock she realised that his long strides had closed the distance between them. That he was kneeling on the bed beside her, reaching for her. His hands grasped her shoulders, drew her against him to lie soft and unresisting in his arms.

'I told you, Tilda. I can't leave it at just one night. I want you. More than I have ever wanted a woman.' His arms tightened.

Her brain reeled and her body melted at the heat of urgency in his voice. And she realised that he had not understood her. That he had not realised she was speaking of Milly. She heard her own voice, a queer strained shadow, say 'But you don't need to marry me for—'

He released her abruptly. 'No! Don't say it, Tilda! Let us have one thing quite clear—you will be my wife, not my mistress. I will not dishonour either of us by debauching you.'

Shock lanced through her as he stood up. 'But why me? You've had so many mistresses... I mean...why marry me?' Against all hope she yearned to hear him say he loved her, adored her, couldn't live without her.

'I haven't had that many!' he said indignantly. 'You make it sound as though I kept a harem!'

Glaring at him, she retorted, 'You've had more than I have, anyway!'

He grinned. 'I should think so! Unless your middle name is Sappho, of course.'

For a moment she didn't understand, but then she firmly suppressed a grin and said, 'I *meant* that you'd had more mistresses than I'd had lovers!'

A very tender smile played about the corner of his mouth. 'Well, that wouldn't be very difficult either,' he noted.

She ignored that. Along with the smile. 'Why? Why me?' She had to force the conversation back on track.

'Because I must,' was all the answer he gave her. She stared up at him, at the hard, set planes of his face, the lambent eyes, blazing with the force of his emotion. And she thought she knew the reason. Milly *had* hurt him. By taking her, he could drown some of his pain. And she would be the most convenient choice. She knew the truth, would not expect too much of him. He would be comfortable with her. They suited.

'We will suit very well, my dear.' She flinched at the tone of calm good sense, echoing her thoughts. 'You know that. My mother will love you as a daughter and I promise to be a good father to Anthea. I have no intention of interfering with your independence. Your fortune will remain yours. Settled upon you. I have no need of it.'

Her eyes widened in shock. 'These are not the terms you would have offered Milly,' she stated with as much composure as she could muster. 'You said yourself that you wanted a bride you could mould to your liking, who would be guided by you. Yet now you offer a completely different bargain. Why?'

Even to herself, her voice sounded cold, clinical. Crispin's mouth tightened. She almost expected one of the bursts of anger she could so easily spark off.

But he spoke gently. 'If I offered you those terms, you would throw them in my face. You are not Milly. You are older, independent and far more mature. And since I want you as you are, I would be a fool indeed to try to change or dominate you. That would end in misery for both of us. You need have no qualms.'

Except for her own peace of mind. Frantically she thought that it would indeed have been easier to be his mistress. The trap was closing about her and she could see no escape. She could not, to save her life, tell him what she had thought he was offering. Not when he had in fact offered her a marriage such as she had not thought possible; a marriage in which she would be valued as an equal.

Almost hysterically, she tried to imagine the words: *Thank you for your offer of marriage, your Grace, but, if you don't mind too much, I'd rather be your mistress.*

It couldn't be done. Not when Milly had practically jilted him for his cousin. She could not deal a blow like that to his pride and self-respect.

Her own cynical mind had dug the pit into which she had fallen. Miserably she remembered thinking that any woman would be happy to give her life into his keeping and surrender herself to his tender care. She had been wrong.

To the woman who loved him it could be nothing but pain to know that he would never love her. That he had loved her cousin and had married her as a sort of second best. Because he was fond of her and she had pleased him in bed.

You wanted to comfort him. And at least he has not offered for you because he feels that he compromised you.

It was marginal comfort at best, but it was better than nothing.

The first person she met, upon leaving her bedchamber half an hour later, was Milly, rushing up to find her.

'Tilda! Darling Tilda! Is it true? Are you really going to marry St Ormond?'

Not entirely sure herself, Tilda yet managed to give a coherent response and submit to her cousin's delighted enthusiasm.

'I was with the Duchess, when Crispin came in to tell her,' explained Milly. 'She nearly fell on his neck! And said something about going to see the Rector at once. But St Ormond told her that since he'd managed to propose without her help, he rather thought he could see the Rector himself.'

Despite herself, Tilda chuckled.

'So that's where he's gone.'

'Gone where?'

'To see the Rector,' explained Milly. 'He was going to collect Guy and go straight down to the Rectory. If all the banns are called at once we can have a double wedding!'

Dear God! thought Tilda. He must be intent on getting it all over and done with as fast as possible.

'Now,' said Milly ingenuously, 'I understand why he has been so gloomy. It wasn't over me at all. He has been in love with you all along. And thought you wouldn't have him! Or that he'd have to offer for me, poor man.'

Tilda opened her mouth and shut it again. There was no way in which she could explain Crispin's motives for proposing marriage. Let alone hers for accepting such a proposal.

Milly looked at her oddly. 'Tilda…you're…you're not doing this for me, are you? Because you think if St Ormond marries you, Papa won't be able to try and force him to marry me?'

That aspect of the situation hadn't occurred to Tilda. Could that be part of Crispin's motivation? Briefly she tried to imagine anyone forcing Crispin to do something he didn't want to do. She failed completely.

Determinedly she manufactured a grin. 'Oh, come now, Milly! His High and Mightiness, the Duke of St Ormond, pushed into a marriage he doesn't want? By a mere baron? You must be all about in your head!'

Milly gave vent to a giggle and Tilda went on. 'We are getting married because we shall suit very well—' she swallowed and admitted part of the truth '—and we…we desire each other, so…'

'Ohhh!' Milly's eyes grew round. 'But he's quite old, Tilda. Do you think—?'

'He's not *that* old!' protested Tilda, aware that she was blushing. Memories of the night she had spent flooded through her. His Grace of St Ormond was hardly likely to find asserting his marital rights beyond his capabilities.

She couldn't say that! 'For heaven's sake, Milly! He can give your papa thirty years, and might I remind you that you have a new sister?'

Firmly, she changed the subject by asking Milly what she should wear for her wedding.

Outside the drawing room they met Lord Pemberton, who fixed his niece with a cold glare.

'I should like a word with you.' His voice bit into her.

Milly cut in blithely. 'Have you heard, Papa? St Ormond and Tilda—'

'I have indeed heard.' He gestured to Tilda. 'I believe the library to be unoccupied.'

Resigned, Tilda acquiesced. He could do nothing. Would not dare. He must know what Crispin's reaction would be.

She entered the library ahead of him and glided to the fireplace. Standing before it she faced him, her chin up defiantly, not a trace of fear evident in her bearing.

'Well, my lord?'

His lip curled. 'Congratulations. I had not thought it possible that the mighty St Ormond would fall victim to the shop-soiled charms of a scheming widow!' He laughed scornfully. 'My mistake! I thought he'd be so eager to avoid the scandal that he'd marry Milly if I told him what I'd seen. But no! He informed me that you were betrothed to him. You must have the skills of Aphrodite—or did you flaunt your fortune under his nose along with your body?'

Sick horror chilled her as the ugly words tore into her very soul. 'What you saw?' Even as she spoke, she knew what he must have seen.

His next words confirmed it. 'St Ormond leaving your chamber at dawn,' he said. 'Slut! No doubt you lured him into your bed as fast as possible on arriving here! The more fool he for marrying you. In my day a man didn't marry a whore! He had her and discarded her as is fitting. How times change! St Ormond has decided to protect you with his name. God knows why, but he has!'

Tilda scarcely heard the rest of the diatribe. Her uncle had seen Crispin leaving. He had tried to blackmail him into marrying Milly on the strength of it. She didn't have to wonder now what had motivated Crispin to come back and offer marriage. He might not love her, but he cared enough to protect her from the scandal that would ensue if Pemberton had spread the story.

He was a gentleman. He had known how inexperienced she was. So he had done the only thing a gentleman could do. Offered her the protection of his name. That knowledge scored itself into her like a brand. He had offered out of obligation—and made damned sure that she didn't realise it.

Her uncle was still speaking. 'And now I understand there's some nonsensical talk of a double wedding! I tell you to your head, girl! I'll not take part in any wedding of yours! Be damned if I will! Take that thought to bed with you tonight. I'll swallow Milly's marriage—if the chit's fool enough to think young Malvern a fair exchange for St Ormond, good luck to her! At least she's not a scheming, mercenary little whore!'

That shook her out of her daze enough for her to lash back. 'You really should try to make up your mind, sir,' said Tilda contemptuously. 'After all, my mother loved a man of no fortune and you refused your consent to the marriage. I wish to wed a man of wealth and title and I am immediately a *scheming, mercenary little whore*. Can it be that your point of view is entirely linked to your own self-interest? But you may rest assured that I have no intention of claiming your escort down the aisle a second time. Nor that I would willingly see you ever again.' She fronted him proudly, her eyes steady, no hint of the hurt he had dealt her showing in her face. Inwardly she bled.

He stared at her for a moment. She could feel his glare burning into her. Then, with a frustrated exclamation, he turned on his heel and was gone, slamming the door behind him.

How she reached a sofa without falling, Tilda never quite knew. But she did and huddled in it, sick and shaking.

He'd offered out of obligation. To save her reputation that her own uncle would have destroyed. He had not even

wanted her to ease his own hurt. He didn't even want her
money. She could give him nothing in return that he
wanted.

Except your body. She shuddered at the thought. If he
made love to her as he had done last night, she would never
be able to hide her feelings. She would never be able to
give herself like that without finally exposing her love.

Tears trickled down her nose unheeded. He'd already
offered her the protection of his name. That was bad
enough. She was damned if she'd accept his pity as well.
She would have to call a halt to this. Before it went any
further. She'd gladly marry him to save him pain—but not
to save her own reputation. She loved him too deeply to
permit that sacrifice.

The irony of her words to Milly struck at her like a blow.
*His High and Mightiness, the Duke of St Ormond, pushed
into a marriage he doesn't want? By a mere baron?*

Lord Pemberton had managed to do just that.

Half an hour later she was still sitting curled up on the
sofa when the door opened to admit the Dowager.

'Ah! There you are! Milly thought I should find you
here.'

Tilda didn't answer at first. Just stared in blank incom-
prehension.

'My dear, I'm so delighted—' She broke off. 'Tilda,
dear, are you quite well? You look so pale. Is your arm
hurting?'

Tilda shook her head numbly. Whatever else was hurting, it wasn't her arm that was troubling her.

The Dowager came across to her and sat down. 'Will
you permit me to say how happy I am to welcome you as
a daughter? That I'm glad it is you that has made Cris so
happy.'

'H…happy, your Grace?' Tilda couldn't think why he

should be happy at all. He'd lost the girl he loved and been accidentally forced into marriage with her cousin.

'Very happy,' said her Grace firmly. 'I haven't seen him like that ever. Certainly not when he told me that he was contemplating marriage with Milly! And you may as well stop being so formal with me. Just call me Marianne, as Hastings does. We shall go along famously, you and I.'

'But…' Tilda searched desperately for the words to tell this kindly, affectionate woman the truth without hurting her. And realised that they didn't exist.

'But nothing,' said the Dowager. 'You and Crispin are going to be very happy together. Don't you dare to sit there feeling miserable or unworthy or whatever silly nonsense your wretched uncle has put into your head! Instead come and tell Anthea. I have put the entire household on pain of instant bandishment if a word of this reaches her ears before you tell her yourself. She is in my sitting room, playing spillikins with Milly and Louisa.'

Anthea! Tilda realised that she had not even given her a thought. Probably because she had known, without Crispin's assurance, that Anthea would be treated as his own much loved daughter. And that Anthea herself would be utterly delighted to stay here with her 'Uncle Cris', whom she regarded in a light bordering on the idolatrous.

Dazed, she allowed herself to be dragged to her feet and shepherded from the room.

'Now, this double wedding idea,' said the Dowager, 'I must say I like it…' She went on happily, outlining all the advantages of the arrangement. No point in waiting about and, since most of the guests would be duplicated, it really made the best sense. Then Guy and Milly could take themselves off on a honeymoon while Tilda and Crispin remained here alone.

'If,' said Lady Ormond, with a faint twinkle, 'one can ever be alone with so many servants falling over themselves to make sure you think they are being useful! But you know what I mean.'

'But…but you'll be here…won't you?'

The Dowager blinked. 'Heavens, no! Didn't I say? I'm going to go and stay with Georgie and Hastings for a few weeks while you and Cris get to know each other.' Her grin became positively naughty. 'My role as chaperon ends after the church, you know! There is nothing more vexatious than actresses or chaperons who don't know when to make an exit! I even thought to take Anthea with me since Georgie's youngest, Jenny, is about the same age. Moore Park is only twenty miles away, so you could come over to see how she is going on as often as you liked.'

'How…how very kind of you,' achieved Tilda. And realised that she was digging the trap deeper with every word, that she was being manoeuvred by the entire Malvern family. That, unless she screamed from the rooftops right now that she would not marry his Grace, the Duke of St Ormond, she would find herself fronting the altar with him, in company with Milly and Guy, in just under three weeks.

There was nothing preventing her from doing just that; announcing that it was all a terrible mistake, that she had never intended to accept him. Nothing stopped her telling the Dowager right now—except her heart. Her foolish, aching heart which could not bear to hurt him any further— because it knew only too well how it felt to be broken.

'Give him a chance, my dear.'

Tilda trembled at the tender understanding in the Dowager's voice. 'A…a chance?'

'Yes. A chance to make you happy. To make up for the past.'

She flinched. Jonathan had once said something very similar to her—and she had accepted it. But she didn't want that from Crispin. She was not prepared to be rescued a second time.

Chapter Fifteen

In the weeks before his marriage, Crispin occasionally wondered if he would still be quite sane on his wedding morning. All the indications were that he wouldn't be. That he would, in fact, be stark raving mad.

To his immense relief, Lord Pemberton stayed only a couple of days, returning home to escort Lady Pemberton to attend the marriage of her daughter. It appeared that Lady Pemberton was perfectly happy to leave her new daughter in the care of a wet nurse, but that she and her lord would only arrive two days before the wedding. But before Lord Pemberton's departure Crispin ensured that notices of both betrothals were sent to the papers and that the banns were called for the first time. He had no intention of cutting his lordship any slack.

The preparations were, thank God, almost completely out of his hands. His mother, sister and aunt had swung into action with terrifying efficiency. So completely did they plan every minute and seemingly irrelevant detail, that Crispin was moved to mutter to his brother-in-law that Wellington should have the lot of them on his staff.

Hastings merely grinned and murmured a few soothing platitudes, while doing nothing to hide his amusement.

But apart from all the upheaval, what really bothered him

was Tilda's subtle, but complete, withdrawal. She was avoiding any private conversation with him by hurling herself into the preparations and learning her way about the house and its ways—which would have been laudable had she allowed him to help. But she declared herself quite happy to be shown by the Dowager and Mrs Simms. And he thought he knew why—she believed that he had offered for her out of duty and honour.

Her withdrawal dated from the day of their betrothal. He had returned from the Rectory, after dutifully downing two glasses of the Rector's best sherry, to find that she was lying down upon her bed. With a headache, according to his mother, who had commented that she understood Lord Pemberton to have had an interview with Tilda in the library.

He had instantly gone up to her chamber, only to find the door locked. Ever since, he had only seen Tilda in company, except for very briefly last thing at night when he escorted her to her chamber. Even then Tilda neatly blocked every attempt he made to win her confidence and he knew that Sarah awaited her mistress within. So he kept his goodnight kiss very brief. Positively chaste. He was having quite enough trouble sleeping as it was, and saw no point in exacerbating the problem. Somehow, given her complete emotional withdrawal, he didn't think it was a good idea to suggest to Tilda that he share her bed.

During the day she was perennially caught up with fittings, for herself, for Milly, for Anthea. If she, or one of the others, wasn't in a state of half-undress, then she was with the Dowager, making endless lists, or consulting over the menu, how many bride cakes would be required. He had never realised just how busy a woman could be over a wedding.

But finally, ten days before the wedding, he came to the conclusion that enough was enough. Tonight he would try and slip through her misty armour. To which end he purposely made no attempt at dinner to inaugurate any conversation with her any more controversial than the weather and the rotation of crops. Afterwards in the drawing room he devoted himself to Aunt Seraphina.

Despite his subterfuge he had the distinct impression, as he escorted Tilda to the stairs, that she wasn't hoaxed in the least by his efforts. She was wound tighter than a watchspring.

Her composure was almost brittle and he knew, the instant he asked her point blank what was bothering her, that she wasn't going to tell him everything.

'My uncle has said that…he is not prepared to give me away again.' Her voice told him nothing, revealing in itself. Cool, devoid of emotion, but he felt her fingers tighten slightly on his arm, as if for support. Sheer incandescent rage flooded through him that Pemberton could so expose her to whispers. This, he reminded himself, was the man who had threatened to make known his niece's supposed affair. Who had actually encompassed his own sister's ruin.

He clung to the reins of his self-control with grim determination. 'A little awkward,' he commented. 'But not insuperable. Have you any ideas?'

She nodded slowly as they went up the stairs. 'I thought that perhaps, since I have been married before, it might be best if Milly and my uncle led the way down the aisle—that I could simply follow them, as if I were merely matron of honour.'

He greeted this with a snort. 'The devil you will! If you think that I'm going to have my bride trailing down the aisle like a lost puppy, you can think again!'

She glared at him, he saw with relief—at least she was actually responding to him instead of holding him at bay.

'No doubt you have a better idea!'

He was about to shake his head when inspiration struck. 'I'll escort you.'

A puzzled frown puckered her smooth brow, making him ache to kiss it away, along with whatever else was bothering her.

'Down the aisle,' he elaborated. A thoroughly wicked grin lit his eyes. 'I'm taller than your uncle. And you're taller than Milly. We'll look suitably ducal and awe-inspiring together—as though we're giving our blessing to the match. And we'll go first.'

'You can't do that!' she protested.

With a lift of one arrogant brow, he asked, 'Who's going to stop me? I'm a Duke. I can do what I damn well like.' He grinned shamelessly at her outraged stare. 'Within reason,' he amended.

'You'd escort me down the aisle?' She appeared stunned at this break from tradition.

He nodded. If nothing else it would mean that he could ensure she didn't bolt halfway. The only problem would be that blasted bit in the service about *Who giveth this woman*... Could it be left out? Tilda was a widow after all. Who *was* supposed to give widows away?

'And who do you think is going to give me away?' she asked tiredly, echoing his thought. 'Were you just going to bestow me on yourself?'

He eyed her forebodingly. 'You're mine already,' he murmured. 'If you care to recall.'

Blushing scarlet, she shot back, 'Were you going to tell the Rector that?'

Raising one brow, he said, 'He is a man of large charity, of course...'

Tilda snorted. 'He'd need to be!'

Crispin grinned and relented. 'Very well. Let's not test his limits. Give me a moment to think.'

He racked his brains. This was obviously upsetting her. Surely he could think of someone—a member of her family, someone with some responsibility for her... He had it!

'Lord Winter,' he said calmly. 'He's your principal trustee, your first husband's heir. Nothing could be more appropriate.'

Blinking, Tilda realised that he was right. Such an arrangement would cause no remark at all, especially since Lord Pemberton would be giving away his eldest daughter.

Heaving a sigh of relief, she looked up at him, all her reserve melted. 'Thank you, Crispin—that was bothering me terribly.'

'Do you want to tell me about the rest?' His voice was a velvety growl.

Her eyes widened as she froze again.

He was smiling down at her, his hand surrounding hers with a steely strength, just as his body had surrounded her—with warmth and safety. She looked up and thought she would drown in the tenderness in his eyes. The temptation to step closer, beg him to wait until Sarah had gone and tell him everything, battered at the barriers she had flung up. Barriers that were there to hold her feelings in. To keep her heart safe.

Even as she fought the temptation, he lowered his head and pressed his lips to hers, slipping his arms about her. His lips firmed, caressed gently, sending her senses spinning, calling forth the burning heat in her soul.

Madness. Even knowing that, she leaned against him, sinking into the kiss, parting her lips and returning the stroke of his tongue. Slow, possessive surges filled her mouth. His hands shifted over her body, holding her to him and she felt the sudden tension that invested his large frame. Powerful muscles tautening, hardening under her hands, against her soft curves.

Her body trembled, remembering how he had felt pressing down on her, how he had touched her and taken her so tenderly… He would come to her now if she asked him— she didn't dare.

She was sinking deeper into him, into a haze of desire and burning need. A tidal wave of emotion threatened to engulf her. If she didn't stop now, she wouldn't be able to. Exerting every ounce of her willpower, she pulled back slightly, breaking their kiss. She could feel the reluctance with which he released her. And it felt as though a part of her had been torn away as he let her go.

Desperately she held herself steady, as though her knees had not turned to jelly, as though her bones were still solid. Her entire body was aflame. More than ever, she realised in shock. And he'd only kissed her.

She had to go, before she changed her mind. Before she begged him to stay.

'Goodnight, Crispin.' She tried to say it firmly, as though she actually meant it. And came to the conclusion that she hadn't been terribly successful, since his brow lifted suggestively and a teasing smile hovered at one corner of the mouth that had been kissing her senseless.

She tried again. 'I'll see you…in the morning.' It was only with a massive surge of willpower that she didn't say *later*.

His mouth hardened. 'Very well,' he said quietly. And reached out to touch her cheek. One finger trailed lightly down in a feathery caress. She held still as fires leapt up under her skin. His fingers firmed under her chin and he bent to brush his lips over hers.

'Goodnight, my darling.' He turned swiftly and strode away down the corridor towards his own apartments. Quickly she went inside. If she watched him go, she'd be calling him back—or running after him.

Time. She needed time to get her feelings under control and make sure that she could keep her emotions hidden even as she responded to him physically. She thrust away the thought that it might prove impossible. Especially if he made a habit of calling her *darling* in just that tone of voice.

Crispin made it to his bedchamber without succumbing to the insidious little voice inside his head suggesting that he should go back to Tilda's room, dismiss her maid himself, and then behave in a manner that his feudal forebears would have applauded. To wit, drag his lady back to his own apartments and have his wicked way with her. All night. And very possibly all of the next day as well.

He swore vehemently as he slammed the door shut behind him. And encountered a startled glance from his valet. With grim amusement, Crispin imagined just how much more startled Stubbs would have been if he'd had Tilda over one shoulder and had calmly told him to leave.

The vision sent a surge of painful heat to his loins. He swore again. Frustration was going to kill him. He'd never known anything like it. In the past, desire for a woman had begun to wane almost as soon as he'd had her. He couldn't remember the last woman, if any, he'd taken three times in one night. Once, at the most twice, was generally enough. And he'd still wanted Tilda—more than ever.

Catching Stubbs's sympathetic eye, he said shortly, 'I'll undress myself. Go to bed and sleep in if you like. I'll be riding early, so I won't need you.' One thing was certain, he was going to have an appalling night's sleep and he might as well cut the torture as short as possible.

As Stubbs left, he flung himself into a chair by the fire. For a man about to marry the woman he loved, he was extremely depressed.

Would he be able to make Tilda happy? Would she come to care for him? Would it have been better to let her go? His heart cried out in protest at the thought. He shrugged fatalistically. It was far too late now.

His mouth twisted in wry self-mockery. He could force or trick nothing from her. Nothing worth having, anyway. Not her confidence, and certainly not her love. He wanted her freely—as she had given herself the other night. Only then would she truly be his.

'Tilda?'

She looked up with relief and forced a smile. The two lists she was checking were beginning to blur into one another and her eyes felt gritty after an appalling night's sleep. 'Guy. How nice. Is there something I can do for you?'

His glance took in the list of acceptances she was checking against the original list and he shook his head. 'Not likely. It strikes me that you are doing quite enough. I must make quite sure that next time I marry, my bride's cousin shares the ceremony and does all the work.'

She chuckled in genuine mirth. 'Milly, I should inform you, is busily sewing my daughter's dress for the occasion. And since Anthea is a terrible wriggler, I can only say, she's welcome to the task!'

'I…I should like very much to speak with you privately.'

The constrained tone in his voice brought her head up sharply. 'Is…is something wrong, Guy?'

'No, oh, no. Just that I…well, I want to…'

The door opened.

'Tilda, the wretchedest thing! That odious mantua maker—oh, hello, Guy!' Lady St Ormond came into the room closely followed by Georgie.

'Hello, Aunt Marianne, Georgie.' Guy coloured up hotly. 'You're obviously busy, Tilda. I won't disturb you.'

She frowned. 'It's quite all right, Guy. Your aunt and Georgie will excuse us if we leave them for a few moments and you can tell me whatever is on your mind.'

Lady St Ormond smiled. 'Of course, dears. The library is empty, I believe. I looked for Crispin there just a moment ago and he wasn't there. I called out in case he was on the gallery, but he must have gone riding, I think. He said something at breakfast about looking at those horrid traps.'

Tilda glanced around the library as they entered, half-expecting to find Crispin at his desk. Far from leaving all the work to his bailiffs and agents, he oversaw everything himself and read widely on agricultural subjects.

The desk stood in the bay window, littered with papers and piled high with books. The chair stood empty.

'Funny he's gone riding at this hour,' commented Guy. 'He nearly always works in the mornings. Unless something is bothering him. Then he likes to go for a ride to clear the cobwebs, as he says. Maybe the curst traps.'

Tilda bit her lip. She could think of something else that might be bothering him. Frustration. She could attest to that from personal experience. He had wanted her last night. As much as she had wanted him. At least she had the dubious satisfaction of having been the one to refuse the delights offered, but it hadn't helped her to gain a good night's sleep. Her pulse quickened at the memory of his mouth caressing hers, the tender warmth of his hands... If Crispin had spent anything like the dreadful night she had suffered, then she could well believe that he might have gone for a ride to clear his head. She groaned mentally. What a fool she had been. She would have to face this hurdle at some stage.

But not now. Right now Guy stood before her looking thoroughly shamefaced.

He spoke very quietly. 'Tilda, I have to apologise to you.'

'You...what? Whatever for?'

'I never thought that Milly would think...that anyone could misunderstand our friendship...she told me what she said to you. That she had thought you might...' If he hadn't looked so guilty, so worried, she might have smiled.

'Guy, you made it perfectly plain that it was Milly who had engaged your interest and affections. You even asked my advice. I'm not really that stupid, you know!' She looked at him earnestly and laid her hand gently on his arm.

He covered her hand with his, smiling down at her. 'I know that, but Milly was so surprised at the way you flirted.

She said you had never been in the least flirtatious before, and, well…'

Tilda blushed as she remembered the reason she had been flirting with him so conspicuously. Lightly enough, she said, 'Blame it on my frivolous old age and soon-to-be-revoked widowhood. All that freedom went straight to my head.' She smiled. 'Now, tell me—is Milly reassured that it is she you want, not me?'

He grinned. 'Lord, yes. She was cock-a-hoop to think that she had been preferred over your beauty and vast fortune, but she was worried that you might have…even knowing that it was Milly I love…'

'No.' She shook her head. 'You're a dear friend, Guy. No more. Even had you asked me, I would not have accepted you.'

His fingers tightened on hers. 'Really?'

'Really.' After all, she hadn't even meant to accept Crispin, and she was in love with him.

He raised her hand to his lips and kissed it. 'Then we wish each other happy? I know Cris is happy. He would never offer marriage unless he wanted to.'

Her smile wobbled a little, but she said, 'Very happy, Guy. Now, I had best return to those wretched lists. Will you excuse me?'

He smiled. 'Of course…cousin,' and bent to kiss her gently on the corner of the mouth. 'Thank you, Tilda. For everything.'

Standing on tiptoe, she returned his salute. 'You are very welcome, cousin.'

They looked at each other and smiled. Tilda holding her smile in place determinedly. Never mind that the tears she battled had nothing to do with Guy, she didn't dare let him see them in case he thought she had lied to him. She couldn't possibly explain the real reason.

'Come along,' said Guy. 'I'll escort you back to the lists.'

Hastily she demurred. 'No, since I'm here I'll just find something to read. I've finished the book I was reading. You go on.'

She heaved a sigh of relief as he left. A moment to steady herself was what she needed. Poor Guy. Had he really thought she might have fallen in love with him? She winked back a tear to think that Milly had such confidence and trust in her love that she could talk to him about something like that.

If only she had the same sort of courage. Another tear formed. This one escaped and slid down her cheek She dragged in a deep breath and wiped the tear away. She had nothing to cry about. She was about to marry the man she loved. And everyone thought that he had wanted to marry her and that he was happy about it.

He shouldn't have had to offer for her. More tears fell, blinding her so that she stumbled slightly. If she hadn't given in to her own desires that night, to her own hurt and need, he wouldn't be in this trap. She steadied herself and found her handkerchief, blowing her nose and mopping up the tears. She couldn't go on like this, dissolving into tears at the least excuse.

Somehow she would have to summon up all Lady Winter's cool composure. Only the composure; she didn't want the bitter cynicism. Crispin didn't deserve that. He had only wanted to protect her by doing the honourable thing.

Shoving the handkerchief into her pocket, she left the library with her head held high.

As the library door shut behind Tilda, Crispin, seated in a large wingchair with its back to the gallery railing, groaned and put his head in his hands. He had ignored his mother, wanting a little privacy to sort out his confusion of emotions. Now they were even more tangled.

Guy had kissed her. Very chastely, he had to admit. But nevertheless he had kissed her. Twice if he counted kissing her hand. He ran his hands through his hair.

He ought to have told them he was there, but he hadn't even realised anyone was in the room until he'd heard Guy say that he wished to apologise. He must have dozed off for a moment. His lack of sleep was catching up with him. Thank God they had spoken softly. That was all he'd heard. But that didn't excuse his conduct in looking over the back of his chair in an attempt to hear more. If he hadn't done that he wouldn't have seen Tilda's hand resting on Guy's arm with his hand covering it.

And he wouldn't have seen him kiss her. As though in apology and farewell. What else could Guy have been apologising for other than raising false hopes in Tilda's bosom?

She had kissed him back. And she had wept after he left.

He swore. If only Pemberton had not interfered, he could have given Tilda time to recover from her disappointment and realise that he loved her. Now he would have to come to her on their wedding night knowing beyond all doubt that she loved, had wanted, another.

She wouldn't refuse him. He knew that. But she was reluctant to give herself no matter how much her body wanted him. She had refused last night. His whole body hardened in a rush as he remembered how sweetly her soft curves had yielded to his passion. Yet she had said no.

He longed to comfort her, ease her pain. His heart ached with the need to hold her and look after her. He didn't dare. He didn't trust himself. She had given herself once, needing comfort for her pain. He had taken advantage of her hurt. He couldn't do that again.

Over the next few days he observed an odd change in Tilda's demeanour. From quiet reserve she shifted almost imperceptibly to outright worry. A faint frown creased her brow and he frequently caught a puzzled look on her face, as though she were trying to remember something, something that just eluded her.

She was thoroughly distracted at times and people had to address remarks to her at least twice to gain her attention. He caught her watching him surreptitiously once and blinked when she flushed a deep crimson. The really odd thing though, he thought confusedly, was that she actually looked as though she were happy at times. She frequently had the oddest, tenderest little smile upon her face as though she nursed a precious secret.

'For heaven's sake, Anthea! Stand still. If I stick any more pins into you, you'll feel like a pincushion!' Tilda gave this exasperated advice through a mouthful of pins as she adjusted the fit of Anthea's dress one last time.

'Sorry, Mama.' Anthea stood still, at least, but plainly her mind was still whirling.

'Mama?'

'Mmm?' Tilda still had a mouthful of pins as she adjusted the hem.

'Will I have some little brothers and sisters?'

Tilda just managed to spit the pins out instead of swallowing them. 'What gave you that idea?' she spluttered.

'I thought that was what happened when people got married,' explained Anthea. 'I asked Uncle Cris when he took me riding.'

Keeping a straight face, as she imagined her betrothed's reaction to his prospective stepdaughter demanding information on that subject, was nigh on impossible.

'Did you?' Her voice only wobbled slightly. 'And what did he say?'

'He said I was enough to be going on with, but he thought it was quite a good idea,' said Anthea, obediently pirouetting as Tilda gave her a gentle push. 'And that he was looking forward to it,' she added, coming to a halt.

Tilda blushed. She wondered just what Crispin was looking forward to: having children—or begetting them? Or what she was looking forward to, for that matter.

'I see,' she managed faintly. 'Perhaps, dearest, you might save these questions for me in future. Young ladies shouldn't ask gentlemen things like that.'

'I know *that*,' said Anthea indignantly.

'Then why in heaven's name did you ask Uncle Cris?'

Anthea looked a little conscious. 'Well, I only knew after he told me. He said it was the sort of thing you'd tell me later.'

Much later. Tilda stuck in the last few pins firmly.

'Very well. Take it off carefully, sweetheart. Take it back to Milly and she will sew it up. What are you supposed to be doing now? Does Aunt Marianne have a task for you?'

Anthea shook her head. 'No. I'm helping Mrs Simms. She wants me to stuff the lavender bags while she sews them.' She wriggled back into her dress and scampered off happily.

Tilda and Sarah exchanged glances.

'How sure are ye, milady?' asked Sarah. 'Might just be late this month.'

'Two weeks?' Tilda snorted.

Sarah shrugged. 'Happens, lass—milady.'

'Not to me it doesn't,' said Tilda firmly. 'The last time I was this late, I had Anthea.'

She sneaked a careful look at Sarah. Wasn't she going to scold or something? Ask her what she'd thought she'd been doing? Read her a lecture? She'd only told Sarah just before Anthea had come in, when Sarah had commented worriedly on the tardiness of her monthly courses. She'd been panicking that Tilda might be inconvenienced on her wedding night.

Instead she was probably going to have to tell her bridegroom that she was pregnant already.

And all her strict and upright maid could find to say was,

'Hmm. Be a spring baby, then. Dare say his Grace is tickled to death.'

'*Sarah!*' Tilda was so shocked that her toes tingled. 'Aren't you even going to ask me what I was doing?'

Sarah's grin was positively disgraceful. 'Be a main waste of breath, lass. I *know* what you was doing.' She looked thoughtful and added, for good measure, 'So did his Grace, I'd have to say.' She shrugged and said, 'Where's the problem? He's marrying you in two days and it ain't as if he only offered because of the child. An' like I said, I'll wager me best dress, he's as pleased as punch.'

Tilda didn't return an immediate answer. Her entire being swirled with confusing emotions. One moment she was elated, overjoyed to be bearing Crispin's child, exulting in the fact. The next instant she was shaking in fear at how close she had come to disaster.

'Ye *have* told him?' Sarah's voice broke in on her thoughts.

Biting her lip, Tilda flushed. 'N…no. Not yet.'

None of the etiquette manuals that she had ever read told a woman how to break this sort of news to her husband, even in the most proper of circumstances. Certainly none of them gave one the least notion of how to go on in this instance. She'd had enough trouble telling Jonathan that she was pregnant—and he'd been hoping for it. Crispin, pleased or not, was in for a shock. Besides, he'd withdrawn himself in the past week, since she had refused to share her bed with him. He made quite sure they were never alone and his goodnight kiss had become the merest peck on the cheek. He even called her *my lady*.

'Ah, well,' said Sarah prosaically. 'Be a nice wedding present, like.'

In the event, Tilda found it completely impossible to catch Crispin alone in the two days remaining before their wedding. The house overflowed with visitors, her aunt among them. Lady Pemberton made it perfectly plain that had she been able to chaperon Milly, the girl would certainly not be marrying Guy Malvern.

She took Tilda to task severely, finishing, 'And your uncle tells me that you *trapped* St Ormond into offering for you! It is all of a piece! A more scheming, ungrateful wench I never met! I hope your husband may not live to regret his foolish choice.'

Tilda smiled. 'I did warn you, ma'am. Obviously my fortune was too great a temptation for his Grace.' She saw no reason to inform her aunt that it was Lord Pemberton's interference that had prompted Crispin's offer of marriage. Nor that he had settled her own fortune back on her with no strings attached. Why he had done such a thing, she couldn't begin to imagine, but she was glad that he had. She could still go ahead with her orphanage and refuge for unmarried mothers.

By the night before the wedding she had given up trying to find a private moment with Crispin. She would be private with him tomorrow night. No doubt Sarah was right and he would be pleased. No doubt he wanted an heir, she told herself. And felt ashamed of her cynicism. No one who had seen him with Anthea could doubt that he liked children, would be a good father. He was not the man to resent it if she presented him with nothing but daughters.

She stood by the open window, staring out over the gardens in the faint starlight, unwilling to go to bed. She had finally sent Milly off to bed. Milly was in a complete daze of excitement and terror that at this time tomorrow night, she'd be in Guy's bed, giving herself and her love to a man who loved her. Tilda shut her heart against the stab of pain.

She had more than she had ever hoped for. And the taste was bitter.

This time tomorrow night...she would not be in this room. The Duchess's suite had been prepared for her. An

enormous bedchamber with an equally enormous bed, a
private sitting room opened off it; and beyond that, down
a short private corridor, was Crispin's room. She'd peeped
in when she'd been taken to approve her own rooms.

The sheer size of *his* bed had shocked her witless. She'd
be lost in it—in more ways than one. Remembering the
vigour of his lovemaking, she didn't doubt that the size of
his bed would be a distinct advantage. Her senses reeled at
the images that spun through her mind. Or would he simply
come to her when he wanted her—as Jonathan had—returning to his own bed afterwards? He had been so formal
and reserved the last ten days. Perhaps he had decided that
a distant relationship would be best.

That might be easier, she told herself. If he didn't stay
and hold her, pet her tenderly, love her with words as he
had the first time, she might be able to conceal her love.
She shut her eyes in despair at the thoughts.

Her bed would feel so cold, so lonely. So empty.

She stared at the bed that she would occupy tonight.
Alone. And didn't know whether she wanted tonight to end
swiftly or never.

Crispin stared out of the window of his bedchamber,
wondering if he had made an appalling mistake, if he
should have simply told Tilda the truth—that he loved
her—because for the life of him he couldn't imagine how
he was going to make love to her tomorrow night without
telling her.

And how would she feel about that? She was putting a
good face on it, but he had seen the sadness in her eyes
whenever she saw Guy and Milly together, the half-hidden
hunger. He had seen her weeping after Guy had kissed her
in the library. How would she feel tomorrow night, knowing that the man she loved was making love to her cousin?

He swore. The last thing he wanted was to take her on

their wedding night knowing that she was breaking her heart for a man she could not have. He couldn't do that to her. And he didn't think he could explain it to her. Not without telling her that he loved her.

Chapter Sixteen

'Dearly beloved, we are gathered here in the sight of God, and in the face of this congregation, to join together this man and this woman, and *this* man and *this* woman, in Holy Matrimony…'

Tilda stared straight ahead, not daring to glance to left or right. Crispin stood to her right and Milly and Guy to the left. She was shatteringly aware of her uncle and aunt behind her. She'd caught a glimpse of her aunt's face on the way past, and her uncle's face as he stepped back from Milly. If looks could have killed, she'd be lying dead at the chancel steps.

The Rector's gentle voice flowed on through the preface. She barely heard him and she was cold, so cold. At least she assumed that was why she was shaking. She trembled even more as Crispin's warm hand covered hers, anchoring it safely to his sleeve.

'…not by any to be enterprised, nor taken in hand, un-advisedly, lightly, or wantonly, to satisfy men's carnal lusts and appetites, like brute beasts that have no understanding…'

She whitened. Why was she here? Because of that very thing. Because she had given in to her desire and his…

'…the causes for which matrimony was ordained. First, it was ordained for the procreation of children…'

At this unwitting reminder, she flushed. They'd managed that bit easily enough. The seed of a new life grew within her. The new life she and Crispin had made. Surely that was a good thing?

'…for a remedy against sin…' Crispin's hand pressed on hers. Very unwisely she looked up. Only to encounter a wicked sideways glance. Hurriedly she dragged her eyes from his and concentrated on the Rector.

'Thirdly, it was ordained for the mutual society, help and comfort, that the one ought to have of the other…'

What help and comfort could she be to him? The question throbbed in her heart. She didn't know the answer, but she vowed in that moment that she would have to try. She'd done her best to be a good wife to Jonathan. She loved Crispin—even if he never loved her, she could still be a good wife. But there would have to be honesty between them—she needed to know why he'd married her.

Her trembling steadied as a measure of confidence returned, and the feeling that she was doing something dreadfully wrong receded. Crispin was so solid and reassuring beside her—they could at least be friends. They had much in common, therein would lie the *mutual society, help and comfort.*

She snapped her attention back to the Rector.

'Crispin Anthony. Wilt thou have this woman to thy wedded wife? Wilt thou love her, comfort her, honour and keep her, in sickness and in health; and forsaking all other, keep thee only unto her, so long as ye both shall live?'

'I will.' The two short words rang with utter sincerity, total conviction. They shook Tilda to the core. Did he mean it? Really mean it? There was no time for speculation, it was her turn.

'Matilda Frances. Wilt thou have this man to thy wedded husband to live together after God's ordinance in the holy estate of matrimony? Wilt thou obey him, serve him and love, honour and keep him, in sickness and in health; and forsaking all other, keep thee only unto him, so long as ye both shall live?'

She opened her mouth to give her assent. Nothing came out. Desperately she cleared her throat. Crispin had turned to her, startled query in his eyes.

'I will.' It came out hurriedly, hoarsely and far too softly, but the Rector was obviously satisfied, because he turned to Milly and Guy, both of whom spoke their responses without the least hesitation.

Then the Rector turned back to them.

'Who giveth this woman to be married to this man?'

Lord Winter stepped forward, and possessed himself of her hand. Firmly, protectively. Lovingly. He flashed her a proud smile as he placed her hand in the Rector's and stepped back. Her heart nearly burst with joy. This time she had been given with joy, with pride. She had been bestowed rather than disposed of—and the Rector was placing her hand in Crispin's.

Heat stole through her and she felt the clasp of his fingers tighten as he spoke after the Rector.

'I, Crispin Anthony, take thee, Matilda Frances, to my wedded wife...' sure and certain, his voice resonated through her as he repeated his vows '...to love, and to cherish...' his voice deepened on *love* and hope rippled through her '...till death do us part, according to God's holy ordinance; and thereto I plight thee my troth.'

Swallowing hard, she made her vows steadily, scarcely able to hear herself for the swirl of confused emotion. He'd spoken his vows as if he meant them—just what was she walking into here? Was it possible that he cared for her?

By the time she had pulled herself together, she had the ring on her finger and the Rector had pronounced them to be man and wife together. Dazed, she looked up at Crispin, whose large hand held hers firmly and protectively on his sleeve. His gaze met hers in searing intensity.

He spoke under the cover of Milly and Guy's vows. 'Mine,' he murmured. The deep, possessive growl shuddered through her. Golden eyes widened in shock. She shivered as he added softly, 'Always.'

The rest of the wedding and the wedding breakfast passed in a whirl. Half the county including Crispin's tenants seemed to have crowded into the church. Most of them came back to Ormsby Park where trestle tables had been set up on the south lawn to cater for the crowd.

After a repast in the State Dining Room, of which Tilda ate very little, Crispin escorted her out to the lawn to meet his tenants.

He had watched her through the meal very carefully and realised that she had eaten practically nothing. So he slipped his napkin into his coat pocket and led her firmly outside on to the terrace.

The catering had been generous and he had not the least difficulty in locating a pasty, still nicely hot. Wordlessly he wrapped it in his napkin and presented it to her.

'What…?'

'It's a pasty, ' he said blandly. 'Very filling, nourishing. Eat it.'

Unwillingly she took it from him. It did smell good. She took one bite and discovered that she was ravenous.

'That's better,' said Crispin cheerfully. 'Can't have the bride fainting dead away, after all.' He quizzed her gently with his eyes. 'Not for lack of food, anyway.'

Hot colour mantled her cheeks, as she thought of all the other reasons the new Duchess might find for being dizzy and short of breath.

Crispin was leading her out to be presented to his people as the Duchess. She must concentrate on them. Do her duty

as his bride. And not think about the other duties of a
bride—the ones on which she had already got a head start.

The last couple to be presented to her was the Marlowes.
The keeper greeted her with pleasure and presented his wife
with pride. 'We'll be celebratin' our twenty-fifth weddin'
day in another month, your Grace. I'll take the liberty of
wishin' you the same happiness. An' I hope I'll be here ter
see it,' he said gallantly.

Twenty-five years, thought Tilda. Dear God, I'll be fifty!
And Crispin would be in his sixties. She peered into the
future. Anthea would be thirty—probably a mama herself.
Dazedly her hand crept to her belly—and this little one—
even this little one would be a man or woman grown. And
there would be others, no doubt.

Smiling, she chatted to Mrs Marlowe, outwardly calm,
as she spoke of stillrooms and preserves, and the best way
to make beeswax polish.

'Aye. I did as you said and watched him.' Marlowe's
voice came clearly to her ears. 'You were right, your Grace,
though whatever made you reckon to *him* has me fair
gapped.'

Crispin was nodding. 'Very well. Leave it. I'll have to
deal with it now. Are there any left?'

What on earth were they talking about? mused Tilda.
Whatever it was, Crispin looked as though he'd eaten
something sour.

'Just the one, your Grace,' said Marlowe. 'Close by the
right of way, near where the path from the gardens comes
out. 'Tis back in the undergrowth a little.'

'You've sprung it?'

Traps. They were talking about traps. Tilda felt guilty.
She'd given no thought to any of Crispin's concerns in the
last weeks. And she'd known that this was bothering him.

'Are you quite well, Tilda?' Guy's voice was concerned.
She looked up at him with a faint smile. 'I'm very well,

Guy. Just a trifle fagged. It is nothing to worry about. Besides, should you not be fussing over *your* wife?'

He grinned. 'I'll do that later, believe me.' For a moment his grin was just as devilish as his cousin's. Tilda had no trouble believing that for all his tender care and adoration of Milly, he had every intention of pleasuring his bride to the full.

As no doubt Crispin had. Her smile became rather fixed as she responded to Guy's banter. How on earth was she to conceal her feelings when they battered at the guard she had set on them, clamouring for their release?

As Lady Hollow came up, Guy took his leave of her and beat a hasty retreat to Milly's side. Even as she smiled at the old lady's cynical and scurrilous advice on how best to deal with the head of the Malverns, her eyes followed Guy and Milly surreptitiously. All very well for them, she thought despairingly. If Milly cried out words of love in the height of passion, her husband would be delighted. Determinedly she returned her attention to Lady Hollow and did not see Crispin watching her with a twisted smile.

Tilda waited with increasing nervousness for her husband. Sarah had long since been dismissed and still Crispin had not come to her. What on earth could be taking him so long? If he didn't come soon she'd be a gibbering mess. She'd never be able to say all that needed to be said.

Maybe he wasn't coming. The thought crept into her heart with chilly inevitability as time stretched on. She cast a glance at the branch of candles she'd left burning beside the bed. They danced and flickered mockingly. So easy to snuff out—had Crispin's passion died as easily? What did she have to offer him if it had?

Miserably she was about to blow out the candles and get into her lonely bed when she realised what she was doing; to wit, feeling sorry for herself. She straightened up and her eyes narrowed.

If she started feeling sorry for herself, that opened the way for others to feel sorry for her. Like her husband. Whatever else she wanted from him, pity wasn't part of it.

Damn it! It was their wedding night and if Crispin didn't want to mark the occasion in the usual way, then the least he could have done was come and tell her so. Her jaw tightened mulishly. He could tell her now. And his reasons had better be damned good ones!

Clutching her robe and temper around her, she stalked to the door that led to his room.

A single lamp burnt on the chimneypiece and she saw swiftly that the room was empty. A night shirt was laid out on the bed and his wedding clothes lay scattered over the floor. So where in the world *was* he?

Avoiding her obviously. Hurt fury shuddered through her. She might as well return to her own room. She could take a hint and she would not demean herself by waiting here for his Grace's pleasure.

Forcing back tears, she turned to go, and a large book on the window seat caught her eye. The last thing she wanted was a book, but reading all night would be better than crying herself to sleep.

She went over to the window, picked up the book and looked at the title. And blinked. What in God's name was Crispin doing reading the sermons of Doctor John Donne? Somehow she'd have thought the love poetry was more his style.

A light breeze from the open window fanned her cheek. The curtains fluttered. Still clutching the volume, she looked out, over the South Lawn towards the woods. Moonlight silvered the scene before her, casting black shadows, leaching the colour from everything.

Full moon, she thought. Nearly as bright as day. Bright enough to go for a walk…as her husband was doing.

Her jaw dropped and she stared in disbelief as her missing bridegroom stepped into view from the deep shadow cast by the house. Stunned, she watched as he strode across the lawn, in breeches, boots and his shooting jacket.

The conversation she'd heard between him and his keeper—Marlowe, wasn't it—came back to her in dizzying clarity. *I'll deal with that at the first convenient moment.* Did he consider their wedding night a convenient opportunity?

Then she spun around and ran to her room.

By the time she reached the side door, Crispin was nearly lost against the bulk of the woods. He wouldn't have had quite such a head start, but she'd had enough common sense to drag on her carriage dress, thick woollen stockings and a pair of list boots. Nothing else. Running fast enough to catch him would warm her quite satisfactorily.

She got within hailing distance just before he reached the trees. And discovered she was too out of breath. So she ran harder, her boots making no sound on the thick damp grass. She didn't dare let him get too far ahead in the trees, she didn't know the woods as he did. And then abruptly he stopped and looked around. And stared. She could feel his shock reaching her in waves.

Some instinct had warned Crispin that he was not alone. He swung around and wondered if he were dreaming. Tilda, her hair down, was tearing after him. She came up to him panting, her breasts heaving. He tried to ignore that, along with his body's all too predictable response.

'What…the…devil…do you think…you're doing?' she managed, stealing his line.

'Going for a walk,' he said shortly. 'Why don't you go back to the house and I'll tell you all about it later?'

'*Damn* you!' she exploded. 'You're chasing poachers on our wedding night? Don't you think that's taking your responsibilities a little too far? Or were you so eager to avoid me that you thought you'd go out and get shot?' She knew that was a trifle melodramatic, but by then she was too angry to care.

Judging by the look on Crispin's face, he thought she was being melodramatic as well. 'I can safely assure you that there's no danger to me. Go back to bed. If I'd thought you'd notice I was gone and worry, I'd have told you.'

'Notice? *Worry!*' She couldn't believe it. 'Just where did you think I'd expect you to be on our wedding night? And if there's no danger, then I dare say you won't mind if I accompany you!'

'No!' His refusal was peremptory.

'Hah! Then it *is* dangerous!' Her eyes glittered at him challengingly in the moonlight. 'Resign yourself to a companion, your Grace. Unless you plan on taking me back to the house and tying me to the bed.'

For a single searing moment Crispin considered doing just that. His blood roared. The images she'd conjured up were erotic in the extreme. Somehow he managed to control himself enough to say, 'An interesting notion, my dear. But my reasons for asking you to stay behind stem from discretion, not concern for your safety.'

'I'm not,' stated Tilda trenchantly, 'interested in discretion. Any more than I'm interested in safety. Try again.'

He swore. Tying her to the bed wouldn't work. He'd never make it out of the bedchamber. In fact, he probably wouldn't make it off the bed.

'Very well,' he grated as he started walking. 'But just remember later that it was your idea in the first place.'

Following him into the woods, she retorted icily, 'Naturally I acknowledge that you did not invite me to accompany you.'

'I meant when I tie you to the bed!' he ground out in savage frustration, painfully aware of the unbridled lust in his voice. And stalked on.

A pregnant silence followed as Tilda grappled with all the ramifications of this. To her absolute fury, the idea of

Crispin tying her to the bed did not cause a single flutter of panic, let alone disgust. Shock was another matter. Delightful, anticipatory shock that rippled up and down her spine in feathery excitement as she contemplated the thought of being completely helpless and vulnerable before him. At his mercy. Not that he'd need to tie her up to achieve that.

Desperately she forced herself to think of something else, before her knees gave out. Like the fact that if he wanted to tie her to the bed, then maybe he hadn't come out tonight because he didn't want her. Which meant that he must have thought she didn't want him.

She stared at his back as he walked ahead of her. Large and dark, positively unyielding. She'd thought she understood his motivation and reasons for marrying her. Quite obviously she'd got things confused. Why on earth would he think that she didn't want him? After the way she'd behaved that night and every other time he'd touched her.

She cursed under her breath as she stumbled slightly. And felt his fingers close like a vice on her wrist.

'Quiet now!' he ordered. 'We're getting close and I don't want you to disturb him.'

As he spoke they stepped out of the narrow path into a broad ride that Tilda recognised at once as the right of way that ran straight through Crispin's lands. Considerably annoyed, she tugged at her wrist. It had absolutely no effect at all. Except that he tightened his grip even further.

'There,' he breathed and gestured with the hand that held the lamp.

At the side of the ride stood a tall horse. Even in this light Tilda could see that it was not the sort of animal an ordinary common poacher would ride. This horse belonged to a gentleman. Or at least someone wealthy.

Releasing her, Crispin put the lamp down behind a bush.

'Wha—?'

'Shh. I'm listening.'

Tilda glared as she rubbed some life back into her wrist. Then she heard it too. Someone else moving about in the woods just beyond the horse. She couldn't think why she was surprised. After all, the horse hadn't come out here all saddled and bridled by itself.

A tall figure, carrying something, came into view between the trees.

'Stay here,' muttered Crispin and stepped out.

'Good evening, Sir Richard. Could I hold that trap while you mount?'

Tilda wondered if she were going mad. Sir Richard-all-poachers-should-be-hanged-Benton? Poaching? It didn't make sense.

There was a metallic crash and curse.

'*St Ormond?* What in the name of all that's holy are you doing out here tonight?'

Sir Richard, thought Tilda in confusion, sounded as though he'd nearly had a heart attack.

'Catching poachers,' he said calmly.

A snort greeted this. 'I'd have supposed you had something better to do with your time tonight of all nights! In *my* day we bedded our brides promptly!'

This was too much for Tilda. She stepped out of the shadows and said sweetly, 'I couldn't agree more. Perhaps, Sir Richard, you might explain just what you are about so that I can persuade my husband to attend to his duties.'

She ignored the outraged expression on her husband's face as she strolled up to them. Instead she concentrated on Sir Richard, who was goggling in disbelief.

Coolly she looked at the heap of metal at his feet. 'A trap, Sir Richard? I thought you disapproved of poaching. So, how do you explain this?'

'Tilda, please let me deal with this…' began Crispin.

'Oh, let be, lad,' said Sir Richard resignedly. 'No doubt you realised I'd take the chance, but I thought you'd be better off dealing with your wife.' He turned to Tilda and

said, 'I beg your pardon, your Grace. I thought if I pushed
St Ormond hard enough he'd crack down on the poaching
on his lands. But I never intended Bull to get away and
hurt anyone. Just a few traps to make him sit up and take
notice. I've been removing them for the last couple of
weeks.'

'Then I take it there'll be no more of it, Sir Richard,'
said Crispin coldly. 'Because if there is…'

A harsh bark of laughter interrupted him. 'You must
have a maggot in your head! My old bones are cursing me
for what I've put them through, crawling about damp
woods in the middle of the night at my age. Now if you'll
pass that damn trap up to me, I'll be on my way.'

With that he mounted his horse, grunting audibly at the
effort. He frowned down at Crispin. 'Well? Are you going
to pass me that trap, boy?'

Crispin shook his head. 'Leave it, sir. I collect it's one
of the old ones we got rid of when I inherited. Marlowe
will collect it. Goodnight.'

The irascible old gentleman glared down at him. 'I'll
wish you the same. Seems to me you'd better get that chit
home and warm her up. Or maybe it's just my old bones.'
With a final disgusted snort, he wheeled his horse and rode
off.

Dazed, Tilda watched him go. Innumerable questions
flashed through her head, but Crispin forestalled her.

'We're going home. Right now.' Determinedly he started
walking. If he concentrated hard, he might just manage to
get her home before he succumbed to temptation and took
Benton's advice. Literally. Before he lifted her skirts and
tumbled her right here in the woods like a village maiden
on May Day.

Chapter Seventeen

'How long have you known that Sir Richard was responsible?' Tilda was completely stunned by the denouement. Firmly she resisted the temptation to press close to Crispin's side as they made their way back through the woods. Small scurryings and an occasional squeal told her that they were not the only creatures in the dark woods. There could be nothing to harm her, she knew, but the darkness pressed in.

'For certain, only this morning, when Marlowe told me that he'd watched Sir Richard removing a steel trap. But I'd suspected, since after his dog attacked you.'

His voice was tight and clipped. Tilda sensed that he would prefer not to say any more, but she needed to know. Needed to know why he'd chosen to come out, tonight of all nights.

'Why did you suspect him?'

'The trapping stopped at once. And Marlowe mentioned to me that he'd noticed that most of the traps were set very close to that right of way. Sir Richard uses that path all the time, especially if he rides over to dine with old Whittlesea—which he does frequently. And he's a little old for crawling around in damp undergrowth.'

'Oh.'

'Of course Marlowe saw him, but never thought to watch him—of all people—until I suggested it. In fact, he tells me he'd generally say good evening to the old devil. He thought I'd run mad. But he watched. And saw Sir Richard removing the traps.'

Tilda understood. 'So you wanted to confront him privately—and by doing it this way, you didn't have to go to him and make an accusation. You could just ask him why.'

A short silence followed. 'That's it,' he said at last. 'You understand me very well. The last thing I wanted was to run the least risk of this getting out. If I'd called on him, there was always the chance of someone overhearing. And I certainly didn't wish to make a straight accusation.'

'But why tonight?' She still felt hurt. Surely he could at least have told her. Couldn't he? They were married. Did he not wish to share things with her? Did he want a fashionable marriage of the type he had intended with Milly? Had that note of sincerity as he took his vows really meant nothing?

His voice darkened. 'This, according to Marlowe, was the last trap. I thought he'd take the opportunity to remove it as quickly as possible. It was risky, being so close to the ride but, after today's celebrations, there was very little chance of being caught.' A note of irony crept into his voice. 'I somehow doubt that he expected either of us to be wandering around the woods tonight.'

That was only too probable, thought Tilda. She would be willing to wager a considerable sum that whatever Guy and Milly were doing right now, they were not out chasing poachers. Bitterly she faced the unpalatable knowledge that rather than bed his bride, her husband had elected to chase poachers. Tears stung her eyes, blurring the faint light cast by the lantern.

Plainly Crispin was in no hurry to consummate their marriage, which suggested that the night he had spent in her bed had not satisfied him in the least. No matter that she had died and shattered beneath him, that she had given herself and everything to their lovemaking—it had meant nothing to him. Certainly his comments about tying her up had been nothing more than a practical solution to keep her out of his way! Her wanton mind had imagined that note of lust in his voice.

Pain lanced through her as she fought to hold back a sob of despair. She should never have come after him. If she managed to get back to the house without crying it would be a miracle.

Stumbling over a tree root, she cursed under her breath and then gasped as she was caught up and held safely against Crispin's side. His powerful arm encircled her; she wriggled but his grip was inescapable. Fire shot through her, burning, melting. And her breathing hitched as her heart raced.

'I can manage.' She tried to sound calm, unconcerned. And succeeded only in sounding snippy.

'You'll be safer with me.'

Still his voice was tight, controlled. As if he'd prefer not to be holding her.

At that moment something snapped inside her. Something that had been gripping the reins of her self-control, holding her back. To the devil with *safe*! She didn't want him merely to look after her and protect her. She was sick of *safe*. She wanted him to love her. Right now she wanted him to ravish her—and all he could do was tell her she would be safe with him!

'I don't want to be safe!' She squirmed furiously. 'That wasn't why I married you!'

He let her go and she swung around to face him. 'Why not just tell me where you were going? How do you think I felt, when you didn't even come to me on our wedding night? When you weren't even in your own room? If you didn't want me, why marry me?' Fury and hurt split over. 'I'm sick of being protected! Of being rescued—looked after. Why can't you just see me as a woman? Why didn't you come to me tonight? What was the real reason?'

She was shaking with the effort not to cry, not to break down completely. Through her tears she stared at Crispin. His face was wreathed in shadows flung by the lantern. His expression was unreadable.

When he spoke it was in a flat, deadened voice. 'I thought, under the circumstances, you would prefer that I didn't force myself on you tonight of all nights. That was why I came out. It was the only way I could stay away from you.'

Tilda stared. 'Force yourself on me! What are you talking about? You're my husband!

She thought his mouth twisted bitterly. 'But not the husband you wanted. I was not prepared to bed you when you were, deep down, longing for another man. I didn't think it fair on either of us.'

What other man? What was he talking about? Did he think she was mourning Jonathan?

Tangled, confused skeins of thought robbed her of speech.

He went on. 'You needed time to recover from your disappointment. I intended to discuss the whole situation with you tomorrow. I should have done it long ago—but the time was never right, so—'

'What disappointment are you talking about?' An incredible suspicion was forming in her mind.

He groaned. 'Tilda, don't pretend with me. It's not necessary, my darling. I knew how hurt you were when Guy offered for Milly. I didn't intend to offer for you that morning—I was going to wait. I knew you'd think I'd offered out of obligation after what had happened—but your uncle was prepared to blackmail me into marriage with Milly by threatening to make public that you were my mistress. He saw me leave your room that morning. So I didn't dare delay.'

She pounced on the last sentence. 'You were going to offer for me anyway?' Shards of doubt, of confusion, stung her. Why had he wished to offer for her? 'You thought I was in love with Guy? But we never...I mean...we were just friends. He flirted with *me* to draw attention from his interest in Milly. I knew that. He never made any pretence otherwise and nor did I wish it.' Her eyes widened. Surely he didn't still think... 'I never slept with Guy...I...thought you knew that.'

'Of course I knew that!' he said roughly. He took a step towards her. She backed warily and he stopped. 'Tilda, are you saying that you weren't in love with Guy? Ever?'

'Never,' she avowed.

He swore. 'Damn it, Tilda, I was in the library that time you and Guy came in. He...he kissed you, and you kissed him back. Then you cried after he left. I...I assumed...'

Shock hit her. 'You were there?'

He nodded. 'On the gallery. I'm sorry. I didn't mean to eavesdrop, but by the time I realised you were there...'

'Guy was apologising for any embarrassment and hurt our flirtation might have caused me,' admitted Tilda. 'Milly and he both wondered if I had taken him seriously.'

'But you didn't.'

'No,' she said quietly. 'Why did you ask me to marry you, if you thought I was in love with him?' An unwelcome thought struck her. 'Or did you offer *because* you thought I was in love with Guy?' Marrying her because he believed it was his duty to protect her from a scandal he had in part created, she thought she could bear...but if...

He swore. 'Yes, damn it!'

A shudder ran through her. 'Not because *you* were in love?'

Tense, searing silence knifed between them. It quivered in the darkness, cold and deadly.

She was about to turn away when his answer came, as if it were ripped from him.

'Yes, that too. Very deeply.'

To hear him say it was worse than the silence. Worse than the prior knowing. This made it real. Gave it life.

'With Milly.' Her voice sounded as dead as his. She'd been mad to force the issue and lay bare his hurt. Believing her in love with Guy, he'd had the sensitivity to hold back from her tonight. She should have accorded him the same courtesy...

'With *Milly*?'

Dazedly Tilda wondered why every tree in the wood hadn't been flattened.

'But you knew I wasn't!'

Shock tore through him. How the hell could she have thought him in love with Milly? After all the cynical and hurtful things he'd said to her on the subject of marriage and his reasons for offering for Milly? And if she hadn't been in love with Guy, why had she been so upset? Realisation struck. She'd made the same mistake that he had. No—the same *mistakes*—plural. And one of those mistakes was not one he was prepared to make ever again.

'Let me get this straight,' he said very carefully. 'I offered for you thinking that you were nursing a broken heart over Guy; and you accepted, thinking that I was wearing the willow for your cousin? Is that it?'

'Well, sort of.' She sounded hunted.

'Sort of?' He couldn't help the edge in his voice. 'No more hedging, Tilda. What does *sort of* mean?'

'I never meant to accept an offer of marriage from you!' she burst out.

'Then what in Hades did you say *yes* for?' he demanded, justifiably incensed.

'I didn't realise you were offering marriage!' she shot back. 'I thought...I thought... *Oh, God!* You'd spent the whole *night* in my bed! I'd behaved like a...a wanton practically every time you touched me—I'd told you I had no intention of ever marrying again; that there was nothing marriage could give me that I couldn't have without it. And I'm as close to illegitimate as makes no difference. I thought you were asking me to be your mistress!'

'I beg your pardon?'

'I...I thought—'

'And you accepted?' Protective fury surged through him. How dare she hold herself so cheaply! How dare she accept such an offer! Even from himself? Come to think of it, how dare she even think that he would offer such a thing to her.

'Why the hell did you accept?'

And then he realised that she was crying. That tears were falling silently, spilling over in soundless pain. His own eyes felt hot as he saw her mouth trembling, saw her face crumple as she turned away.

Swearing, he took two strides and caught her. There had been enough distance between them. He enfolded her in his arms, cradling her against his body. And gloried in the way she surrendered and melted, soft curves moulding to his hard muscles. She clung to him, pressing herself closer, as though she wanted to be a part of him. And she would be. Very soon.

The surge of rampant desire he had been holding in check for weeks ripped through him. He knew a fierce satisfaction that he could give in to it now, seduce her to it. She had never loved Guy—she would be his and his only. Finally he thought he understood, thought he knew why she had held him at bay, why she had been so unhappy. But he wasn't taking any chances this time. He was going to make quite certain.

Tenderly he stroked her hair. 'It's all right...we're both idiots,' he whispered. 'We should have been more open with each other. But the main thing is that we understand now...and we're married. You're mine, Tilda. Always.' He rained kisses on her soft curls, threading his fingers through the silken strands, spreading them over her shoulders.

Gently he found her chin and teased her into lifting her tearstained face.

She could feel herself melting, but before he could kiss her, she put a hand over his mouth. She had to know the truth. 'Cris. You said before that you...that you were in love...' She gasped as he began kissing the palm of her hand, as he sucked gently at her fingers, taking them one by one into the wet heat of his mouth.

'I said...that...because I was...am,' he murmured between bites.

'Who...with?' Her knees were so jellified she could barely frame the question and a thousand darting fires had sprung up under her skin. And an aching, yearning hope that she dared not surrender to—that threatened to destroy her if it were denied.

'You mean, *with whom*?' His voice was unsteady. 'Haven't you understood that yet, my blind little love?'

He bent his head and took her lips in a kiss that was inexpressibly tender, his mouth moving on hers in passionate demand. And she yielded to it with a sob of joy, her lips parting under his in utter surrender as he gathered her closer. Fiery delight winged through her, scorching as she felt his arms tighten around her, felt the pressure of his lips deepen, felt his tongue plunge into the hot sweetness of her mouth in fierce possession.

Wildly she returned his kisses, tangling her tongue with his, exploring his mouth.

At last he lifted his head and breathed. 'Do you understand now, my darling?' With a groan he hauled her closer. 'But why? In God's name! *Why* did you accept my offer if you thought I wanted you as my mistress?'

'Because I loved you so much,' she whispered. 'I thought that it was all I'd ever have of you...and when I realised what you had offered, I was terrified...thinking that I'd never be able to hide how I felt in a marriage.'

She felt him stiffen. 'You loved me? You accepted what

you thought was a *carte blanche* because you loved me? And the night we made love—it was me you wanted? Not comfort?'

'Just you,' she murmured against his cheek. 'Only ever you. I couldn't bear to hurt you—insult you—by telling you what I'd thought. Especially as I thought you'd been hurt by Milly.'

A moment's silence ensued.

'I think,' said Crispin in a very careful voice, 'that we had better keep moving. We definitely need to be somewhere more private.'

'We…we do?' Her voice was breathless. 'Where?'

'Bed,' came the uncompromising answer.

'I thought you wanted to keep moving.' Tilda was puzzled at the detour. They were deep in the darkness under the willow tree by the lake and Crispin had drawn her into his arms.

'I said we needed to be somewhere more private,' he murmured, feathering a kiss over her trembling lips, biting softly at the tender lower lip and stroking it with his tongue.

Tilda gasped and he filled her mouth—a slow, purposeful penetration, a promise of things to come. She sank against him, into him, her body melting in surrender to his strength. She moaned and sobbed as he traced the line of her jaw with his lips, found the wildly beating pulse at the base of her throat and laved it with a hot sweep of his tongue. Fire streaked from her aching breasts to her belly and lower so that she shifted her thighs against him in frantic need. One corner of her dazed mind knew that she'd never be able to walk to the house if he kept this up.

He was nipping at one ear lobe, his warm breath driving her wild but she somehow managed to say, 'You…you said you wanted to take me to bed…' She sucked in a startled breath as his hand shifted to her bodice and began undoing buttons.

'I'll settle for just taking you.' His voice was a possessive, predatory growl, drifting down to her out of the dark.

For a moment she didn't understand. And then, 'Here?' A shock of wickedly knowing delight lanced through her at the thought that he was going to tumble her right here by the lake.

'Right here,' he affirmed. 'And now.' She could hear the devilish smile in his husky voice and the barely leashed desire.

Deft fingers had reached the buttons at her waist and he paused to slip one hand inside, to caress soft warm curves that heated and melted. His fingers teased and cupped the sweet mounds of her breasts.

'No chemise,' he observed. 'How very convenient.' On the word he bent his head and drew one puckered and aching nipple into the heat of his mouth. Tantalisingly he licked and teased until she cried out and arched against him, begging for more. She felt his lips curve in triumph and then he suckled, hard. She screamed softly, her knees buckling, and felt his arms tighten.

He released that breast, but only to treat its burning twin to the same sweet torture. This time she tried to control her scream, but he suckled harder until she sobbed her pleasure. Only then did he raise his head to say, 'No one will hear you out here. ' Undoing a few more buttons, he added, 'Except me.' His tone suggested that he didn't mind in the least if she screamed.

Wild with need, her fingers flickered over the buttons of his shirt, then gripped it, pulling it free of his breeches. His teeth flashed in a delighted smile as he stepped back and shrugged out of his shooting jacket.

She blinked as he flung it around her shoulders, sliding first one and then her other arm into it.

'Wha—?'

'You'll need it,' he growled.

She stared up at him in confusion, scarcely able to think

for the desire scorching through her veins. He was pressing her backward even as she wondered what he was doing.

'The ground's damp,' he said, with a wicked grin, as she brought up against the hard trunk of the willow. Her hands pressed against his chest; she wondered dazedly which was the harder, his body or the tree. She thought the tree might—just—have the advantage. His weight held her trapped as he took her mouth again, plundering, devouring.

He groaned in delight as he felt her soaring response, the wild sweetness of her kisses as her tongue danced with his, as her body clung and moulded. A shudder ran through him as he felt small hands slip under his shirt, stroking, exploring. One slid up over the hair-roughened muscles of his chest, found a nipple and circled it curiously. He felt his whole body tighten, shift from hard to harder; and then, as she found his other nipple, to sheer agony.

He lifted his head and through the haze of heat clouding his mind, concentrated on the buttons at the front of her gown.

'How far do these go?' he rasped.

'Hmm?' Plainly she was as dazed as he.

'Do they go all the way to the hem?' he ground out.

'Uh…yes.'

Every instinct howled with triumph. That, he thought, was a great deal more than convenient. It was inspired. He fastened his lips to her throat and slid down, tasting, feasting all the way into the creamy vale between her breasts and over the gentle swell of her soft belly until he knelt before her to deal with the last few buttons. So that she stood fully bared to his gaze, to his hands. And to his mouth.

She was tugging at his shirt and he raised his arms to allow her to pull it off. He felt her fingers sink into the muscles of his shoulders, entwine themselves in his hair. Felt her stooping to join him.

Instantly his hands gripped her bottom. Hard. Holding her upright.

'I told you,' he growled. 'The ground's damp.'

'But…' The protest strangled in her throat as she realised just what he intended. That the extra padding of his coat was not to protect her from the ground, but from the tree. Sheer wanton excitement speared through her at the mere thought.

Shudders of need rippled downward as he surged to his feet and lifted her against him. She was frantic with need, her body arching wildly as he gripped her bottom. Instinctively she wrapped her legs around his waist, opening herself to him.

'Please…oh please…' She sought his mouth with hers. He took it fiercely as he let her slide down on to him, as his loins surged, thrusting deeply into the heated, silken sheath that welcomed him.

They were one. His weight pinning her to the tree was hers, his hands beneath her bottom kneaded and supported her. And his mouth melded to hers, swallowing her cries of pleasure as he moved powerfully against her, inside her, his hair-brushed chest shifting against her swollen breasts even as he surged deep within her body so that she no longer knew where she ended and he began.

She broke and shattered in his arms, helpless and blind in the storm that tore them apart and left them clinging to each other in its wake. Tilda was barely aware of him lowering her to the ground and wrapping her safely in his arms. Warm hands caressed and soothed, a husky voice murmured words of passion, of love. And she floated, sated and content.

'I hope, lady mine, that you intend to let us get back to the house now.' His teasing question breathed into her ear as she drifted in a pleasurable golden void, bounded only by his arms and chest as he held her tenderly. They sat leaning against the tree.

'Hmm.' Her mind wouldn't focus. She didn't even want it to.

'The house,' he growled insistently.

Part of her mind revived. 'Why?'

His body shifted restlessly against her. 'So I can get on with my husbandly duties, of course.'

'Oh.' Now why hadn't that occurred to her? Possibly his style hadn't been in the least cramped by their present location. But he'd said something earlier, about the ground being damp. She wouldn't want him to catch a chill.

'Again?' There was no hint in her voice that she found the idea of carrying out her wifely duties again in the least distasteful. Quite the opposite, thought her gratified husband.

'Of course again,' he said. 'I can assure you that the last month has been hell on earth. And I have every intention of reaping my just rewards.' He dropped a kiss on her hair. 'Besides, we'd better get started on all those brothers and sisters Anthea requested. These things take a little effort as I'm sure you know.'

'Do they?' She couldn't help the mischief and sheer smug triumph in her voice.

Warily he asked, 'Don't they?'

'Not as much as you might have thought,' she whispered, sitting up so that she could see his face. Stunned shock followed by a strangely intense glitter blazed in his eyes. Then they were hooded as he looked down.

Slowly his hand shifted down from her breast to curve wonderingly, possessively, over her belly. Fingers traced and marvelled at the soft swell. She saw him swallow, then his eyes were back on hers.

'You're having my baby?' His voice was molten. 'Then that night…?'

Breathlessly she nodded.

'When…when did you know?' he whispered. His fingers still caressed and stroked her belly, as though he had to touch to believe.

She trembled at the loving awe in his touch. 'A week ago…I should have told you earlier…'

Dazed silence hung between them. At last he said, 'Thank God for your uncle, then.' And pulled her back into his arms, cradling her against him.

'My uncle?' Tilda couldn't see any reason to be grateful to Lord Pemberton.

'Oh, yes,' said Crispin. 'If he hadn't tried to blackmail me that morning, I wouldn't have offered for you. Not then. I was going to wait, give you time since I thought you were in love with Guy.' He groaned. 'Fool that I was! But I knew if your uncle saw you first, you'd never accept my offer. You'd think I'd only offered out of obligation… And if I'd waited—then found you were increasing…' His arms tightened, his voice became muffled against her hair. 'You might never have quite believed that I married you for love. It's been hard enough. Did Pemberton tell you he'd seen me? What he'd tried to do?'

'Yes,' she whispered. 'I was so confused, I couldn't think straight. I'd thought you were hurt about Milly, but then I did wonder if you were offering for me to protect me…and I just couldn't ask…'

'You didn't trust me?'

She clung, realising his hurt. 'It wasn't that. After that night, I knew if we were alone together, if I tried to speak to you about why you really offered for me, I'd probably give myself away. I didn't want you to know I loved you, I didn't want you to feel sorry for me. And then you seemed to withdraw…so I decided to wait until tonight to tell you I was having your baby and try to find out why you married me…' She pressed closer. 'When you weren't in your room…'

'This reticence of yours is going to be a problem,' he

observed drily. 'I'll have to do something about it. Because I like hearing you say that you love me, and pity hasn't got a chance with all the other things I feel for you. So get rid of that idea.'

'Very well,' said Tilda dutifully. Then, curiously, 'Just what do you intend to do about my reticence?'

His lips curved wickedly and a matching gleam sprang to his eyes. 'Oh, I think I'll just encourage you to tell me what you're feeling.'

One hand slid over her hip, teasing, heating her.

She gasped and wriggled in sudden excitement.

'Not good enough, my sweet.' His voice was low and hungry. His fingers explored further and she cried out in pleasure, her fingers sinking into his shoulders as he stroked and probed, releasing a flood of searing desire. He could feel it flowing through her.

'Better,' he murmured as she twisted against him. 'But I can see you need lots of practice.' He drew a deep breath. 'In bed!' Determinedly ignoring her outraged protests and his own inclinations, he hauled her to her feet and started to do up the buttons of her dress. And realised that wasn't a sensible move.

It was far too tempting to undo them again.

'You do them up,' he said firmly, looking around for his shirt. He pulled it on over his head. It smelt of damp grass. God only knew what Stubbs would think. Or of the inevitable grass stains on his leathers, he thought as he buttoned them up. He could only hope the truth wouldn't occur to him. Not that Stubbs wasn't discreet. He just didn't think that he could deal with the pokered-up face his valet used to conceal amusement.

And he definitely didn't relish the idea of any of his staff catching them sneaking back into the house at dawn. No. Returning to the house now was the best option. Before things got out of hand. Once in his bedchamber he had every intention of making sure that things got thoroughly out of hand.

Crispin awakened in the grey light of dawn with his exhausted, sated bride settled safely where she belonged. In his arms, in the ducal bed. He'd finally got past Tilda's reserve to the achingly sweet, loving woman it had hidden. The wildly passionate wanton. To discover that she was his, body, heart and soul. She'd given him the two most precious gifts she had to offer; herself—completely and unconditionally. And she was carrying his child. Boy or girl—he didn't give a damn. The knowledge sent his heart soaring.

'Crispin?' It was the softest of murmurs.

'Mmm?'

She wriggled even closer, snuggling her cheek into the curve of his shoulder, his arm tightened possessively.

'Did I mention that I love you?'

'The subject did come up,' he said with a throaty chuckle. 'But I'm quite happy to be reminded.' A short, considering pause as he slid his hand lovingly over her curves. 'Frequently. I take my vows seriously—there was something in there about being fruitful in the procreation of children.'

A deliciously voluptuous, sleepy chuckle greeted this. 'You've already dealt with that, your Grace.'

'Practice,' asserted his Grace virtuously, 'makes perfect. Besides, I said I'd worship you with my body, my darling, and I intend to do just that.' And he suited the action to the word.

*   *   *   *   *

Colonel Ancroft's Love

by

Sylvia Andrew

Sylvia Andrew has an Honours Degree in Modern Languages from University College, London and, before ending up as Vice-Principal of a large comprehensive sixth-form college, taught English for foreigners in Switzerland, Cambridge and in Compton Park, an international finishing school for young ladies which was housed in a beautiful country mansion leased from the Devonshire family. The house and grounds have provided inspiration for several settings in her novels. She and her husband Simon now live in a small market town in the west of England, which is full of the Georgian architecture which they both love. And just a few miles from their home is the marvellous Dorset Jurassic Coast World Heritage Site. In 2000 Sylvia wrote a historical celebration of the town's splendid fifteenth-century parish church in a millennium *son et lumière*, which was a great success.

She and Simon belong to the Georgian Group, the National Trust and English Heritage, all of which help them to satisfy their love of historic houses and wonderful landscapes. Simon lectures all over the place on architecture and wild orchids, while Sylvia tries to do nothing, and usually fails, since she is heavily involved in the local museum. She just can't keep away from old maps, newspapers, photographs and census returns! Her other passion is theatre performances of Shakespeare. She and Simon have one married daughter, whom they visit quite often, and a very precious grandson called Joe.

Prologue

Brussels, June 15th 1815

Colonel John Ancroft watched from the gallery as his two best officers joined the throng in the Duchess of Richmond's ballroom. He didn't envy them. The evening was stiflingly hot and the room was crowded. He saw with approval that Adam Calthorpe was talking to the Countess Karnska, doing his best to reassure her after the rumours of the French advance. Ivo Trenchard was, of course, making for the loveliest woman in the room. Tom Payne was whirling some poor girl round the ballroom with more energy than style. The Colonel nodded. The situation was normal—that is, as normal as it could be in these extraordinary circumstances. He went back into the small room and fingered the papers lying there. Reports, none of them precise, none reassuring. Where the devil was Bonaparte? Some of the scouts put him just a few miles away on the border, but everything was vague, nothing clear. One thing, however, was quite certain. The two greatest generals in Europe, Wellington and Napoleon Bonaparte, would very soon come face to face in battle.

Possibly as early as tomorrow. Even now, while the cream of European society was dancing and laughing below in the Duchess of Richmond's ballroom, Wellington was closeted in the Duke of Richmond's library, together with his corps commanders, his generals, and his senior Staff Officers, drawing up battle plans. When they were ready and the situation made clear, it would be up to him, Colonel Ancroft, to see that Calthorpe, Trenchard and the rest of the men under his command carried the marching orders to the regiments stationed outside Brussels. Till then he had nothing to do but cool his heels in this cramped little room in the Duchess's house, listening to the music drifting up from the ballroom.

The Colonel was a severely disciplined man. He seldom let himself dwell on the past, or think of the future. The past was too painful, the future too uncertain. But tonight he allowed his thoughts to wander. If he, John Ancroft, survived the coming battle, what would he do with his life? Where would he go? It would have to be London. He would buy a house in London. There was certainly no home for him in Yorkshire. While his uncle lived, still nursing the implacable hatred that had taken possession of him after the death of his only son, Marrick Castle was closed to him.

He frowned. Marrick... He had avoided even thinking about Marrick for years, had deliberately shut out the sunny memories of his childhood, playing with Philip, riding with Philip, wrestling with Philip, of being second only to Philip in his uncle's regard and affection. He had been very young when his own parents had died within months of each other, and he and Philip had been brought up together at Marrick like brothers. As they grew older there had been rivalry, of course. Two lusty young men, anxious to prove their manhood, were bound to cross each other from time to time. But before Gabriella Ainderby made her appearance it had all been basically good-natured. It was love for Gabriella which had brought about the fatal change in the cousins' relationship, and since that time he had almost forgotten what love was… Fourteen years ago, but the memory still had so much power to hurt…

This wouldn't do! He suddenly got up and went back on to the gallery, staring down at the mass of people, willing himself to think only of the present. Trenchard was nowhere to be seen—he was probably out in the garden with Madame de Menkelen. No, the lovely Isabel de Menkelen was down there, dancing with someone else. Ivo must be losing his touch… Calthorpe was now with Tom Payne. A nice boy, Lieutenant Payne, but wayward. He would make a good soldier when he learned to submit to discipline…

'Colonel Ancroft!'

He turned. One of the Duke's aides was standing respectfully behind him. 'His Grace wishes to see you, sir. In the library.'

So the summons had come, the action was about to begin. And not a moment too soon. He followed the young man down the stairs and disappeared into the library.

In the great battle of Waterloo that followed, Colonel Ancroft fought with courage and daring. Twice he was wounded and twice he went back to stay with his men. In the end he was carried off the field half conscious and weak from loss of blood with a dangerously deep sabre cut in his thigh. He was more fortunate than Tom Payne and thousands of others. He was one of the survivors, but it was two years before the surgeons finally pronounced him fit. By the beginning of 1818 he was living, as he had planned, in London.

Chapter One

London, May 1818

Colonel Ancroft stood at the window of his house in Mount Street, contemplating the scene. Two street vendors were having a lively discussion in the street below. He watched them for a few minutes to see if they would come to blows, and wasn't sure whether he was relieved or disappointed when they settled their difference and went on their way without incident. He sighed, turned, and surveyed the room. What should he do next for entertainment? Count the stripes on the wallpaper? He walked restlessly about the room, finally coming to a halt at the writing table. After staring at it for a moment he sat down with a gesture of impatience, poured himself a glass of wine, and took up his pen. He would catch up on his correspondence.

By the time his man came into the room the Colonel was absorbed. He eventually turned and said irritably, 'Well, don't just stand there, Betts. What is it?'

'Mr Fennybright is here, Colonel.'

There was a short silence during which the Colonel got

up and straightened himself. He took a breath, then said, 'Very well. You'd better show him up.' As Betts turned to go he added, 'And fetch more wine. That decanter is almost empty.'

A minute or two later Betts returned, accompanied by an elderly gentleman whose dress and demeanour made it obvious that this was a lawyer. The lines on his face showed humour and benevolence, though at the moment the expression on it was solemn enough.

'So, Fenny! I take it that you have some news for me.'

'Your uncle passed away three days ago, my lord. I arrived in London early this morning and have come straight here.'

After a short silence John Ancroft said, 'So that's it. It's over.' He walked to the window and stared out. Without turning, he asked, 'Were you there at the end? Did… did my uncle leave any message, send any word?'

The lawyer shook his head. 'None, my lord.'

'Did he mention me at all?'

Mr Fennybright hesitated. 'Not…not anything to the point.'

'Come, Fenny, come! You needn't be discreet—I can guess what the gist was. Someone will tell me, why not you? There was no relenting, no word of forgiveness, I take it.'

'Lord Coverdale was old and ill, my lord. He…he was not himself.'

'Damn it, tell me, Fenny!'

'His lordship never became reconciled to the tragic death of his son, not even on his deathbed.'

'*What did he say?*' Then, as the lawyer hesitated again, John Ancroft turned to him and said brusquely, 'I intend to know, Fenny! His exact words, if you please!'

'Forgive me,' said the lawyer in troubled tones. 'You

will not enjoy what you hear.' In response to a gesture of impatience, he took a breath and said, 'Very well, my lord, since you insist… In spite of anything we could say, his late lordship remained implacable. His exact words were that he…he cursed his misfortune that not all of Napoleon's armies had managed to rid the world of the villain who had murdered his son. That his sole regret in quitting this life was that you had survived him to inherit the title for which you had killed your cousin.' John Ancroft turned back abruptly to face the window. After a lengthy silence, the lawyer added earnestly, 'It was a shocking scene, my lord. No one present believed anything of the sort. Indeed, there isn't another soul in Yorkshire or anywhere else who believes that Lord Philip Ancroft's death was anything but an accident. But none of our remonstrations—not even those of his chaplain—could persuade Lord Coverdale to withdraw his words. He died soon after. I'm…I'm deeply sorry, my lord.'

John said harshly, 'You needn't be. My uncle was wrong in one thing—I never thought of or wished for the title. But there was some truth in the rest. I *was* responsible for Philip's death. For two deaths—Philip's and… and Gabriella's. And then Rose died, too…'

'No, really, my lord! You must not say such things! You ought not even to think them! Your wife had been ill for years before she died. And I remember, if you do not, your kindness and generosity to her. Even though—'

'Even though she hated the sight of me? No, that's wrong. Hatred was too strong an emotion for poor, gentle Rose. But she saw as little of me as she could. God knows, I wasn't there very often, but she couldn't disguise her unease in my company, even for half an hour! Towards the end she had hysterics whenever she saw me. And she brought little Harriet up to feel the same. It was no wonder that the child regarded me with such horror. Between them, my wife and my uncle convinced her that I was a murderer.'

'That was very wrong of them,' said the lawyer gravely. 'Wickedly wrong. You would never have wished your cousin Philip any real harm. How can anyone talk of murder? You weren't even near him when he wrecked his curricle and killed himself and Miss Ainderby!'

'I drove him to it. No! Don't try to say anything, Fenny. The truth is that Philip and I were both in a fury when he got into that curricle, and, instead of stopping him, I goaded him further. There's no excuse for my behaviour. I was older than he was and should have had more control.'

'You are too hard on yourself, my lord. No one, not you, not even his father, could control Philip Ancroft when he was in a rage. And as for Miss Gabriella Ainderby... A lovely young lady, but—'

'No!' The sudden exclamation stopped Mr Fennybright. 'Leave it, Fenny, leave it!' After a pause John went on, 'You've been a good friend to me, Fenny. You have never wavered in your support of my case, I know. But I have always understood my uncle's reaction. He had good reason to hate me. In the end it was all he had left—his hatred of me. It's what kept him alive—that and his desire to outlive me.'

'I'm afraid that might well be true and I am sorry for it. I think the death of his only son turned his mind. May God now give him rest.'

'Amen to that,' said John sombrely, as Betts came into the room with a decanter and glasses. 'You'll take some wine with me?'

The two men sat down and sipped their wine in silence. After a moment John said thoughtfully, 'You know, there was a time in the early years when I hated myself as much as my uncle hated me. Nothing would have pleased me more than to satisfy his hopes.'

'My lord?'

'Don't pretend you don't know what I'm talking about. We've known each other too long. You know as well as I do that I never wanted to succeed to this damned title! In those early days in the army I would have been only too happy to oblige my uncle by getting killed in action. But the French failed us both.' There was a touch of self-mocking humour in his voice as he went on, 'He was bitterly disappointed, and all I got for my pains was swift promotion for what they called my admirable disregard for personal safety!'

'Was that why you stayed on the field at Waterloo? Even after being so severely wounded?'

'Curiously enough, no. By that time, I had begun to value life a little more. No, I stayed with the action at Waterloo because Wellington needed every man. It was a very tight thing, Fenny. But we survived. And won.'

'Are you now fully recovered?'

'Yes, yes! A slight touch of fever now and then, but otherwise perfectly sound. I wish now I had not sold out of the army. Last year I saw no future in a military career, but now... Apart from the odd occasion when I act as aide to the Duke when he is in England I'm at a loss.'

'That will fortunately no longer be a problem, my lord,' said Mr Fennybright briskly. 'You now have a large number of responsibilities waiting for you up in Yorkshire, for which a strong hand is needed. The sooner you take charge the better.'

John stared down at his wine. 'What makes you think I want to take charge at all?'

Mr Fennybright was so shocked that for a moment he

could not speak. 'But, you must!' he exclaimed finally. 'My lord, you must!'

'*Must*, Fennybright?' asked the Colonel, a touch coldly.

The lawyer took a breath and said firmly, 'Yes. Must, my lord. Forgive me, I have no desire to offend you, but I've looked after the interests of the Ancrofts, here and in Yorkshire, all my working life, as my father did before me, and his father before that, and I would be failing in my duty if I did not remind you of your obligations. You are now the fourth Marquess of Coverdale and a considerable landowner. You have responsibilities, which an honourable man, such as I know you are, would never avoid.'

'A *considerable* landowner, Fenny? I should have thought my uncle would have left me very little!'

'He was not able to dispossess you! Most of the Ancroft property is entailed. My lord, as one of Wellington's most highly regarded officers, you know the meaning of duty. You have now inherited large estates in Yorkshire, together with property in London and elsewhere in the country. You have hundreds of people dependent on you for their continued fortunes. And then there's your daughter Harriet, too. I cannot believe you mean to fail them!'

John got up and walked like a caged tiger about the room. 'Dammit, I swore I would never go back again after that last visit! My uncle's point-blank refusal to receive me, my wife's hysterics when I insisted that we met, the fear on the child's face when I approached her... Call me a coward if you wish, Fenny, but I cannot face a return.'

The lawyer put down his glass and said firmly, 'But you must! Lady Harriet would soon get to know you better. And she needs someone who is more than a father in name alone.' He paused. 'The rest of the people up there would give you the heartiest of welcomes. Your uncle

was a recluse and deeply suspicious of change. The estate
has been managed well enough, but time has moved on,
and change is *needed*. Only you can see to that.'

John gave him a hard look. 'I don't know…' he said
slowly. 'I never thought—not for one moment—of ever
living in Yorkshire again.'

'I beg you to reconsider. It…it would give your life
the direction you said it lacked.'

'You may be right,' said John slowly. He sat in thought
for a moment, then said decisively, 'Thank you for coming, Fenny. I can't answer you at the moment. You must
give me time.' As the lawyer got up to go, the Colonel
added, 'By the way, I'd be obliged if you kept this news
to yourself for the moment. For the past seventeen years
I never acknowledged my connection with the Cover-
dales. The Honourable John Matthew Ancroft, heir to the
Coverdale title, didn't exist as far as the army was concerned. My family history has been my own affair, and,
with very few exceptions, I have not talked to anyone
about it.' He added with a bitter smile, 'Hardly surprising,
is it? So, until I give you the word, I will continue to be
known as plain Colonel Ancroft. Understood?'

'As you wish, my l—Colonel. I am at your disposal.
Will you call in at my chambers at Lincoln's Inn? Or
would you prefer me to come here in a few days' time?
There are business matters to discuss, whatever your de-
cision.' Betts appeared at the door, and the lawyer bowed.
He paused and said, 'My lord—'

'Colonel, Fenny, *Colonel*!'

'Colonel Ancroft, I have known you, as you say, all
your life. I have been proud that the firm of Fennybright
and Turner has continued to serve the Ancroft family with
loyalty and discretion, even during the last seventeen difficult years. I have always looked forward to your return.

Not just to England, but to Yorkshire—to Marrick. That's why I have always kept you informed of events up there. I am not the only one who would be bitterly disappointed not to see you take your proper place.'

John did not reply to this, but said merely, 'See Mr Fennybright out, Betts. Then bring up a bottle of brandy.'

Betts returned after a few minutes, carrying a salver on which was a bottle of brandy and two glasses.

'Two? Are you thinking of joining me, Sergeant?'

'No, sir. Captain Trenchard called while you were with Mr Fennybright. The Captain said he would come back later. Shall I pour out some brandy, Colonel? Or will you wait for the Captain?'

'There's no need to look like that, Betts. If I want a drink now, I'll have one and be damned to you!'

'As you wish, Colonel. Doctor Hulme won't be best pleased, though. He said—'

'I know what the confounded doctor said, Betts! When I want a nanny I'll send for one. Meanwhile, you can do your duty and pour me out a brandy. There's too strong a taste of the past in my gullet. I need to drink to the future, though at the moment I have no idea what it will hold!'

Falmouth, May 1818

At the same time as the Colonel was receiving his law-yer, the landlord of the Green Bank Hotel at Falmouth, three hundred miles to the west, was reverently receiving his latest guest and promising her the best parlour his inn could provide. The inn was a popular one with travellers from the West Indies, but it had seldom seen a more strik-ing, or, what was more to the point, a more clearly wealthy one. The lady was tall, generously built, with hair the colour of burnished chestnuts. Her dark green pelisse was cut with style, and her shoes, gloves and the fall of lace at her throat were all of the highest quality. A dashing hat worn to the side was trimmed with a beautifully curled ostrich plume. She was accompanied by her maid and a retinue of porters carrying a large trunk and numerous bandboxes and valises. Ignoring the curious and admiring glances that followed her, the lady walked with perfect self-possession through the hallway, up the stairs and into the parlour.

The landlord watched anxiously as her green eyes passed over the room, and breathed a sigh of relief when she sank gracefully into the settle by the empty fireplace. Her voice when she spoke was perfectly modulated—warm, husky, with an unmistakable air of authority.

'Thank you, landlord. A fire, please, as soon as possible, and then you can show the bedrooms to my servants here. Oh, and send up a bottle of brandy, if you please.'

'Brandy, ma'am?'

She surveyed him coolly. 'That was what I said, I believe. Your best.'

For a few moments all was bustle—the servants from the inn made up the fire, stored boxes and cases in the bedrooms under the guidance of the lady's maid, while the lady herself took off her hat and pelisse and settled by the hearth.

Presently the travellers were left to themselves, and the lady's maid, a buxom lady in her late forties, was back in the parlour with her mistress. A second servant who had just appeared, a man a few years older than the maid, was standing in silence by the door. Burly, thickset, with powerful shoulders and a decidedly pugnacious air, it would have been hard to decide what his role in the household was. He had none of the polish of a footman or major-domo, but at the same time appeared to be more at ease in the parlour with the two women than any ordinary groom would have been. There was nothing remotely servile in his manner.

The maid bustled about the room like a small whirlwind, scolding all the while.

'No wonder that landlord stared, Miss Caro! Sending for a bottle of brandy! You're in England now, miss, and proper ladies in England don't drink brandy. Not unless they're ill.'

The lady laughed. '*Proper* ladies don't in Jamaica, either, Maggie. What makes you think I should become proper just because I've crossed the Atlantic? Don't be such a killjoy! We've arrived! I want to celebrate!' She jumped up, spread her arms wide and laughed again. Then she said to the man at the door, 'Bring two more glasses over here, Joseph. We'll all celebrate!'

As she poured out the brandy she looked at her companions and said, '*Smile*, you two! Here we are in England at last, and my villainous cousin and his men have been left behind, four thousand miles away on the other side of the Atlantic! There isn't another boat for two weeks. We're safe!'

Maggie shook her head. 'We've not finished our journey yet, not by a long chalk. They were telling me on the ship that it's three hundred miles to London, and we've a long way to go after that.'

'Yes, yes, I know. But the roads must be better over here. I believe the mails can reach London from here in less than three days, so even travelling at a comfortable pace it shouldn't take us more than a week. Joseph, drink up! You must set about hiring a suitable carriage and horses for us. A post chaise, I believe it's called. If there isn't one to be had here, try the King's Arms.'

'*Hiring* a carriage, Miss Caro?'

'Yes. We must get to London as soon as we can. Once we are there we can take the time to look for our own equipage. I have my directions, Joseph! Off you go!' Joseph turned. 'Wait! I almost forgot. There's something else. Take this letter to a Mr Trewarthen at the address on the envelope. If the lawyer back in Jamaica has done his job properly, there'll be money to pay our shot here and have something in hand.'

'Will that be all now, Miss Caro?'

'Of course. And, Joseph! I'd like to set off tomorrow, so do what you can.' The man nodded and went out and the lady turned to her maid. 'Maggie, you can go along to the bedroom to pack a couple of the bags with clothes for a week. Leave the trunk and the rest of the luggage locked. We won't need them on the journey. I shall keep the small case with me, as usual.' She gave her maid a sharp look. 'What the devil's wrong with you, Maggie? Do cheer up! Aren't you pleased to be back in your native land again?'

'This isn't my native land, Miss Caro! This is Cornwall. I was born in Derbyshire! And it's over thirty years since I left England. I'm not sure whether I'm pleased or sorry to be back.' She rallied and said in her former scolding tone, 'But one thing I *am* sure of—and that is that you'd better watch your language when you're in England. No ''confoundeds'' or ''devils'', if you please! And none of the scandalous words you picked up in New Orleans, either! You don't want to set people's backs up, the way you did in Kingston. You haven't got your grandfather now to silence the critics.'

The lady's face changed. 'No,' she said briefly. 'No, I

haven't. Very well, Maggie. I know you mean well, and I'll try, I'll try. Don't say any more. Go and deal with the luggage.'

When the maid had gone out, the life and vitality drained from Caroline Duval's face. She sank onto the settle and leaned back, closing her eyes. After a moment she rallied and murmured, 'My apologies, Grandfather! A moment of weakness, I'm afraid. But don't worry. I'm doing my best. I don't intend to let you down.'

She got up purposefully, walked over to the door and locked it. Then she went to the table, and pulled towards her a worn leather case something like a small hatbox. She opened it, using a key that hung on a chain round her neck. At first sight the contents consisted of two very stylish headdresses, frivolous confections of net, lace and feathers. These she put to one side. Then she took out two sealed envelopes. And then, very carefully, she lifted out a leather pouch that had lain hidden on a bed of soft wool underneath. She opened it, unwound a length of fine linen, then slowly held up a richly jewelled cup, a chalice. It was not large—a mere five or six inches tall—but when it caught the light from the window streaks of blue, red and green fire flashed out from it, almost hurting her eyes with the intensity of their light. She gazed at it for a moment, marvelling again at its beauty, its air of mystery. The cup was old and very beautiful. It had been an object of veneration for centuries. And now, after an absence of over sixty years, it was on its way back to where it belonged...

Then she gave a sigh and, after removing a small purse which lay at the bottom of the case, carefully re-wrapped the treasure and set it back in its nest. The envelopes and hats were replaced, the case securely locked, and the purse slipped inside her reticule. Then she unlocked the door and sat down again to wait for Joseph's return. The first stage in the fulfilment of her beloved grandfather's last orders had been achieved. She had brought the Ainderby Chalice back to England, as Peter Leyburn had wished.

Now for the second stage, the journey to London and a place called Lincoln's Inn, where she was to look for the chambers of Fennybright and Turner. One of the partners, Samuel Turner, was the son of an old friend and ally of her grandfather. He would help her with the third and most difficult stage—the safe restoration of the chalice to its former home in the wilds of Yorkshire.

Chapter Two

Joseph returned after half an hour and reported that a well-sprung post chaise would be waiting for them at whatever time they chose to leave the next morning.

'Good! You've done well, Joseph. What's this?' 'This' was a note from Mr Trewarthen, the lawyer, inviting Mrs Duval to dine with him and his wife that evening.

Caroline frowned. 'Confound it, I shall have to set Maggie to shaking out one of my evening dresses! I hoped not to have to unpack them! But I'll have to go—it would be uncivil not to. Tell her, would you, Joseph?'

'Aye. And then I'll take a walk round the town, Miss Caro. I might hear a thing or two.'

'Such as what?'

'Where the villains are—there's always one or two. They're not all at home in Jamaica, missy. And there was a character outside this inn when I came back… I'll just take a little stroll.'

'You think it necessary?'

'That's what I'm here for, isn't it? To look after you?'

'And I'm glad of it.' Caro Duval smiled warmly at the man. 'After all, it's what you've done most of my life.'

'Aye, nigh on. I'll see Maggie, shall I?'

'Yes, do that, Joseph. Tell her I'll be along in a few minutes.'

Joseph left and Caroline turned her attention to what she should wear that evening. Though it was only an invitation to dine from a small country town lawyer, it would be her first encounter with society in England, and she was not yet sure of the local customs. Would the Trewarthens be shocked if they saw she was not in mourning for her grandfather? Then, with a totally characteristic toss of her chestnut locks, she laughed and said, 'Oh, devil take it! I'll wear whatever comes out first!'

In the event Caroline tried after all to conform to notions of propriety. The dress she wore to the Trewarthens' dinner party was of plain white silk. True, it had been imported from Paris just a few months before, and was somewhat daringly cut, but then so were most of her dresses for the evening. Maggie produced a shawl of black lace which she draped carefully round Caroline's neck and shoulders. But when she stood back, she frowned.

'I'm not sure that's any better,' she said doubtfully. She was right. Caroline's shapely form and creamy skin were enhanced rather than concealed by the lace.

'Stop fussing, Maggie! I haven't anything more suitable. And what does it matter anyway? I shall never see these people again.'

'All the same, Miss Caro. You behave properly! There's no point in offending people unnecessarily. Not here in England.'

Mindful of Maggie's words, Caroline kept her manner and her conversation polite to the point of insipidity that evening. The company was naturally curious about her life in Jamaica, and she answered their questions as best she could, though she was sometimes forced to use discretion rather than strict truth.

It wasn't always easy, for she and her grandfather had behaved pretty much as they chose in their little world on Jamaica. Those ladies on the island who regarded themselves as the arbiters of taste and behaviour might disapprove of the Leyburns, but they knew better than to be critical in public. Peter Leyburn's position as one of the island's foremost citizens was secure. It was based not only on a huge personal fortune, but even more on his connection through his wife, Caroline's grandmother, with the Willoughbys, one of the oldest and most respected families in the West Indies. It would be brave, not to say foolhardy, to risk antagonising someone so influential, and no wife or mother with the interests of her family at heart would risk it.

Without her grandfather's support and protection Caroline would have been much less fortunately placed. Always beautiful, high-spirited and strong willed, she had committed the ultimate social sin of running away with a handsome adventurer at the age of seventeen. She had returned a penniless widow just eighteen months later. There was talk of scandalous company she had kept in New Orleans—but this was never confirmed, and Caroline never spoke of it herself.

The ladies of Kingston would have ostracised Caroline Duval from decent society forever if they had dared, but Peter Leyburn, proud of his granddaughter's stubborn refusal to let the episode break her spirit, saw to it that she was once again accepted by the world as his granddaughter and heir, and the ladies were eventually forced to give in. However, they neither forgave nor truly welcomed Caroline. In their opinion she was too bold, too unrepentant…and far too attractive. What eligible young man would look twice at their own carefully brought up daughters when Caro Duval was there with her slow smile, her air of mystery, her graceful, swaying walk and the hint of danger in her green, green eyes? And they were right. Most of the men in Kingston, eligible or not, had sooner or later fallen victim to Caro Duval's spell.

Nothing of this featured in Caroline's account to the Trewarthens' guests of life on the island of Jamaica. In reply to their eager questions, the history of the island, its agreeable climate, the beauty of its mountains were all carefully described. Even the liveliness of its social life was briefly given its due. But no mention was made of Caroline's own determination to ignore the gossip, to maintain a pose of mocking indifference to sly snubs and cold sideways looks from the ladies. She had only laughed when she heard them calling her the Widow Duval behind her back, and though she was sometimes forced to put gentlemen, who should have known better, back in their place, she never lost her temper.

In truth, her looks and manner were deceptive. After that first mad escapade, she had never felt the slightest temptation to stray. She had fallen in love once, and the lesson had been short, swift and severe. It had been enough to cure her for life. Behind the charming façade, the delightful laugh, the challenge in her green eyes, lay a cynical scorn for most of society. Her adored grandfather had been the only man in the world for whom she had any real respect. With very few exceptions, she regarded all other men as fools or knaves.

But none of this showed in her manner at the Trewarthens. As she returned to the inn, accompanied as ever by the faithful Joseph, she congratulated herself on behaving exactly as a stranger, a widow and newcomer to

England would be expected to behave—with modesty, decorum and courtesy.

She would have been surprised and, being Caroline, highly amused, if she had heard the conversation which took place afterwards in the Trewarthens' bedchamber.

'A very fine woman!' said Mr Trewarthen. 'A real lady and very well informed. I found her account of Jamaica most interesting.'

Mrs Trewarthen sniffed. 'You are mistaken, Mr Trewarthen! In my opinion that woman is a hussy if ever I saw one! Did you see the neckline of that dress? Why, half an inch lower and you could have seen down to her waist!'

'Oh, come! You exaggerate, Mrs Trewarthen! Mrs Duval is certainly…er…well endowed, but the dress was perfectly modest.'

'I dare say you have a better idea of that than I have,' said Mrs Trewarthen tartly. 'You didn't seem able to keep your eyes off it. But her hair, too! You must agree that her hair is a most extraordinary colour. It has to be dyed!'

'You are not usually so uncharitable, my dear,' said Mr Trewarthen mildly. 'I thought her manners and appearance perfectly ladylike. Whatever has she done to offend you?'

Mrs Trewarthen stopped and thought. Then she said slowly, 'Nothing, I suppose. She was polite enough. But there's something about her. I didn't like her. It was as if…as if she was secretly laughing at us all.'

'You are talking nonsense, Henrietta! Mrs Duval is a widow who has just lost her grandfather, and is over here on the mournful task of carrying out his last wishes. She never met us before tonight. How could she *possibly* be laughing at us?' He looked at his wife sternly. 'I think we should stop this. It is not for us to criticise or question the affairs of a valued client. Mr Peter Leyburn's letter asked us to assist his granddaughter in any way we can, and that is what I have tried to do. Now, shall we go to bed, my love?'

The next morning the party from Jamaica was all set and ready to go at an early hour. Before following Maggie into the carriage, Caroline had a word with Joseph.

'Do we need so many men? Driver, postilions *and* a groom?'

'I thought it best, Miss Caro. We have to cross Bodmin Moor, and they say that's a terrible lonely road. Too many men is better than too few, to my way of thinkin'.'

'You're being very cautious, Joseph. Are you suspicious? What about the man you saw last night? Have you seen him again?'

'I can't say I have, Miss Caro. But all the same…'

'All the same, what?'

'I think someone was keeping an eye on me down at the stables.'

'Oh, come! Who could it possibly be? I'm quite positive that none of the other passengers on the boat was in league with my dear cousin Edmund. Respectable people, the lot of them. And Edmund himself, and all his men, were left behind in Jamaica. We saw them standing on the quay as the boat left Kingston.'

'That fellow Trewarthen knew you would be coming,' said Joseph obstinately. 'Why couldn't someone else have been forewarned, too?'

Caroline stared at him for a moment. Then she shook her head. 'I don't believe Mr Trewarthen has been indiscreet. And anything else would mean that Edmund had unbelievable foresight. No! I cannot think that is so. You're being over-cautious, Joseph.'

Joseph was persistent. 'Well, what about the crew of the ship we came on? Shall I ask around at the quay? If one o' them wanted to follow us, he'd have to leave the ship. Someone might know—'

'We haven't time,' said Caroline firmly. 'I wish to be in London as soon as possible. In any case I think it would be a waste of effort. No, don't argue! It's highly unlikely that we are being followed, and I intend to set off straight away. This carriage is so heavily laden we shall have difficulty in keeping up anything like a decent pace. Help me in, then on to the box with you.'

The carriage lumbered out of the yard of the inn and on to the high road. Caroline sat back and breathed a sigh of relief. They were on their way. Five or six days and they would be in London.

But progress on the journey was slow. The roads in this part of the West Country were not particularly good, and though the coach was comfortable it was not built for speed. By the time they were crossing Bodmin Moor they were all weary, and Caroline began to long for a warm fire, a good meal and a comfortable bed. She decided to abandon her intention of making for Launceston, and when the driver drew up at a small posting inn, she got out and inspected it. She was reassured to see this was a stopping place for the mail coach, so the place must be respectable. It had a good menu and several rooms. The inn, small as it was, would do.

'Don't bother changing the horses! We'll stay here for the night,' she said with decision.

Joseph looked doubtful. 'It's a lonely place, this. Better to stay in a town, Miss Caro.'

'It can't be all that bad if the mail calls here,' said Caroline impatiently. 'We all need a rest, Joseph. Maggie

has a bad head, and I am stiff and tired myself. I see that
there's a good stable behind the inn with accommodation
for postboys and grooms. We'll leave the trunk and valises in the coach—they'll be safe enough with you and
the men sleeping above—and with an early start tomorrow we can easily make up the distance. Maggie will tell
you which bags to bring in.' Refusing to listen to any
further protests, she entered the inn.

The landlord and his wife were obviously respectable,
with rosy, country faces and smiles for their unexpected
windfall. There were no other guests, and Caroline was
shown two rooms that were cramped, but clean. After a
moderate meal and a glass of excellent brandy she retired
for the night and the rest of the party did the same.

But in the early hours of the morning they were all
woken by shouts and the sound of scuffles in the stable
yard. Caroline jumped out of bed and opened her door.
Maggie was on the landing with the landlady. The lamp
in the landlady's hand revealed a face full of distress.

'Oh, ma'am! I don't know how to tell you, that I don't!
It's never happened before, I swear! Not like this. Them
villains off the moor—you never know what they'll do
next, and that's a fact!'

'What is it? What has happened?'

'Your carriage, ma'am! It's been broken into! All your
lovely things—all thrown everywhere, all over the yard.
Oh, ma'am!'

'What? Maggie, fetch Joseph!'

'Your man is already there, ma'am. He gave the alarm.'

Caroline put on some clothes and hurried down. The
landlord, looking as distressed as his wife, led her through
to the yard. She stopped in shock. Every trunk and valise
had been taken out of the carriage and their contents

strewn over the yard. Dresses, shifts, stays, fans, shoes, shawls lay in the dirt and dust in hopeless confusion.

'It's that Burnett family, ma'am,' said the landlord grimly. 'I helped to get one o' 'em transported last year and they've borne a grudge ever since. This is their revenge, I suppose.'

'Are you sure?' asked Joseph.

The landlord nodded. 'I'm sure,' he said. 'Who else would do such a thing? Wanton destruction, that's what it is.' He looked at Caroline. 'What can I do to put things right, ma'am?'

Caroline was looking at the mess with growing anger. 'I take it that the culprits are well away? Have you sent anyone after them?'

'I have. But once they're on the moor it's not easy to find them. It might take a week or two. But we'll catch them, though, sooner or later and when we do…'

'I trust they'll be adequately punished. But I don't have time to wait to see it, landlord. Meanwhile…'

'What shall I do about this?' He turned to look at the mess in the stable yard, and burst out, 'Dang it, if I had those miscreants in front o' me now…' He smacked one fist into the other in fury.

Caroline felt much the same, but said briskly 'You can tell your people to gather my garments up out of public view, as quickly as possible, then have them brought to my room. My own maid will sort out what can be saved. The rest can go on the rubbish heap. Come, Maggie! Goodnight.' Caroline was so angry she could not have said another word. The clothes were not important, but the thought of strangers, rough men, having handled them was intolerable. She would probably throw most of them away. The inconvenience and delay would be considerable. Why on *earth* had she not followed Joseph's advice and stuck to staying in the towns?

By the time dawn was breaking Caroline and Maggie had put aside those garments that could be laundered, and had rejected most of the rest. A number of delicate things, such as fans, sandals and parasols, had been so trampled on in the fight that they were ruined. Fortunately she still had the contents of the valises they had brought into their rooms with them, so they were not totally without a change of clothing.

'Well, this is a fine welcome to England, I must say!' said Maggie as they sat down, exhausted, to take some refreshment provided by an anxious landlady. 'What shall we do now?'

Caroline drew a breath. 'The people here can appease their consciences by washing and pressing this lot,' she said, touching one bundle with her foot. 'They can do what they like with the rest.'

'But, Miss Caro! Are you going to wait here until that's all done? I thought you wanted to be in London before the week was out?'

'I do. We shall leave this morning as planned. As soon as the clothes have been properly dealt with, the landlord can put them in my trunk and send it all by carrier to London. It shouldn't take very long. The trunk will probably arrive before I've completed my arrangements with Mr Turner. Don't look so doubtful, Maggie. We can always buy new things if necessary. Now, finish your chocolate—it's time we were off!'

The landlord was only too glad to promise whatever Mrs Duval wished, and by eight o'clock they were on their way again.

* * *

In spite of the landlord's belief that the attack had been prompted by his enemies, the experience at the inn had made them cautious. They decided only to travel in daylight, and always to stay in large towns. The roads improved as they drove towards the capital, and though Joseph still kept a close watch he saw nothing to worry him. As they pulled up at the Star and Garter in Andover on the next to last night of their journey, Caroline was in better spirits. Hounslow, where they were to spend the following night, was the largest coaching centre in England and only ten miles from London. She would soon make the acquaintance of Samuel Turner, and some of the burden of this long journey would be taken from her.

But Joseph returned with a long face from a walk round the town. 'I can't swear to it, Miss Caro, but it's my opinion there's a character in town I've seen before.'

'When? Where?'

'On the quay at Falmouth. I think I saw him the night the carriage was broken into, too.'

'So you think the landlord was wrong? It wasn't the Burnett gang?'

'I never thought it was. No use saying anything, though. No evidence.'

'Joseph, what do you think we should do?'

'Well... The road isn't the best for us. There's a bit of a deserted stretch just before we get to Hounslow. Three or four miles of it and it's lonely. They say here it's the haunt of highwaymen.'

'It's not highwaymen I'm afraid of! But surely the road is busier than the roads in Cornwall? And if we take care to use it in daylight?'

'Aye. We'll do that. But we'd best take a few other precautions. I'll have my pistols close at hand.'

'I'll make sure mine are within reach, too, but don't

tell Maggie. I don't want to listen to another of her lectures on what is ladylike. And there's something else I shall do, too... Right, Joseph. Now for a good dinner, a night's sleep and an early start.'

They reached the edge of Hounslow Heath by late afternoon when it was still quite light. Caroline took heart. The road led in a reasonably straight line across bracken-clad heathland. Surely nothing could happen here! But they had hardly gone a mile when she heard Joseph give a warning shout and when she looked out she saw a band of six or seven mounted men thundering up behind them. They swept past, there was the sound of shots, and the carriage came to a sudden halt. The doors on each side were flung open and two men jumped in. It all happened so quickly that there was no time to get out her pistol to defend herself.

'There's the case!' said one of the men. 'Get it!'

One of the men made a lunge for the leather case that never left Caroline's side. She kicked out at him and he gave a shout of pain as he lost his balance and fell through the open door. 'Joseph!' she yelled. 'Where are you? Come and help me! *Merde, alors!* Where are the *confounded* men I hired?'

The second villain made to snatch the case from her arms. Maggie dragged him back valiantly, but he turned and slapped her and she fell back with a cry on to the seat.

'Maggie! Maggie, are you all right? Where the *hell* are those men?' Caroline turned on Maggie's attacker, but this time he was ready. He gave her a violent chop on the forearm and she involuntarily released her grasp on the case. In a flash he had snatched it up and had disappeared out of the carriage. Caroline scrambled out after him, but she was too late. Her attacker had thrown the leather case up to one of his accomplices and was already mounting his horse.

'Right! Away! Let's be off before anyone comes! We have what we want,' he called. In a flash they were all away over the heath. She turned to urge someone to follow, but saw Joseph sitting on the ground swearing, while the groom bound up his arm with a rather dirty handkerchief.

'Joseph!' Caroline ran to her servant's side. 'What's wrong?'

'My arm, missy! They got me in the arm.'

'He didn't ought t'have tried to stop them,' said one of the postboys gloomily. 'Always best to let 'em 'ave wot they want. They don't hurt you then. He shot one o' 'em, y'see. Winged 'im. That made the others real angry and they shot back.'

'Give me your kerchief! Come on, hand it over!' She passed it to the groom, who added it to the bandage on Joseph's arm. 'Why the devil didn't you come when I called?' she went on. 'And why didn't anyone chase after those men? What did we hire you for?'

'Beggin' your pardon, ma'am. We're just postboys. We're not bloomin' 'eroes. We wouldn't last long if we objected to all the coves trying to make a dishonest livin' on the 'igh road. It's company policy to stand aside, see? If you want protection, you travel with the mail!'

Caroline looked at them, seeing them properly for the first time. In spite of their name, there wasn't a boy among them. Wizened old men, the lot of them. Even the groom. She and Joseph had made a serious mistake.

'Can you get into the carriage, Joseph? You must see a surgeon. I suppose there's one in Hounslow?' she said, turning to the men. They nodded rather doubtfully.

'Right, then we'll set off again. Don't look so worried! Those men won't be back. They've taken what they wanted.'

Joseph, looking ghastly, was helped into the carriage, and in a short while they were travelling on towards Hounslow. Maggie had fully recovered, but Joseph lay back against the squabs, his lips tightly compressed. Blood was seeping through the makeshift bandage the groom had applied, in spite of all Maggie's attempts to stem it with more cloths.

Caroline drew the folds of her cloak around her and shivered. Edmund must have an accomplice on this side of the Atlantic. Those men were no ordinary bandits. They had taken nothing but the leather case. And Joseph, her old friend and staunch protector, had been injured, perhaps badly. Her heart stopped for a moment. Joseph mustn't die! Not Joseph! She leaned forward and put her hand on his knee. He opened his eyes and nodded faintly.

'Nothing fatal, missy. Don't worry.' Then he shut his eyes again.

Caroline was not reassured. As they drew into Hounslow she was desperately considering what she should do.

Hounslow was noisy, chaotic and, apart from coaching requirements, had very limited resources. The place consisted of a large number of posting inns strung along the road and little else. But the groom proved himself of some use by finding them rooms in one of the quieter places, run by a Mrs Hopkins, a widow whose heart was as large as her anatomy. She instantly took them under her wing.

'That poor man!' she said, gazing at Joseph. 'Fancy being attacked like that in broad daylight! I can't understand it!'

'I was hoping to find a surgeon,' said Caroline. 'I think the bullet is still lodged in his arm.'

'You won't find that here!' said Mrs Hopkins roundly. 'There isn't a surgeon in Hounslow I'd trust with my dog! Drunken sots, the lot o' 'em. If you'll take my advice, you'll take him to London.'

Joseph had been put to bed in one of the ground floor rooms and the groom was in the process of re-binding the arm when Caroline went in.

'I've stopped the bleeding for the moment, ma'am,' he said. 'But he needs a surgeon. The bullet is still there.'

'Could he travel? I'd like to take him to London.'

'Tomorrow? Yes.'

'Then would you please reserve places for three on the first coach to leave Hounslow in the morning? Ask Mrs Hopkins if you can book them in her name.'

'That'll be the Bristol Mail. I'll do my best, ma'am.'

As soon as the groom left Joseph woke and tried to sit up. 'I don't need a surgeon!'

She pushed him back against the pillows. 'Don't be a fool, Joseph. Of course you do!' She looked at him remorsefully. 'I owe you an apology. You were right.'

'It's not for you to say anything, Miss Caro. The master trusted me to get you and that case safely to Yorkshire. And I failed at the first hurdle!' Joseph turned his head away.

'No, no! You haven't failed! We're not dead yet!' Caroline leaned forward and whispered. 'They didn't get what they wanted.'

'You needn't try to comfort me! I saw them riding away with it!'

Caroline smiled mischievously. 'They took the case. And they took what was in it. Two hats, and a pewter tankard from the Star and Garter at Andover. I don't think they'll be happy with any of those, do you?'

'Is that right?' Joseph's worn face broke into a grin. 'Where's the other?'

'Well, Joseph, haven't you noticed? Look at me!'

She stood up and removed the large shawl she had been wearing. In spite of his discomfort Joseph began to laugh. 'Miss Caro! What a lass you are!'

Caroline appeared to have changed overnight. The face was the same, but her shapely figure and slender waist had quite disappeared. The lady who stood before Joseph looked ten years older and three or four stone heavier.

'How did you do it?'

'Petticoats—Maggie's, as well as my own. And part of the bedding from Andover. I left a very handsome tip for the landlady there. You needn't worry, Joseph. My grandfather's bequest is safer than ever.' She patted her middle.

'What happens when they find out?'

'That will take some time. The case was locked, and I doubt the men who stole it will stop to open it before they hand it over. By that time I hope we shall be safely hidden in London.'

'You must go on without me, Miss Caro. Take one of the mails that pass through here. Go tomorrow. Find Mr Turner.' Joseph had been sitting up again, speaking feverishly, but now he slumped back. 'But who'll look after you?' he groaned.

'Don't think for one moment that I shall leave you here. We'll all go together. Listen to what I've decided...'

The groom had done well. He had managed somehow or other to book the places Caroline had asked for and early the following morning she joined the overnight mail from Bristol to London. No one could have recognised the elegant creature who had arrived at Falmouth six days before in the stout lady who, together with her 'sister' and 'brother-in-law', was to attend a funeral in London. The morning was chilly and all three were well wrapped up. Caroline was dressed in a voluminous black cloak, her glorious hair hidden under a cap and bonnet, all acquired from Mrs Hopkins. Joseph was wearing a black coat that had belonged to the late Mr Hopkins, his arm easily accommodated in its ample width, and Maggie had managed to find a cloak in her own luggage which was suitably drab. No one in the stable yard took the slightest bit of notice of them as they left.

Just over two hours later they were in the Swan with Two Necks in the centre of London. Caroline saw Joseph comfortably settled with Maggie in charge, then she sat down to write a message to the lawyer. She sealed it and gave it to one of the grooms to take to Mr Turner in the chambers of Fennybright and Turner at Lincoln's Inn as quickly as possible.

They had barely finished breakfast when Mr Turner appeared. After introducing himself, he said, 'All is arranged as you asked, Mrs Duval. A room is being prepared for your man in my own house. The chaise waiting below will take him there immediately, and a surgeon will call on him as soon as it arrives.'

'You're very kind, sir. Maggie, you go with Joseph.' She went over to Joseph and took his hand. 'I shall follow very soon. I have to explain things to Mr Turner before I leave the inn, but Maggie will take good care of you.'

After Joseph and Maggie had gone Caroline turned to the lawyer. 'First I must give you a letter from my grandfather. May I ask you to read it?'

Peter Leyburn first thanked the lawyer formally for his services since taking over from his father ten years before. He then went on,

'You may sometimes have asked yourself how I came to know your father. We met in Yorkshire many years ago, long before I came to Jamaica. He knew my history, he knew my real name—which is not Leyburn. In return for a small favour I once did him he kept my secrets and gave me help whenever I needed it. I think you could say we were friends. But he is dead and I am now dying…

In the past ten years I have found you to be as trustworthy and as discreet as your father, Samuel, so I am asking for your help in paying one final debt. My granddaughter has agreed to take my last bequest to my family home in Yorkshire. I did them a great wrong, and am now doing my utmost to put it right.

Caroline is a courageous and resourceful woman, and Joseph Bellerby a loyal servant. He will protect her to the death. But England is strange to her, and the journey to Yorkshire is a long one. I ask you to see that she has everything she needs. I cannot think there is any real danger, but if she needs extra servants, extra guards, then make sure she has them.

I know my granddaughter. She understands how important it is to me that what she has is delivered safely to Yorkshire. You see? I will not even now write down the true nature of what she carries, nor its exact destination. Only she knows that. You, and anyone else who is curious, may call it my "remains", for it is all I have left to do in this life.

Do this and you will earn my eternal gratitude— wherever I am. I rather think my ultimate destination is not a happy one. But perhaps if Caroline succeeds

in her task there may be some hope of intercession
for me.

You will also earn a large sum of money, which
has been set aside for the purpose. Otherwise, apart
from one or two trivial sums, Caroline has inherited
everything. I leave her affairs in your care. If she
marries, her husband will take over from you. But
since I doubt that my granddaughter will ever risk a
second marriage, your commission may prove to be
a long one.

Look after her, Samuel. In memory of your father,
if not of me. With my thanks and my regards,

    Peter Leyburn'

The lawyer laid down the letter. 'Your grandfather pays
me a great compliment.'

'I think it may prove to be a great burden!' said Caroline with a wry smile. 'Especially in view of what has
happened.'

'No, I assure you. I regard it a privilege to help you in
any way I can. Your grandfather's "small favour" saved
my father from ruin. I could never repay that debt.'

Caroline nodded, then went on. 'I'm afraid he was mistaken in one thing—there *is* danger.' She got up. 'Mr
Turner, I would like to tell you more about this, but these
are not very suitable surroundings, and I'm worried about
my servant Joseph. His injury was caused by men who
are determined to stop me from carrying out my grandfather's wishes. So far they've been on our track wherever
we've gone. I *must not* be seen leaving this inn in your
company. My disguise was good enough for an early
morning coach journey, but not for London in broad daylight.'

'You're disguised?' asked Mr Turner in astonishment.

Caroline stared at him, then burst into laughter. 'It must be better than I thought! Yes, Mr Turner, I'm in disguise.' Still laughing, she pulled off her bonnet and cap.

'Good God!' Then the lawyer said, covered in confusion, 'Oh, I beg pardon, Mrs Duval! What must you think of me? But... But... The difference!' He gazed in fascination at the riot of chestnut hair tumbling down Caroline's back.

'Good! I seem to have succeeded. So, if you agree, we shall now part company. If you permit me, I shall call at your house to see Joseph. Can you warn your people to expect me?'

'Of course,' said Mr Turner, still looking slightly stunned. 'I'll send a boy to Mrs Turner immediately. She will be delighted to welcome you.' He looked doubtfully at Caroline's hair.

'Ask her to expect a Mrs Hopkins. And never fear! I'll tidy myself and be back in disguise before I venture out. May I call on you at your chambers this afternoon? "Mrs Hopkins" will come to consult you about her husband's estate.'

'Of course. Is there anything else I can do?'

Caroline grew sober. 'I can see that you are somewhat overwhelmed, Mr Turner. Perhaps you even think me mad to act like this?'

'No, no! I am sure you have the best of reasons...'

'I assure you I have. Those men on Hounslow Heath weren't ordinary thieves. They knew what they were looking for, and it's only by the merest chance that they didn't get it.'

'Then I'll help you all I can. Shall we say three this afternoon?'

'Three o'clock it is. Mrs Hopkins, remember. I'll tell you more then about the man who is trying to prevent me from reaching Yorkshire. If you could meanwhile think of a way in which I could go north with adequate protection, I should be most grateful. Joseph's arm will, I fear, take some time to heal.'

Mr Turner took his leave of this extraordinary client and returned to his chambers. After sending a message to his wife, he sat down to ponder. This was a strange co-incidence! His partner, Edward Fennybright, was at this very moment strongly urging John Ancroft, the new Marquess of Coverdale, and another of the firm's most important clients, to take up his duties in Yorkshire. If he succeeded, then there would an escort for Peter Leyburn's granddaughter that could hardly be bettered... Colonel Ancroft was one of the Duke of Wellington's aides, and a notably brave and resourceful officer. He pulled a face. He was now also a peer of the realm, a Marquess, with huge estates in the north of England. How on earth could one persuade such a man to take on an escort's duties? The idea was preposterous...

But after his interview with Caroline that afternoon he decided that he would try. Without wishing to go an inch beyond a perfectly professional relationship, he had found her totally captivating. She was as her grandfather had described her—resourceful and courageous. And, with him at least, she had been frank. He had not been put off by an undercurrent of cynical amusement in her conversation. He had seen her concern for Joseph Bellerby, and heard the change in her voice when she talked of her grandfather.

But from her account of the events since her grandfather's death there was real danger in her mission. It would not be long before this cousin of hers made his way over to England to join his accomplices. From all accounts he was determined to capture whatever it was Caroline Duval was carrying. She would need all the protection he could find for her on her journey up the Great North Road.

In the meantime, she would need somewhere safe to stay until Joseph Bellerby could travel, somewhere not far away, but outside London, perhaps. There was a house in Barnet…

Chapter Three

'Have you gone mad, Fenny? It's quite out of the question. The journey to Marrick would be tedious enough without adding a sorrowing widow to the party. What the devil are you thinking of?'

Mr Fennybright sighed. Colonel Ancroft's reaction to Sam Turner's suggestion was very much as he had predicted. 'I beg pardon, Colonel. I should never have mentioned it, and indeed would not have done if Mr Turner had not been so concerned for the lady.'

'Who is she, anyway?'

'At the moment she is known as Mrs Hopkins,' said Mr Fennybright carefully.

'"Known as"? "At the moment"? What does *that* mean?'

'It is for her own protection. The lady is under some threat. She…she believes she is being pursued.'

'Worse and worse! A *nervous* sorrowing widow!'

'It is true that her own groom was shot on their road to London.'

Colonel Ancroft stared at him and said slowly, 'So she has some reason to be anxious. Is he dead?'

'No, but badly injured. She is waiting for him to recover a little before she takes the road north. She is determined to take him with her.'

'I don't believe it! You are actually asking me to undertake a journey of over two hundred miles, which you know I'm reluctant enough to take, in the company of a nervous widow and a fellow who hasn't the sense to avoid being shot by some highwayman or other. Is that it?'

'The lady has a maidservant, too, of course...' said Mr Fennybright, scrupulously exact as ever.

'What is wrong with the maid? Smallpox?'

'You are pleased to jest, my lor—Colonel. As far as I know there is nothing wrong with the maid. And Joseph Bellerby, the groom—'

Colonel Ancroft sat up. '*What* did you call him?'

'Joseph Bellerby, Colonel.'

'Bellerby... The Bellerbys were a large family on the Marrick estate—and it's not all that common a name. Tell me, why does the mysterious Mrs Hopkins wish to travel north?'

'I concluded from the little Mr Turner told me that she is taking her husband's remains to the family home.'

Colonel Ancroft regarded him sardonically. 'This gets better and better! A nervous widow, a wounded man, a maid with smallpox—oh, no, the maid is perfectly fit—and now a corpse! What devilish rigmarole *is* all this?'

'There's no corpse, my l—Colonel. I suppose there must be ashes,' faltered Mr Fennybright, wishing he had never mentioned Sam Turner's wretched client. But he went on bravely, 'The lady is perfectly genuine, and so are her difficulties. I've seldom seen Mr Turner so concerned.'

The Colonel thought for a moment. Then he sighed and said, 'I make no promises. But I'll listen to what Mr Turner has to say.'

*   *   *

In the following meeting Mr Turner used his considerable powers of persuasion. No one who knew dashing Caro Duval would have recognised her in the picture he drew of a nervous, vulnerable woman on a mournful mission, in a strange country, with only an elderly maid and a wounded man for company. He gave the Colonel a most affecting description of the lady's shock when the men she had hired to protect them on the road to London had let her down, and her reluctance now to trust strangers. He ended by appealing, in the most respectful manner possible, to the Colonel's chivalrous instincts as an officer and a gentleman.

Indeed, he was so convincing that Colonel Ancroft found it impossible to refuse him.

'Excellent! You are very kind, Colonel Ancroft.'

'May I now know her real name? And her final destination?'

'Er…as I have told you, my client is convinced that she is in danger. She wishes to keep her assumed name and a measure of disguise, until she is safely outside London.'

'Come, come! My tongue won't wag. Is this theatre really necessary?' said the Colonel impatiently.

'So the lady believes. But in strict confidence, Colonel, she is Mrs Caroline Duval of Kingston, Jamaica. Her goal is somewhere within twenty miles of Richmond in Yorkshire. I am unable to be more accurate—that is as much as I know of her precise destination.'

He saw that the Colonel was beginning to look doubtful once again and hastily added, 'Mrs Duval is the granddaughter of the late Mr Peter Leyburn, who was a highly respected member of Jamaican society and one of my firm's oldest clients. I can vouch for her respectability.'

'Very well, very well. I've said I shall do it and I shall.

I have engagements in London till the middle of July, but wish to leave soon after that.'

'That would suit very well, I am sure. The groom will hardly be fit to travel much before then. Do you wish me to make arrangements for you to meet her? It would need some notice—she is not living in London at the moment.'

'Please do.'

In the event, the Colonel did not meet Mrs Duval till shortly before they were due to leave. But they corresponded—to the satisfaction of neither. The Colonel was happier writing reports or lists of commands to his officers, rather than composing letters to a lady of quality. His style was courteous but stiff, and he found it impossible to avoid a distinct flavour of command. Caroline was anxious not to antagonize someone who had said he was ready to help her, but she found the old-fashioned formality of his tone a rich source of amusement. At the same time the assumption of authority, which it did not disguise, caused some resentment. She said as much to Mr Turner when he visited her in Barnet.

'What a block of wood your Colonel is, Mr Turner! It's quite obvious he has no idea how to handle the female sex! Perhaps I can amuse myself on the journey north by teaching him some graces. He certainly needs them!'

'I am sorry you're disappointed in Colonel Ancroft, ma'am. It's true he has been little in society, but he is a capable man, and one of great courage. Surely in your present situation these qualities are more use to you than an ability to please the ladies?'

'You're right, of course. Still, I suppose his career as a soldier has led him to expect unquestioning acceptance of all his suggestions, too. Well, I'm sorry, but that I cannot do. I've been too used to ordering my own life to leave everything to someone else. He writes to me as if I'm in my dotage, unable even to think for myself.'

'Mrs Duval, please, I beg you to be careful. The Colonel is not an easy man, but that is understandable. He has some consequence in the world, and is used to exercising authority. He will not take kindly to argument. And in order to persuade him to accept your company I had to present you to him as being older, rather more timid, and certainly more helpless than I think you are. Try not to spoil my picture before you have even met him!'

But, try as she might, Caroline was quite incapable of leaving matters completely in the Colonel's hands, however capable he might be. And just as much as she resented his commands, did *he* resent her attempts to interfere.

'Who the devil does the woman think she is, Fenny?' demanded the Colonel. 'Anyone would think *she* was doing *me* the favour! She has already questioned my decision to use my own horses. She doesn't wish to waste any time, if you please! Can't she see that I planned it so for her sake? Has she any idea how demanding it is to be constantly on the move for over two hundred miles? And just as I thought we had agreed on that, she now wishes to know how well sprung my carriage is and what accommodation it provides. She's anxious for her groom. A confounded *groom*! One might have expected a servant to travel in a wagon if he wasn't fit to ride!'

'I understand that the groom has looked after Mrs Duval since she was a child,' said Mr Fennybright soothingly. 'He means a lot to her. Shall I ask Mr Turner to arrange for some other conveyance for the groom?'

'No, there's no need. As it happens, there will be no shortage of room, though she's damned lucky that it is so. I intend to ride most of the way. I hate to be inside when the weather is warm. There'll be enough room in the carriage for luggage, *and* maids *and* grooms—*and* widows, too! At least she has finally stopped questioning the route I intend to take. Tell me, Fenny, was I foxed when I agreed to all this?'

'Mrs Duval was not questioning the route so much as wishing to learn what it was, Colonel Ancroft.'

'Why does she need to know? Confound it, there wasn't a man in my command who would have raised so many questions. I'd have had him in irons if he had! And the obstinate woman still won't tell me where she wishes to finish!'

Some spirit of mischief inspired Caroline to act and dress the part when she and the Colonel finally met. She would have gone in disguise anyway, the chalice, as always, in a specially designed cradle round her middle. But if the Colonel expected an elderly widow, then an elderly widow he would get! Basing her impersonation on a very tiresome woman back home in Jamaica, Caroline walked with the aid of a stick. Under her cap and bonnet her face was half hidden by a fringe of pathetic grey curls. And she practised talking like Mrs Jameson, whose plaintive voice had an irritating habit of fading away at the end of every sentence. When she demonstrated all this to Maggie before they set out to meet the Colonel for the first time, the maid shrieked with laughter. Even Joseph smiled.

'You're wicked, Miss Caro!' Maggie cried. 'That's Mrs Jameson to the life! But it's too much! You won't deceive the Colonel!'

'Oh, yes, I will, Maggie. I know his type. Our Colonel is a man of fixed ideas. He's expecting a tiresome, melancholy, elderly frump, and that's what he'll see. I don't expect to deceive him for long. Even Colonel Ancroft will eventually penetrate my disguise. But I hope that won't be before we are a good few miles along the road to Yorkshire. Now, if you will pass me those spectacles and the veil I'm ready.' Since the spectacles Maggie had acquired for her had such strong lenses that she could hardly see anything at all when wearing them, she slid them into her reticule, ready to put them on just before meeting the Colonel.

But at the last minute they were very nearly overtaken by disaster. Outside the lawyer's chambers Caroline had to lift up her heavy skirts to get out of the carriage. She realised her mistake when she met the boldly appreciative eye of a gentleman standing nearby. She hadn't been able to disguise her ankles! Unusually flustered, she looked away and turned towards the entrance, but a sudden gust of wind blew her veil high into the air. She dropped her stick during the subsequent struggles to put it back in place. Hot and exasperated, she forgot herself so far as to swear roundly in some of the more lurid language she had picked up in New Orleans. Then she called angrily, 'Maggie! Come and fix this damned veil for me!'

Startled out of his lazy appreciation of her charms, the gentleman's jaw dropped and his eyes opened wide. This was too much for Caroline's ever-ready sense of the ridiculous. She started to laugh. When an answering gleam of amusement appeared on his handsome face, she gave him a conspiratorial look, then lowered her veil with a sigh of relief. He wasn't about to denounce her. He picked up the stick, gave it to her with a bow, then went away, still laughing.

Her escape was even narrower than she could have

dreamed. The handsome gentleman was one of Colonel Ancroft's closest friends in London. Captain Lord Trenchard had in fact only just taken his leave of his former commanding officer. But Caroline was undeservedly lucky. Though the Captain had guessed who she was, and what she was doing in that particular spot, he decided for reasons of his own not to unmask her.

After the formalities had been completed inside the lawyer's chambers, Caroline sat with her back to the light and covertly studied Colonel Ancroft. He was not at all what she had imagined. She wondered if London had more than its fair share of interesting men. The one outside had been quite startlingly handsome, and though this man here was not his equal in looks his appearance was very distinguished. In his late thirties, she guessed, with silver wings in his coal-black hair and cool, silver-grey eyes. He was broad-shouldered, if a little thin, but as tall and as upright as her grandfather, and he had the same look about him, too—as if he wouldn't tolerate what her grandfather had called shufflers and shirkers. Indeed, this man's whole aspect was unbendingly severe. A cold man, she guessed, without much humour. *He* wouldn't have laughed at her lapse outside. She sighed. Colonel Ancroft might be younger and better looking than she had imagined, but he didn't look like much of a kindred spirit. The journey was going to be very long!

She had been so busy examining her escort that she had missed some of the conversation, and when she started listening again she was surprised to hear the Colonel say with quite a bite to his voice,

'*Colonel* Ancroft, Mr Turner. *Colonel!*'

So our friend is sensitive about his rank? she thought. Well, well, well! Who would have thought it? There's some fun to be had, after all! She then applied her mind to the discussion and was pleased to see that, though the Colonel might be severe, he appeared to be efficient. When the chance arose, she said tentatively,

'I am so grateful to you for taking so much trouble, Captain Ancroft. You have no idea what a comfort it is to me to have a man in charge. I've been so long alone...' Her voice trailed away and she put a lace handkerchief to her eyes. Then with a little sniff she whispered, 'Thank you so much!'

'Not at all, Mrs...Hopkins. I am...delighted to be of assistance. But if you will forgive me—it is *Colonel* Ancroft. Not Captain.'

'Oh, I'm so sorry! What must you think of me—'

'It is perfectly all right, Mrs...er...Hopkins—'

'No, no! It isn't! I'm so stupid, you see. I have never had much to do with the military. Before my loss I lived a very sheltered life, Captain Ancroft.'

The Colonel looked grim. 'So it would appear, ma'am,' he murmured. He turned abruptly to Caroline's lawyer. 'Well, Turner? Are the details clear? I shall call for Mrs Hopkins on Tuesday at twelve noon. We shall set off as soon as the carriage has been loaded.' He turned to Caroline. 'Unless noon is too early an hour for you, ma'am?'

'Well...' she said doubtfully. 'I think I could be ready. Yes. Twelve noon. On Wednesday.'

'Tuesday, ma'am, Tuesday!'

'Are you sure? I thought you said Wednesday...' Caroline sounded worried, but behind her veil she was grinning.

He controlled his obvious annoyance and said patiently, 'No, it was Tuesday. I shall call for you on Tuesday. But pray do not trouble yourself, Mrs Hopkins. I shall send a groom to Barnet on Monday to remind you.'

'You are very thoughtful,' said Caroline. Then she added kindly, 'Er...I see you do not like addressing me as Mrs Hopkins, Captain Ancroft. Once I feel we are safely clear of London, you may call me Mrs Duval.'

The Colonel had obviously had enough. 'And you, ma'am, may call me Colonel!' he snapped.

In spite of her teasing Caroline was ready for the Colonel the following Tuesday, as, true to form, his carriage drew up at noon precisely. A coachman was on the box, and two grooms sat behind, all in dark green livery. The inside of the carriage was empty, for the Colonel was riding a superb bay with his groom at his side. The Colonel, his carriage and his servants all standing at the gate made an impressive display.

The servants began to load the carriage. Caroline invited Colonel Ancroft into the house to wait. He stopped when he saw Joseph standing by the door.

'I guess this is Joseph Bellerby. Are you fit again, man?'

Joseph held himself as upright as he dared. His arm had become infected and had taken longer than they had expected to heal. Even now it was often more painful than he would admit. But he was as anxious as Caroline to see their mission over. 'Pretty much, Colonel,' he said. 'I think I'd be of some use in a fight.'

'I'm sure you would, Bellerby. But let's hope it doesn't come to that! I should like to hear more from you about the attacks on the road from Falmouth. Are you quite certain it was not just a strange coincidence?'

'As certain as a man may be, sir.'

Colonel Ancroft nodded. Then, seeing Joseph's pallor, he said brusquely, 'Into the carriage with you. My man will see you comfortably installed. We shall speak another time. It's time the loading was finished. Are you ready to start, Mrs…Hopkins?'

'Of course, Captain.' Caroline let a nervous titter escape her. 'Oh, I'm sorry, do forgive me! *Colonel* Ancroft!'

It suited Caroline very well that the Colonel rode alongside. The day was warm and her heavy veil and widow's black outfit, not to mention the padding round her middle, were causing her some discomfort. Once in the carriage with Joseph and Maggie, she took off her veil and the cape she wore over her dress and sat back with a sigh of relief. She looked out of the window. Colonel Ancroft was riding some distance ahead.

'So, Joseph, what do you think of our Colonel Ancroft?' she asked.

'I've not yet seen enough of him to judge, Miss Caro. But he's not a man I'd care to cross. I shouldn't play too many games with him if I were you.'

'Oh, I'm safe enough! Colonel Ancroft has too low an opinion of the female sex and too high an opinion of himself to believe that any woman could make game of him.'

Maggie shook her head. 'I'm not so sure. Joseph's right, Miss Caro! There's more to the Colonel than you think! Those lawyers, even Mr Turner, treated him with a lot of respect. And it's clear that he's a man of wealth. Look at this carriage! Your grandfather didn't have a better one.'

'Aye, and the horses, too,' Joseph added. 'They're prime cattle, every one.'

'That's not to say anything! Kingston was full of men who were rich and flattered by the lawyers, but it didn't mean that they were particularly clever. I've known only one man whom I couldn't take in when I tried, and that was my grandfather. I don't doubt that the Colonel is highly respectable and very worthy, but he's too solemn for my taste. Teasing him is quite irresistible! If only this damned disguise wasn't so uncomfortable!'

'And when are you thinking to discard it?' asked Maggie.

'Tomorrow or the next day. When I've thought of somewhere safe to keep this.' She tapped the bundle round her waist.

'If you'll take my advice, you won't leave it a moment longer than you have to,' Maggie warned. 'That gentleman is by no means as stupid as you think him. You can always tell a man by the way his servants behave, and Colonel Ancroft's servants treat him with great respect. What's more, they like him, too.'

When they stopped at Hatfield, Caroline was surprised to see one of the Colonel's grooms leading his horses away and an ostler from the inn coming out with a different team.

She only just remembered to speak in her adopted voice as she called out, 'What's happening, Colonel Ancroft? I thought you wished to travel with your own horses?'

'I decided that it would make the journey too tedious, Mrs…Hopkins. To use the same horses for every stage would mean long delays. Your man is more fit to travel than I had feared, and, as I understand it, you are in some haste to be in Yorkshire, I believe. We shall use post horses.'

'But this was not what was arranged!'

'Are you now saying that you wish to take four or five days longer than necessary on the road, after all?'

'No. But I wish you had informed me beforehand of your change of mind!'

'Why? What would you have done differently?'

'Why, nothing, I suppose. But I should like to have known in advance, all the same!'

The Colonel regarded her thoughtfully. Then, with a sort of patient indulgence which set Caroline's teeth on edge, he said, 'I apologise. But I really didn't see the necessity. You have asked me to see you safely to York-shire, and that I will do. Why should you be worried with the details? Now, with your permission, we shall continue. I've sent ahead to book rooms at Buckden for the night. We really shouldn't waste any more time.'

Once in the carriage again Caroline sat fuming. It did not pacify her to know that the Colonel was in fact merely doing what she had wanted all along. He had no right to make a change in their plans without telling her. None at all!

'I don't understand, Miss Caro,' said Joseph, observing her obvious annoyance. 'The Colonel has decided to oblige you. Why are you so put out?'

'He should have consulted me first!' said Caroline angrily.

'But what would you have said if he had?' Maggie asked, looking puzzled.

Caroline looked at her two companions, started to speak, stopped, then suddenly laughed. 'Yes, yes, yes. You're quite right, both of you. I'm being unreasonable. All the same…'

'If you don't mind my saying so, Miss Caro, you have only yourself to blame. The sort of ninny you pretended to be would have been very happy to leave all the decisions to someone else. The poor Colonel was only doing what he thought best. He doesn't know what you are really like.'

'*Poor* Colonel? What's this, Maggie? What has the Colonel done to arouse your sympathy?'

'Well, it might have escaped your notice, but it hasn't escaped mine. That poor man is not looking at all well. From what Mr Fennybright's clerk told me, he's only just recovered from the wounds he received at Waterloo. Two years it took! They must have been terrible. Riding in this heat can't be good for him, and he looks as if he's paying for it.'

'Nonsense! You're imagining things! Colonel Ancroft is an iron man, nothing would affect him. He wouldn't permit it!'

Maggie pursed her lips and said no more.

It was getting late when they reached Buckden. Joseph was looking exhausted and Caroline was relieved when the Colonel oversaw his transfer to a small room off the stables with a comfortable bed in it.

'Thank you,' she said. 'I'm surprised the inn can provide such a suitable room.'

'Normally they don't,' he said briefly.

'You arranged for it in advance?' she asked in astonishment.

'All the inns where we shall be staying have been warned to make similar arrangements. Bellerby isn't young, and that wound of his has obviously not yet healed. He's a good man and deserves your concern.' He stopped and wiped his forehead. Caroline looked at him properly for the first time. He had not sounded as incisive as usual.

'I believe you're not well yourself, Colonel,' she said.

'Nonsense. I'm perfectly fit, ma'am. I've arranged for

supper to be served in your room in half an hour. Now, if you'll excuse me, I shall bid you goodnight.'

'Wait! Are you not to have any supper?'

'Thank you, no. I'm not at all hungry. Goodnight.' Before she could say any more he had bowed and turned away.

Maggie took some supper to Joseph, then she and Caroline ate together in the small parlour which had been reserved for them. After the meal they went upstairs. Caroline looked doubtfully at the door of the Colonel's room, which was just along the landing.

'I wish he had eaten something,' she said. 'I think you might be right, Maggie. He isn't well.'

'He has his man to look after him, Miss Caro. He'll be all right. I'm more concerned about Joseph at the moment. He seemed a bit feverish when I took him his food. I'll just go down to see him again after we've taken those things off you.'

Maggie removed the bonnet and cap, then helped her mistress out of her widow's stiff black dress.

'Oh,' Caroline sighed. 'That's better! My head was aching under that bonnet. And the air is so cool on my arms! Now, help me to unwind this, but be careful!'

The bindings round her waist were taken off, and the pouch with its precious contents was put carefully on the table. Caroline took a deep breath, then stretched like a cat. 'Is that what women feel like when they are carrying a child? So misshapen, so heavy and awkward? And so hot!'

'They have their reward at the end,' said Maggie with a smile.

'You're right, of course.' Caroline walked over to the

window and gazed out. It was rapidly getting dark. 'I don't expect I shall ever have a child, Maggie.'

'Why shouldn't you?'

'Because a child needs a father! Preferably one who is married to its mother. And unless I go stark, staring mad, I shall never again put my head in that particular noose.' Maggie nodded sympathetically. She knew more about Caroline Duval's marriage than anyone other than the girl's grandfather.

Caroline returned from the window and sat down. Still in silence Maggie prepared her for bed, brushing the grey powder out of her hair, both of them thinking of the past.

Except for the period of Caroline's disastrous marriage, Maggie had looked after her all her life. After her own baby had died, she had been asked to nurse little Caroline and in her grief she had taken the child to her heart. For the first seventeen years she had been both confidante and nurse. She had listened to her childish secrets, had comforted her when, not quite nine years old, she had lost her father, mother and only brother in a freak storm at sea. And as her charge slowly grew into a young woman, a bright future had beckoned. Caroline Leyburn was one of nature's darlings. She was rich, beautiful, and intelligent. But more than this she had a warm heart, an enchanting openness, an ability to infect everyone who met her with her own vivid zest for life.

But then, at seventeen, Caroline had fallen headlong in love, and no one could persuade her that the man she had chosen was unworthy. Neither Maggie nor anyone else had been able to protect the girl against the practised charms of Laurent Duval. She believed everything Duval told her. And he, a gambling adventurer, had seen in Peter Leyburn's heiress a golden opportunity.

Of course, thought Maggie sadly, they had all handled

the situation with sinful stupidity. She had remonstrated in vain. Peter Leyburn had threatened to cut his grand-daughter off without a penny, forecasting that Duval would desert her if he did. When Caroline simply refused to believe him, he had lost his temper and made the biggest mistake of all. Without warning, he had had Duval summarily shipped out of Jamaica and back to New Orleans. Caroline, in love, and intensely loyal, had packed her bag in a fury, filled her purse with gold, and had left in the middle of the night, heaven knew how, to follow her lover. They hadn't heard a thing from her for eighteen long months. Nor had they ever again heard from Duval.

Maggie was one of the few who had seen Caroline Duval's condition, both physical and mental, when she first arrived back. Duval was dead, the money had disappeared long before, and Caroline was destitute. It took months to restore her spirits and health, and over a year of her grandfather's energetic encouragement before she was ready to face the world again. Then, confident and defiant, she took her place in society, hiding her cynical contempt for most of those in it behind a curtain of laughing mockery. Her great love for her grandfather and her affectionate concern for her two servants were the only signs that were left of the delightfully open, lovingly trustful child she had once been.

Maggie sighed. Surely there must be someone somewhere who could find that child again. Caroline had so much to offer. But even if the right man appeared, Caroline herself would be his greatest enemy in his attempts to unlock her heart. Maggie sighed again and returned to the present.

'There, that's done,' she said. 'I'll just go to take a look at Joseph. I won't be long.'

But in fact she was back within minutes, looking very

worried. 'He's very restless. And he has a fever. I think he's in pain, though he'll never admit it.'

'I'll come,' said Caroline with decision. 'Where's the medicine chest?' She got up and put on her wrapper.

'You can't leave the room dressed like that!' said Maggie, scandalised.

'Why not? Who will see me? It's quite late—there's practically no one about. And it's dark. I haven't time to put on all those black clothes again!'

'But your hair!'

'Damn my hair!' said Caroline forcefully, shaking her mane of hair back over her shoulder. 'Are you coming or not, Maggie?'

Together they descended the stairs, each with a candle. The inn was silent.

They spent some time making Joseph comfortable until he was nearly asleep. Maggie, who had remained uneasy, suggested that Caroline should go back to her room. 'I'll just stay till he's fast asleep,' she said. 'But you go. I shan't be happy till you are out of sight, Miss Caro.'

Caroline looked at Joseph. He seemed peaceful enough. 'Very well. Don't be long.'

She crept out of the stable and went quietly up the stairs. At the door of her room she paused. Muffled cries could be heard coming from the Colonel's room. Then sounds of stumbling. Suddenly the door was flung open and Colonel Ancroft appeared in the doorway. He was still in his shirtsleeves, but without a cravat and with his shirt open to the waist. In the dim candlelight Caroline could see a forehead gleaming with sweat, flushed cheeks, and eyes which were black hollows in a pale face. The hand clutching the doorpost was trembling.

She forgot her lack of disguise. 'Colonel!' she exclaimed. 'What's wrong?' She hastily put her candle down on the table nearby and came towards him.

Chapter Four

Colonel Ancroft didn't appear to have heard her. After a moment of stunned disbelief, his face was suffused with a look of ineffable tenderness. Before she could stop him he had come towards her and taken her gently in his arms. 'Gabriella!' he said huskily, gazing down at her. 'I can't believe it! My love! You're here again! I thought I'd lost you forever. Where have you been? Oh, sweetheart, I've missed you so much!'

Caroline gazed up in amazement. The Colonel's face was transformed. The discipline, the strong jaw, the firm mouth were all there still, but no trace of severity, no coldness. He was smiling, his eyes glowing with feeling. Suddenly she saw a younger, less forbidding, Colonel Ancroft, his soul in his eyes, a young man deeply, over-whelmingly, in love. Her heart twisted. Lucky, lucky Gabriella!

He stroked her cheek, then with a deep sigh of contentment, bent his head and kissed her, almost tentatively at first, as if he wasn't sure that she was real. Then, as she stood unprotesting in his arms, his kiss grew deeper, more passionate.

'Come, Gabriella,' he whispered. 'Come, my dearest!'

Slowly he drew her into his room and shut the door. Caroline moved with him as if in a trance. She found herself in the grip of feelings she thought she had banished forever, a slow stirring of the senses, a warmth in her blood, a leaping response to a man's touch on her body. What was happening to her?

She murmured incoherently against his lips, but when he kissed her again, this time with more assurance, she was lost. Still clasped together, still locked in a kiss, they moved slowly towards the bed. Her wrapper fell to the ground and her shift followed it as he pushed them both off her shoulders. When they reached the side of the bed he sat down, holding her so that she stood between his knees. 'Such a slender waist,' he said, worshipping her with his eyes, hands and lips. 'Such beautiful... perfect...breasts.' He drew her closer and rested his head against her. 'Oh God, Gabriella, I want you so. It's been so long. Let me show you again how much I love you, my bride.' Putting his arms around her, he pulled her slowly but irresistibly down on to the bed beside him till their bodies were closely entwined. He kissed her hungrily, his hands pulling her ever closer till they were almost one. For a moment Caroline felt happier than she had felt for many years, lost in pure sensation... But she came suddenly to her senses as she realised with a shock that the Colonel was so burnt up with fever that he was hardly aware of what he was doing. This mustn't go any further!

She pulled back. 'No! Let me go! You're making a mistake!' she cried, struggling to free herself. 'I'm not your bride. I'm not Gabriella. Please let me go!'

He held her for a moment desperately trying to focus his eyes on her face. 'Not...not Gabriella?' he said incredulously. 'But you must be! Who else could look so much like her, and *not* be Gabriella? Oh, no! Now that I've found you again I shall never let you go, never!' He stroked her cheek and murmured, 'You've no need to be afraid, my love. I want to cherish you, live with you, spend the rest of my life with you, just as I promised all those years ago. You have no reason to be afraid. But don't try to tell me you're not Gabriella—I couldn't feel like this about anyone else in the world.' He started to kiss her again.

'Confound it, I am *not* your Gabriella! Let me go, sir! Let me go, I say!' Caroline wrenched herself free and leapt up. She picked up her shift and wrapper, then, still holding them against her, she turned to him. Making an effort to speak calmly, she said, 'You're ill, Colonel Ancroft. Let me fetch your man.'

The man on the bed lay rigid for a moment. Then he nodded painfully 'I think I must be. The sun was so hot…I…I'm sorry… I thought you were someone I knew. You look so like her… But now I hear you, you don't *sound* like Gabriella. I must have been dreaming… Or in a delirium. I'm sorry!' Then he turned his head away and said with a groan of despair, 'And, indeed, I know that Gabriella is dead. I saw her die. She and Philip together…'

Stifling an impulse to comfort him, Caroline hurriedly dressed herself. When she turned to face him again his eyes were closed, his face ghastly in the candlelight. It was as Maggie had said. The long ride in the hot sun had taken its toll of a body only just out of convalescence. He had probably woken out of a dream, a nightmare, even, and in his sickness had mistaken her for Gabriella. She wondered fleetingly who the girl was and what had happened to her. She had clearly meant everything to him.

Caroline would never have imagined John Ancroft capable of such intense feeling, such passionate love.

He opened his eyes and looked at her as if seeing her for the first time. He seemed more sensible. She bent over him. 'Where is Betts?' she asked.

'I sent him away. He...he's in the stables... With... with... *Who are you?*' he asked desperately.

For the first time Caroline saw the danger she had put herself in. Colonel Ancroft mustn't find out like this what sort of game she had been playing with him... She thought, then said, nervously backing away, 'One o' the maids, sir. If you'll excuse me, oi'll just fetch yore servant.'

When she went to her own room Maggie was there, looking shocked. Caroline shook her head and gave the maid a rueful grin. 'It's not what you think, Maggie, dear! Joseph isn't the only one who is suffering tonight. Colonel Ancroft has a fever as well.'

'I'm not at all surprised. I told you.'

'We have to find his manservant.'

'I know where he is,' said Maggie. 'He's sleeping in the stable rooms. It seems the Colonel asked him to keep an eye on Joseph. I'll fetch him, shall I?'

She went to the door, then turned. 'The Colonel didn't see you like that, did he, Miss Caro?' Caroline was silent. '*Did he?*' Maggie looked appalled. 'He *did*! Oh, heavens! What did he say? What are you going to do?'

Caroline gathered her wits together, and said as calmly as she could, 'Go and fetch Betts, Maggie. It's all right. Colonel Ancroft didn't recognise me. I told him I was one of the servants. Make haste. I suspect this is not the first time he's been ill like this. Betts will know what to give him.'

*   *   *

Betts was not unduly worried by the Colonel's attack. Caroline heard him talking to Maggie as he came up the stairs. 'You needn't worry about the Colonel, Miss Maggie. He'll be as right as rain in the morning, you'll see. A dose of 'is medicine and a good night's sleep—they'll fix 'im. Strong as an ox, the Colonel. Mind you, I thought 'e was gettin' over these attacks. 'E 'asn't 'ad one for months. It must've been the sun.'

Betts's voice died and the door of Colonel Ancroft's room was opened and shut. Caroline breathed a sigh and prepared to go to bed.

But she found sleep impossible. Her mind was filled with the extraordinary events of the night. John Ancroft had suddenly revealed himself to be a man of feeling, a man who had suffered greatly, still suffered. The man she had dismissed as a wooden block had tonight become a vulnerable and passionate human being. What was his story? Had Gabriella been his wife? Caroline doubted that. It had sounded more as if she had been betrothed to him rather than married. How had she died? And what part had this Philip played in the tragedy? That there had been a tragedy of some kind she had no doubt.

For the first time she began to consider John Ancroft seriously, and she came to the conclusion that he was more of a mystery than she had realised. He was obviously very wealthy, though he hadn't appeared so when she first met him. He dressed simply enough, yet his carriage, his horses and his servants' livery were all of the highest quality. He was severe, a disciplinarian, one would have said, yet his servants' respect was mixed with liking, and Mr Fennybright had seemed fond of him! Then again, he clearly knew this Great North Road well, but had not travelled it for some time. And tonight... Well, that was something altogether astonishing, a revelation indeed! A world away from the man she had dismissed as a simple, rather unimaginative soldier.

All of which brought her to herself. However hard she tried, she simply could not account for her wanton behaviour tonight. Somehow or other this new John Ancroft had broken through the shell that she had built to protect herself from any further humiliation and despair. The Widow Duval had had no heart. In the years since Laurent Duval's betrayal there had been many men who had begged in vain for her kisses. She had driven them mad, laughed at them and secretly despised them for it. But tonight… It was unaccountable! What spell had caught her? Tonight she had been helpless in John Ancroft's arms, had met passion with passion, given rein to feelings she had long since forgotten, been eager to lose herself in a man's caresses. She had damned nearly given herself to him! This was danger of the highest degree, she told herself. Had she not sworn that she would never again place her self-respect, her emotions, her body at the mercy of another being? How could she have forgotten? How had it happened? Caroline tossed restlessly in her bed, unable to find an answer.

But after a while her ability to treat herself and others with mocking irony came to her rescue. It was unlikely she would be put to any further test. Tonight's situation was one that was most unlikely ever to be repeated. She grinned as she thought over the more intimate moments of her encounter with the Colonel. Betts had said his fever would have gone by the morning. But how would he behave? Would he try to seek the 'servant girl' out or would he do his best to avoid her? Would he have a guilty conscience, or would he regret that the situation had come to an early end? Or was it perhaps possible that he would remember nothing at all? Caroline was not in the slightest afraid that she would be unmasked. The candlelight had been dim, her appearance had been so different from what he knew of her, even her voice was several tones deeper than the one she normally used in speaking to him. No, she was safe.

She finally went to sleep with a smile on her face. But she dreamt of a man's strong arms holding her with such tenderness, and his deep voice telling her how much he loved her, and calling her his bride. And when she woke she had tears on her cheeks.

If Caroline had not known the truth of the matter, she would have said the next day that the Colonel had a hangover. His manner was even stiffer than usual, his voice more peremptory, and he held himself carefully as if he ached all over. She was concerned for him, but said nothing. Betts had approached Maggie as soon as he saw her. 'Best not say anything to 'is nibs,' he said. 'The Colonel's as fit as a flea this morning, 'cept for being a mite short-tempered. But 'e's very touchy about 'is illness. He don't like people to know about it, see? So, mum's the word.' As the Colonel looked suspiciously his way, he raised his voice and said cheerfully, 'Mr Bellerby seems better this morning, miss. 'E'll be fit to move on, never fear.'

When Caroline appeared the Colonel gave her a brief bow. 'Today's journey will not be so strenuous,' he said. 'We are travelling the same distance, but if we can get away in the next hour we should have two or three hours in hand over yesterday. We'll take a more leisurely break at midday. Your man should be able to cope.'

From the safety of her veil Caroline looked at him closely and marvelled. It was difficult to see the passionate lover of the night before in the man standing before her. Except for the fact that he was paler than usual, and a small frown creased his forehead, this was all Colonel Ancroft, her wooden soldier! She restrained a sudden desire to smooth his brow, and said in the high, light tone she used for 'Mrs Hopkins', 'Thank you, Colonel. I believe we are going to Grantham, are we not?'

'Yes,' he said curtly. 'The inn there is excellent.'

The little party moved off. Caroline took one last look at the inn as the carriage drove out of the yard. It was hard to believe that she had not imagined it all...

The day promised to be warm again, and John Ancroft hoped to heaven that he would manage better than he had on the previous day. Fifty miles to Grantham should be a reasonable day's stint, especially if they could take an hour's break in the middle. If his memory served him correctly, the road was bordered with trees for a good stretch of the way. He gritted his teeth and climbed into the saddle.

Betts was looking concerned, damn him! Betts was an old woman. The Colonel would be travelling in the carriage if Betts had had his way, and that was something John Ancroft refused to contemplate! The ride might be uncomfortable at first until his head cleared, but anything was better than travelling in a closed carriage with the Duval woman! He needed to do some thinking, and the less he heard of that whining voice the better he'd be pleased!

The day was still young, a soft breeze kept the air fresh, and the trees along the roadside gave plenty of shade. Today's ride would be pleasanter than the one from Barnet to Buckden. For the first half-hour John concentrated on staying upright in the saddle, but after a while his head cleared and his mind began to work again. What the devil had been going on the previous night? Had it all been a nightmare brought on by his fever? He had been a fool to ride so far in yesterday's unbroken sunshine. The bouts of fever that had plagued him ever since his spell in the marshes of southern France had been growing less frequent and less severe, and he had begun to hope they had gone forever. Yesterday's attack had taken him by surprise.

Things might have been better if he could have fallen straight into bed after reaching Buckden, but because of his idiotic commitment to Mrs Duval, he had first had to see that the ladies and Joseph Bellerby were suitably accommodated. Mrs Duval had seemed fit enough after the journey, though she had looked hot. That was much her own fault. She'd do better to lose some weight! And it was surely not necessary for her to wear that absurd veil whenever she was in public? He had little sympathy for such a woman, and why he had given in to Fennybright and agreed to see her to Yorkshire he could not imagine.

But Joseph Bellerby had looked exhausted. Why couldn't his mistress have left him in London where he could have been comfortably looked after? All the fuss about danger, and pursuers and God knew what else. What nonsense it was! The woman had a grossly overactive imagination.

As a result it had been far too late by the time he had escaped to his room. Betts was seeing to Bellerby, so he had been alone. He remembered taking his cravat off, and undoing his shirt, feeling worse and worse all the while. His memory of what followed was unclear, but he supposed he must have collapsed. John Ancroft frowned. What *had* happened afterwards? Had he dreamed it all or had it been real? That servant girl… No, not a girl. A woman. A beautiful woman with full breasts and lovely limbs… There had been no one like her in the inn this morning, though he had searched for her as discreetly as he could. If she *had* been real, then she must have thought him either mad or an unprincipled villain.

Ever since Fenny had convinced him that he ought to go back to Yorkshire he had been having dreams, but never one as vivid as this. Even now in broad daylight he could feel his body tightening as he remembered... God damn it, he hadn't felt so unsettled, so frustrated for years! She *must* have been real! He could still remember the feel of her body against his, the long legs, the deep bosom, a waist so slender that he could circle it with his hands... And that glorious hair... Or had the hair been part of his dream, part of his conviction that she was Gabriella?

She had been holding a candle when he first saw her. No wonder he had gone mad—the shock had been almost more than he could take. Her hair—Gabriella's hair—had flamed in the candlelight, the dark, red-brown tresses surrounding the loveliest face he had ever seen or ever wished to see. Gabriella's face, with Gabriella's eyes. Had that been just an illusion? A figment of his fevered imagination? She had seemed enough of a living creature afterwards...

But if she had indeed been a real person and not a ghost, why had she allowed him to make love to her without a word? No false protestations of modesty, no haggling, none of the usual hesitation before money was exchanged. Her response had been silent, immediate and total. There had been not the slightest demur before they had very nearly reached the point of no return. She *must* have been one of the serving wenches. Was she a trollop or was she a tease? She hadn't looked like either. Perhaps he had offended her by mistaking her for Gabriella? Surely not! In his experience serving wenches of that sort

were not so nice in their feelings—they couldn't afford
to be. On the other hand, she hadn't stayed for a reward
either, but had been concerned for him, had promised to
send his man to look after him. He would ask Betts who
had come to tell him that he was needed.

But Betts could only say that Mrs Duval's maid had
come to see to Joseph and had told him the Colonel
seemed to be ill. There hadn't been any mention of a
servant from the inn. One thing was sure. It certainly
wasn't Miss Maggie in his bedroom last night. She was
almost as unlikely a candidate as Mrs Duval! For the first
time that morning John Ancroft smiled. Now there would
be a substantial armful!

Cheered by the absurdity of such a thought, John sat
up straighter and started to enjoy the ride. The inn at
Buckden was behind them. He might never know the truth
of what had happened there, and he must dismiss it. He
resolved one thing more. If he was to live at Marrick and
survive, then he must lay Gabriella's ghost for good,
along with all the other poor ghosts.

They passed the monumental milepost at Alconbury
where the road through Huntingdon joined them, paused
for a while in Stilton, then stopped for quite a time in the
town of Stamford. Colonel Ancroft found a comfortable
seat in the shade for Joseph Bellerby, then suggested that
the ladies might care to take a stroll round the town.

'Oh, Captain! Is it safe?' asked Caroline.

Colonel Ancroft gave her a hard look. 'I would correct
you yet again, if I didn't suspect you mean to tease,
ma'am. I am quite sure it is safe. We are now something
like ninety miles from London, and there has so far been
no sign whatsoever of pursuit. Are you quite certain you
have not made a mistake? It is my opinion that the pre-

vious attacks on you were unfortunate, but unconnected. In fact, I would say that disguise is really no longer necessary—I suggest that I now call you by your proper name, and though I must respect your feelings, I think you would be cooler if you removed your veil. Is it really necessary?'

With a touch of genuine panic Caroline said, 'Quite necessary. Absolutely necessary, Colonel. But you may call me Mrs Duval.'

The Colonel gave a slight shrug of the shoulders, then said politely, 'As you wish. Shall we walk, Mrs Duval?'

'You mean to come with us?'

'Of course. After half a day in the saddle, I need to exercise my legs a little! And do you think me so churlish as to leave you to walk unescorted round a strange town?'

'Oh, no, Colonel!'

'Then shall we set off?'

Their tour of the town proved very pleasant. Caroline was impressed with the Colonel's knowledge and said so.

'I have travelled this road many times before, ma'am.'

'Oh? Are you a native of Yorkshire, then, Colonel Ancroft?'

'Yes, Mrs Duval.' The Colonel's tone was not encouraging, but Caroline persisted. Since the night before she had developed a healthy curiosity about her wooden soldier.

'I suppose you have many friends there.'

'I have been away from the area for some years.'

'Why is that? Has the army been so demanding?'

'That and the fact that I...I had a disagreement with my uncle, which made it awkward for both of us if I was anywhere near him.'

'Do you have any other family?'

'One daughter.' This time there was a warning in the

Colonel's voice which said her questions had gone far enough, and Caroline was silenced. In truth, she could hardly have said anything more. Her breath had been taken away by this startling revelation. So her wooden soldier *had* been married to Gabriella. His 'bride' had been his wife, and the mother of his child!

They said little during the rest of the walk. The Colonel pointed out one or two items of interest, but the enjoyment had gone. They were all glad to get back to the inn, where an excellent meal was waiting for them.

They stayed the night at Grantham as planned, but nothing untoward occurred. Joseph needed no attention—he was feeling and looking considerably better. The Colonel excused himself early, and Caroline and Maggie retired to their room before nine o'clock.

'So, Mrs Duval,' said Maggie as she helped Caroline out of her heavy clothes. 'No need for further disguise, eh?'

'Don't be absurd, Maggie. Of course there is! The Colonel is not so stupid that he wouldn't recognise his servant girl if he saw me as I really am. There's no help for it. I'll have to keep this confounded disguise for the rest of the journey. I shall probably die of heat!'

'You're in a right pickle, Miss Caro. It wouldn't be so bad if you hadn't made fun of him with your "Captains" and your silly voice. He might forgive the servant girl trick, if it weren't for the rest.'

'Oh, no, he wouldn't! You don't know the half, Maggie.'

Maggie was now engaged in her nightly task of brushing the powder out of Caroline's hair, but at these words she stopped, brush in mid-air. Her eyes met Caroline's in the looking glass. 'Why wouldn't he?'

A slow blush began in Caroline's cheeks and spread down over her neck and shoulders. Her whole body seemed to be on fire.

'Miss Caro! You said that nothing had happened last night!'

'No, I didn't!' said Caroline with a touch of defiance. 'I said the Colonel was ill, and that he hadn't recognised me. But you needn't look so shocked, Maggie. Nothing of any consequence happened.'

Maggie put the brush down. 'Now you just tell me exactly what went on! Did he…did he attack you?'

'Of course not! He's a gentleman.'

'Hmph! From what I've seen, being a gentlemen wouldn't have stopped him. But in this case I believe you. The Colonel seems a very honourable man. Are you going to tell me what happened or not?'

Caroline gave Maggie a carefully edited version of the events in Colonel Ancroft's bedchamber the night before. It seemed unnecessary to go into detail about her own behaviour…

'So you see, Maggie,' she concluded, 'our Colonel has a tragic past. There's a mystery about it which I would dearly love to solve.'

'I'd talk to Mr Betts if I thought it would do any good, but it wouldn't. He's as close as an oyster about his master. If I hadn't actually had to fetch him last night, he would never have told me about the fever attacks. In any case, I don't think he knew the Colonel before their army days.' Maggie looked severely at Caroline. 'What is more, Miss Caro, if I were you I'd stop wondering about him. You need to concentrate on your own problems, not go borrowing trouble from others. Yours are big enough, heaven knows!'

'Don't be such a Job's comforter! If this heat continues,

it is quite likely that wearing these clothes will carry me off with an apoplexy—then you'd be sorry! If only I could think of something to do... But I cannot, cannot confess all to the Colonel. What *would* he think of me.'

'Why should he think ill of you, if, as you say, nothing happened? I'm beginning to think you've been less circumspect than you've given me to understand, Miss Caro!'

'I let him kiss me.'

There was a short silence. Then Maggie said slowly, 'I don't understand. You've never so much as hinted that you found the Colonel attractive. You've even made fun of him, called him your wooden soldier. What has caused such a change? Why, you've hardly let any man get close enough to hold your hand, let alone kiss you, ever since—'

'Yes, yes, ever since I came back from New Orleans. And I can't answer your question. I don't know. I don't know, Maggie. It wasn't just that I felt sorry for him. He...he seemed...he seemed different. Not Colonel Ancroft at all.' She paused, then said with a return to her normal manner, 'Still, it won't happen again. No one was hurt, Maggie. Let's forget it.'

'As long as the Colonel does, too,' Maggie said soberly.

'Yes, well as long as he doesn't see me as I really am he won't dream of connecting me with that girl. Now, since I am condemned to wearing them for the remainder of the journey, what can we do about these clothes?'

'I suppose you could leave off the heavier petticoats,' Maggie suggested. 'I doubt anyone will notice.'

'Well, I will! After all, I'm now Mrs Duval. She has more courage than "Mrs Hopkins". And who knows? It may get cooler as we go further north.'

* * *

But Caroline's optimism was unfounded. The weather seemed to get warmer with every day that passed. By the time they reached the inn just beyond Doncaster she was in serious trouble. Maggie did her best to cool her down with the limited facilities the landlord could provide, but the bath the servants brought up to the room was too small, and no amount of sponging could reduce Caroline's discomfort to any real extent. That night she lay limply on the bed, still feeling dirty, sticky and hot, wondering if she could survive the journey. Yet to reveal herself to John Ancroft was a step she still could not contemplate…

She slept fitfully, and woke ridiculously early, long before anyone, even a servant, was stirring. The sun was streaming through the cracks in the shutters—it would be another hot day.

She sat up in bed. Maggie was still sound asleep at the other side of the room. From outside the window Caroline could hear the sound of water, and she remembered that the night before they had driven alongside a laughing, gurgling stream for the last mile or two. The sound had driven her mad. Now temptation was too strong. She must seek it out!

Mindful of an extra need for caution, she decided to wear her black widow's dress and to take her cap and veil with her to put on if necessary. The cumbersome bindings which made her dress so very uncomfortable could be left behind, though. If anyone saw her she could manage somehow or other to bulk her appearance out. She wrapped the chalice carefully and hid it under Maggie's bed, taking care not to wake her. Then, picking up a cake of soap, a towel, and her cap and veil, she slipped out of the room and down the stairs like a shadow. She was soon outside, running through the field at the back of the inn in search of the stream.

After a minute or two she found the perfect place, where a small waterfall was splashing on to a platform of rock above a deep pool. A scent of summer hung in the air from the flowers and shrubs edging the pool, and over-hanging trees and tall plants hid the spot from general view. She hid her bundle of clothes in a bush, and then in rapturous delight she walked slowly, testing the ground, feeling every ripple, into the clear, cool, scented water. It was sheer heaven! She swam about for a few moments, then climbed up and stood under the waterfall. After a moment she fetched her soap and washed her hair, twisting and turning in the stream of water, loving the feel of it as it poured through her hair and over her body. She stretched her arms in the air and laughed out loud for sheer joy…

The man picking his way carefully through thorns and spines heard the laughter and stopped short. He had re-membered the pool with the waterfall from past visits, and after a sleepless night the temptation to enjoy the freshness of an early morning swim had been too great. Slipping on breeches and shirt for decency's sake, he had snatched up a towel and escaped. But for some minutes now he had been making his way slowly and painfully through an undergrowth of thistles and thorns! Either the path was more overgrown than it used to be, or he had missed it altogether.

When he heard the laughter he stopped and looked up. And caught his breath. Stones, thistles, thorns—all were forgotten in the enchantment of what he saw. It was an incarnation of every man's fantasies. A slender nymph under the waterfall, holding her head back to let the stream of water ripple over her mane of hair, her arms raised in sensuous delight.

Chapter Five

John Ancroft stood spellbound for a moment, then with an effort he turned his eyes away. This was no nymph, no creature of legend. This was a young woman who had come to this secret place to bathe. And he was no peeping Tom to indulge in lascivious enjoyment of her nudity. He would have to forgo his own bathe and leave like the gentleman he claimed to be. With a last, regretful glance he turned to go…and stopped.

The girl was now lifting her wet hair to shake it dry. Dark chestnut tresses glowed like fire in the early morning sun… Memory flooded back and with amazement John saw in her the servant who had been with him in the inn at Buckden. Was he going mad? Had his memories of Gabriella so distorted his mind that he saw her image in every red-haired female he met? This girl could not possibly be the same, Buckden was a hundred miles to the south. No, this was some local village maiden, and he was a fool with an obsession. He must get away from here. Quickly. He flung a last glance at her…

'Oh!'

The exclamation of dismay came from the girl in the

pool. She had finished with the waterfall and was starting to wade towards the bank. She had just seen him.

'Oh, heavens!'

The horror in her voice shamed him. 'I mean you no harm,' he assured her. 'I came upon you by accident—' He was unable to go on. Now he saw her better he realised that the long legs, and slender waist and hips seen under the waterfall had deceived him. This wasn't a young girl. This was a mature woman—all woman, too, just like the Buckden female. Unless he really was going mad, there really couldn't be two so alike, and so like Gabriella! This *must* be the woman from Buckden! But how had she got here, and why? He took a step forward, then stopped to consider. Was it possible that Mrs Duval had been right, after all, to be afraid? Was someone keeping track of their movements? And, absurd as it might seem, was this woman part of the plot? He saw her again in his mind's eye, stretching and twisting under the waterfall in such spontaneous, innocent enjoyment. No, that wasn't possible! But he owed it to Mrs Duval to make certain.

'Just a moment,' he said sternly.

'Stay away!' she said. '*Please*, stay away!'

'I mean you no harm. But I want to talk to you. Just to be sure. Where are your clothes?'

'No! I don't want you to... I don't need my clothes.'

'You don't?' John smiled grimly, more than ever convinced that there was more to this than he had thought. 'So you mean to talk to me as you are?'

She pulled her hair forward over her shoulders. 'Why not?' she asked. 'I can talk to you from here, though I should prefer you to go away. What do you want, sir?'

'This is absurd! I'll get your clothes and then—'

'No! I don't want you to! Stop! Stop, I tell you!'

John had caught sight of a bundle of clothing tucked into a bush. Ignoring her protests he went towards it. 'Here, I'll pass them to you and you can dry yourself and put them on. Don't worry. I'll stay well clear. I won't ask you to talk to me until you're decently clad.' He bent down, picked the bundle up and held the clothes out to her. A towel, a black, ungainly dress…and a cap and widow's veil. 'But these aren't yours—' he began. He looked back at the girl and frowned. 'Just what is going on?' he asked sternly. 'And what are Mrs Duval's clothes doing on this path?'

The situation was potentially catastrophic. Any moment now the bubble of deceit would burst. But none the less Caroline felt laughter welling up inside. It might well be hysteria, but the sight of John Ancroft in breeches and half-open shirt, holding out that dreadful dress, the veil and the streamers from the cap hanging down limply below his knees, was testing her gravity to its limits. Did he think she had somehow got rid of Mrs Duval? Was he about to arrest her forthwith on suspicion of abduction, or even murder? Before he did anything he'd have to find some other clothes for her first!

It was no use. She burst into a rich laugh. And the expression on the Colonel's face, astounded, outraged, angry, only made things worse. She choked again with laughter. He made a sudden move towards her.

'No, no,' she spluttered. 'You don't have to fetch me. Throw me my towel and yours and I'll come out without your help.'

But in spite of her laughter Caroline was facing some unpleasant facts. Her little game was very nearly over. Indeed, the moment John Ancroft had seen her in the pool her charade was doomed. She cursed the misfortune that had brought him to this very spot at this particular time. Her only hope was that he would not altogether abandon their journey north when he heard the truth.

He passed her the towels, and then drew back a little, though it was clear he did not trust her enough to let her out of his sight. Ignoring the silent observer, Caroline waded nearer and covered herself without undue haste. Then she stepped out of the pool. She was sober again. Standing before him, swathed in the towels, bare legs showing beneath, she said humbly, 'You see before you, Colonel Ancroft, a penitent. I'm afraid I have been playing a dreadful trick on you.'

'Indeed, ma'am?' he said coldly.

'Yes. Though I did not start out with the intention of deceiving you, I assure you. Mr Turner—'

'Excuse me a moment. Am I to understand that I have the honour of addressing Mrs Duval? The *real* Mrs Duval?'

Caroline's ever-ready sense of the ridiculous was roused once again. What would an onlooker make of this excessive formality between two people who, to say the least, were much less than formally dressed? She was practically naked, and he wore only breeches and shirt. Her wet hair was hanging halfway down her back, and his was standing on end, as if he had not combed it but dragged it through the bushes. Any impartial onlooker would swear that they must be escaped Bedlamites! She forced herself to rise to the occasion, however, and replied gravely, 'You have, sir.' Her voice shook as she went on, 'But the honour is mine, I assure you.'

It was no use. She could not stop herself. Laughter burst out again and rang across the pool.

He waited in icy silence till she was calm again, then said, 'I am afraid I do not find any of this amusing, Mrs

Duval. If you will put these things on, I suggest that we return to the inn. Then, after we are both more suitably dressed, I shall listen to your explanation with interest. In an hour's time?'

He turned away. Caroline put on the black dress and wound her hair into a knot. She followed the Colonel back towards the inn in silence.

The inn was stirring when they returned, and they received several curious glances, but neither paid any attention to them. Caroline went swiftly up to her room, and was met by Maggie at the door.

'Miss Caro! I was just about to come to look for you. Where have you been?' She held Caroline away from her and studied her dress. 'What's this? And your hair is wet, too!' Her voice changed. 'Miss Caro! What have you been up to?'

'There's no time to explain properly. The Colonel caught me out, Maggie. He knows I was pretending. He wishes to see me in an hour, and I dare not be late. He is—'

'Angry?'

'Icily furious. I only hope I may not have turned him against us forever!'

Maggie did not waste time in 'I told you so's'. She said simply, 'Then you'd better be sure you are ready and looking your best. Take those things off.'

'With pleasure. There's one advantage at least in this business. Those clothes have had their day! They can be thrown away and burnt!'

'That's not much to rejoice in if the Colonel decides to abandon you.'

'Oh, I hope he does not! Somehow or other I must persuade him not to think too badly of me.'

Maggie glanced curiously at her mistress. There was more than simple anxiety at being stranded in Miss Caro's voice. What was going on? This concern for a man's opinion was not at all like her. She made no comment, however, but simply fetched one of her mistress's own dresses, one of the ones bought in London to replace those lost near Bodmin.

'Sit down and I'll do my best,' was all she said.

Caroline's hair was already drying. It was easy enough to wind it into a topknot and persuade some of the curls to form a frame round her face. The pale lemon-yellow muslin gown was a perfect setting for Caroline's colouring, and its simple cut flattered her magnificent figure. Maggie stood back and studied her work. 'You'll do,' she said.

'Let's hope the Colonel thinks so,' said Caroline with a wry smile. 'Pass me that bag, please.'

'This one? But it will ruin the look! It's far too heavy and big! Take the silk reticule, Miss Caro. Your grandfather's bequest will be safe enough with me.'

'I am sure it would. But I think I need to take it with me.'

Head held high, she went downstairs. John Ancroft was waiting for her at the bottom. He studied her in silence, but somewhat to Caroline's disappointment, he showed no sign of appreciation at her changed appearance.

Instead he said coolly, 'We shall take a walk, Mrs Duval. I am sure you would not wish the world to hear what we have to say to each other, though I assume your maid and Bellerby must be in your confidence. A pity. I had thought Bellerby an honest man.'

'He is! Colonel, I hope you will not blame either of my servants for this!' Caroline said. Her deep voice was calm, but quite firm. 'It would be unjust to think ill of them when they were doing their best to protect me.'

'Really? Well, you may try to convince me of that when we are more private.' The Colonel's tone was still very cold.

Yes, thought Caroline. You may listen to my reasons for the disguise, John Ancroft. I might even be able to persuade you that it really was necessary, and, in the end, you might even forgive me for it. But what you will *not* forgive is the business with the 'servant girl' in your room the other night. You will regard that as a betrayal. Proud, reserved John Ancroft cannot bear the thought that anyone, least of all Mrs Duval, has witnessed what he felt for Gabriella or seen his private agony. *That* is my real crime.

But nothing in her manner indicated that she was afraid. This was Caroline at her fighting best, the young girl who in the end had refused to let Laurent Duval defeat her, the Caroline who had roused her grandfather's support and admiration, and the woman who had ignored private condemnation and won back her place at the head of Kingston society.

They walked to the top of a small prominence where some kindly soul had placed a bench so that walkers could sit and enjoy the view. Here they stopped and she sat down.

'I'm waiting,' said Colonel Ancroft. Those who had been under his command in the Peninsula—those who still lived, that is—could have told Caroline that this was the Colonel's hanging voice. He regarded her without expression, his silver-grey eyes as cold as the Arctic in winter, his mouth a hard line, his manner one of someone who was prepared to listen and to judge. And afterwards to sentence.

Caroline decided to waste no effort in further pleas for forgiveness. What she had done had perhaps been ill advised, but it was not criminal. In any case, Colonel Ancroft was unlikely even to listen to apologies. So she drew a breath and plunged straight in.

'I dare say you concluded that I was merely suffering from an excess of nerves when I asked Mr Turner to find me an escort to Yorkshire. But I assure you, by the time I reached London I had every reason to think myself in danger. I have in my possession something which is badly wanted—fanatically desired—by a distant cousin of mine, a man called Edmund Willoughby. He pursued me in Jamaica for it, but I managed to escape him and believed myself to be safe when we reached England. The last I had seen of him was from the deck of the packet boat as it drew out of Kingston harbour. He and some of his men were standing on the quayside, unable, I believed, to harm us any more.'

'Harm you? How?'

'In Jamaica he had threatened me, killed one of my servants, and had ended up by imprisoning me in his villa outside Kingston. With Joseph's help I managed to fight my way out.' Caroline stopped. It had been such a near thing. She still could not think of it without feeling sick.

'What did this fellow want of you? A forced marriage?'

'No, indeed! He is already married. His object was more mercenary than that.' She regarded him thoughtfully. 'You look unconvinced. I think this is the moment when I have to trust you with a secret. I doubt you will continue to help me otherwise.'

'I think that's quite likely,' said the Colonel coldly. 'I enjoy being a dupe no more than the next man.'

'My cousin Edmund wants something my grandfather gave me before he died. Something which is worth a king's ransom, and which I promised to guard with my life. If you find that too dramatic, then I am sorry. It is so. Apart from…this morning, it has never been out of my sight since we left Jamaica.'

The Colonel cast a glance at the bag on her knee. 'I take it that you now have it in that bag? Why haven't I seen you carry anything like that before?'

Caroline's lips twitched. 'You saw evidence of it every time you looked at me, Colonel Ancroft. I had it round my middle. It was what made me so very…well built.' John Ancroft's expression changed slightly and a fleeting grin softened his mouth. A very faint ray of hope, the merest glimmer, awoke in Caroline's breast at these signs of amusement. The Colonel had a sense of humour, after all! She didn't comment, but carried on.

'We were wrong about having escaped Edmund. One of his men must have been on the ship with us, and as soon as he set foot in Falmouth he conscripted help on behalf of his master. The attack in Cornwall was a clumsy effort to search our luggage. The second attack, the one during which Joseph was wounded, was much better managed. The thieves knew what they wanted, and where it was kept. They left us, believing they had been successful. As they would have been, if Joseph had not seen someone acting suspiciously the night before. After that second attack we used the short time we had before they discovered their mistake to set up our defences. And so, I called myself Mrs Hopkins and put on her disguise.'

'At the same time finding a safe place for this.' He touched the bag. 'No doubt you will eventually explain where your husband comes into all this?'

'My husband?' Caroline said blankly. 'Why, nowhere, sir!'

'There is no husband?'

'There was. But he has been dead for years.'

'So where are his ashes?'

'What are you talking about, Colonel? I've no idea!'

'That was part of the deceit, too? I was told that you were bringing your husband's ashes back to his family home.'

'Not by me!'

'No, my lawyer, Mr Fennybright, told me. But I refuse to believe that Mr Fennybright would set out deliberately to deceive. Especially not me. So how did it happen? Perhaps he was misled? I've always believed Samuel Turner to be as honest a man as Fennybright, but did *you* persuade him to spin us the affecting story of an elderly widow, setting out on a mournful task of taking her husband's ashes back to his birthplace? If so, I congratulate you. It was a masterpiece. I would never have considered this exercise if Turner hadn't appealed to my instincts as a gentleman. So, Mrs Duval, did you manage to persuade Mr Turner to mislead both his partner and myself, or was he himself deceived?'

'But I didn't do anything of the kind! It's true that I'm a widow. It's true that I was nervous about the journey— with good reason, as you have heard. And it's true that Mr Turner was most anxious to help the granddaughter of one of his oldest clients and friends. Were you very reluctant when Mr Fennybright approached you?'

'Extremely so! In fact, at first I refused outright.'

'That must be it! I can only think that Mr Turner was told this, and embroidered the tale a little. Perhaps he thought a dead husband more affecting than a dead grandfather? But I promise you, Colonel Ancroft, the only deceit lay in pretending to be older than I was in order to disguise my identity from my enemies. I did not ask, much less persuade, Mr Turner to deceive his partner. I'm sorry if you think I did.'

'And the ashes? Are your grandfather's ashes in that bag you carry?'

Caroline stared at him, 'Most certainly not,' she said forcefully. Then her irrepressible sense of humour got the better of her and her lips quivered as she added, 'The last thing I would want to do is to travel round England with a bag of ashes round my middle! Very hazardous, I should imagine. And *most* disrespectful!'

This time the Colonel remained serious. He was still very angry, after all. What *could* Mr Turner possibly have said to give him such a false impression? No one knew what was inside her precious bag, but there had never ever been any mention of ashes! Ashes… Remains… Remains! 'Ah!' she exclaimed. 'I think I understand. Was the word used by your Mr Fennybright not ''ashes'' but ''remains''?'

'It may have been.'

'I think Mr Turner may have deliberately obscured the truth—not exactly deception, but a lawyer's play with words. My grandfather wrote to Mr Turner that what I carry could be described as his ''remains'', since returning it to Yorkshire was all that was left for him to do in this life. That must be where Mr Turner got his idea. But it isn't anything like ashes. My grandfather was respectably buried in Kingston cemetery some months ago—with a great deal of ceremony, too.'

She felt a sharp pang at the memory and looked down, willing herself not to show what that death had meant to her.

'I'm sorry.' Briefly the Colonel's voice was gentle. But it soon hardened again as he said, 'So, you're travelling to Yorkshire for your grandfather's sake, not for that of your husband. And it appears that you were right to be nervous.' He paused. 'Was there no one else to do this? It seems a very odd thing for your grandfather to have asked of you, a woman.'

'I was the last of the Leyburns in Jamaica. There was no other he could trust. My grandfather and I... My grandfather and I were very close, Colonel Ancroft. I was willing to do anything for him, and he had good reason to believe me capable. I...I am not without experience in dealing with unscrupulous men.'

The Colonel looked her over. 'You do not surprise me,' he said drily. 'And I'm sure you have your own methods.'

Caroline was undisturbed. Worse things had been said to her in Kingston. She gave him a wicked smile as she replied, 'If you mean what I think you mean, Colonel Ancroft, then I have to tell you that a woman uses what weapons she can. Brute force is not often at her disposal.'

He nodded an acknowledgement, but didn't comment on this. Instead he went on, 'Why did you not trust me with the full story before we left London?'

Caroline hesitated. 'I wouldn't have trusted anyone. Even Mr Turner doesn't know the full story.' She looked him in the eye. 'Tell me what you would have done, Colonel. I was as near distraught as I can be. My servant, my *friend*, had been badly wounded, Edmund's men were very close, and I had come as close as I ever wish to losing my grandfather's most treasured possession, something I regarded as a sacred trust. I was a stranger in England, my only connection here my grandfather's lawyer. I was told you were a brave and honourable man, and can now believe it is true. But I didn't *know* then.'

There was a silence. Then Caroline added, 'I can't be sorry for my deception. But I do beg pardon for the smaller deceits I practised—calling you "Captain" and teasing you with my irritating voice and silly questions.'

The Colonel sat down beside her. 'Yes, why did you?'

Caroline hesitated, then shrugged and said with a touch of exasperation, 'You irritated me. Your letters were so patronising! As if I was a helpless idiot. I couldn't tell you what I really thought, so I teased you.'

'But dammit, from what I was told you *were* a helpless idiot! That was why I agreed to help in the first place! I didn't want to accept the commission, but could hardly refuse Turner, when he appealed to me as a gentleman to see you safe in Yorkshire!'

'I suppose you're right. I shouldn't have done it. Though...' she looked at him between her lashes '...it did enliven some dull moments.'

'I suppose it did.' He gazed at her and almost smiled again. But then he got up, walked a few paces to the edge of the slope and stood there contemplating the view. After a moment he turned round. 'When will you tell me where you wish to go?'

'You're still prepared to take me?' He nodded. Caroline felt such an enormous sense of relief that she was hard put to it not to hug the man standing before her. But she restrained herself. She must be careful not to do anything to remind him of the incident in the inn at Buckden. That had not been mentioned, and she had an idea the Colonel intended to forget it. It would not be wise to bring it to his mind.

He sat down again. 'Now, where?'

'A place called High Hutton. It is not far from Marrick Castle. In the next river valley, in fact. Why, what's wrong, Colonel Ancroft?' The Colonel had risen to his feet once more and was now staring down at her with a shocked look in those grey eyes.

'What game is this? You said your grandfather's name was Leyburn.'

'Yes,' said Caroline. 'Peter Leyburn.'

'And you said this was his family home, I believe?'

She nodded in bewilderment. Why was John Ancroft so upset?

'It may surprise you to know, Mrs Duval, that there are no Leyburns in that valley. Is this another of your tricks?'

Caroline stood up to face him. 'Colonel Ancroft, I've been as frank with you as I dared. I don't tell lies, nor have I made a mistake. My grandfather asked me to go to High Hutton. I'm sure he told me that he came from there. You can't know the area as well as you think!'

The Colonel gazed at her angrily. Once or twice he started to speak, then stopped. Finally he shrugged his shoulders and said, 'I'll take you to High Hutton, ma'am. You will discover for yourself that it's the only building of note for miles around. There are *no Leyburns* in the valley of the Alne! Certainly not at High Hutton. For the last three hundred years High Hutton has belonged to the Ainderby family.'

'Aind—!' Caroline closed her lips tight. The name had taken her unawares. This was the name of the chalice. It was the last secret of all, the one she had sworn to keep until the moment she put the Ainderby Chalice into the hands of its rightful heirs. She must not betray it by another syllable.

To her relief Colonel Ancroft's next words showed that he had mistaken what lay behind her involuntary exclamation. 'Yes, *Ainderby*,' he said. 'Not Leyburn.'

Very wary now, she said, 'Perhaps these Ainderbys were friends of my grandfather?'

'Perhaps. We shall see.' The Colonel's expression was

forbidding. 'And now, I think we should go back to the inn. We're making a very late start.' He turned towards the path down the hill.

Caroline sighed and looked at him in exasperation. Why would he not talk to her about his own affairs? It was clear to her that his feelings towards the Ainderbys were far from friendly. Perhaps his own family was at odds with them. Were they neighbours of his? So far she had no idea where the Colonel lived, or what he would do when he got there. He had a daughter somewhere. Was it to visit her that he was coming north? Or did he intend to live with her in Yorkshire from now on?

They went down back to the inn without speaking. Caroline was sad. For a moment she had felt close to John Ancroft, but he was now as remote as ever. What had she said? Though she racked her brains she could think of nothing. She had been honest and sincere in her apology. He had appeared to accept it. He had not mentioned the embarrassing question of the 'servant girl', preferring, it seemed, to put it behind him. So what had happened to make him angry again?

Humour came to her rescue. For a man who had twice been in very compromising circumstances with her, he was remarkably unfriendly! When she thought of all the gentlemen who would have given their left arm even to dream of being in a similar situation, she was quite put out! It was not at all what she was used to.

As a result of their walk on the hill they were indeed late setting out. Colonel Ancroft had reserved rooms at the Angel in Catterick, but he decided that a change of plan was necessary. There was some wild country in front of them, which meant that they would not be able to keep up the speed of previous stages. He sent a groom on ahead to cancel the rooms in Catterick and reserve others in Boroughbridge, which was some twenty miles nearer.

It was as well he did so. The weather, which had become increasingly sultry, suddenly degenerated and they were forced to take shelter more than once from severe thunderstorms.

In the middle of the day they decided to stop for a while at the Swan in Ferrybridge. Colonel Ancroft told her that it was reputed to be the most luxurious inn in England, and afterwards Caroline was of the opinion that this might well be so. They sat in comfort while the storm raged outside, enjoying an excellent meal. And when they came out afterwards they found that the weather had changed yet again. The sun was shining and the air smelt fresh, washed clean by the rain of the previous hour. Caroline decided that she had had enough of the carriage. The roads might well be muddy after the storm, but she would take advantage of the fact that she could now be seen as a comparatively young, energetic woman, and ride for a while. Besides, she hoped to learn more about Colonel Ancroft. Riding at his side must be more productive than sitting in a carriage with only Joseph and Maggie for company! So she went back into the inn, got Maggie to look out a change of clothing and appeared again, just as her escort was beginning to show some impatience. He frowned at her green habit, dashing hat and riding boots, his eyes lingering involuntarily on the chestnut curl hanging over her shoulder.

'Do I infer that you intend to ride, ma'am?'

'If you will permit, Colonel,' said Caroline demurely. But her air of submission was somewhat spoilt by the enchanting smile which followed.

The Colonel frowned. 'The roads will be dirty.'

'I'm not afraid of dirt, sir.'

He regarded her impassively for a moment, then said, 'I'll see if they have a suitable mount for you,' and wheeled away.

In a few minutes Caroline was riding alongside him on an elegant bay, rejoicing in her new found freedom, and admiring the view.

It was a weird, wild countryside with a strange beauty of its own. She had seen nothing like it in Jamaica. To the left was a sheer drop from the road into a wide valley, and now and then they could see coal mines in the distance. She asked the Colonel about them, and found him remarkably well informed for a man who had spent the previous seventeen years abroad in the army. She said so.

'Since I decided to come north, I've been reading about them, Mrs Duval. I thought it better to learn what has been happening since I was last here.'

'When was that?'

'Nine years ago.'

'Quite some time, then. Your daughter must have missed you.'

'She has been very well looked after. I doubt she has missed me at all. Do you see that ruin over on the horizon there, Mrs Duval? It was once an abbey.'

'That is something England has which Jamaica lacks. History, Colonel Ancroft. We're a very new country compared with yours. Are there many old buildings in Yorkshire?'

The Colonel took this subject up with obvious relief. He took a quarter of an hour to list some famous abbeys and priory churches to be found in the county, together with a brief history of each.

'Thank you, Colonel. My goodness! What an authority you are on your county. First coal mines, now abbeys! Is your own home anywhere near here?'

'No,' he said. 'It is more than fifty miles away. But there are coal mines and abbeys to be found all over the north.' He gave her a slightly amused look, then said blandly, 'I don't believe I mentioned the Cistercian abbey near Ripon. Fountains Abbey. It's particularly pictur-esque. It's a pity that our journey does not allow time to visit it. Are you interested in history, Mrs Duval?'

Caroline was forced to follow his lead. The Colonel, it appeared, did not wish to talk about his home. Nor any-thing else remotely personal. Just wait, my friend, she thought. We Leyburns do not give up so easily! I'll find out about you yet.

They rode in silence for a while. Then her companion said abruptly, 'You said that what you carry is valuable. Would it be safer with me? I'm very ready to look after it for you, Mrs Duval. These roads aren't always safe, even without pursuers! What is it? A necklace? Some other jewellery?'

'Thank you, but no. I'll look after it myself. I promised my grandfather, you see.'

'You were obviously very fond of him.'

'I adored him. My parents died when I was nine, and my grandfather and I were left behind to keep each other company. He was a wonderful man, though he could be ruthless when he chose. At one time in my life I...I made a catastrophic mistake. And afterwards, though he had been bitterly hurt by my behaviour, he took me back with not a single reproach. It's not too much to say that he saved me from destruction.'

'You were fortunate to have someone at hand.' He spoke harshly, bitterly even. Once again Caroline's inter-est was roused. But she knew better than to probe. It was not the moment. But with every hour that passed she was becoming more intrigued by Colonel John Ancroft. He was like no man she had ever met—except perhaps her grandfather. She had an idea that the Colonel was more scrupulous than her grandfather, who had occasionally revealed a devious side to his nature. But she was not at all sure that the Colonel would be less ruthless if and when he thought it necessary.

Chapter Six

John Ancroft stole an occasional glance at his companion as they trotted along in the sunshine. This was his first real opportunity to study her since he had discovered what she really looked like. He allowed his thoughts a free rein. She was very beautiful. In the clear light of day, he could see that she didn't in fact resemble Gabriella quite as closely as he had thought. It was true she had the same richly dark chestnut hair, the same pure green eyes, the same flawless skin. She was tall as Gabriella had been, and if Gabriella had lived to full womanhood he rather thought she too would have been a seductively full-bosomed, slender-hipped creature such as Caroline Duval.

But there were differences. Gabriella had had an innocence about her to which this woman was a stranger. Gabriella had given herself to him just once. She had shown such sweet abandon that he had been enraptured, especially as he knew that she had not done so lightly, or loosely, but because they were so in love that neither of them could have resisted. And because, as they both knew, she was so soon to be his wife.

But Caroline Duval… Why had she seemed so willing to join him in his bed at Buckden? *She* had not been suffering from a fever. And why had she then drawn back? Had he offended her in some way? Dammit, why couldn't he remember more clearly? What *had* happened that night...? But the memory remained obstinately elusive, and after a moment he gave up the struggle and returned to his musings.

They both had plenty of spirit, she and his Gabriella, but humour was not a part of Gabriella's make-up, whereas he suspected it was deeply ingrained in Caroline Duval. Gabriella had taken life seriously. She *might* have developed the same attractive little laughter lines round her eyes, but he doubted it. Besides, Gabriella, he thought with a pang, had always been so proud of her beauty, so anxious to preserve it, had stated her determination to stay young forever. As she had, of course. Eternally young in memory...

With determination he turned his thoughts back to the woman riding beside him. He had been amused by her efforts to question him, but he was damned if he would make it easy for her after the way she had teased him earlier! She was an intriguing mixture, all the same. Though she was obviously curious her questions had been basically harmless—such as any politely interested new acquaintance might have asked. After the scene at Buckden he wouldn't have been surprised if she had probed, been intrusive. But she had behaved honourably since that night, never showing by word or look that he had very nearly seduced her, nor that she had been a witness to his embarrassing parade of raw emotion. What other woman would have resisted the temptation to look conscious, or to give him sly looks, or significant nods? Or, worse still, to give herself the pleasure of offering advice or sympathy? But Caroline Duval had done none of these. If she had been a man, he would have called her a true gentleman.

Other qualities she had, too. Courage for example, and pride. When he had caught her under the waterfall she had been shocked, and frightened, of course. That wasn't surprising. But how quickly she had recovered, refusing to let herself be cowed, or show embarrassment or shame. Nor had she used the occasion to behave provocatively, either. Her laughter had been quite genuine, and clearly stemmed from a keen sense of the ridiculous. He grinned. She was right! It had been a bizarrely comic situation. Why hadn't he appreciated it at the time?

He rode on through the countryside considering this and his smile faded. Because he had been so angry, that was why. For a few moments he could have throttled her. It was many, many years since he had been in such a rage. Not since...not since Philip had died. It wasn't the simple fact of her deception. That would have annoyed him, but it would not have put him into such a fury that it had taken all his control not to give way to it. It was the thought that this woman had been privy to his passion and his pain, had witnessed feelings he had kept hidden from the world for years, that she had taken advantage of his weakness to deceive him into believing Gabriella had returned from the dead... That had been intolerable.

But had he been fair? *She* hadn't tried to persuade him she was Gabriella. He had persuaded himself. That much he could remember. But what sort of woman was she, to come into his bedchamber without protest? As far as he could remember he hadn't dragged her in. His memory of that night was fogged by the effects of fever, but he couldn't remember a struggle, only a sensation of overwhelming delight at rediscovering Gabriella, his love, followed by devastating grief at losing her all over again.

Strangely though, the remaining impression of the woman who had been in the room with him was not one of someone looking for excitement or sexual gratification of any kind, but someone who had treated him with dignity and compassion. And she had made no reference to the episode since. The woman was an enigma! He had never known anyone like her.

'You're frowning, Colonel Ancroft. Do you not approve of my riding with you like this? Is it "not done" in England?'

She was looking at him with that little air of mockery which seldom left her. Those green eyes seemed to hold an invitation to laugh with her at the world and its absurdities. She might *ask* about the rules of society, but he was not at all sure that she would allow them to *affect* her. If he were to tell her now that what she was doing would be severely frowned on by the *ton*, he was almost sure she would shrug her shoulders, and continue to ride with all the confidence and self-possession in the world.

Colonel Ancroft would have liked to test his supposition, but there was unfortunately nothing at all untoward in their riding together in full sight of the rest of the party. 'It is perfectly proper, Mrs Duval,' he said. 'Are the rules in Jamaica stricter, then?'

'I suppose they are. But my grandfather was somewhat scornful of the establishment, and I'm afraid he taught me to be the same. He used to say that one should abide by one's own code of conduct and be damned to the rest.' She added carefully, 'That was what my *grandfather* was used to say.'

For some reason Colonel Ancroft did not doubt that it was what Caroline Duval was used to say herself, too. But he merely remarked, '"To thine own self be true." Was that it? Make up your own rules. Didn't it make for difficulty in such a restricted world as I imagine Jamaican society must be?'

Caroline Duval laughed. 'Oh, yes! But then, I had everything to win and nothing to lose, you see.'

'I'm afraid I don't understand?'

'I was a black sheep, Colonel. The ladies of Kingston would have seen the Widow Duval drummed out of the regiment if they could have managed it. You're looking concerned. There's no need, I assure you. With my grandfather behind me, there was never any risk of it, and now... Now I'm a reformed character and *perfectly* acceptable anywhere.'

She gave him a wicked look. Reformed character, indeed! A sudden memory of this woman standing before him in the bedchamber, the perfection of her body, the feel of her skin against his cheek, took him by surprise. He looked away before she could read the flare of desire in his eyes. She was a witch! He fought to find something unexceptional to say.

'I'm sure you had many admirers, too.'

'Among the gentlemen, you mean? Oh, yes.'

'Were you... Have you never been tempted to remarry?'

This time Caroline Duval was not laughing. She said emphatically, 'Never! Not once! I make many mistakes, Colonel Ancroft, but I try very hard not to make the same mistake twice.'

He was surprised at her vehemence. The late Mr Duval, it seemed, had not been a success.

Then she said with a look of challenge in her eyes, 'Since I've satisfied some of your curiosity, Colonel Ancroft, won't you satisfy some of mine?'

He regarded her warily, but decided he would trust her

not to delve too deep. 'I might,' he said cautiously. 'What do you wish to know?'

'Where you live—and, before you say London, I mean here in Yorkshire.'

With only a fractional hesitation he said, 'Marrick.'

'Really? Grandfather described the castle there as something of a landmark.'

'He was right. It is quite large and prominently placed.'

'I see! So you *do* know the area! Have you been away long?'

'Seventeen years. Though I have been back briefly once or twice since then.'

'The last time nine years ago. You see, I do not forget what you have told me! Is your daughter at Marrick?'

'Yes, for the moment. She will go to London next year to be presented to society. She's seventeen next February.'

Caroline turned an astonished face towards him. 'Your daughter is sixteen?' When he nodded she said, 'You must have been ridiculously young when she was born?'

So she wanted to know how old he was? He didn't mind telling her. 'Thank you for the compliment. I was twenty-two.' With amusement he watched her working it out. 'I'm thirty-eight,' he added helpfully.

She laughed and blushed. 'I had already concluded as much,' she said. He was fascinated. He hadn't imagined Caroline Duval *could* blush, but she was damned attractive when she did.

'I shan't enquire how old you are, Mrs Duval. It isn't something a lady likes to be asked, I understand,' he said quirking an eyebrow at her.

'I'm twenty-six. And you may save any gallant exclamations of surprise, Colonel. The fact doesn't disconcert me in the slightest.'

He found himself saying, 'But then, from what I have observed, I think it would take a great deal to disconcert you, Mrs Duval.'

Once again colour rose in her cheeks. She raised an eyebrow and said quizzically, 'Are you reminding me of an episode…no, *two* episodes we would both rather forget, Colonel Ancroft?'

Her directness surprised him. He had made his comment without thinking, regretting what he had said as soon as the words were uttered. What the devil was it about this woman? After swearing to himself that he would never mention the incident at Buckden to anyone, least of all to Caroline Duval, here he was embarrassing them both by his words. He snatched a glance at her. The look in her eyes was mockery, not embarrassment! The wretched woman was laughing at his discomfiture! Well, he thought grimly, two can play at that game, my lovely one!

'You're surely omitting at least some aspects of those "episodes", if you think I would rather forget them, Mrs Duval. I have every man's appreciation of beauty,' he said smoothly. 'Especially natural beauty.'

He saw with some satisfaction that he had surprised her. Her face flamed, she sat upright in the saddle, and said hotly, 'Why, you *sal*—!' Then she stopped and bit her lip, nervously fingering her whip.

Colonel Ancroft laughed aloud at these signs of temper. He was willing to swear that Caroline Duval was not often caught off balance like this. She continued to gaze at him angrily for a moment, then a reluctant smile appeared and she nodded in acknowledgement.

'My congratulations, Colonel! I haven't often had a taste of my own medicine returned so quickly. I suppose I deserved it.' Her amusement this time was quite genuine with no trace of malice. 'But it was almost worth it just to see you laugh! Shall we now cry quits?'

He nodded, still chuckling. 'I must apologise. It was not a gentlemanly thing to do.'

'But irresistible, I'm sure,' she said drily.

They were just coming in to Aberford, their next stop.

'I think I must ride in the carriage for the next stretch,' said Caroline. 'More than my *amour propre* is hurting. It's months since I've been on a horse for such a long time. Thank you, Colonel Ancroft, for an instructive... and amusing ride.'

The Colonel helped her dismount, then watched her walk, somewhat stiffly, into the inn, the smile still lingering on his lips.

The decision to stay the night at Boroughbridge rather than to press on to Catterick turned out to be a good one. The inn was commodious and comfortable, and it served them with a delicious meal. The trout had been freshly caught in the river, the veal collops were done to a turn, and the pastry in the gooseberry tart melted in the mouth. In the interest of her own self-esteem Caroline had taken considerable pains with her appearance, and she felt she was looking her best. The evening was warm, but her short-sleeved dress of fine white lawn was elegantly cool. A Paisley shawl was draped over her arms.

Colonel Ancroft gave her a slight smile when she appeared, but once again made no comment. Caroline was slightly piqued. This was a man who didn't believe in empty compliments, it appeared! Over dinner they conversed on unexceptional matters, the scenery, the local activities, aspects of Jamaican life... It was all strictly impersonal. After the challenges of the journey it all seemed rather flat to Caroline. She would have enjoyed a further sparring match with the Colonel, but he was obviously not in the mood.

The inn had some old London newspapers and John spent some time after dinner perusing their columns. He gave a sudden exclamation.

'What is it, Colonel?'

He cleared his throat and said, 'I'll read it out. ''Mr Edmund Willoughby, one of Jamaica's most prominent citizens, has now left London after a disappointingly short stay. Mr Willoughby landed in Falmouth a month ago after a highly uncomfortable voyage from Kingston, during which the packet was delayed by violent storms in the Atlantic. He was forced to spend some time recuperating at the home of his English relatives in Kent, and had time for only one week in the capital. It is understood that he intends to see something of the countryside during his sojourn in England.''' He lowered the paper. 'Is this your cousin?'

Caroline nodded. 'English relatives—I wonder if Edmund found his ally among them?' Then she asked suddenly, 'But tell me, how old is that newspaper? When did Edmund leave London?'

'Several days ago, I should imagine. Does he know your destination?'

'He knew it was somewhere in the north, but that's all. My grandfather didn't really trust him, any more than I do. He knew very well that Edmund wanted what I am carrying, though I don't think he realised to what lengths my cousin was prepared to go to get it. But Grandfather was always cautious about this thing. He never discussed it.'

John respected her wish for secrecy, but he could not help wondering what it was she was taking to High Hutton. The whole affair was puzzling. She was always so careful not to give any clue as to what it might be. He had asked her whether it was jewellery, and offered to take care of it, but she had refused the offer without answering his question. What *was* her grandfather's connection with High Hutton? Was he a repentant thief? Had he been a pirate on the Caribbean in his early days, perhaps, and now wished to make amends by returning some valuable trinket to the Ainderbys? Or was it something of sentimental value, a souvenir of someone he had loved? He asked, 'Has it been in your family a long time?'

'I think so. But I don't know for sure. I don't even know how Edmund learned of it. I had no idea myself of its existence until Grandfather told me about it, shortly before he died. But I'm quite certain that Edmund cannot know precisely where we are going, only that it's somewhere in the north of England.'

'Then there isn't any immediate danger. There's more than one road out of London to the north, and though I've had my men keeping watch, there hasn't been any sign of pursuit.'

Caroline was still not altogether reassured. 'I can't fail now! I mustn't!' she said agitatedly. 'Colonel Ancroft, how far is it to Marrick and High Hutton?'

'About thirty miles or more to Marrick. And another eight or so to High Hutton.'

'Then we're close enough to outrun Edmund. We must leave Boroughbridge at first light tomorrow,' she urged.

'I agree. I'll warn the men to be ready.' He smiled at her. 'Try not to be so anxious. We can't do anything before tomorrow, but we'll start in good time, I promise. Now! The inn has some excellent brandy. Allow me to order a glass for you. I've noticed you enjoy one occasionally, and it will help you sleep.'

Caroline made an effort. She gave him a challenging

look. 'I suppose you disapprove of my drinking brandy? Maggie does.'

'Why should I? Though surely rum is a more usual tipple in Jamaica?'

'Neither rum nor brandy is considered suitable for a lady, not even in Jamaica.'

'But as you told me—you make your own rules, do you not? Drink the brandy, Caroline. It will help to calm you. It's very unlikely that your cousin will find us, especially once we've left the main road north. And if he does, we can deal with him, I fancy.'

They left the inn as planned early the next morning and were soon driving over a handsome stone bridge over the River Ure. They would leave the Great North Road just beyond Catterick, which was a mere twenty odd miles away. Caroline was restless. It would have helped if she could have ridden with the Colonel, but they had both agreed that that was out of the question. She must stay out of sight in the carriage.

'Do what you can to keep Bellerby happy,' John said. 'I think he's fretting at his inability to help. That arm is not healing as fast as it ought.' He regarded her critically. 'And you'd better sit well back,' he said with a frown. 'Your appearance is too distinctive. It's a pity you chose to throw away your widow's weeds.'

'Do not say so!' she begged. 'I was never so glad to be rid of any garments before! I'll sit well back in the carriage, I promise.'

It was as well she did so. After making good time along a straight road from Boroughbridge, they arrived at Catterick Bridge. From here the Great North Road went on to Carlisle and then into Scotland and Gretna Green. But,

much to Caroline's relief, Colonel Ancroft and his party
would at last leave the main road and turn west towards
Richmond. Marrick Castle and High Hutton lay among
the hills beyond.

They had stopped to change the horses before turning
off, and found they had to wait. Another carriage, one
travelling south, was already at the inn, the ostlers busy
harnessing up a new team. The landlord came hurrying
out to apologise for the delay, and offer the inn's hospitality while they waited. His face changed comically when
he saw the Colonel.

'Eh, Master John! Well, I never!' He turned to the
house and shouted, 'Annie! Annie! Come 'ere, lass,
quick! It's Master John come back after all these years.'
He took the hand John was offering, and shook it enthu-
siastically, grinning from ear to ear. 'Ee, it's good to see
thee, lad! Where's tha been, all this time?'

His wife came out and gave him a shove in the ribs
with her elbow. 'I'm ashamed of thee, Barnaby, I am that!
Where's your respect?' She turned and curtsied. 'My lord,
you'll 'ave to forgive my husband. He means no 'arm,
but he forgets what's due to you now. May I say we're
reet glad to see your lordship. We'd be honoured if you'd
step inside a moment. And the rest of your party.'

'Thank you, Annie, but another time. My passengers
are impatient to be at Marrick. And don't blame Barnaby.
It's a wonderful welcome he's given me. Besides, it must
be difficult to show too much respect to the scrubby boy
he taught to ride. I've had many a cuff on the ear from
him.' Annie laughed, and John turned to put his head
inside the carriage. 'I ought to explain,' he said to Caroline, 'that Barnaby and his wife were once in service at
the castle. Barnaby was head groom there, and taught us
to ride.'

'Aye, you and Lord Philip both.' Barnaby's red face clouded over. 'That was a poor business,' he began, 'but there! His lordship was always too hasty for his own good... But we're glad you've decided to come back to us at last, Master John.'

'I say! Ho, there! Landlord!' The peremptory call attracted everyone's attention. Both John and Barnaby turned to look. An exquisitely dressed gentleman was stepping down from the other coach. His blue velvet coat and pale fawn breeches looked so out of place in these parts and at this hour that they all stared. Then John's eyes narrowed. He turned again and gave a quick glance at Caroline. Like everyone else she had looked out to see who had called the landlord, but she was now shrinking back against the squabs. Her face was white. 'Edmund!' she mouthed at him. John nodded and stepped forward, covering the window with his broad shoulders.

'Well, did you hear me? Landlord, I say!' snapped the exquisite.

'In a minute, sir!' said Barnaby amiably.

'No, dammit! Now! Come here, I want to ask you something.'

Barnaby looked at the Colonel, who said quietly, 'Be careful what you tell that gentleman, Barnaby.'

Barnaby ambled over to Edmund Willoughby. 'What can I do for you, sir?' he asked pleasantly. 'Are my men not doing their job to your satisfaction?'

'It's not that,' said Mr Willoughby impatiently. 'I want to ask about some travellers you might have seen. A Colonel Ancroft. I need to talk to him. Do you know anything about him? Have you seen him? I understand he belongs somewhere in these parts.'

'In these parts, you say? I don't think so, sir,' said Barnaby, the very picture of a slow-thinking landlord of a wayside inn. 'Give me a moment to think… And I'll ask the lad, too.' He looked round. 'Where is he, the young varmint? He should be dealing with the other gentleman's carriage. Unless you watch them every minute of the day they're back in the taproom! Excuse me, I'll be back in a moment.' He went to the door of the inn and roared, 'Jem! Where are you? Come out here and start your work before I use my belt on you!' He went over to John, apparently to apologise, but lowering his voice he said, 'What is it, my lord?'

Colonel Ancroft said quietly, 'I heard. I don't want him to find me, Barnaby. Put him off. He doesn't know the new title, so you can impress him with that if you have to. But no mention of Ancroft.'

Barnaby bowed and cuffed the ear of a puzzled stable lad, who was just coming round the corner. Then he went back to Mr Willoughby.

'Now, sir, I'm all yours. What was the name of the party?'

'Ancroft.'

'And why would you be wanting him, sir?'

'The er…the villain has abducted a cousin of mine. I suspect he's taking her to Gretna. They must be stopped before he succeeds! Have you seen them?'

'What makes you think they're anywhere round here?'

'They had rooms reserved in Catterick last night. I waited for them but they didn't arrive. I must find them. There'll be a substantial reward, landlord. Have you seen them at all?'

'I can't say I have, sir. We've had very little traffic through here these last days. Perhaps they're at Boroughbridge? We've had some weather recently, and that might have delayed them. Try Boroughbridge, sir.' He turned away.

'Just one moment! What about the fellow over there? Who is he? Don't just stare like that, you fool! Check them. There's someone who appears to be travelling north, *and* he has a female in the carriage with him, too!'

John Ancroft stiffened and strolled towards him. He stood looking coldly down at Edmund Willoughby. 'May I have your name, sir?' he asked.

'Certainly! And I hope to have yours. I am Edmund Willoughby of Kingston in Jamaica.'

'Ah! Jamaica, eh?' drawled John. 'I suppose that explains it.'

'Explains what, sir?'

'The uncouth manner you use in talking of myself and my wife. Colonial manners. I suppose I must forgive you.' And John turned away with insulting indifference.

Mr Willoughby coloured angrily and said, 'One moment! You have not yet told me who *you* are, sir! May I have your name?'

John raised an eyebrow and looked Edmund up and down. 'Certainly!' he said finally in a bored tone. 'Tell him, Barnaby.'

Barnaby said in tones of hushed respect, 'You're talking to the biggest landowner for miles around, sir. This is his lordship, the Marquess of Coverdale. It's more than my inn's worth to annoy him. So, if you don't mind, sir, I'd like you to be on your way. It doesn't do my business any good at all to have strangers coming here and insulting their betters.'

'Why, you impertinent—'

'On your way, sir!'

With bad grace Mr Willoughby got into the carriage and told his man to give the order. In minutes he was on his way south again.

John Ancroft watched him go, and then turned to the

landlord. 'Barnaby, you rogue!' he said grinning. 'You should be on the stage!'

'Oh, I can crawl with the best o' 'em, my lord—when it suits me.'

'I'm obliged to you. Now, we must make haste to reach the shelter of Marrick before Mr Willoughby discovers his mistake.'

Barnaby eyed him curiously, hesitated, then said somewhat awkwardly, 'May it please your lordship… Annie and I would like to give you our best wishes, my lord. You and your good lady. We didn't know your lordship was married, you see.'

'I'm not, Barnaby. The lady is merely a friend. I said it in order to put that villain off the scent. And before that dramatic imagination of yours gets to work, I'm not off to Gretna with her, either. Thank you. If the gentleman comes back again, don't provide him with any horses!'

'Don't you worry, my lord! And if I do, they'll be broken-down nags not worthy of the name! Give my regards to Marrick! They'll all be reet glad to see your lordship there.'

'Oh, will they?' muttered John to himself as they set off again. 'I doubt it, Barnaby. I doubt it very much.'

Just three miles further on, they stopped again in Richmond. A team of John's own horses which had been sent down from Marrick were to be harnessed up for the last stage of their journey. Caroline was fascinated by the warmth of the welcome the Colonel received from nearly everyone who saw him. John Ancroft may not have been seen in Richmond for nine years, but he had not been forgotten.

As they entered the inn he said to her, 'I've sent a groom to warn my steward up at Marrick to have rooms prepared for us all. The roads were pretty bad when I was last in the district, and from what I hear they're now worse, not better. High Hutton is nearly inaccessible at the best of times, and the recent rains have made the road up the valley dangerous. We'll stay the night at Marrick and then consider what's to be done.' He nodded reassuringly. 'You'll be as safe at Marrick as anywhere in the kingdom. It was once a fortress.'

Caroline nodded. Once again he had taken the law into his own hands without consulting her first. But this time she was ready to trust his judgement. However anxious she was to see her mission over, his better knowledge of the country must prevail. However, she could not resist teasing him once more. Putting on a mournful face she said wistfully, 'And I had *so* hoped you were taking me to Gretna, as my cousin said! Especially as you've told the world that we are already married!'

'Mrs Duval—'

'There's another thing! Last night you called me Caroline. But now I'm back to being Mrs Duval again. What have I done to displease you? Apart from running away with you to Gretna.'

John gave her a reluctant grin. 'You forget, I know you better now. You won't disturb me with your teasing. I know your views on marriage, and they agree with my own. But I think we're friends enough for me to call you Caroline, if it's your wish. My name is—'

'Oh, I know your name! It is the Marquess of Coverdale! And to think I thought you Captain Ancroft, a simple soldier in the service of the King...'

'You always knew I was a Colonel. And the Coverdale title is very new. My...my uncle died in April.' His face changed. 'I should perhaps warn you that I'm highly un-

certain of our reception at Marrick. I only hope it won't
affect you.'

'But everyone I've seen is delighted that you're back!
How can you be uncertain?'

He hesitated and seemed to be debating within himself
what to say. Then he walked to the window and peered
out, examining the weather. He then turned back to her.
Caroline was puzzled—John Ancroft was not usually so
indecisive. She waited.

He said suddenly, 'Caroline, do you feel able to ride
with me a part of the way to Marrick? All of it, even. It's
no further than our ride to Aberford, and the weather
seems promising. I think I need to talk to you.'

'Of course, I should be delighted! It won't take me long
to change. I'll call Maggie at once.'

Once they were out of the town and on the road he
kept up a good pace, and they had soon left the carriage
far behind. The scenery became increasingly wild as they
went on through a narrow valley. A river flowed alongside, its banks lined with thick woods, all in full leaf, and
above the road, the upper slopes were covered in grass,
interspersed with grey limestone rocks. Everywhere,
small streams and rivulets rushed down to join the river
at the bottom, filling the air with a constant sound of
running water. And in the distance hills of grey and green
were bathed in the afternoon sunshine. John seemed to be
feasting his eyes on it, like a man starved of the sight for
too long.

Some way along the valley they left the road and turned
on to a narrow track which led to a grassy knoll above.
To Caroline's relief, a halt was called, and they dismounted. John gave the grooms a signal to fall back, and

they were left effectively alone. He led her to the edge of the knoll.

'I hope you don't object to this seclusion?'

'I'm no nervous maiden, John! And I imagine you have a good reason to want privacy. No, I don't object.'

'Good. Over there. Can you see?'

Caroline looked in the direction he was pointing. On a rocky outcrop some distance away she saw a large castle bathed in the afternoon sun. Even on a sunny afternoon it looked formidably uncompromising, grey and stark among the rocks. 'That is Marrick Castle,' he said.

'It's an impressive sight. How it dominates the countryside!'

'Yes. Marrick and High Hutton between them. For centuries, the Ancrofts and the Ainderbys have held most of the lands round here. They've been in turn enemies, friends, rivals, and allies.' He paused. 'And some have loved.'

Caroline caught her breath. Was she to learn something about the Ainderbys at last?

John Ancroft glanced at her and said, 'I should like to tell you something of our family history. This isn't idle gossip. I've invited you to stay at Marrick, and want to prepare you for whatever is waiting for us there.' He took a breath and began again, 'You said people were pleased to see me. Yes, I think you're right. The ordinary folk round here are pleased to welcome me back because they believe there'll be better times ahead. My uncle was a recluse for many years before he died, and the estate has been badly neglected. There's no shortage of money to make the reforms necessary. It was rather a complete abdication of interest on his part. They all hope that I'll do better by them.'

'But they seem to *like* you, too!'

'I suppose they remember me from happier times, when I was a lad among them. The folk round here are rather like your Joseph Bellerby—their respect has little to do with rank or position. You have to earn it. And if they once decide you're worthy, then they're yours for life.'

'I think you said once that you'd quarrelled with your uncle?'

'Yes. And this is why. He had a son, my cousin Philip, his only child. He and I were brought up as brothers. But there was an accident and Philip was killed, together with Gabriella. My uncle blamed me for it, and I must say he had some justification.'

The bare words, uttered without expression or feeling, hovered in the air between them. If Caroline had not heard the devastation in John Ancroft's voice in that bedchamber in Buckden when he talked of Gabriella's death, she might have thought that the tragedy now meant little or nothing to him. But the contrast between these matter-of-fact sentences and the anguish she had witnessed at Buckden could not have been greater. What she was seeing now was John's public figure. The private agony which she had accidentally provoked that night was not for the world to see. Never for the world. *'I saw her die,'* he had said. *'She and Philip together.'*

But was John Ancroft now saying that he believed himself responsible? Responsible for Gabriella's death! The depth of the agony she had witnessed that night suddenly became more comprehensible. She waited.

He took a deep breath and went on, 'In my fever at Buckden I mistook you for Gabriella. You...you strongly resemble her, you see.'

Caroline was silent. There was nothing she could say.

John went on, 'There are still some older people at Marrick who were there at the time of the accident.

They're sure to see this resemblance, even if they don't comment.' He turned and looked at her. 'In fact, Caroline, I suspect your grandfather may have had a closer relationship with the Ainderbys than you know. The physical likeness is striking.'

'I...I remember your saying so.' Caroline said awkwardly.

He gave her a swift tortured look. 'Yes,' he replied. 'Yes. Indeed. May I go on? Or are you tired? I've at least explained why you may be subjected to some strange looks. Perhaps that's enough.'

'No, please! Tell me a little more. Tell me about Gabriella's daughter. Your daughter.'

'Gabriella's! No, no! You're mistaken. Harriet is my *wife*'s daughter.'

Caroline looked at him in astonishment. 'Gabriella wasn't your wife?'

'No.' He paused. 'No. We were to have been married within the month when she was killed. My wife's name was Rose. Harriet is *her* daughter.'

'I see...'

He gave her a little smile. 'I'm quite sure you don't. But that's another long story and a sad one. I won't go into it more than I have to. My wife, you see...my wife...had been in love with Philip, and thought I had killed him deliberately. She persuaded Harriet to believe the same.'

'Your *own daughter*? But how did she manage that? Harriet wasn't even born when the accident happened!'

'No. Not till the following February. You mustn't blame my wife, however. She had help from my uncle... Oh God, Caroline, if you knew how difficult this is! But I must prepare you!' John turned away again and gazed out over the valley, as if to draw strength from it. He began again. 'After Philip died, my uncle's affection for me turned to a hatred which was so virulent that he would have harmed me in any way he could short of murder. He poisoned my wife's mind against me, and then set about turning Harriet away from me, too. With considerable success. Since she was old enough to understand, Harriet has disliked and feared me. As far as I know, she still does. That's what I wish you to know.'

Chapter Seven

'John! Oh, John!' There was no trace now either of mockery or of laughter in Caroline Duval's face. Nor was there the sentimental pity he had always feared from others. Her expression was a mixture of shock and pure compassion.

He was moved, but refused to show it. After seventeen years of steeling himself against the softer human emotions he was not about to melt at the sight of the first beautiful woman to show him compassion! On the whole he preferred her mockery. That could be dealt with far more easily!

'Pray don't be too sorry for me,' he said a little stiffly. 'There's no need. I hardly know the child. She was only seven when I last saw her, and even that was for a short two minutes. I have only told you this unhappy tale, to prepare you for her attitude towards me.'

'But what about the child?' Caroline cried. 'What about Harriet?'

'I believe she's a well-balanced, reasonably happy girl. Considering her beginnings, remarkably so. Mr Fennybright was good enough to find an excellent lady of education and breeding to be her companion, and I have regular reports from both the lady and Fennybright himself. No, Caroline, you need have no misgivings about the child. She's very bright. Shall we move on?'

As they made their way back on to the road, John Ancroft was wondering whether he had been wise to reveal so much. He could have satisfied many other women with a good deal less. But Caroline Duval was no fool. However short her time at Marrick, she could not fail to notice the situation. It was better to give her the facts rather than to see her speculating about his family affairs.

Besides, in a curious way, his dislike of revealing anything of his private concerns was balanced by a sense of relief at having unburdened himself, shared his trouble with someone he could trust not to offend him with excessive sympathy or pity. He was quite certain that his story was safe with Caroline Duval.

They arrived at the steep drive up to Marrick Castle not long after. Built on a rock, Marrick was accessible only by this drive, which ended in a bridge over a moat. The moat had long since been emptied and a wild garden planted in its hollows, but the wooden bridge and massive arch that had once been part of the defences were still in use. When they entered the main courtyard John's face clouded over at the sight of what looked like hundreds of servants gathered there. But his expression grew more amiable when an elderly man with a shock of white hair came towards him.

'Thomas!' he said, dismounting and shaking the man by the hand. 'Thomas Beckford! How d' ye do?'

'Very fair, my lord. But it's a grand day for Marrick!'

'Is it, indeed? It's an idle day for Marrick from the looks of things! What are all these people doing here?'

'Eeh, my lord! What do you think? We had to give the

new Marquess a welcome. There wasn't a soul for miles around but wanted to come when they 'eard you'd be back today, my lord.' Thomas's eyes passed to Caroline, who had been waiting in the background. The old man's eyes widened briefly in shock, but he quickly controlled it and became once again the well-trained servant.

'Mrs Duval, this is my steward, Thomas Beckford.' Turning back to the steward, John said, 'I hope you have some rooms ready for Mrs Duval and her people?'

'They're quite ready, my lord. If his lordship would come this way? Mistress Duval?'

The steps up to the great Hall were lined with servants, all bobbing and smiling at their new master. Some were even cheering. John spoke to some of the older ones and nodded to others. Walking behind him, Caroline had cause to be grateful for his warning. Not everyone was as discreet as Thomas Beckford. Numbers of people craned their necks and stared as she passed, and she heard a growing buzz of conversation behind her. But she lost none of her usual grace and composure as she followed John up the steps. Whether it was her likeness to Gabriella, or her possible relationship with the new master that was disturbing them, they would soon enough learn that she was but a temporary visitor to Marrick, with no part to play in their future.

Two people were waiting at the top of the steps, a girl and an older woman. But as they approached, the girl suddenly broke away and fled into the room behind. The woman who had been beside her looked vexed for a moment and turned, clearly debating whether to go after her. But then she changed her mind, came up to John and curtsied. 'Lord Coverdale, may I welcome you back to Marrick? I am Mrs Abbington.'

'Thank you.' John turned to Caroline. 'Mrs Duval, may

I present Mrs Abbington? Mrs Abbington has looked after Harriet for many years, and from all accounts very well, too.'

'Not so well as I should, apparently. You must excuse Lady Harriet, my lord. She must be over-excited. I'll fetch her presently.'

'No need for hurry, ma'am. I'll see her when she is ready. Now, will you perhaps show Mrs Duval to her room? I expect she needs a rest.'

'Certainly. Mrs Duval?' The companion led the way across a huge hall to a baronial staircase. 'I've arranged for you to be in the blue bedroom, ma'am,' she said as they traversed a long corridor decorated with stags' heads and pieces of old armour. 'I think you'll like the view.'

Eventually, after what seemed like miles, they came to a comfortable bedchamber with blue curtains and bed hangings. Caroline not only liked the view—she was struck dumb by it! Row after row of green and grey hills, purple now in the sun's lengthening shadows, stretched into the distance. To the right a foaming stream hurtled down over boulders and rocks to join the river in the valley far below. Over to the left, beyond a deep cleft, was an outcrop of rocks, overrun with tiny rivulets and infant waterfalls. 'It's breathtaking!' she cried. 'I don't think I've seen anything so impressive since I left Jamaica.'

'Jamaica? I didn't realise... You're a long way from home, ma'am!'

'Yes.' Caroline sobered, as she remembered that the task she had come from Jamaica to fulfil was still not complete. She took the strap of the bag that never left her, pulled it wearily over her head, and laid the bag down on the bed.

'Could you please find my maid, Mrs Abbington? And the valises.'

'I'll see to it with pleasure, ma'am. Er... Unless his lordship decides differently, we dine early at Marrick. Dinner is served at six.' Mrs Abbington gave a little bob and left her. Caroline was suddenly exhausted. So much had happened during the past twenty-four hours. And now, just over those purple hills lay High Hutton and the end of her quest. One more day and it would all be finished with.

And then what would she do?

After a refreshing nap she dressed carefully in another of her new gowns and came downstairs with fifteen minutes to spare. At the foot of the stairs she hesitated, but then a maidservant, whose shy smiles could not quite disguise her curiosity, led her through the Hall and into a line of rooms that had been laid out on the southern side of the castle. The sun had moved round, but there was still plenty of light, in spite of mullioned windows. She stepped forward into the room...and walked into what was clearly a family crisis.

John looked much as he had at their first meeting in Mr Turner's chambers—stiff, upright, cold, reserved. Her wooden soldier to perfection.

Mrs Abbington was nervous and distressed. She was holding Harriet Ancroft firmly by the arm, saying, 'Harriet, I will not allow you to behave so rudely! What do you suppose your father thinks of you—or me, either—when you show him such ill manners? Now, please prove that you do know how a lady should behave. For my sake, if not your own.'

The girl looked pale and tearful. 'Must I, Abby?'

'Yes,' replied the companion firmly. 'Now, if you please.'

Harriet Ancroft showed resistance in every line of her thin young body as she bobbed a curtsy to her father and then held out her hand, stretching her arm out to its full length. 'Welcome to Marrick, Father,' she said woodenly.

Caroline was briefly amused. Like father, like daughter, she thought. And as the pair stared stonily at one another, she saw that Harriet really was like her father, with the same dark hair and silver-grey eyes, as well as the same expression! But her amusement turned to dismay when she saw the girl snatch her hand back as soon as it was touched, her face suddenly a study in revulsion.

'Harriet!' said Mrs Abbington severely.

John turned away and said wearily, 'Leave it, Mrs Abbington, leave it. The girl hardly knows me, after all. Let her go back to her room, if she wishes.'

Caroline spoke up. 'But surely not before I have a chance to meet her?' She came forward and said to the girl, 'I'm disappointed. I was hoping to talk to you. Your father is so proud of you that I wanted to see you for myself.'

'Proud? Of me?'

'Why, yes!'

'How can he be? He hasn't been near me for nine years!'

'Hasn't he? But he gets frequent reports, I understand, from Mrs Abbington here, and also from Mr Fennybright. You know Mr Fennybright, do you not?'

The girl looked uncertainly at Caroline. She obviously liked what she saw, and indeed, Caroline was a very attractive sight in a gown of apricot silk and Honiton lace. Harriet decided to answer her. 'Yes. Yes, I do.'

'Shall we talk about what Mr Fennybright says over dinner? Or have you other things you'd like to discuss?'

'Abby says you come from Jamaica. I'd like to hear about that.'

'Why, there's nothing I like better than to talk about Jamaica. But what am I thinking of? Shouldn't your father introduce us first?'

John gave Caroline a straight look, as if to say that he knew what she was up to, but said simply, 'Mrs Duval, as I am sure you've guessed, this is my daughter, Harriet. Harriet, Mrs Duval is on her way to High Hutton, but I decided it was too dangerous to go over there tonight, so she is staying here.'

'It is! The Alne has flooded the road as much as three feet deep in places. You mustn't attempt it, ma'am! Besides, there's no one there.'

'What's that?' asked her father. 'What do you mean?'

The girl ignored him and addressed Caroline. 'The Ainderbys are in Kirkby Stephen. They'll be away for weeks.'

Caroline was stunned. All this way, nearly five thousand miles, weeks of travel, danger and discomfort...and after it all she was to be baulked at the last moment. Curiously, it had never once occurred to her that there might not be anyone at High Hutton to receive her.

'What are they doing in Kirkby Stephen?' John asked. 'Does anyone know when they plan to return?' Caroline listened apprehensively for the reply. When it came it was a shock.

'They are not expected back before the end of August, I believe,' said Mrs Abbington. 'They're visiting Mr and Mrs Paul Ainderby.'

'Paul is Martin's younger brother,' said John for Caroline's benefit. He said to Mrs Abbington, 'So Paul has moved to the other side of the Pennines? That's surprising. I thought the two brothers were fonder of each other than that.'

'Really?' Mrs Abbington sounded doubtful. 'From what I have heard, Lord Coverdale, they have been at odds for years. Mr Paul Ainderby went to the other side of the Pennines, they say, to get away from his family. This visit is an attempt at reconciliation. It will be the first time for many years that the two have met.'

Caroline was dismayed. 'But this means that I have to wait a month before I can see them!'

John turned to her. 'So it seems. It appears that we shall have the pleasure of your company for longer than we had thought!' He paused, then added lightly, but with a significance that was meant only for her, 'But you'll be safe enough here, Mrs Duval. Marrick has fended off many an attack in its time. Perhaps Harriet would tell you something of its history as a fortress? I know she has always been fascinated by the stories of the many who have found a safe haven here.'

'How would you know anything at all about me?' the girl demanded belligerently.

'Harriet!' exclaimed Mrs Abbington. 'What *has* come over you? Please use more respect when speaking to your father!'

'Because I listen to what Fenny tells me and I read the reports which Mrs Abbington sends,' said John patiently.

Harriet was diverted into a more natural manner. 'Fenny? You call him Fenny, too?'

'Ever since I was a boy,' said John, giving her a smile. But this was going too far. Harriet scowled, and turned to Caroline.

'I could show you round tomorrow, if you wish, Mrs Duval.'

Aware that John's real purpose had been to remind her that she herself would be safe here at Marrick, Caroline nevertheless pulled herself together, gave Harriet Ancroft one of her dazzling smiles and said, 'You're very kind, Lady Harriet. Thank you!'

Harriet blinked, then a wave of colour flooded her pale cheeks. 'May I lead you in to dinner, Mrs Duval?'

Caroline had plenty of opportunity to study Harriet Ancroft over the next week. The reports of her had not lied. She was a clever, accomplished girl, and when away from her father she had excellent manners. Her life had been more secluded than most, and she sometimes showed a certain awkwardness, a lack of grace, in company. But she was very bright, and really came to life as she took Caroline round the castle, recounting its history, dwelling with a child's relish on some of the more gruesome details, then switching to a young girl's delight in romance as she told stories of the love affairs that had unfolded within its walls. In return Caroline described life in Jamaica to her, and answered her many questions about the island. In the evenings the dinner table was lively with their talk. Once or twice Harriet actually forgot herself and addressed her father without prompting.

Caroline was even free of responsibility for the chalice for a while. John had persuaded her to leave her precious bag in the castle's strong room, a chamber without windows and heavily guarded from any possible intruder by thick doors and bars. The relief, though temporary, was enormous. It meant she could walk and ride with Harriet unencumbered by a constant reminder of the duty waiting to be performed. What was more, with the chalice in Marrick's strong room she was free for the first time in months of the fear of having it stolen from her by Edmund or one of his minions. Not that anything had been heard of her cousin since he had left the inn at Catterick Bridge, and she sincerely hoped he was still searching the inns further south.

She saw little of John. He was constantly in conference with his steward, his bailiffs, his farm managers, and, of course, the lawyers. Marrick was a huge undertaking and in urgent need of attention. So Caroline waited patiently for the Ainderbys' return, and meanwhile enjoyed the sunshine and cool breezes of the Yorkshire dales. And the company of Harriet.

She was without Joseph Bellerby. His arm was now almost as good as ever, but he had asked her to give him leave of absence.

'You're safe enough here, Miss Caro. For the moment you don't need me to look out for you. I've family living not far from here, and I've not seen them for nigh on forty year. I'd like to pay them a visit.'

Caroline eyed him in surprise. 'I didn't know you came from here, Joseph?'

'Aye, that I do. I came out to Jamaica to work for your grandfather when I was nobbut a lad.'

'How did you come by that?'

'An uncle o' mine had gone out with the master to Jamaica many years ago. When Uncle Ben got older, 'e sent for me to replace 'im. That's 'ow.'

'Why didn't you tell me this earlier?'

'It weren't my place to go chatterin' about your grandfather's business, Miss Caro! A very close man, the master. But now... Well, the master's dead, and I'm gettin' older myself. I'd like to see my brothers and sisters again before I die.'

'Well, you're not going to die for a good while yet,

Joseph dear, but I think you should see your family! Of course you can go! How long do you want?'

'I'm not sure. You can send me word when you want me. But I'll be back in time to go with you to High Hutton.'

If Joseph had been a local lad he might know more than he had told her. Caroline asked carefully, 'What do you know about High Hutton, Joseph?'

Joseph's face took on an obstinate look. 'Not much. But enough. It's best you wait and see, Miss Caro. That's what the master wanted.'

'But surely you could tell me!'

'It's best you wait, Miss Caro.'

Caroline sighed. 'Very well. I know I can't move you when you have that look on your face. Enjoy your holiday. And take care of that arm!'

He nodded and went. Afterwards Caroline asked Maggie if she had known that Joseph came from Yorkshire.

'He's never said, Miss Caro. He was already working for your grandfather when I came to look after you, and even when he was young he would never use two words when one would do. He and your grandfather were as tight-lipped as each other as far as their own business was concerned. But I thought once or twice he must be a Yorkshire man.'

'I shall be glad when this is all over, Maggie!' exclaimed Caroline crossly. 'I don't like so many mysteries.'

'I thought you were getting on rather well with his lordship?'

'Maggie,' warned Caroline. 'You needn't take that tone again. Lord Coverdale and I understand one another perfectly. We have no secrets now, and I even believe we are friends of a sort. He has certainly done more than

anyone could have expected to help me. I can't imagine
what we would have done if he hadn't invited us to stay
here until the Ainderbys are back. But don't start looking
for anything more than ordinary kindness in his actions.
You know my views on marriage, and I think his are
pretty similar.'

'He'll need an heir for this title of his...'

'Then he can look elsewhere for someone to marry! As
far as I am concerned it is never again, Maggie. *Never*
again!'

Maggie shrugged and started to take the pins out of her
mistress's hair. 'It's a pity, that's all I can say. A great
pity. What are you going to do when you're old?'

'I don't know!' Caroline looked at her defiantly for a
moment, then she grinned and winked at her maid through
the looking glass. 'I might find a handsome, poverty-
stricken poet, forty years younger than I am, and pay him
to keep my bed warm. What do you say?'

'Miss Caro! If I didn't know you better... You
shouldn't say such things!'

'Then you shouldn't try to frighten me with questions
like that, Maggie. How the devil should I know what I'll
do?'

After a few days Mrs Abbington, who suffered from
headaches in the heat, was content to leave Harriet and
Caroline together on their afternoon walk. Caroline was
sorry for the woman but glad of an opportunity to talk to
Harriet alone. Some of the things the girl had said had
made her wonder if the situation between her and her
father was as hopeless or as simple as John believed.

They took one of the paths leading down from the castle towards the valley. When Caroline was doubtful about
going so far, Harriet begged her not to spoil things.

'It's not really very far. I've often been down there by myself, and it's very pretty by the river. So cool and green.'

Since the day was still quite hot Caroline allowed herself to be persuaded and they set off down the path.

'It's a pity your father had to go to Richmond. It would do him good to relax with us occasionally,' said Caroline after a while. 'He works too hard. I noticed he was limping quite badly when he came back from Catterick last night.'

'Was he?' The girl's voice was noncommittal.

Caroline persisted. 'You know he was severely wounded, do you?'

'No, I didn't.' Harriet's reply came so quickly that her companion suspected it might not be true. The girl went on, 'Why should I care if he was wounded? Thousands of men were wounded at Waterloo. He wasn't the only one.'

So she knew where her father had been wounded! A poor liar, Harriet. But Caroline was careful not to say so. Instead she nodded. 'I suppose you're right. At least he wasn't killed. But doesn't it worry you to see him working so hard now?'

'Why shouldn't he work hard? Marrick is what he always wanted. And now he has it.'

'*Did* he always want it?'

'Of course he did! He killed his best friend, his own cousin, for it.'

Caroline seized the opportunity that Harriet had given her. She decided it was worth the risk of being thought a busybody in order to get the girl to tell her what she knew. 'Good heavens!' she said. 'Did he? Who told you that?'

'My mother. My Uncle Coverdale. Philip was my father's cousin, Uncle Coverdale's son. His only child. And my father killed him!'

'I can hardly believe it! What happened?'

'I'm not quite sure. All I know is that Philip was killed when his curricle crashed.'

'I see. It was an accident, then?'

'Oh, no! I am sure my father meant it to happen. Uncle Coverdale said so.'

'But how could he do that? Was your father in the curricle with Lord Philip?'

Harriet looked at her mutinously. 'I don't know. I don't suppose he was, or he would have been killed as well. Besides, Gabriella Ainderby was with Philip, so there wouldn't have been room. But Uncle Coverdale would never talk about it. He said it was enough for me to know that my father killed his son so that he could inherit the title, and that I must never, ever forgive him. My mother said the same. And I won't.' She paused, then said, 'I'm not sure why you are so curious about it, Mrs Duval.'

'Because I like and respect your father! And I'm curious to know why a bright, intelligent girl, such as yourself, has never tried to find out enough to form an opinion of her own! From what I've heard, you seem to have accepted what your uncle said without once giving it any real thought.' Caroline paused a moment, then went on carefully, 'That was perfectly understandable when you were a child. But you're not a child any more, my dear, and your father is now back in Marrick. It seems to me that he would like to get to know you better, but you put him off. Why? Because of this accident. Haven't you ever asked anyone else what happened?'

'The servants weren't allowed to talk about it. Besides, I don't need anyone else's version,' said Harriet mulishly.

'It's enough that my Uncle Coverdale said that he was to blame. My father, I mean. I hate him!'

Caroline looked shocked. 'But he *is* your father! And I've found him to be an honourable man, not a villain. Have you ever seen his army record?'

Harriet turned her head away, 'Yes,' she said. 'I... I have. Mrs Abbington showed me what the newspaper said of him. He's very brave.'

'Then why are you so convinced of his guilt? I don't know any more than you exactly what happened. But I do know that your father has been deeply unhappy about it ever since.'

'He doesn't look it.'

'Your father, my dear Harriet, is not a man who wears his heart on his sleeve.'

Harriet scowled at her. 'He has no heart! Why has he kept away so long? Why didn't he come when my mother died? Why is he leaving it to Fenny to organise my come-out? Because he is not interested. He has no heart! No, Mrs Duval! You are quite wrong to defend him. Please let's talk of something else!'

There was little point in pushing it any further, thought Caroline. She had done what she could. But what the girl had just said confirmed some of her suspicions. Part at least of John's crime in his daughter's eyes was to have ignored her existence for so long. 'I'm sorry,' she said swiftly. 'I was wrong to ask. Come, do I hear the sound of water at last? I'm so hot I could throw myself in!'

They wandered along the bank under the shade of the trees, and soon Harriet was more of a child again, laughing at the antics of the river creatures, and building up an impressive collection of stones, bracken leaves and other objects she could use in her painting lessons.

* * *

They went down to the river again the next day. And the next. The weather was still very hot, and the cool shade of the trees overhanging the water was more than welcome. It was on that day that Harriet herself brought up the subject of her father.

'I've been thinking about what you said,' she said abruptly.

'What was that?'

'About my father. About what happened in that accident. So I asked Thomas Beckford. Are you shocked, Mrs Duval? Abby always told me that I shouldn't gossip with the servants, but how else could I find anything out?'

'This was in a good cause. Did Thomas tell you anything?'

'He didn't want to at first. I told you, the servants had been ordered not to talk about it. But I could tell he wanted to, really. He likes my father, and I had the impression that he didn't like what my uncle had told everyone about him. So I asked him about the accident.'

'Was he there at the time?'

'Yes. He said that just before it happened my father was very angry with Philip. The curricle was standing in the courtyard, and the two of them came down the steps quarrelling about the girl he was engaged to. The girl my father was engaged to, I mean. The one who looked so like you. Gabriella Ainderby.'

'Did Thomas say that, too? That Miss Ainderby looked like me?'

'Oh, yes. But I knew that already. All the servants talk about *that*. They think my father is in love with you.'

Caroline smiled and shook her head. 'They're completely mistaken. He kindly agreed to escort me to High Hutton. And that's all. I promised my grandfather I would deliver something there, and when that is done, I'll thank your father for his help, and return to London. A little later I'll go back home to Jamaica.'

'I wish you and he would—'

It was not surprising that Harriet might hope for a match between John and herself, thought Caroline. The girl liked her, and the idea of a mother as well as a father would appeal to someone who had had neither for so long. But it was out of the question for more reasons than one. She must put the idea right out of Harriet's mind.

'Don't. I'm sorry, Harriet, but that's impossible.'

'Why? I thought your husband was dead?'

'He is. But I'll never marry again, not even if your father asked me. Which he won't. You must forget the idea. Now, tell me about your conversation with Thomas Beckford.'

'Thomas said my father was nowhere near the curricle when it crashed. Philip had got into the curricle, and shouted something at him. My father shouted back that he was welcome to go to damnation—I know I shouldn't say things like that, Mrs Duval, but that's what Thomas said he said—that Philip was welcome to go to damnation in his own way if he wanted to, but he was to leave Gabriella alone. He forbade Philip to take her in the curricle with him. Miss Ainderby was on the steps behind him.'

'And Lord Philip was too hot-headed to listen?'

'Yes. He shouted that he would soon show my father, and told Miss Ainderby she was to get in if she wanted to come. And as soon as she did, he took off. But he drove too fast down the drive and lost control on that first bend.'

'You see? It doesn't sound to me as if your father had anything to do with it at all!'

'But Uncle Coverdale said he did! Was he telling lies?'

Caroline paused and thought. It was important to get this right. She stopped and took the girl's hands in hers. 'Harriet, in my opinion Lord Coverdale didn't think he was. He had convinced himself that what he said was the truth.'

'How can that be?'

'I think it must be something like this. When people we love die, especially if they die when they're young, we have to find someone or something to blame. Your uncle was mad with grief for his son. He told himself, I believe wrongly, that your father had wanted Philip's death, and from there on it was a short step to believing that he had actually contrived it.'

'But my mother believed it, too!'

It wouldn't help Harriet to learn that her mother had been in love with another man, and equally distraught at his death. Caroline shook her head. 'I can't help you there. I don't know enough about your mother. But I *have* come to know John Ancroft. I can't believe him guilty. Remember, he too lost someone he loved in that accident.'

Harriet walked away and sat down on a log at the edge of the river. 'I don't know!' she cried. 'I don't know *what* to believe!'

'Why don't you ask your father?'

'I couldn't!'

'Yes, you could! My dear girl, you must! You must give him a chance!'

Harriet was silent. But she seemed to be thinking, and Caroline was content to leave it there. It was getting late, and Mrs Abbington would be looking for them. They retraced their steps along the river and up the path to the castle.

* * *

That evening before dinner she saw Harriet, rather pale but very determined, go up to her father and say something to him in a low voice. He looked surprised, but nodded immediately. And after dinner, instead of staying in the dining room with a glass of port as usual, he followed his daughter out of the room. They went into the library together and shut the door.

Caroline sat with Mrs Abbington for a short while, then decided that the tension was too much. She got up and said, 'Would you like a stroll in the garden, Mrs Abbington? It's a beautiful evening.'

To her relief Mrs Abbington shook her head. 'I have never trusted the night air, Mrs Duval. If you'll excuse me, I think I shall soon go upstairs. I still have that wretched headache. Can I ask your maid or one of the other servants to accompany you?'

'That's really not necessary. I'm sure I shall be quite safe, and I don't at all mind being alone. Goodnight. I hope your head is better tomorrow.'

Draping her stole more firmly round her shoulders Caroline went through the long doors that led out on to the terrace. She paused for a moment breathing in the scented air, and gazing at the dying light of the sun behind those purple hills. Then she descended the steps that led into the garden at the side of the castle. Harriet had told her how an earlier Ancroft had created this garden for his new bride, who had come from the south of England and missed the softer climate of her home. It was surrounded by a wall, and in its shelter grew numerous fruit trees, herbs and flowering shrubs, chosen to please her. Now, a hundred years later, their perfume still filled the evening air.

Caroline wandered along its paths till she came to an ornamental bench in a corner. Here she sat down and thought. It looked as if the long-standing animosity Harriet had felt for her father was about to end. She was a newcomer, a stranger, but she had become close to both father and daughter in these past days. She was happy for them. It was what she had hoped for, and father and daughter would both benefit from a new beginning. They each needed someone close to them.

So why this feeling of sadness? Self-pity? She hoped not! That was not something she allowed herself. During those far-off nightmare months in New Orleans she had sworn never to feel sorry for herself, never to weaken. Faced with Laurent Duval's duplicity and his unbelievable cruelty, she could easily have gone under if she had not held on to her inner determination to survive. It had been a close thing. She had the feeling that his death had released her just in time. Bruised in body and battered in spirit, but free at last of his viciousness, she had sought out her grandfather again, and he had taken her back with no questions and no reproaches. She had looked into the abyss in New Orleans, but had not succumbed. Her grandfather's love and confidence had restored her.

Since that time, whatever the scandalmongers may have hinted, whatever food she gave them for gossip, there had never been any substance in the rumours they had so gleefully spread. Since Laurent Duval's death no man had held her, touched her, as intimately as John Ancroft had held and touched her in the inn at Buckden. She had often aroused desire in the men around her, but before that night in Buckden she had never felt any desire herself. She had thought herself no longer capable of it.

In Jamaica she had led an independent life and, despite what the world thought, a decent one, deriving amusement from the antics of the people round her, and depending on no one but her grandfather for support. She had loved no one but him, and since his death Maggie and Joseph had had her affection, but no one had had her heart.

Was this her future? With only Maggie and Joseph to comfort her?

And if Joseph decided to stay in Yorkshire...

She sat contemplating this. She would have to encourage him to stay, if that was what he wanted. He was getting old, and she doubted now that that arm of his would ever truly heal. She would have to let him leave her... A tear slid down her cheek. And another. Confound it! This would not do! She jumped up impatiently.

'Don't go!'

She whirled round, startled. John was coming towards her. He must not catch her with tears on her face! Thankful that the fading light would hide any trace of them, she said as normally as she could, 'I thought you were with Harriet!'

'I was. We've had a...surprising conversation. And a very illuminating one. I actually believe that she no longer regards me as a monster.'

'That's very good news.' He was coming nearer and she turned slightly away.

'I think I might have you to thank for that, Caroline.' His voice was in her ear, he was very close. Too close...

'Nonsense!' she said huskily. 'It was only a question of time.'

He turned her round and looked at her narrowly. 'Good God! You've been crying!' he exclaimed. 'Why?'

'What nonsense! Of course I haven't,' she said angrily, pulling herself free. 'Something was in my eye. It's out now. Tell me about Harriet.'

'There's still some way to go, but she is at least questioning what my uncle told her.'

'May I ask something?'

'Go ahead.'

'I don't understand why your wife believed it too. Surely she knew it wasn't so. Didn't she owe you her loyalty?'

'Rose? She was never very strong. And in the end she was deeply unhappy, and seriously ill. She died when Harriet was eight.'

'But surely if she loved you—'

'She never loved me! Philip was her life. Oh, you needn't look like that, Caroline! I knew she was still in love with Philip when I married her. I was trying to make some sort of reparation, to give…to give Philip's child a name.'

'Harriet?'

He nodded. 'The child doesn't know, of course. As far as she and the world are concerned, she is my daughter.'

'What about you? How do you regard Harriet?'

'You know, it's strange. In spite of her antipathy I've always thought of her as mine, regretted the fact that she appeared not to love me. When I first married Rose I hoped that we would eventually be able to live together in amity, to create a home for the child. But I couldn't have been more wrong.'

'I see.' She stole a glance at him. He was staring into the distance, a frown on his face. Then he shrugged and turned back to her.

'Why did you do it?' he asked.

'Do what?'

'Persuade Harriet to talk to me.'

'Because she needs you!' At his look of doubt she said more firmly, 'She does, John! I've been talking to Mrs Abbington. Harriet was careful to keep it from Lord Coverdale, but in the past few years she's collected everything she can find about you and your career. She has a secret cache in her bedroom. At least some of her resentment arises from what she sees as your indifference to her. You must believe me. I feel for her. She needs you.'

'You *feel* for her? So the Widow Duval has a heart, after all?'

'Oh, no! Don't try to give me virtues I don't possess.'

John took her chin in his hand, 'I wasn't talking of virtues,' he said softly. 'Only of hearts.' He kissed her gently on the lips. Then smiled and kissed her again.

Caroline was surprised by the sudden rush of feeling that leapt into life as his lips touched hers. It had happened again, she thought hazily. The same witchery was at work, the magic that had brought her almost in a trance to his arms in Buckden. But there was a difference. John Ancroft had believed then that Gabriella Ainderby was in his arms. Tonight he was kissing Caroline Duval, and fully aware of it. For one moment the knowledge was like heady wine. Had she really thought she was no longer capable of desire? Then what was this, this heat in her blood, the feeling of weakness along her limbs? What would he do if she responded as ardently now as she had that night in Buckden? Would he kiss her as deeply, as intimately as he had that night? The temptation was almost too strong…

'Thank you,' he said gently, in a totally matter-of-fact tone, 'for your concern for Harriet. Now tell me why you were crying.'

It was like a shower of cold water. She came back to earth and removed herself carefully from his arms, telling her pounding heart to be still. 'I've told you,' she said defiantly. 'I wasn't crying!' He held her eyes, and after a moment she turned away and gazed at the garden. What the devil had she been crying about? She gathered her wits together and said, 'I think I'm going to lose Joseph Bellerby. He's gone to visit some members of his family near here, and I'm afraid he'll want to stay with them forever. He's getting old, and it's understandable that he might want to die in the place he was born, surrounded by his own family. But if he does...' She swallowed. 'I mustn't stand in his way, but I'll feel lost without him. I've known him all my life. He's the last link with my grandfather.' The tears were too close again. She shook her head angrily.

John took her hand and said firmly, 'My dear Caroline, don't meet trouble halfway. The Bellerbys are a quarrelsome lot. They're always falling out among themselves. After a week or so spent in the bosom of that family, your Joseph will almost certainly be glad to get away from them. But if he isn't... We must think of something else.'

What did he mean by that? What could he mean? Had there been something in his tone...? Confound it, thought Caroline, she was in danger of getting altogether too serious! It was time to pull herself together. With a brilliant smile she turned again and replied, 'Why, thank you, Lord Coverdale! Are you by any chance thinking of offering yourself in Joseph's place? Because if you are, I ought to warn you that I am a very hard...mistress...' She chuckled at his shocked expression and with a graceful wave of the hand went into the house, leaving John Ancroft staring.

Chapter Eight

John watched her go. She really was like no woman he had ever known! One minute weeping over the loss of a valued servant, the next making remarks meant to outrage him and laughing at him when she had succeeded! His lips twitched. She was very witty—a mistress of the double meaning. Yes, exactly! Mistress. There was that word again, raising all sorts of speculations in a simple soldier's mind! How many men had known Caroline Duval as their mistress? Ten? Twenty? Or none at all? It was impossible to guess. Her behaviour at Buckden had suggested that she was experienced—though not promiscuous. When it came to the final barrier she *had* drawn back. On the other hand, she had been remarkably self-possessed at the waterfall, had made no desperate attempt to hide herself, shown no maidenly panic. It was almost as if she was used to being looked at in a state of nudity. She had, of course, been married—apparently very unhappily. But who had been at fault in that?

He stood there for some minutes, his thoughts in a tangle. Harriet must be his chief concern. He would be very happy if he and Harriet could indeed make a life together. But what about a wife? A mother for the girl?

It might be better than a paid companion, especially if Harriet liked her—as she liked and trusted Caroline. That lady's behaviour in the past may not have been above reproach, but it was evident that she had the girl's interests at heart. And as a wife she would certainly be interesting!

John stopped short. What was he thinking of? Putting a woman like Caroline Duval in the place that was to have been Gabriella's? She might look like Gabriella, but how could he regard her as any kind of replacement for his lost love, the girl who, to him, was still the embodiment of everything a man could want in a wife—beauty, innocence, virtue, constancy… It was impossible! He could not do it!

But Caroline Duval, said the little voice inside him, has her own virtues. Not conventional ones, perhaps, but worth taking into account. Courage, humour, pride, compassion… All of these. And, whatever she might say to the contrary, she had a heart. If a man could capture her heart… He was lost in thought for some time. But then he shook his head. Time to sort out his thoughts and speculations when her business at High Hutton was resolved. Then would come the reckoning.

The next morning, Harriet pressed him to stay at home and accompany them on their walks.

With real regret John said, 'I'm sorry, my dear. I simply have to go to Richmond again this morning. If I could, I would very much like to spend the whole day with you, but I can't postpone my business there. What do you plan to do this afternoon?'

'If Mrs Duval agrees we shall go down to the river again. I need some different bracken for my watercolour.

The fronds I gathered yesterday are all exactly the same shade, and I want some variation.'

'How would it be if I joined you there this afternoon? I think I could get back early enough.'

The contrast between Harriet's enthusiastic response and her previous attitude towards him could not have been greater. Deeply pleased, he went off to Richmond, leaving her debating with Caroline what they should do that morning, while Mrs Abbington listened and looked on with approval. There was no doubt that Caroline had made friends there!

But others who were not at all friendly were also interested in Caroline's activities. Though neither Caroline nor Harriet had been aware of it, they had been under observation for the past two days by two ruffianly men, unscrupulous cutthroats. Dan and Billy Parker were always available for hire to any man who paid them well enough—and Edmund had promised them a great deal if they found and captured Caroline Duval. After a wide-ranging search they had tracked her down to Marrick, and were now ready to strike. For the past three days she had come along the river path every afternoon in the company of a young girl, and with no other protection. The two would almost certainly come today, too. From a suitable vantage point from which they could see without being seen, they noted John's departure along the road to Richmond. Then they sat down to wait patiently for their quarry... A large sum of money was practically in the Parkers' pockets!

Harriet and Caroline came down from the castle as planned, their pale muslin dresses easily seen as they walked through the trees, conversing animatedly all the way. The girl was a different person altogether, the scowls and sulks a thing of the past. She talked excitedly of her father, of what he had said the night before and the plans they might make for the future. A London season figured largely in her conversation.

The two were so absorbed that they did not at first register the unkempt, villainous-looking men blocking the path in front of them, one with a cudgel, the other with a wicked-looking knife. But it was soon clear that the men were looking specifically for them.

'That's the one,' said the man with the cudgel. 'The tall one with red hair. That's the Duval woman.'

'Harriet!' shouted Caroline. '*Run!* Quickly! Run back to the castle!'

'No, you don't!' said the first man before Harriet could even turn. 'We need you, too, sweetheart! You get her, Billy! I'll take this one.'

He made a lunge at Caroline and grabbed her round the waist. Billy caught Harriet with no trouble at all. The poor girl was too scared to put up any kind of resistance. Nothing like this had ever happened to her before, and she was paralysed with fright. Unfortunately, Billy enjoyed such a situation and liked inflicting pain. Though it would have been simple for him to drag the girl along the path, he took a handful of her hair and used that to pull her along, cruelly tugging and twisting it as he went. Harriet screamed with pain, tears running down her cheeks. Caroline was distraught. She yelled curses at them both and struggled frantically to get free, desperate to help Harriet. But Dan was too strong for her, though, unlike poor Harriet, she did not give in without a fight. Kicking, biting, screaming, she fought every inch of the way, and Dan had bruises on his shins and more than one scratch on his face before he was finished.

The riverbank was deserted, and the men were obviously well prepared. They knew exactly where they were going, and in a short while, too short for any hope of rescue, they arrived at a ramshackle stone building, in a small clearing just off the river bank. It looked empty. Here Caroline and Harriet were bundled unceremoniously down into a dark cellar and the door was shut and barred behind them.

Dan uttered a sigh of relief and wiped his face with his sleeve. 'You'd better make yourselves comfortable!' he shouted through the cellar door. 'You'll stay there till we've found our client. You've got a fine turn of language there, missus. Try it on the rats!'

'Bye, bye, *sweetheart*!' yelled Billy. 'I'll do yer hair for you again, when I see you next!'

Their raucous laughter at his joke died gradually away as they left and there was silence outside. They were left to the smells and airless darkness of the cellar.

'Harriet?' said Caroline apprehensively into the darkness. 'Harriet, are you all right?'

'I...I think so. It was very painful for a while, but I'm not really hurt,' the girl replied.

A hand touched Caroline's arm. With enormous relief she took firm hold of it and drew the girl to her. 'Splendid,' she said. 'That's one thing we don't have to worry about, at least.'

A giggle broke out near her. 'It's not much.'

'It's a beginning,' said Caroline firmly.

The giggle changed into something dangerously like a sob. 'What do those men want? Why were they so cruel? Are we going to die, Mrs Duval?'

'Of course not! They just want to keep us here until they can fetch my cousin Edmund.'

'But why? And who is your cousin Edmund?'

'It's a long story. I'll tell you when we're back in the castle. Don't waste your energy asking about it at the moment, Harriet, we have to find a way out.' Sensing the girl was near hysteria, Caroline kept her voice as calm and businesslike as possible. 'Now, is it my imagination or is there a glimmer of light over there? I think it might be a window or some kind of outlet. Let's go to see. Keep tight hold of me and try to follow where I tread. Right? Thank goodness we have our walking boots on! Silk slippers would be no use at all!'

They made their way slowly, gingerly to the source of light. Harriet went rigid and clutched Caroline's hand even more desperately, as various scratches and scutterings told them they were disturbing the cellar's usual occupants. But they pressed on and at last reached a small, very dirty, window. It was covered with cobwebs inside and weeds outside, but it was a window all the same.

'There! What did I say? Perhaps it's a way out for us, Harriet! There are some bars, but one of us might get through them... Let me see...' She took off her fichu and wiped one of the panes of glass.

Disappointingly, the bars were set too close together to allow either of them to pass through. Harriet gave another little sob.

'Oh, no, Harriet. This isn't the moment to lose heart! We're not finished yet! We can't travel but our voices can. Now I'm letting go of your hand, but don't you let go of me! Hold on to my skirt.' Caroline bent over and fumbled in the dark, swearing colourfully as she tried to unlace her sturdy boot. Then she stood up, wrapped the fichu round her hand and said, 'Turn your face away, Harriet, and keep as far back as you can!' Then swinging her boot, she dealt the window a hefty blow with its heel.

One pane broke and a welcome stream of air came into the musty gloom.

'So far, so good! At least we now have some air. Now for another!'

'How many panes are there?'

'Four, but I don't have to break them all, Harriet. We only need one each.'

'What for? Oh! To shout, you mean?'

'The sound should carry quite a way in this valley. With luck it may even echo. How good are you at shouting?'

'I can try.'

'Brave girl! Don't bother with "Help!"—"Yahoo!" or "Holla!" will carry further. Which would you prefer?'

'I like "Holla!" better.'

'Then come nearer the window and stand by me. That's right. Now, are you ready? When I say "three". One, two, three!'

They yelled with all their might through those two small windowpanes, then waited. All they could hear was a mocking echo sent back by the opposite side of the valley. *'Holla...a...a...a...a.'* When that died away there was silence.

She could feel the girl beside her shivering and said encouragingly, 'We'll try again in a moment. Swallow, to ease your throat first. It's so dusty here, and you need all the volume you can muster.'

'Oh, Mrs Duval...' Harriet's voice wavered.

'Swallow, Harriet! Don't give up! I expect your father will soon be on his way. He said he would try to meet us, you remember. He'll come to our rescue, don't you worry! He'll be so proud when he hears how well you held up. Ready again?'

They yelled again. But again there was no response.

'We'll have a little rest, then we'll have another shout. Are you cold?'

'A b...b...it. It's so d...d...amp in this cellar.'

'Then come here and let me put my arms right round you to keep you warm.'

A small voice said, 'Mrs Duval, you're so brave! How do you know what to do? Did you learn it in Jamaica?'

Caroline's rich chuckle sounded in the gloom. 'Not exactly. It's not regarded as part of a conventional upbringing even out there in the colonies!' She thought, then decided to distract Harriet by telling her about herself. The girl must be wondering what Dan and Billy had in store for them. She said softly, 'I don't tell everyone this, Harriet dear, so once we get out you'll keep it to yourself, I know. When I was only about a year older than you are now I ran away from home. I thought I loved someone enough to leave my grandfather, and all my friends. And I thought he loved me. I was wrong. It was the biggest mistake anyone could have made. Seventeen, with no money, and no one to protect me, I found myself in some very rough company. I had to fight to survive. On the way I learned some...unusual tricks. But I came through. And *we* shall too, I promise you.'

'I would never have guessed... Does my father know?'

'No. You're the only one in England I've told. So not a word. Now. Shall we try again?'

They yelled again. And this time they were rewarded. As well as the echo they heard the sound of a horse coming towards them.

Refusing to believe that it might be Edmund and his accomplices coming back to deal with them, Caroline called yet again.

A man's voice said urgently, 'Call once more, I can't see you! Where are you?'

It was John. For a moment Caroline was weak with relief, then she pulled herself together and shouted, 'Down below you. We're in the cellar!'

The grass was torn away from the window, and more light came in. 'Caroline! What the devil are you doing there?'

'Mind the broken glass! Don't ask questions, just come inside the house and unbolt the door to this place. Hurry! They'll be back soon.'

As John came round and they heard the sound of bars and bolts being drawn Caroline muttered furiously, 'What are we doing here, indeed! What does he think we are doing? Hunting rats?'

The door was opened and John came down the steps. He stopped in shock. 'Harriet is here too!' he exclaimed. 'What the devil is going on?'

Harriet stumbled and would have fallen, but John rushed to catch her. She burst into tears and he hugged her tight. 'Harriet, my dear girl…!'

'Don't waste time! We must go!' cried Caroline. 'Those men will be back with Edmund any minute now!'

'Too late, lady!' said a voice at the top of the cellar steps. Dan came down slowly, his cudgel in the air.

Caroline was amazed at the speed with which John responded. He thrust Harriet towards her, leapt up on to the steps and, ducking and twisting, dragged Dan down off them. The two men grappled with each other, and the cudgel dropped to the ground. Harriet screamed. Caroline, watching anxiously, drew her back into the shelter of the flight of steps and hissed, 'Be still! Your father knows what he's doing. He's a bonny fighter! But you mustn't distract him.'

A vicious fight ensued, but John slowly gained the upper hand. It was difficult in the half-dark to see exactly what was going on, but in the end the two men were on the ground, John's fingers round the other's throat, squeezing the breath out of him. Dan's struggles were growing weaker...

Another figure appeared in the door at the top. With a shout of surprised anger Billy rushed down, his knife ready. Harriet screamed again and John looked up. He was just in time to see Caroline, green eyes intent in the semi-darkness, waiting for Billy to reach the bottom step. Then she pounced on him from behind, throwing her fichu over his face and pulling his head back with it. Before he could turn, she had twisted his arm up his back. Billy gave a howl of agony and dropped the knife. Caroline laughed.

'Now who's hurting?' she growled. 'No! Don't try to move your arm, Billy, *sweetheart*! Nor anything else. I know what I'm doing, I've been taught by a master, and I'd *hate* you to break something. And that's what'll happen if you even *breathe* too hard.'

'Let go of me! Let go! Dan! Dan, you've got to help me! She's hurting me! She's going to break me arm!'

Caroline gave a laugh. 'I might, too. I have to do something, Billy *sweetheart*. And unlike my poor friend, *your* hair isn't long enough to get hold of. But confess now. Isn't this much more *fun*?' She gave a small tug and Billy howled again.

John had finished with Dan. The big man lay unconscious on the floor. He came over and picked up the knife. 'You can let him go,' he said.

Caroline stood back and John took over. He propelled Billy, who staggered whimpering over to his brother. 'You needn't worry,' he said drily. 'I haven't killed him. He'll come round in a minute or two.'

The stuffing had gone out of Billy. He sank down in a

heap beside his brother, holding his arm and rocking himself, still moaning, not taking the slightest notice as John
helped his two ladies up the stairs.

John shut the cellar door behind them and made it secure. He carried Harriet outside and put her on to his
horse. 'Hold on tight!' he said. 'It's quite a walk. We'll
have to take the long way round up the drive.' He looked
somewhat oddly at Caroline. 'My congratulations,' he
said drily. 'But did you have to be so hard on the poor
fellow?'

'You weren't there when he hurt your daughter!' she
said briefly. 'I was. I ought to have been a lot harder!'

They made an interesting sight as they came painfully
through the archway. Harriet was exerting herself to sit
upright, but her hair was in wild disorder, and her white
muslin dress black with dust. John, walking beside her
and watching her carefully, had grazed knuckles, a streak
of blood down his cheek and a tear in his jacket. Caroline
was almost unrecognisable. Her hair was in as bad a state
as Harriet's, and looked much worse. Its chestnut masses
rioted down her back and over half her face, but failed to
hide that she had an incipient black eye, and that her dress
was torn and even dirtier than Harriet's. A filthy fichu
was draped over her shoulders in an attempt to hide the
worst of the damage. After a moment's shocked silence
everyone in the courtyard rushed to the rescue. The three
of them were taken to their bedrooms. Scullions were
ordered to fill kettles and set them on the fire, and a train
of footmen was soon hurrying upstairs carrying steaming
cans of hot water, together with a variety of restorative
drinks.

After an hour of Maggie's shocked ministrations, Caroline, clean, dry and once again her elegant self in a green

muslin dress, received a message from John requesting her presence in the library as soon as she was ready. When she went down she found that John and Harriet were already sitting at the table, but there was no sign of Mrs Abbington.

'I sent some of my men out to release your attackers and take them to Richmond,' John began. 'But when they got there the cellar was empty. They're now searching the area.'

'Edmund must have arrived before them,' said Caroline.

'You're assuming that your cousin is involved and I think you're right, Caroline. But there's so far no evidence to connect him with it. Until we know more, I suggest that we say as little as possible. I've merely told anyone who asked that you were attacked on the river path. Harriet assures me she hasn't talked to any of the servants, nor mentioned your cousin to Mrs Abbington or given any reason for the attack. They are all under the impression that you were set upon by itinerant thieves. Have you said anything?'

'Only to Maggie. And she is discreet.'

'Good. Then we'll keep any speculation to ourselves.' His face altered and his voice was harsh as he continued, 'Harriet has told me what happened before I came on the scene.' He stopped, took a breath, then went on, 'I would very much like to get my hands on that pair again. Especially the smaller one. Billy. He deserved everything you did to him.'

'And more,' said Caroline. 'I can now confess to Harriet that I was not at all sure what would happen when they came back.'

'Quite. Thank God I came along when I did.' He

paused and said more calmly, 'But I was surprised you were so unprotected. I had assumed that you were always accompanied on these walks of yours.'

'Joseph Bellerby would normally have been with me. He's away at the moment, as you know. I can't tell you, John, how much I regret putting Harriet into danger. If I had known—'

'Harriet herself knows she was wrong not to have a groom or one of the other servants with her. She won't let it happen again.'

Caroline sighed. His tone was sternly uncompromising. Harriet and her father had evidently had words before she had arrived. She hoped this episode was not about to spoil the budding relationship between father and daughter.

But Harriet said, 'I won't, Papa. I promise. It was too frightening. But it was exciting, too! Mrs Duval was very clever.'

'Clever enough to get you both half-killed!' growled John Ancroft.

'But she saved you! When that second man came down the stairs I thought he was going to murder you, Papa!'

At first John regarded Caroline coolly. Then, reluctantly, he began to smile. 'I suppose I must thank you. There was certainly little I could have done to prevent him. Where on earth did you pick up a trick like that?'

'In a hard school, I assure you.'

John turned to his daughter. 'Er…Harriet, Mrs Duval possesses some remarkable skills—but they aren't the sort I would wish you to acquire, however strongly you admire her. They will hardly serve you in the kind of society I hope you'll encounter in London.'

'I've already told your daughter,' Caroline interrupted. 'I have a somewhat reprehensible past. I hope and pray she is never forced to rely on herself alone, as I was, to survive.'

John eyed her speculatively. 'I wonder if I shall *ever* know the real Mrs Duval,' he said. 'That widow's disguise was only the first layer, it appears.'

'Nonsense. I've told you. I'm now perfectly respectable.' Caroline turned to Harriet with a smile. 'For a beginner, you were remarkably good! But remember what I said in that cellar. I very soon bitterly regretted the day I left the protection of my home. You, Harriet, will never be so foolish. And now you must put it all behind you, and concentrate on other things. Your début, for instance. For that there are other, more pleasant, skills to learn. Can you waltz?'

Caroline's attempt to give Harriet something else to think about worked almost too well. The girl's face lit up and she said eagerly, 'Oh, could you teach me? Please do, *dear* Mrs Duval!'

Caroline laughed. 'I'd love to. But you'll have to be a quick learner! I shan't be here all that long. If your father wishes, I can show you the first steps before I go.'

'Then I could teach you the rest,' said John blandly.

When the two ladies looked at him in astonishment he burst into laughter. 'What made you both think I wouldn't know how to waltz? Do I appear to be so dull? My dear girls, no one would survive for long on Wellington's staff if they couldn't waltz! There's nothing his Grace loves better than a ball!'

'Then you must teach me, Papa! You and Mrs Duval together! And...and can't we have a party? We ought to celebrate that you've come back.'

'That's something to celebrate?'

Harriet flushed. 'I...I think so, Papa,' she said shyly. 'I think I've been wrong about you...'

'We've both made mistakes, child,' John said seriously, holding out his hand to her. 'Let's make a new beginning.'

Harriet came round and put her hands on his shoulders. She kissed his cheek. 'With a party? A ball?'

He laughed. 'Perhaps we shall. Why not? Marrick shall show what it can do! But first...' He grew serious again. 'We still have to sort out the question of Mrs Duval's delightful cousin.' He turned to Caroline. 'He must be stopped,' he said. 'But I think you'd rather avoid a scandal, wouldn't you?'

'Of course. Especially as it might involve you. But is it possible?'

'We'll have to see. If I can once get hold of him, I think I can frighten him into leaving you alone for good. Especially if he realises that his efforts have all been all in vain.'

'Can you convince him of that?'

'Believe me, I can, and will!' Harriet was still standing beside him. He put his arm round her waist and drew her closer. 'When Edmund Willoughby sent men to attack my daughter,' he said grimly, 'he started a fight I shall be only too glad to finish. You can forget about Edmund Willoughby, Caroline.'

'You sound quite bloodthirsty. Are you planning to dispose of him?'

'We'll see. Probably not. But I can see that he goes back to Jamaica too frightened to do anything more dangerous than look after his plantation, or whatever he does there. Would that do? Or would you like him sent to another island?'

'I think Jamaica will suit. Without the incentive of... of...'

'Of your grandfather's treasure?'

'Yes. Without that he'll leave me alone when I return.'

There was a short silence. Then John said slowly, 'To Jamaica? I hadn't realised... When do you plan to do that?'

'First I must go to High Hutton.'

'Yes, yes! But after that?'

'I shall probably travel a little. Perhaps do a season in London. But I'll go back to Jamaica eventually. My home is there.'

'Of course.' There was another pause. Then he said briskly, 'Of course! So, you're happy to leave everything to me?'

'Yes. This time I would! At the moment I have no desire whatsoever to see my cousin.'

Harriet had been looking on wide-eyed during this conversation. Her father turned to her and said, 'My dear, this must all seem gibberish to you. And I can't at the moment explain it.' He cast a glance at Caroline. 'I don't know the whole of it myself. But once it is over, with Mrs Duval's permission, I promise to tell you as much as I can. Will that do? Meanwhile what can I say to make sure you keep what you've heard so far to yourself?'

Caroline's heart lifted as she saw Harriet gave him a mischievous grin. 'That you'll promise to teach me the waltz, Papa?' she suggested.

John laughed. 'That's easy enough!'

'And that you'll give a party at Marrick.'

'That takes more effort...but, yes! Done!' he said.

The men sent to search found no sign of Dan and Billy. Nor was there at first any sign of Edmund. It was the next day before they found him. He was lying half in, half out of the river, ugly bruises on his cheek and covering his body, stripped of most of his clothing. He was carried up to the castle and put to bed.

The surgeon was sent for and after examining him carefully, he said, 'He's been subjected to a severe beating, as you can see.' He directed a look of enquiry at John.

'I suspect he was waylaid and robbed on the river path,' said John gravely. 'My daughter and a friend staying with us at the moment were attacked yesterday on the same stretch of river. We are at this very moment searching the surrounding countryside for the villains who did it. Will he live?'

'Oh, he'll live. I've given him a sedative. He's asleep, not unconscious. A couple of days of bed rest, and apart from some aches and pains he'll be fit enough. Unless there are complications, it won't even be necessary for me to come again. But it was lucky for him that your men found him in time. Another few hours and he might well have died. Who is he, do you know?'

'There was nothing on him to identify him,' said John carefully. 'But you needn't concern yourself with that. I'll see he's looked after and sent on his way when he's ready.'

The surgeon left and John was left gazing down at Edmund Willoughby. A weak face, he thought. And a mean-looking one. Eyes too close together and a small, petulant mouth... What should he do about him?

John put Betts in the bedchamber and told him to watch over his visitor, to look after his needs and to keep his own mouth shut. He was to be informed the moment the 'guest' seemed fit enough to talk. Except for a few moments when he took some water and a little soup, the invalid slept through the whole of the next day, but John was sent for the day after.

* * *

Edmund Willoughby was sitting up and looking a great deal better. 'It's about time! That damned servant wouldn't say a word! Who are you and where am I?'

'I'm Coverdale and you are in Marrick Castle.'

Willoughby regarded him sourly. 'Oh, yes, I remember now. Colonel Ancroft at Catterick Bridge. So you *are* one and the same. Clever that. You fooled me. How did I get here?'

'My servants were looking for the men you hired to attack Mrs Duval. They found you lying near the river bank and brought you in.'

A shifty look appeared in Willoughby's eyes. 'What men? I haven't hired any men to attack anyone. What do you mean?'

John said in a bored voice, 'Come, Willoughby! Some lies are possible to sustain, but not that one. You weren't set upon by gypsies! What happened? Did you refuse to pay your friends when you found out that Mrs Duval and my daughter had escaped? I'd say you were extremely unwise if you did.'

'They beat me!' said Willoughby sulkily. 'The damned scum beat me! How dared they! Of course I refused to pay them! They hadn't done anything!'

John sat down next to the bed. He spoke softly, but the menace in his voice caused Edmund to cringe back against the pillows.

'They had done a great deal, my dear fellow. They had frightened and distressed two vulnerable women, one of them still a child. They had treated them roughly, locked them in a cellar without air or light, and then left them to their fears. I suppose it's fortunate that I happened to come along to rescue them. If anything serious had happened to either of those ladies you, my friend, would have paid with your life! At least! As it is, someone will have to pay for what *did* take place, and I'm very much afraid you are the one.'

Willoughby grew even paler. 'You mustn't threaten me, I'm a sick man. It isn't fair!'

'I'm not *trying* to be fair, Willoughby. Those women were under my protection, one of them my own daughter. When you injured them you injured me, and I intend to have satisfaction.'

'You can't challenge a sick man!' Willoughby cried, sliding down in the bed. 'I'm a stranger in England, a foreigner. I refuse to fight you!'

John's lip curled. 'I don't intend to fight. Why should you think killing a worm like you would bring me any kind of satisfaction?'

'Well, what are you going to do?' Willoughby sat up and said eagerly, 'If you want money, I have some in London. A great deal. Let me go and I'll send it, I promise. I promise! I'm sorry for what I did. Really sorry. I didn't mean them to hurt Caroline, or your daughter. I didn't even know your daughter was with her! And you could say I've been punished already, couldn't you? Look at these bruises! If you let me go, I swear I'll go away and you'll never see me again.'

'Why should I believe a cur like you?'

'Because I'm telling you the truth! Nothing is worth what I've been through in the last year. I should never have chased her to England.'

'Why did you?'

'I wanted that chalice! I can't expect you to understand, Coverdale. No one who hasn't seen it could.' For a moment Edmund Willoughby seemed to have forgotten John's presence. There was a new note in his voice, a kind of awe. 'It was the chalice... I saw it once in Peter Leyburn's study. He always kept it locked in a special sort of cupboard, but one day he had it out when I came in. He was holding it in his hands and staring at it so intently that he didn't know I was there. The light... The colours... I have never seen anything like it before or since. It took hold of me. He was so furious that I had seen it that I think he might have killed me if he had dared. But I didn't care. I wanted it. I wanted it so badly that I offered him anything, begged him to give it to me, to leave it to me when he died. It became an obsession. But he always refused even to listen. Then when he died he left it to *her*!' He thumped the pillow angrily. 'I should have taken that chalice when she was still in Jamaica! It ought to have been easy, but somehow or other she always got away from me. That's why I followed her here.'

'It's now beyond your reach, Willoughby. Forget it. You'll never have it. Peter Leyburn didn't leave it to Caroline Duval, either. He sent it back to where it belongs.'

'Where is it now? Have you seen it?'

'That's something I'm not going to tell you. And, no, I haven't seen it. I didn't even know what it was until *you* told me. Caroline has always refused to talk of it.' He leaned forward and said earnestly, 'There is no chance that you will ever see it again, Willoughby. Put this madness out of your mind. You have more urgent concerns at the moment.'

Edmund seemed to grow smaller in the bed. 'What are you going to do with me?'

John looked at him for a moment. Then he said contemptuously, 'You're not worth a great deal of trouble. If I were to hand you over for the punishment you deserve, your cousin would suffer almost as much. I think I shall send you under suitable escort to be put on the next packet boat to leave Falmouth. But don't think you can take up where you left off in persecuting Mrs Duval. If I hear of any further harm to her, I shall make you pay. I assure you I can do it, Willoughby, even if you are as far away as Jamaica. Believe me.'

'Oh, I've learned my lesson. I'll be glad to go back. So Caroline is under your protection, is she? I didn't think you'd be fool enough to have married her, whatever you said at that inn. Well, make the most of it. She never stays long with the same man.'

John's lips tightened. 'Caroline Duval is under my protection as a guest! Nothing more! No! I don't wish to hear another word.' He got up. 'You'll leave tomorrow at first light, whether you feel fit or not. You've had my warning. I'd remember it if I were you, Willoughby.' He went to the door and called Betts in.

'Colonel?'

'Organise an escort to take this man to Falmouth as speedily as possible. He is to sail for Jamaica as soon as there is a packet, or any kind of boat, to take him. He is to be guarded until the ship sails. I'll provide you with the necessary funds tonight. Understood?'

Betts's training stood him in good stead. His 'Yes, sir! Right, sir!' gave no indication that the order was in any way extraordinary. Not even by a raised eyebrow. When the Colonel was in this kind of mood, a wise soldier did what he said without comment or delay.

Betts did well. Edmund Willoughby left Marrick the next morning in one of the castle's carriages. He was apparently being looked after by his valet, another man-servant, a coachman and two grooms. On the journey down to Falmouth such an ostentatiously large entourage aroused frequent comment. What was the gentleman afraid of? He didn't appear to be particularly happy with his men.

But Edmund Willoughby still had a score to settle with Caroline. His last act before boarding the packet boat was to sit in the parlour in the King's Arms under the watchful eye of his escort, and write a letter. He sealed it, addressed it and gave it to Betts to take back to Yorkshire.

'I've written a letter to thank your master,' he said. 'See that he gets it.'

Chapter Nine

While Edmund was making his journey back to Falmouth and on to Jamaica, Marrick bustled with activity. After long years of silence and seclusion the castle hummed with excitement, as preparations got under way for the grand reception and ball at which John Ancroft, fourth Marquess of Coverdale, would renew his acquaintance with the neighbourhood. It would be an occasion, too, for Lady Harriet Ancroft, his daughter, to mix in society before her début in London the following year.

An army of servants was drafted in to prepare the castle for the ball, and Mrs Abbington was faced with a mountain of new, unforeseen duties.

'I am really not sure how I shall manage, Mrs Duval,' she confided to Caroline in a worried voice. 'Such a large number of guests wish to stay the night that I can't work out where to put them all. Many of the bedchambers have been shut up for years—they will all need to be aired, and cleaned and prepared. And as if that weren't enough, Lord Coverdale wishes to have a sit-down dinner for forty before the ball. He'll expect me to make sure refreshments are available throughout the evening, as well.'

'That really isn't difficult, Mrs Abbington,' said Caroline, in an attempt to encourage her. 'Thomas Beckford is a very good steward, and you have an excellent chef in the kitchens.'

Mrs Abbington was not to be comforted. 'But they aren't used to such large affairs! It's years since anything like this was done at Marrick, and they all need a lot of direction. There's a thousand things to do! How I am to plan it all I do not know. The main reception rooms have to be dusted and polished, chandeliers taken down and cleaned, curtains shaken, floors scrubbed, ornaments washed... Quantities of silver, china, linen to be looked out and checked...' Mrs Abbington came to a halt and held her hand to her forehead. 'And my head is aching so.'

Caroline looked at her with a great deal of sympathy. Mrs Abbington was a quiet woman, excellently suited to acting as companion to a young girl, and running a household that never had visitors or any kind of entertainment. The previous regime under Lord Coverdale had suited her very well. But she was now faced with a different world, and it was clearly too much. It was no surprise at all to hear the day after this conversation that Mrs Abbington had taken to her bed with a violent, and permanent, headache.

The situation was potentially desperate, and Caroline felt obliged to offer to step into the breach. Till now she had done her best to stay in the background while these preparations were going on. She was not a member of the family, merely an unexpected guest who would leave as soon as the Ainderbys came home. But things were different now and, in the circumstances, what could she do but agree to take over? This was something she loved and was well used to doing. Her grandfather may have despised Kingston society, but his business and political interests made it imperative that he entertained frequently, and often lavishly. A dinner for fifty, a musical evening for a hundred, a ball for two hundred—she had managed them all with ease. She was not at all daunted at the prospect of opening up a large castle in Yorkshire. To tell the truth, she was stimulated by the new challenge!

At first the servants looked askance at this guest who seemed to have taken over the household so firmly. But the new Lord Coverdale made it clear that he supported Mrs Duval in her efforts, and Mrs Duval herself soon impressed them with her command of the situation. The lady clearly knew what was needed, and, what was more, she saw to it that everyone else did, too!

John watched and marvelled as the castle slowly emerged from its years of sadness and neglect, and the servants learned to move swiftly and efficiently about their work. 'Mrs Duval says' was heard all over the castle, whether it was the gardener watering plants with anxious care—'Mrs Duval wants plenty of greenery for the ballroom, my lord'—or the chef trying out new recipes—'Mrs Duval is hoping for a worthy centrepiece, my lord.' Furniture was ruthlessly redeployed or moved away altogether, and when he questioned the men, they said with all respect, 'But Mrs Duval wants the hall cleared for dancing, my lord! As well as the ballroom.' John lost no time in putting a ban on any interference with the furniture in his library! Who knew what 'Mrs Duval' would want next?

And Caroline Duval seemed to achieve it all without the slightest loss of her calm, slightly lazy-looking grace. She appeared to find plenty of time to coach Harriet, too. John watched her patiently teaching the girl how to approach the different ranks of the *ton*, a curtsy with the correct degree of formality for some, a polite bob for others, a hand extended to yet others. He listened as she went through the proper forms of address, and laughed with his daughter as Caroline acted out a crotchety duchess, or a plum-voiced bishop to make the lesson fun. Harriet had been well educated by Mrs Abbington in the niceties of ordinary behaviour, but John was amazed to see that she was now being taught the manners of the cream of society. Taught by an expert, too. The most exclusive seminary for the young ladies of the *ton* could not have found fault with what Caroline Duval was teaching Harriet Ancroft! And in spite of her easy-going manner she was strict. Harriet was not permitted any lapses. Some of her own philosophy, it was true, sometimes surfaced, but nothing to take exception to. If Harriet stammered or apologised after she had been clumsy or forgetful, Caroline would say firmly, 'Never apologise, never make excuses. Hold that head of yours up, Harriet, and keep calm. The world will take you at your own valuation. Stay courteous, stay polite, but never, never cringe!' John looked and wondered. Once again, this woman had him puzzled. Loyal granddaughter, actress, impudent wanton, superb manager and chatelaine, and now a first-class mentor to his daughter... Where the devil was the *real* Caroline Duval?

Of course time was made, too, to teach Harriet all sorts of dances. A fiddler was brought up from the village, and John and Caroline between them demonstrated the steps needed for most of the country dances, and one or two others besides. The waltz was kept as a special treat, to reward Harriet when she did well with the others.

'It will do no harm for you to know the steps, Harriet. But from what I have heard, and I think your father will bear me out, you must not dance it in public until you have the approval of certain ladies of London society, the famous patronesses of Almack's. Is that not so, Lord Coverdale?'

'Quite right. There won't be any difficulty in obtaining their approval, however. Sally Jersey is an old friend of mine. But you must wait until you've got it.'

'I will, I will! But please show me how it goes! Dance with Mrs Duval, Papa! I can play the piano and watch at the same time. Go on!'

So John took Caroline by the hand, bowed and began to waltz with her. His touch was impersonal, the distance between them perfectly judged, close enough to guide, but a respectable distance apart. Nothing could have been more proper. Yet John was aware of every movement of her body, as they swayed gracefully round the room. For all her height she was as light as thistledown in his arms, matching his steps perfectly. He was sorry when they finally came back to the piano and a shining-eyed Harriet.

'That was wonderful!' she exclaimed, jumping up and clapping her hands. 'Now you must teach me!'

'You'll never have a better teacher,' said Caroline laughing. 'Your papa, Harriet, is the best partner I think I've ever danced with!' She turned to John. 'My congratulations! Wherever did you learn to waltz like that?'

'My dear lady, the two chief qualities necessary to be a success as an officer in Wellington's army were first to be able to march well, and second to be able to waltz even better!'

'There must have been one or two others,' she murmured. 'Ability to fight, perhaps? To command men? And…courage under fire?'

'Yes, but those were trivial matters compared with keeping the army on the move and the ladies happy, I assure you!'

'Shameful! You mustn't disillusion us, Colonel! We thought you all heroes.'

'He *was* a hero! I read about him. He was often a hero! They kept saying it. ''Bravery under fire.''' Harriet turned to her father. 'I was always afraid you would be killed, Papa. I know that's what Uncle Coverdale wanted, but I could never want that. I was always afraid for you.'

John stood looking down at her. He said finally, 'Strange. If I had known that, there might not have been so many commendations for bravery under fire.'

'What do you mean?'

'Never mind. Come, Harriet! If Mrs Duval will kindly oblige on the piano, we shall begin your lessons.'

After a while Harriet was sufficiently adept to start learning the turns. This needed another demonstration, and John and Caroline duly set off dipping and swaying down the room. To this point they had kept their steps simple for Harriet's benefit, coming back, not by changing direction with a turn, but by following round the curve of the room. But this time John pulled Caroline to him as he guided her into the turn. The contact was closer than he intended and gave them both a shock. He had to restrain a mad impulse to pull her closer yet, to hold her as he had held her in Buckden... For a moment the world was forgotten in a surge of desire. It gave him a certain amount of satisfaction to see that Caroline's eyes had widened and she was breathing rapidly. He wasn't alone, then, in this sudden and inconvenient onset of feeling... With an effort he pulled himself together, took up the correct distance once again and came down the room with her.

'That looked easy enough,' said Harriet.

'It was far from it,' muttered John. 'If you only knew, child!'

Caroline said hastily, 'It looks easy until you try, Harriet. Look, I'll show you where to put your feet.'

'Er…' said John. 'I must apologise. I've just remembered an appointment. I'll have to excuse myself for this afternoon.'

'Papa!' exclaimed Harriet in tones of deepest disappointment.

'It's all right, Harriet!' said Caroline swiftly. 'We can do the steps of the turn nearly as well without your papa. I can leave the piano—we don't really need music for it. We can count. Now, come over here.'

John looked back as he came to the door, and met Caroline's gaze. By Heaven, she was laughing at him again! The wicked look in her eyes told him that she knew perfectly well why he had no wish at the moment to demonstrate an intimately close turn—with his daughter!

They had taken to having a short stroll round the garden after dinner, using the tranquillity of evening to discuss the day's activities and plan for the next, and that evening John found himself waiting more impatiently than usual for the moment when Harriet would excuse herself and go up to visit Mrs Abbington and he and Caroline would be free to go outside. At last it came. They went out on to the terrace and started down the steps.

'The invitations have been sent out?' asked Caroline. This was one task which she had found impossible, and John had taken it over.

'The last of them went out today. I've had one delivered to the Ainderbys, though I'm not sure they'll be back in time to come. Still, they had to be invited. You may

meet Martin Ainderby before you go to High Hutton. Will
that disturb you?'

'I don't think so. I would still wait till we go over to
High Hutton to talk to him. A ball wouldn't be the time
or place to mention the...what I'm bringing.'

'You can call the thing by its right name, if you wish.
Your cousin told me what it was.'

She grew pale and said fiercely, 'Did you ask him? He
had no right to tell you if you did!'

'No, I did not ask him. It was obvious that you didn't
wish the world to know, and I respected that wish. I'm
surprised that you think I would!'

'I'm sorry. You're right. The world was not to know,
not even someone like you. My grandfather was very insistent. He was furious when Edmund saw it. He made
me promise to tell no one else. Only the Ainderbys were
to know anything at all. I've kept my promise. Now I
hear that Edmund has let it out the first time he meets
you, and all my trouble has been wasted. What did he
say? Have you...have you looked at it?'

This time John was really annoyed. 'Of course not!' he
snapped.

'No, of course you wouldn't.' She gave him an apologetic smile. 'I just thought that if Edmund had talked
much about it you might have been tempted. It's incredibly beautiful, you see. Mystically so. I can almost understand Edmund's obsession with it. Grandfather was the
same.' She frowned as she said thoughtfully, 'You know,
he was a strong man, my grandfather. I never saw him
miserable or depressed. But when he talked of that...
that...'

'Chalice?'

'Yes. The chalice. He was always disturbed. And every
bit as fanatically determined as Edmund. It was to go to

High Hutton, those were almost his last words! Promising to bring it here was the only way I could make him easy in his mind. Oh John, I wish I knew what lies behind it all!'

'I can't help you,' he said taking her restless hands in his and holding them still. 'I was only twenty-one when I left Marrick, and before that time we'd had very little to do with the two Ainderby brothers, though they were much the same age as we were. My uncle had quarrelled with their father, and we never visited. I had a hard time persuading my uncle to allow my engagement to Gabriella.'

'How did you meet her, if you saw so little of her brothers?'

He shook his head. 'Gabriella wasn't their sister. She was their cousin.' He started to walk slowly down the path, still holding Caroline's hand.

'Tell me about her,' she said softly. 'Where *did* you meet her?'

The scents of the garden surrounded them in the warm air. The light was fading, and it seemed a time for confidences. For the first time in years John felt an urge to talk. 'I met her at a ball in Richmond when she was a couple of years older than Harriet is now. She was there with her mother. I thought her the loveliest thing I had ever seen, and fell in love there and then.' He smiled down at her. 'I had plenty of rivals for her favours. But in the end she took me.'

'How soon did you get engaged?'

'Two months later. We had to overcome considerable opposition. Gabriella's mother didn't like it any more than my uncle did.'

'Why not? You must have been a most eligible young man. Belonging to one of the most important families in this part of Yorkshire, handsome, well set up... What more could a mother want?'

'My fortune wasn't particularly handsome! My connections were good enough, I suppose, but at that time...' He paused. 'At that time I had no prospect of a title, and my own estates were not large. Mrs Ainderby was ambitious. She thought her daughter would be throwing herself away if she married me. But then she suddenly relented. Almost overnight. I never asked her why, I was only too happy that she had. We got engaged at the end of June and were to have been married in the last week of July. But by that time Gabriella was dead.'

They walked in silence for a while.

Then Caroline said hesitantly, 'What was she like, your Gabriella? She looked quite like me, I know. But what was she like as a person?'

He thought for a moment. 'She was still very young, of course. I've sometimes been reminded of her when I see Harriet now. All that openness, that shining innocence... She loved meeting people—company, dancing, concerts, going to balls. And wherever she went she was always surrounded by admirers.' He turned to Caroline. 'But I was always sure she was mine. And the night before we got engaged she told me she had always felt the same.'

He stopped and looked at her. 'I'm sorry! This can't be very interesting for you. I don't know what has come over me! I haven't talked of Gabriella for years. The last time was in Spain and I at least had the excuse of being wounded.'

'Who was your confidante that time? A lovely senora?'

'Far from it! An ordinary-looking Englishman, Adam Calthorpe. He was in the army with me. We were wounded together at Talavera, and we talked through the night to keep our minds off our aches and pains. Adam's a great fellow, I'd like you to meet him.'

Caroline laughed. 'That's most unlikely! Unless I come across him in London.'

'You might if you're still in England next year. He and his wife had a baby son last December, and missed this year's season. They'll almost certainly be in London next spring. In fact, I had considered asking Adam's wife, Kate, to help me with Harriet's début.' He paused. But he wanted to know. 'Will you be?'

She didn't understand him. 'Will I be what?'

'Be in London next spring?'

'I...I don't...I'm not quite sure,' she said, clearly disconcerted. 'I've no reason to hurry home. But I can't make any plans for the future until I've delivered the...the chalice.'

They had reached the farthest end of the garden. The sounds of the house hardly penetrated this far, and the countryside was still as the sun slowly sank, leaving the hills in shadow.

John took her hand again. 'Caroline, I want to thank you. For everything. For all the effort you're making to make this ball a success.'

'That's nothing! Really, John, I mean it. I enjoy the work.'

There was a brief silence, then he said awkwardly, 'You've done a lot for me personally, too. You've been generous about what happened in Buckden. You must have been curious, but until tonight you have never asked about...about Gabriella.'

'Was I wrong to do so now? Has it stirred up the unhappiness I saw that night?'

'No. I think it might even have done good. It's strange. I nearly didn't come back here at all, you know. If Fenny hadn't persuaded me that it was my duty I doubt I ever would have. I had decided I couldn't bear all the reminders. But somehow... That journey with you, meeting Harriet again, realising that I can be a father to her... And seeing Marrick and my people again... A lot of the unhappiness has disappeared. I can even talk of Gabriella with less difficulty. I suppose you think that after seventeen years it's time!'

'I can't answer that. We have to deal with what we can, when we can.' She hesitated, then went on, 'You, at least, didn't suffer the humiliation of learning that the person you had loved was completely worthless, as I did. But I got over it. And talking to my grandfather helped. It gave me confidence in myself, restored my pride again—along with a certain scorn for the way in which the rest of the world judges by appearance.'

'As I did with you?'

She looked at him for a moment. Then she said sombrely, 'I think you still do. But perhaps that's as well.'

It was most unlike her to sound unhappy. He drew her to him. For a short while they stayed like this, his only aim to give comfort. But then the intimacy of the dark, secluded garden, the heady scents of the flowers, the warmth of her body resting against his, slowly combined into an irresistible mixture. The urge to hold her yet more closely, to press her to him, kiss her was overpowering. He tightened his hold and she looked up, startled.

'John—' Any other words were lost as his mouth covered hers and an explosion of passion left them breathless. They clung to one another, locked together in a swaying embrace. The kiss went on and on, neither wanting to put an end to this swirling, intoxicating delight. This was what he had been waiting for! Caroline felt so right in his arms, he wanted to hold her like this forever. Her response excited him further, and he strained her to him. He was trembling when he finally raised his head. He held her face between his hands, searching in the dark to read the expression in her eyes. She looked desperate.

'I don't want this,' she whispered despairingly. 'It's too…it's too dangerous.'

He was surprised into a laugh. 'Don't be absurd. What do you mean? How can it possibly be dangerous?'

'You mustn't laugh. I mean it. I…I don't seem to be able to take you lightly, John. I can't treat you like the others. You get too close. Much too close.'

John was disarmed by her evident distress. He relaxed his hold, but still kept her in the circle of his arms. 'There's no need to be afraid. I don't want you to take me lightly.' There was a silence. Then he said slowly, 'Caroline, when your visit to Ainderby is over, would you consider staying on here for a while? Nothing would please Harriet more, I know, and I… I'd like time for us to get to know one another better. Harriet needs someone like you in her life…and I believe I do, too. You've said that you can't consider the future until you've taken the chalice to High Hutton, so I won't press you now. But afterwards when you're free…'

She pulled away. 'I…I don't know… I'd have to think. What you're talking of…it sounds as if it might become altogether too serious for me. Too close, too close.' She threw him a quick look. 'And yet…it's so tempting… I've so dreaded the thought of being alone.'

He wanted to take her in his arms again, but she held him off. 'No, don't! That doesn't help, it just obscures the issue. I mustn't let my senses rule my head! Once was enough.'

'Senses? Not heart?'

She shook her head ruefully. 'You keep looking for my heart. But I'm not sure I have one to lose. Not any more.'

He gave a slow nod. 'That's something that might be said about both of us, perhaps. But surely there are compensations? Interests in common, friendship, humour. And wouldn't you say that there's a certain…feeling between us?'

She pulled a face. 'I can't deny any of those—especially not the "certain feeling"! But I need more than that to convince me.'

'What?'

Caroline shook her head. 'Leave it, John! Give us both time to consider. Shall we go back to the house? It's getting cold.'

John had to acquiesce. Perhaps he was not altogether sorry. His invitation to Caroline to stay longer at Marrick had come almost as much of a surprise to him as it had to her. The magic of the night, of that kiss, might well have had a lot to do with it. But even when he thought about it in the cool light of day it kept its appeal. Caroline, it was true, would never be able to replace Gabriella, but she was a woman of beauty, intelligence and passion. His daughter was on the way to loving her and, from what he had seen, Caroline Duval would in her totally individual way be a good mother. Whatever her own standards of behaviour might have been in the past, she was strict enough with Harriet. Yes, he could do a lot worse than consider Caroline Duval as his future Marchioness…

He was annoyed therefore when Caroline announced on the day before the ball that she was proposing to remain in the background for the whole of the evening.

'What do you expect us to do?' he asked. 'Who will

give the servants the necessary orders, receive the guests, be in charge?'

'I've asked Mrs Abbington. She says she's well enough.'

'But, Caroline—'

'I don't think you've thought about this. Mrs Abbington has been Harriet's companion and managed the household for many years. She will be regarded as the proper person to act as your hostess tomorrow night. You needn't worry. She'll do it well. And I'll make sure that there are no crises.'

'But you've done all the work!'

'In the eyes of the county I'm merely an unexpected guest, waiting for the Ainderbys to return. Unless you want all kinds of unwelcome speculation about my position here, you'll pay me no particular attention, nor give me any undue importance. I mean it, John. I know what gossip can do, and the last thing I want is to spoil what ought to be a perfect evening for Harriet. Don't you agree?'

'You don't mind about spoiling my evening?'

'You'll be busy looking after Harriet, and making sure your guests are happy and well fed. You're a great man, now, John! And *noblesse oblige*, you know!' She laughed at his disgusted expression.

But her laughter was stilled when he said, 'I hear the Ainderbys will be back tomorrow, though I doubt they will be in time to come here for the ball. Shall I send a message asking if we may visit them the day after?'

'Yes,' she said, suddenly breathless. 'Yes, of course! So they're coming back at last... And my journey to Yorkshire will finally reach its end. It seems almost strange to think that it will soon all be over.'

'Your grandfather's part will be over. But not his

granddaughter's. I still hope to see her continue to play a part in Yorkshire, Caroline, though perhaps not at High Hutton.'

Caroline dressed early on the evening of the ball, then sent Maggie to see to Harriet. When Maggie had gone she sat down in an armchair by the window, put her head back against the cushion and gazed out on the hills. Tonight was a climax of a sort. She had done her best for a girl she had come to love, and now she could only be an onlooker. Harriet was bound to be a success, here and in London. Perhaps she should make sure she was in London for Harriet's début whatever happened up here in Yorkshire in the next few days. What *would* happen? She guessed that John Ancroft might well ask her to marry him, and wondered what she would say if he did.

There were, as he had said in the garden, sound reasons for considering it. Interests in common, friendship, humour…and a certain 'feeling' between them. He had meant a strong physical attraction, of course. And when he had asked what more she wanted to convince her she had been unable to tell him. Not out loud… How could she have said, 'I'm sure you won't hurt me physically as Laurent Duval did. But physical hurt was more bearable than what he did to the real me, Caroline. If I let myself trust you, let you near me, how can I be sure you won't hurt me as he did, betray my trust, my belief in you? To give anyone, but especially a man, such power over me fills me with horror… I would need very strong reasons to risk that a second time. I'm not sure the ones you gave me are enough.'

She had sworn never to marry again, and part of her still rejected the very idea. But John was not Laurent Duval. She believed she could trust him not to hurt her as

Laurent Duval had hurt her. He had a basic respect, a basic kindness, which had been totally absent in her late, unlamented husband. And most women would think her a lunatic to turn him down. Refuse the prospect of marriage to the Marquess of Coverdale! Quite mad! In the eyes of the world it would bring so much—a great position, wealth, security, Marrick and other houses all over England.

But she had never set a great store by position. She had all the wealth she could ever need. If security meant money to buy servants and houses, then those were hers already... But marriage to John would bring so much more. Harriet as a daughter, a family, perhaps children of her own, a home. And John.

She got up and walked about the room the train of her grey silk dress rustling behind her. John. Her wooden soldier. Someone she had seen in every possible state of mind—cold reserve, despair, black anger, and amusement, laughter. A man of authority, yet liked by those under him. Someone who was at ease with Barnaby and Thomas Beckford, but who had clearly mixed with the great and the good of Europe. A strict man, but very kind. How could she have ever thought him simple? And this man, against all the odds, seemed to respect her, value her. So much so that he might ask her to marry him. Dared she risk it?

It was time to go down, and she was still no nearer a decision!

Harriet looked enchantingly pretty in a white dress with pink silk roses round its sleeves and hem. She was carrying a small bouquet of pink roses in a silver filigree holder, which John had presented to her before the evening began, and her dark hair was held in a delicate silver clasp given to her by Caroline. The guests were disarmed by her shy charm, and her silver-grey eyes shone like stars as she joined in the country dancing with grace and enthusiasm. Her presence at the ball could be counted a great success and augured well for her London début.

Caroline herself had stuck to her decision and stayed severely in the background. She had dressed herself for the part, getting Maggie to skewer the rebellious waves of her hair into a discreet twist with a small diamond aigrette and a fall of Venetian lace covering the many pins that held it in place. Her dress of grey silk *gros de Naples* had half-sleeves and a train, its neckline trimmed with more lace. The stones in her diamond necklace, though not extravagantly large, were of the first water. She looked unostentatiously elegant. A woman of distinction. She was careful to allow John to put his name on her card for only two dances, and refused to go into supper with him.

'I am surprised at you, Lord Coverdale! Do I have to remind one of Wellington's stars that the host takes in the senior-ranking lady present? Lady Randolph, you may be sure, will be well aware of her status, and expect no less! Do your best to charm her for Harriet's sake, if not your own!'

Lady Randolph was a formidable dowager who terrorized her family and everyone else who came within her orbit. She loved gossip, and with the aid of her cronies was always *au fait* with the latest scandals. She would make an excellent ally in restoring Marrick's position in the neighbourhood, but it would be dangerous to offend her. Fortunately John saw the sense of this, remembered his manners and led Lady Randolph into supper with all the address and polish at his command. Caroline, watching, was once again impressed with a new facet of John's

personality. When Lord Coverdale chose, he could be a
real charmer! The old lady was delighted.

After supper the dowager captured Caroline, sailed
with her into an alcove and subjected her to a polite, but
ruthless examination. A lesser woman would have been
afraid, but Caroline remained undaunted. She was a past
mistress in fending off unwelcome questions, and expected to enjoy the promised verbal fencing match. In the
conversation that followed Lady Randolph learned a great
deal about Jamaica, but very little about Caroline Duval.
After a while she decided that subtlety was getting her
nowhere and tried a broadside attack. She suddenly said,
'Hmph! I suppose you realise that you're the image of
Gabriella Ainderby? Is that why Coverdale is so taken
with you? Are you and she related?'

'Not as far as I know. But I've heard the name, of
course. Was Lord Coverdale engaged to her at one time?'

'Yes, more's the pity!'

Caroline was startled. 'I beg your pardon?'

'It was a sad end for her, but it would have been a
sadder one for him if she had lived.'

'Lady Randolph, I'm not sure what you are trying to
say.'

'I'm not *trying* to say anything, Mrs Duval! I'm *telling*
you that he would have been a sight unhappier married
to that girl than he was when she died.'

Caroline decided that she must change the subject. She
badly wanted to know more, but this old harridan must
not be allowed to see how very interested she was. She
said sympathetically, if a little disingenuously, 'Miss Ainderby is dead? That must indeed have been a sad blow
for Lord Coverdale. But his daughter must now bring him

a great deal of pleasure. I think she looks charming, don't you? Do you have granddaughters, Lady Randolph?'

'Three,' snapped the dowager. 'All dull as ditchwater. But I'm happy to say that they have never given their mother a moment's worry. They've all made very good matches.' She gave Caroline a crocodile smile and leaned forward. 'Which is more than could be said for the Ainderby girl! What a time Mrs William Ainderby had with her! And all the other Ainderbys, too! Of course it's water under the bridge now—mother and daughter have both been dead these many years. But I happen to know that the family would have thrown them out of High Hutton within the month if Gabriella had not managed to get herself engaged to John Ancroft. And I tell you this, there were a good few of us who were very sorry for him when she did!'

Caroline's mind was reeling, but, not without difficulty, she held on to her air of polite interest. She would not betray herself to this woman! She said calmly, 'Lord Coverdale was saying tonight that he thought the Ainderbys were back at High Hutton. Have you heard?'

Lady Randolph looked at her sourly and decided to give up. She knew when she had met her match. Mrs Duval was either not interested in old scandals about her host, or she was too clever to let it be seen. Either way, even *she* felt she could not in decency drag in the subject of Gabriella Ainderby for a third time. She switched to other, more recent scandals.

Caroline was released soon after by one of the other guests, a Mr Dalton. He was some years older than John but still very handsome with bold, dark eyes and a dashing moustache. He asked her to dance. She was so relieved that she gave him a brilliant smile and got up immediately. She excused herself to the dowager, who smiled briefly in response and immediately looked round the room for another prey. As Caroline accompanied her rescuer into the ballroom he said with a grin, 'You seemed to survive the ordeal remarkably well, Mrs Duval. Lady Randolph's victims are usually more crushed when they leave her.'

'I've met quite a number of Lady Randolphs in my time, sir. I rather enjoy their company—for a while! But I admit I was very glad when you came over.'

'Really?' He seemed to be assessing her. For a moment there was an element of familiarity in his gaze which didn't altogether please her. They danced for a while, then he said, 'I expect others have already said how like Gabriella Ainderby you are. It gave me a shock, I can tell you, when I first saw you. It might have been Gabriella herself come back to haunt us all.'

'*Am* I so very like her?' she asked coolly.

He went on, 'Of course you are! The same red hair, the same wicked eyes, the same charmingly enticing smile! How much further does the resemblance go, I wonder?' With a shock Caroline felt her hand being squeezed.

'I think I must have misheard you, sir,' she said pleasantly, removing her hand from his grasp. 'At least, I hope I did. I'd hate to believe that these are Yorkshire manners. My name is Caroline Duval, not Gabriella Ainderby. I am from Jamaica, and at present Lord Coverdale's guest. Is that enough for you? Now, we'll talk of other things. Do you live far from here, sir? I find the roads very uneven in quality. How difficult is it to get about in winter?'

He gave her an odd look, but remembered his manners enough to follow her lead. Though he still eyed her speculatively from time to time, there were no more over-familiar remarks.

Caroline was puzzled. She knew that her normally

rather striking appearance could lead to misconceptions about her behaviour. She had sometimes played on it out of sheer mischief. But this evening she had deliberately set out to make herself unexceptional. Nothing could be more sober, or more respectable, than her grey dress, and her restrained hairstyle with its lace cap and diamond aigrette. What was it about her likeness to Gabriella Ainderby that caused such a strange lack of good manners?

By the end of the evening Caroline was seriously worried. More than one gentleman had been sufficiently misled by her superficial resemblance to Gabriella to assume she was an easy target for their gallantries. She had soon disabused them. That was not the problem. But it was possible that her presence in Marrick might stir up more potential grief for John than he had yet experienced. For seventeen years Gabriella had lain quietly in her grave, forgotten, as far as she could see, by all but John. But her own resemblance to the girl was stirring up old memories, old scandals. John Ancroft had put Gabriella on a pedestal, and worshipped at its foot for seventeen years. What if his image of her had been false?

She avoided talking to John by the simple expedient of going upstairs to bed while he was still dealing with his guests. In her present state of mind it would have been difficult to know what to say to him. But though she was very tired, sleep eluded her. She tossed and turned, her mind swinging like a pendulum between her two enigmas. The impression she had gained tonight of Gabriella Ainderby was very different from everything John had told her about the girl. Where was the truth? And as she got nearer to High Hutton and the delivery of the chalice, she began to wonder about its history. So many mysteries surrounded it. Would she learn the truth about *that* tomorrow?

The chalice and Gabriella Ainderby. She was not sure that the truth about either would turn out to be very welcome.

Chapter Ten

Caroline got up early the next morning, pale and heavy-eyed, still wondering how she could talk about the ball the previous night without letting John see how concerned she was. He was already downstairs and dressed for riding.

'I wondered about you when you disappeared last night,' he said, looking at her with a frown. 'Have you been doing too much?'

'No, no! Of course not. But you were busy when I wished to go to bed, and I thought it best to leave you and Mrs Abbington to deal with the guests. When are the people who stayed overnight leaving, do you know?'

'Oh, we're a hardy lot in Yorkshire! We don't keep London hours. Some have gone already, and the rest will depart soon after breakfast. Caroline, Harriet has been invited to a party the Lawsons are giving tonight at Brough. I'd like her to go. The Lawsons have a large family, some of them around her age, and it would be good for her. And it fits in quite well with our plans. We shall be out for most of the day, and I don't think this visit to High Hutton is a suitable occasion for her. Do you mind?'

'I think it's a wonderful idea!'

'Good. Good!' He looked pleased. 'I'll tell her. Er... shall we set off for High Hutton about eleven o'clock? I think everyone will have left by then.'

'Certainly.'

He looked at her closely. 'You *are* tired! Shall we postpone the visit?'

'By no means!' exclaimed Caroline in a panic.

'If you're sure?'

'Absolutely certain!'

'I had thought we would ride cross-country. It's a long way round by road. But it looks as if it might be better to take the carriage after all...?'

'No, I should prefer to ride. I haven't had enough fresh air recently. It might do me good.'

'In that case, why don't you have a rest before then?'

A rest in her room would keep her out of John's way for a little longer. Caroline said thankfully, 'I think I will.'

He accompanied her upstairs, and escorted her to her room. 'Maggie, see that your mistress lies down for a while. I think she's been overdoing it, whatever she may say!' He turned to Caroline. 'Stay up here till it's time to go. I'll say goodbye to Harriet for you. And try not to worry so much about today.'

'He's right, Miss Caro. You look washed out. Let me take that dress off and fetch your wrapper. I'll draw the curtains in a minute, too. By the way, Joseph is back, and says he'll go with you.'

'Did he enjoy the visit to his family?'

Maggie smiled broadly. 'Perhaps for the first day or two. But after that he was glad to get away. The rest of the Bellerbys are a noisy, quarrelsome lot from what he said.'

'So he doesn't wish to stay in Yorkshire after all?'

'I don't think so.' Maggie paused. 'That is, not with

his family. But I don't know what he'd do if you decided
to stay?' She looked at Caroline inquiringly.

'Don't you start,' said Caroline wearily. 'It's all so confused. And I still have to deal with the Ainderbys.'

'I expect his lordship will see to any problems. A very
capable man, his lordship. And a gentleman with it. Anyone who had him to look after her could count herself
lucky!'

'You think so?'

'I'm certain of it!'

'If only I could be sure... The prospect is tempting,
but how could I ever marry again? To hand over such
power...'

'You could trust his lordship, I'd stake my life on it!'

'Wouldn't we all miss Jamaica?'

'Not if you were happy. And married to the Colonel.'

'Not so fast! There are a few problems to solve first!'

'Such as what they say about Miss Gabriella Ainderby?'

Caroline sat up. '*What* was that?'

'Miss Ainderby. You should hear what the servants
here have to say about her. The older ones, that is. They
remember her quite well, and she was a proper little mad-
am, from all accounts. Wasn't happy until she'd got a
man where she wanted him—wrapped round her little finger. Then once she had him so as he didn't know whether
he was on his head or his heels, she lost interest. But up
to that point she'd try anything. She was up to all sorts
of tricks. It didn't stop with kissing, either!'

'Be quiet, Maggie! I won't listen to this!'

But Maggie was not to be stopped. 'Our poor Colonel!
The servants here say *she* was the one who really caused
the accident, not him! The two cousins were both in a
rage, but that was because they'd quarrelled over her! The

Colonel was angry with Lord Philip because he thought he was flirting with Miss Ainderby, but it was the other way round. Miss Ainderby wouldn't leave Lord Philip alone! You may take it from me, Miss Caro, Gabriella Ainderby was far from being the saint the Colonel makes her out to be!'

'Oh, Lord!' Caroline put her face in her hands. Maggie could be right. The people last night had given her the same impression. She looked up. 'How can we stop him from finding out?'

'If you ask me, it's time he did find out.'

'No! I can't bear to think what it would do to him.'

Maggie was silent. Then she said slowly, 'I think you're much fonder of the Colonel than you admit, Miss Caro.'

Caroline stared at her. 'Am I? I don't know! I never thought I'd ever fall in love again with anyone. Not after that first time. But what if you're right? Oh, Maggie, what a coil I'm in!'

'And I think the Colonel is pretty sweet on you, Miss Caro. He's a changed man since we were in Barnet. If he knew you loved him, he might not mind about Miss Ainderby as much.'

'You think so? If I could only be sure of that.' She leaned back against the pillows. 'Since you already know so much, you are probably aware that Lord Coverdale has asked me to stay on here for a little. Just as a guest, for the moment. Do you think I should?'

'Yes, I do, though it's not my place to say so.'

'Whenever has that stopped you from saying what you wanted?' asked Caroline.

Maggie ignored this. 'You said yourself you'll be lonely in Jamaica without your grandfather. And the Colonel is a good man. You'd be safe in his hands.'

A yawn caught Caroline unawares. 'He has a friend in you, at least.' Then she added sleepily, 'I'm not so sure that I want to be in any man's hands, Maggie. Not metaphorically, at least. I wouldn't at all mind being in a good man's hands literally...'

'Miss Caro! You watch what you're saying! If you're going to be a Marchioness, you'll have to learn how to behave!'

Caroline didn't reply. Her short night had caught up with her. She was asleep.

However, she was ready when one of the servants came to say that Lord Coverdale was waiting for her. She came downstairs in her green riding habit and met him at the bottom of the stairs.

'You look much better,' he said. 'Do you feel it?'

'Thank you, yes. You have my bag there, I see.'

'I took it out of the strong room five minutes ago. I suppose you will carry it, won't you?'

'Yes. For this last stage.'

'Don't be nervous. I'll be there whenever you want me. The Ainderbys are not monsters.'

'I'm sure they aren't! And I'm not nervous! It's just... Oh, confound it, John, I'm *horribly* nervous! I hate not knowing what's ahead!'

'Is there any kind of message or letter for them?'

'Two letters. One to give them, and one for me to open at the same time.'

'Then let's be on our way! The sooner we're there, the sooner you'll know. And remember! Whatever happens, I'll be nearby.'

'I...I'd like you to be present. All the time.'

He turned and gave her a long look. 'Thank you,' he said at last.

* * *

It was another warm, sunny day, but there was a cool breeze on the hills. It made for very pleasant riding. The climb was quite steep, and at the top they dismounted and gave the horses a rest. Below them the river ran like a silver ribbon threading its way through the surrounding trees. Above them the sky was a deep, clear blue. Caroline stood with Joseph just behind, looking down over the hills and dales which spread in every direction, a patchwork of green and grey, brown and purple, with here and there a single square of pale green or gold, where the farmer had planted wheat or some other crop.

'So, Bellerby. What do you think of Yorkshire after all these years?'

'It's a grand place in summer, your lordship. But the winters are none so great. Jamaica is warmer then, I'm thinking.'

'Did you find out from your family when it was that your uncle left these parts for the West Indies?'

Joseph shot a glance from under his brows. 'It were a long time ago. Too long for most folk to remember,' he replied evasively.

'Joseph! That's not an answer!'

'Better to wait, Miss Caro. After *that's* handed over.' He nodded to the bag round her middle.

'The sooner the better! Shall we go?' John waited while Joseph helped Caroline into the saddle, then set off once again.

The Ainderbys were waiting for them in the main doorway at High Hutton, and as she and John rode up with Joseph close behind, Caroline inspected them with interest. Martin Ainderby was tall, as tall as John or her grandfather. He would have been a handsome man but for a general sourness in his expression. Beside him was his

wife. She was a plain woman, with a short, rounded figure, wispy hair, and an air of defeat about her. Not a
prepossessing couple, thought Caroline. By now she was
used to expressions of surprise when people up here saw
her for the first time, but the Ainderbys' reaction was
stronger than any she had seen before. Shock and amazement, yes, but mixed with something approaching antag-
onism. She was even more apprehensive about the coming meeting, but waited calmly to be introduced. This
John did, and they were invited in. They were in a large
hall with rooms opening off at either end. The door at
one end was open with an inviting glimpse of an airy,
sun-filled room. But Mrs Ainderby walked over and shut
it before turning to her visitors again. She said,

'You've had a long ride. I expect you'd like something
cool to drink. Martin, would you take Lord Coverdale and
Mrs…Mrs Duval into the library, while I find one of the
servants? Will your groom have his in the kitchen, Lord
Coverdale?'

'Thank you kindly, ma'am. I'll wait here in the hall, if
you don't mind,' said Joseph stiffly.

Mrs Ainderby looked surprised, but said nothing. Instead she pointed to a chair by the door, and went off,
presumably in the direction of the kitchens. The others
followed Martin Ainderby into the room at the other end.
There was a slight pause while they sat down, then Mrs
Ainderby came in again, accompanied by a servant carrying a tray of drinks. There was another pause, during
which Caroline felt herself being eyed uneasily by their
hosts.

Mrs Ainderby gave her husband a glance. He cleared
his throat and said, 'I was a little surprised at your note,
Coverdale. You said Mrs Duval wished to speak to us,
but as far as I knew…' he threw Caroline a glance '…as

far as I *know*, we have never met the lady before.' He turned to her. 'Am I wrong?'

'No,' said Caroline. 'Unless you have been to Jamaica, sir? I have never been in England before this spring.'

'Really?' He seemed about to say more, but changed his mind. After a short pause he went on, 'Then, how can we serve you, Mrs Duval?'

Caroline carefully opened her bag and took out two letters. 'Forgive me if I appear to be acting mysteriously. But I must ask this. May I confirm that you are Martin Ainderby, the eldest son of Thomas Ainderby, of High Hutton?'

Martin Ainderby coloured angrily. 'Of course I am, ma'am! Who else could I be? What *is* all this about?'

'I'm sorry if I've offended you, but I had to make certain. The truth is, I am not sure myself what it is about. My grandfather died last year in Kingston, Jamaica, Mr Ainderby. Almost the last thing he did was ask me to deliver this letter to you. And, if the others will excuse me, he also gave me a letter addressed to me, which I was to read at the same time. Here they are.' She handed one letter to Martin Ainderby, and held the other in her hand, waiting till both could be opened at the same moment.

Martin Ainderby took his letter over to the light and stood by the window reading it. Caroline stayed where she was. The two other people in the room waited in silence and suspense.

John watched Caroline anxiously. She had grown very pale, and was obviously agitated. She had first scanned her grandfather's letter rapidly, then with a smothered exclamation had gone back to the beginning again, devouring the page with her eyes.

Martin was no less affected. He read more slowly, and when he had finished he came back to the table in the centre of the room and put the letter down on it.

'Where is it?' he asked heavily.

John had never seen Caroline in such distress. She could hardly speak. 'I'll show you,' she said, and started to open the bag again.

'No!' said Martin. 'Not here! You'd better come with me. You too, Ellen!' When John got up, he said fiercely, 'Not you, Coverdale!'

'I'm coming,' said John evenly. 'I don't know what this is about, Ainderby, but I can see that Mrs Duval has had a shock. I insist on coming with her.'

'And I wish him to come,' said Caroline. 'Lord Coverdale is to know…everything.'

Martin looked from one to the other, and saw their determination. Without another word he went over to a large bureau that stood in a corner, unlocked it and took out a heavy bunch of keys. 'Follow me,' he said briefly. 'Bring the bag with you.'

He led the way across the hall. Joseph, sitting stiffly on his chair, followed them with his eyes. He looked troubled. Martin took up a lamp from the table, lit it and went through a leather-covered door. John made sure he was close to Caroline as they followed him through the door and went a good way along a narrow passage, till they came to another door, which Martin opened with one of the keys. On the other side, they were in a part of the house that was obviously much older than the rest. Another door, another lock, then steps downwards. The air was cold but dry. There was some ventilation, though no window was visible.

Martin put the lamp down in a niche in the wall and turned up the wick. John saw that they were in a small stone chamber with an altar-like table at one end. A large oak cupboard stood on the table. Its wood was black with age, but its handles and locks shone bright in the lamp-light. Another lamp stood to the side, evidently kept permanently lit. Martin turned this up, too. Then he turned round and faced Caroline.

'If this is a trick, you will be cursed forever. If it is not a trick, then your grandfather is cursed.'

'My grandfather has returned the chalice. He is not cursed,' she said steadily. 'I have it here, ready to give you.'

'Do you swear secrecy, Coverdale? Otherwise you will have to leave this chamber now.'

'I'll swear whatever you suggest. But I'm not leaving this chamber while Mrs Duval remains. Get on with it, Ainderby. It's damned cold down here. I give you my word that I'll keep your secret, whatever that is.'

Martin selected a small key and opened the black wooden doors. John drew in his breath. It was an amazing sight. The inside of the cupboard was a blaze of reflected light. Brilliant streaks of red, green, blue, the bright sheen of gold streamed out, dazzling in their intensity. When his eyes were more accustomed to the display he saw that the cupboard had three shelves. In the centre of one of the shelves was a large gold dish, a paten, tilted on to one edge. On another was a krater-like bowl, also of gold and also tilted. Both objects were encrusted with jewels. The centre shelf was empty, a pool of darkness amid all the splendour.

Caroline went over to a side table and took a leather pouch out of her bag. She undid the pouch, took what was inside out of its linen wrappings and held it up. Her hands were quite steady. In them was one of the most beautiful objects John had ever seen—a graceful chalice of gold, chased and, like the objects in the cupboard, embellished with jewels that caught the light of the lamps and threw it back at them in a blaze of colour. It was obviously very ancient.

'The Ainderby Chalice!' Martin breathed the words with reverence and awe.

Caroline stepped slowly towards the cupboard and placed the chalice on the middle shelf, where it shone even more brilliantly than its fellows. Then she stepped back and made a curious little bow. 'It is done, Grandfather,' she said in a low voice. Then she came back and stood by John.

For a moment he was speechless with astonishment. Caroline Duval had carried this priceless artefact, centuries old and, as she had said, worth a king's ransom, all the way from Jamaica, worn it next to her body, carried it in a pouch over her shoulder... How could she have taken such enormous risks! It might so easily have been lost forever or damaged beyond repair during her long journey. She saw him looking at her.

'It was well protected in its own case for most of the time,' she said almost apologetically. 'But the case was stolen during the attack on Hounslow Heath. Since then I have protected it as best I could. I couldn't confide in anyone, not even you. Don't condemn me, John.'

'I don't condemn you. But I should like to know how your grandfather came to have it in the first place.'

She said expressionlessly, 'He stole it.'

'*Stole* it? But how? This place is like a fortress. And how could he have known about it? I was brought up only eight miles away, and have never heard a breath of anything like this.'

Martin regarded him coldly, obviously regarding his presence as an unwelcome intrusion. 'The presence of these relics has been kept secret ever since they were entrusted to the Ainderby family by the Abbot of Belvaux Abbey. They were part of a treasure brought back from the Holy Land many hundreds of years ago, and were ancient even then. The Abbot wished to protect them from King Henry's men, when the Abbey was dissolved. He himself was later hanged for his part in the Pilgrimage of Grace.'

'What was the Pilgrimage of Grace?' asked Caroline.

'A rebellion in the north against the King. For nearly three hundred years we have kept them faithfully here in this chamber, and only members of the Ainderby family have had access to it,' said Martin. 'But their access has been free and untrammelled.'

Caroline turned to John. Her distress was real, but she had control of herself. Her deep voice was calm and clear. 'My grandfather's real name was Peter Ainderby. He was the youngest son of William Ainderby, this Mr Ainderby's great-grandfather. He…he ran away to Jamaica when he was twenty, taking the chalice with him. He says in my letter that he was very wild as a youth, and at the time was full of resentment about an inheritance, which his father had denied him because of his behaviour. He was ordered to leave High Hutton and on a mad impulse took the chalice with him. He realised almost straight away that he had done something very wrong, but once it was in his possession he found he couldn't give it up. I told you. It had the same effect on him as it had on my cousin Edmund.'

'He was a thief!' said Martin harshly. 'He betrayed the family's trust.'

Caroline spread her hands in a gesture of appeal. 'But he sent it back! Doesn't that count for something?'

Ellen Ainderby had been silent till now. But she sud-

denly spoke. 'You'd better go,' she said. 'We don't want
you here! Your grandfather was a thief, and you bring
back too many unhappy memories.'

'*I* do?'

'Yes! You're too like your cousin Gabriella.'

'Of course,' said John. 'Caroline, you're an Ainderby!
That's why there's such a likeness. You and Gabriella had
the same great-grandfather.'

'And the sooner she is out of this house the better.'
Ellen turned to her husband. 'Get her out of here!'

'You can't blame Caroline for her grandfather's crime!'
John exclaimed. 'She's brought this chalice back to you
at great personal risk. You can't be so unjust!'

'No,' Caroline said nervously. 'Leave it, John. I agree
with Mrs Ainderby. I bring too many unhappy reminders.
Please let's go. Now!'

Martin took a last look at the chalice, then closed and
locked the cupboard. The little party retraced its steps
back to the hall. Joseph was standing by the door, and he
gave Caroline a look of inquiry.

'It's back,' she said briefly. Then she added, 'You
knew. You knew, didn't you, Joseph?'

'My uncle told me afore he died. He went to Jamaica
with the master when he were a lad, and knew most of
what had happened. He told me, but I kept it quiet for
the master's sake. Lately I've done my best to help you
put it right, Miss Caro. It were what he wanted.'

Caroline stood by the door, not quite knowing what to
say. The day's revelations had left her feeling drained.
Joseph, her grandfather, and Gabriella... She wanted to
leave High Hutton as soon as possible, suspecting that the
Ainderbys had something to say about Gabriella that she
would not want John to hear. The sooner they could go
the better. She turned to Martin. 'I've done what I came

to do,' she said. 'You must be happy to have your treasure
restored, and I am happy that my grandfather's wish has
been granted. So we'll take our leave. Mr Ainderby? Mrs
Ainderby?' With relief she started for the door, not caring
how abrupt her farewell had sounded.

'What is that girl doing in the house again?'

The voice rang across the hall. They all turned round,
startled. An old woman dressed in black and walking with
the aid of a stick came out of the door that Mrs Ainderby
had closed so carefully an hour before.

'Mama! Why aren't you still asleep?'

'Never mind that, Martin Ainderby! I told you to throw
that girl out of my house, and, as soon as I turn my back,
you've got her here again!'

The two Ainderbys both started to speak at once. Ellen
Ainderby won. 'My mother-in-law is confused,' she said.
'It's better you should go.'

'As for you, ma'am,' said the old lady, scornfully raking her daughter-in-law with a glittering eye. 'I'd have
thought you had more pride! Hasn't that girl brought you
enough pain? Ready to see your husband making love to
that…that hussy all over again, are you? Under your very
nose again? Well, I shan't get rid of her a second time!
You'll have to put up with it!'

'Wait!' said John sharply. 'This must stop. I can't stand
by and listen to such insults to the lady I brought here, a
friend of mine.'

Old Mrs Ainderby gave a raucous laugh. 'Friend, is she
now? I thought she was to marry you, John Ancroft.'

Martin went over and took his mother's arm. 'Mama,
you're mistaken! This is Mrs Caroline Duval from Jamaica. Let me take you back to your sofa—'

She shook him off angrily. 'Don't you try any tricks
on me! I'm not blind, boy! I can see who she is! She's

Gabriella Ainderby, and if you don't send her packing she'll cause you as much trouble as she did before. What about your wife? She's looking sour enough. Is she to watch once again while you make a fool of yourself over that girl? Shame on you!'

John had gone pale. He was staring at the old lady as if he couldn't believe what he was hearing. 'Mrs Ainderby, are you talking of your *niece*, Gabriella? Is what you are saying about *Gabriella*?'

'Of course I am! Look at her! White as a sheet. She don't want you to know, but it's time someone told you, John Ancroft. She wrecked my family and she'll wreck yours! That girl can't leave anything in breeches alone till she's made him her slave. My poor Martin went out of his mind over her, and my other son Paul, too! Why do you think they don't speak any more? I sent her packing. I told her mother. I'll give you a week to find somewhere else to live, I said. I don't care where, but your daughter is to leave High Hutton and not come back.' She gave another cackle. 'She didn't waste any time, either! She'd got her daughter engaged to you before two days were up. What happened? Why isn't she your wife? Did you see through her before you married her? Your cousin Philip did, but you were as innocent as a newborn babe!'

'Mama!' Martin was trying in vain to take his mother away, but John stepped forward and held his arm.

'Gabriella is dead, Mrs Ainderby. She won't do you or yours any further harm. But...' He turned to Martin. 'Tell me what she's talking about! It doesn't make sense. What does she mean about Gabriella?'

Martin looked uncomfortable. 'She shouldn't have said anything. You must forgive her, Coverdale. She's old, and a little out of her mind.'

Ellen Ainderby had been growing increasingly agitated.

Now she suddenly spoke up. 'She's *not* out of her mind! Except that she is confusing Caroline Duval with Gabriella Ainderby, and that's natural enough. For one moment I thought myself that it was Gabriella at the door! No, Martin, I *will* speak! Most of what your mother's been saying is perfectly true! I'm glad that that chalice is back at High Hutton, but I wish to heaven that that woman had not been the one to bring it! She reminds everyone of that accursed cousin of yours! She reminds *me* of how Gabriella ruined my marriage, how you and I have never been happy since. And she reminds *you* of how you and Paul fought over her, and how the two of you haven't been friends since. Aren't I right? Aren't I?'

Her husband looked away in pain. It was more explicit than any acknowledgment. Ellen Ainderby drew a shuddering breath, and turned back to John.

'Your precious Gabriella demanded *every* man's homage, and didn't care how she got it, or who was hurt until she did. It sickened me to my soul to see the air of innocence she put on. Innocence! She was a *serpent*!'

'No! I don't believe you! Not Gabriella! It can't be!' But John's desperate cry lacked conviction.

Ellen went on remorselessly, 'You'd have found out sooner or later, Lord Coverdale. She was after your cousin even while she was engaged to you, but he at least knew her for what she was. I was *glad* she died! You deserved better.'

John turned away and walked to the door. He swung round. 'I...I can't—' He broke off and shook his head.

Martin said dully, 'I'm sorry, Coverdale. My wife shouldn't have spoken as she did, but what she says is the truth. I'm sorry you had to hear it from us. I...I don't think there's any more to say. Excuse me. Come, Mama. You must rest again.' He left them in the hall.

Ellen Ainderby was back in her shell, once again a quietly unhappy woman. She said, 'I'm not sorry. Except that you've seen what our life here has been for the past seventeen years. Goodbye, Mrs Duval. Lord Coverdale.' She followed her husband.

John looked at Caroline and saw her expression. He said incredulously, 'You're not surprised! You knew! You knew all this and you didn't say a word! I trusted you with my deepest feelings, you knew how I felt, but you didn't say a word!'

'How could I?' asked Caroline helplessly. 'You loved her.'

He gazed at her in silence for a moment, then he turned away. 'Bellerby will see you back to Marrick,' he said curtly. 'I...I need to think. Bellerby!' He strode off in the direction of the stables. The last Caroline saw of him was of a figure galloping off as if all the hounds of hell were after him.

Caroline and Joseph rode back to Marrick in near silence. As they came in through the archway she saw that the carriage that had taken her cousin Edmund to Falmouth was there. Betts, John's man, was beside it.

'Good evening, ma'am,' he called. Caroline roused herself.

'Betts! You're back again. Come and see me when you are ready. I'd like to hear how my cousin fared.'

'I will that, ma'am. As soon as I've reported to the Colonel.'

'I'm not sure you'll find him in the castle, Betts. He went for a ride, and I doubt he's back yet.'

'I'll have a look, ma'am. If he isn't, shall I come to see you?'

'Please. But not if you're too long about it. I'm rather tired.'

'Very good, ma'am. You may rest easy, though. Mr Willoughby is safely at sea somewhere on the Atlantic Ocean.'

'Thank you. Till later, then.' Caroline dismounted and went slowly up the now familiar steps. The castle seemed deserted. During the day the servants had dismantled all the arrangements for the ball, put nearly all the furniture back in its usual place, and swept and cleaned the rooms. Now most of them had gone. Mrs Abbington was with Harriet at Brough. Unless John came back soon she would be alone for dinner.

Maggie was waiting for her when she got to her room, but when she saw her mistress's face she forbore to ask questions.

Only later, when Caroline had rested and was getting ready for the evening, did she risk it.

'You saw the Ainderbys, Miss Caro?'

'Oh, yes, Maggie,' said Caroline wryly. 'I saw the Ainderbys. I've done what my grandfather wanted me to do. Did you know that he was really an Ainderby? That Peter Leyburn of Kingston, Jamaica, was really Peter Ainderby of High Hutton in the county of Yorkshire?'

'No, I didn't know, but I thought there must be something like that about it. He was always something of a mystery, your grandfather, and you couldn't be so like Miss Gabriella Ainderby just by coincidence. So, it's all done?'

'Yes, it's all done...' And Caroline astonished her maid by bursting into tears.

'There, there, now!' Maggie soothed her mistress as a

nurse would soothe a child. 'There, there, Miss Caro! It's over! You can put it behind you now.'

'It's not that, Maggie,' sobbed Caroline. 'It's the Colonel!'

'You told him about your grandfather? He was annoyed? Surely not! Not just about a little thing like a name!'

'There was more to it than a name, but no, that wasn't it. He was very sympathetic about my grandfather. But… oh, Maggie, the Ainderbys told him about Gabriella! He knows now what she was really like. They said everything that you told me this morning.'

'What happened?'

'He sent me back with Joseph and rode off by himself. I don't know when he'll return.'

Maggie was silent, then she said, 'It's not altogether a bad thing, Miss Caro. He would have heard about her sooner or later. Better now. Then he can put it all behind him before he settles down properly.'

'He took it badly. He was even angry with me. He thought I should have warned him.'

'Oh, he won't hold that against you, once he's himself again. He'll see for himself that you couldn't. Don't worry, Miss Caro.'

There was a knock on the door. Caroline started up. Maggie said, 'There! That's probably the Colonel now, come to see that you got back safely.' But when she opened the door Betts was there.

'Mrs Duval asked me to see her, miss,' he said.

'Betts!' called Caroline 'Come in! Is your master back yet?'

'Not yet, ma'am. But he'll probably be here any minute. It's getting a bit late for dinner. A very punctual man, the Colonel. I came to tell you about Mr Willoughby.'

'Yes! He's now on the high seas?'

'He is that. From what he said, he wasn't looking forward to it, neither.'

'No, he isn't a good sailor. How did he seem otherwise?'

'Resigned, you might say. I don't think he'll forget what the Colonel said to him. Powerful impressive the Colonel can be. You'll be all right now.'

'Thank you! Could you ask your master to let me know when he is back?'

'I will. Thank you, ma'am.' Betts gave her something like a military salute and left, winking at Maggie as she stood by the door ready to close it.

'Maggie, see if the kitchens can put dinner back by an hour. Lord Coverdale arranged it for seven, but he can't possibly be ready by then.'

Maggie went and Caroline was left to her own thoughts. This should have been a day of relief, the dinner tonight a celebration of a burden lifted. But she could not rid herself of a sense of impending disaster.

Betts went back to his master's quarters. The Colonel was still not back. He busied himself about the bedchamber, sorting out clean linen and a change of clothing for the evening. He looked round. Everything was laid out ready. With a shake of the head for his forgetfulness, he fetched Mr Willoughby's letter from his own bag, and laid it on the dressing table next to the Colonel's brushes. No doubt Mr Willoughby had little of importance to report, he was probably just grateful for the standard of comfort the Colonel had provided for him. More than he deserved. All the same, the letter should be handed over as soon as the Colonel came in.

Chapter Eleven

John Ancroft rode furiously along highways and bridle paths, over fences and hedges, heedless of danger. He was desperate to get away from High Hutton, to leave the Ainderbys and their tales of Gabriella far behind him, to escape from what he had heard. Once or twice he very nearly ended it all as he took a fence too recklessly or rode without caring under low-branched trees in the woods. He paid as little attention to his safety as he had in those early battles in the Peninsula, when all he had wanted was to satisfy his uncle's desire to see him dead. But fate protected him now as it had protected him seventeen years before. In the end the thought of Harriet and her need of him slowed him down, forced him to take more care.

Then, once he started to think, he realised that, run as he might, he could not escape from the truth. He believed what the Ainderbys had said. For seventeen years, he had lived with a fairy tale, a mirage. He had cherished an image of a girl who had given herself to him in love and innocence, who had died forever young, forever unsullied. He had seen himself as the most fortunate, and at the same time, the most unhappy of men, a man who had gained a peerless bride, only to lose her a few short weeks before their marriage. And it had all been an illusion.

He came to a halt and found himself high up on the hills gazing down on Marrick, the pain almost more than he could bear. What a damned, blind, insanely stupid dolt he had been! Why hadn't he seen Gabriella for what she was? It was clear to him now that Philip had known, had tried to show him how faithless Gabriella could be, but he had refused to look. Before the accident, on that last fateful day, Philip had quite deliberately flirted with Gabriella, and he, John, had been so blind that he had accused his cousin of envy, of wanting Gabriella for himself, of being unfaithful to Rose. In the face of these accusations Philip had lost his temper. He had always been quick to take offence, and John usually used his influence to calm him down. But that day John had shouted back, and soon they had both been in a black rage with each other, the worst they had ever known. Gabriella had brought devastation to the Ancrofts as well as to the Ainderbys. Almost her last act had been to trip lightly into that curricle, quite indifferent to the havoc she had caused between the hitherto devoted Ancroft cousins, perhaps even enjoying her power. In the accident that followed he had lost a man he had regarded as a brother, for the sake of a worthless, empty-hearted little whore. For a while he felt the pain of loss as acutely as he had seventeen years before. But this time it was for Philip alone.

After a time his thoughts turned to Caroline Duval. He was certain she had known about Gabriella before the Ainderbys' revelations, but how? Was it such common knowledge at Marrick? Or had she been talking to guests at the ball, the old Randolph harridan, for example? *Why* hadn't she said something to him? She could have saved some of this pain! It would have been hard to hear the truth about Gabriella from anyone, but to hear it like that, from the Ainderbys, to witness what she had done to them... Why hadn't Caroline warned him? He tried to remember what her excuse had been. 'How could I?' she had said. 'You loved her.'

Damn the woman! Why couldn't she have seen that living in a fool's paradise was far worse than any reality, however painful? He had thought that his relationship with Caroline Duval was based on truth. After those two dramatic encounters on their journey north, when so much had been revealed, he had believed that the only secret between them was exactly what it was that she carried to High Hutton.

So much had been revealed... Or had it? Was it only her body that had been revealed at Buckden, and at the waterfall, and nothing of her *real* self? He had been so wrong about Gabriella Ainderby. Could he not be equally wrong about Caroline Duval? After all, she had begun their association with an attempt to deceive him. Perhaps the resemblance between those two was more than one of appearance... Perhaps Caroline Duval's real reason for attempting to hide the truth about her wanton cousin Gabriella was because she feared it might damage her own hopes for a future at Marrick—as Marchioness of Coverdale.

John's heart twisted as he gazed down at Marrick. Recently he had actually begun to hope that his return to Yorkshire, to Marrick, would mean an end to seventeen years of living in the wilderness, a return to life itself. He had begun to laugh again, to feel the warmth of affection, to look forward to a future with a woman he felt he could love. Had it all been deceit on her part, self-deception on his? Did Caroline Duval have a heart? He had begun to hope so, though she herself had always denied it. Or did the beauty she shared with Gabriella hide the same corrupt mockery of one?

The shadows were lengthening, the sun well to the west. It was time to go back, time to find out.

Betts hurried up to him when he entered his room, prepared to scold. 'I've been a touch worried, Colonel! It's getting late, and Bellerby told me you had sent him back with Mrs Duval, so I knew you didn't have a groom with you. If you'd met with an accident…'

'Well, I didn't and if I'm late for dinner it's not the end of the world.'

'Mrs Duval has set it back an hour, Colonel.'

'Good! So get on with it, man, instead of scolding me as if you were a nursemaid, not a valet! Fetch some brandy, while you're about it. I'm damned tired.'

Betts hastened to do as he was bid. The Colonel did indeed look tired. And not at all his usual neat self. Dishevelled, he was. Very dishevelled. Judging his priority, he brought the brandy first, then produced as if by magic quantities of hot water and towels. Within a short time John was sitting down at his dressing table looking altogether more himself.

'What's this?' John held up the letter which Betts had carried back from Falmouth.

'Mr Willoughby asked me to deliver it to you, Colonel.'

'Willoughby, eh? You saw him off, did you?'

'Yes, sir! Mr Willoughby won't trouble you or Mrs Duval no more. He's on the high seas.'

'Good,' said John. 'Shall I read it now, or leave it till later?'

'There's still some time before you need to go down, sir,' said Betts helpfully.

'Bring me another brandy, Betts, and I'll read it now.'

'Mrs Duval wanted to be told when you got back, sir. Shall I go to tell her?'

'Do! This won't take long.'

Betts left, and John sat sipping his brandy, reading Edmund Willoughby's letter.

Coverdale,

I could see you were taken with Caroline Duval. That doesn't surprise me. She's a handsome creature, and you're by no means the first to fall. But perhaps I should tell you one or two things you ought to know before you get too involved with her. Take it as an attempt to show my gratitude for your leniency towards me in the matter of my unfortunate treatment of your daughter.

She and that old reprobate, Peter Leyburn, kept Kingston society pretty well under their thumbs. As a result, half the tricks Caroline Duval got up to, especially in New Orleans, never reached the ears of society. If Duval was her name. There was some question as to whether she had ever actually been married to Laurent Duval, but we'll let that pass.

For instance, has she told you that she posed without a stitch on for some of the most disreputable so-called artists in Louisiana? When she came back to Kingston old Peter spent a fortune on buying up as many of their portraits of her as he could lay his hands on. There was a time when you had to pay half a year's income in a certain house in Kingston just to see the one that he had overlooked. But believe me, it was worth the money... Even the most jaded palates were stimulated.

Has she told you about the duel fought over her, and how one of the participants died? He had a wife and children, too... But that was in New Orleans, so in the lady's mind it probably doesn't count.

She was more circumspect in Kingston, though there are a good few unhappy wives who could tell you something about her. But perhaps you really should ask her about Senator Coburn's son, though I doubt she will admit to anything. When he committed suicide they blamed it on his gambling debts. Her part in the affair never came to light. However, if his mother is to be believed, she had a great deal to do with it.

I could go on. There's quite a lot more. But perhaps I have written enough to show you the sort of woman you have in your house, keeping company with your daughter.

Believe me, it is not easy for me to reveal these family embarrassments to you. I hope you take it in the spirit it is meant. I return to Jamaica, knowing, as one connected to the family, that the names of Leyburn and Duval will always call forth the sideways looks and raised eyebrows so painful to a gentleman of my standing. I must bear it as I can.

I have not forgotten your kindly warnings. You may be assured that when my cousin eventually comes back to Jamaica I will not hurt her. In fact, I will do all I can to protect her as my uncle Leyburn protected her—though without his resources I fear it will prove extremely difficult.

Betts has been insisting for some minutes that I end this letter and join him on the quayside ready to embark. I cannot say I have liked his attitude towards

me. Anyone would think I was a prisoner!
      With best wishes for your future happiness
      Yrs etc.

                              Edmund Willoughby

John's first impulse was to tear the letter up and throw
it away. It had obviously been written by a man eaten up
with resentment and anger, a man who had failed in his
attempt to capture the chalice, and was now wreaking
what revenge he could on his cousin and on the man who
had helped her.

But then he took up the letter and read it through again.
He had asked himself a while ago if Caroline Duval had
a heart. Was this the answer to his question? Edmund
Willoughby's malice was evident, but he seemed to have
some evidence. John's doubts of Caroline redoubled as
he considered Edmund's accusations...

She had posed for portraits without a stitch on. That
was possible. Had he not seen for himself that she remained perfectly composed when caught under the waterfall? If what Edmund claimed was true, she was well
used to being seen, stared at—studied even—when she
was naked.

A duel had been fought over her. He had not had a real
opportunity to study Caroline Duval's behaviour when
other men were present. At the ball the other night she
had certainly behaved with circumspection. But was that
her normal behaviour or had she been anxious to impress?
If she had teased hotheaded gentlemen of Louisiana as
Gabriella had teased hardheaded Yorkshire men, there
might well have been a quarrel that led to a duel. But
would she allow a married man, a father, to lose his life
over her? Before today he would have sworn it was impossible. But not now. Not now, by God! He had been

deceived by Gabriella. Perhaps Caroline Duval had deceived him as much.

Her behaviour in Kingston. That was more serious. In Kingston she was not an impetuous seventeen-year-old, but a woman who had been married, a widow, the pampered granddaughter of a very rich man. Surely by then she would know what effect her actions might have on others? She was far from stupid or unthinking. Yet to drive a young man to suicide...?

But he must not get carried away by Edmund Willoughby's letter. He must be fair. If asked whether the man could be trusted, he would reply that he couldn't. Not at all! It was perfectly possible that a disappointed, frustrated man would exaggerate small incidents, enlarge gossip to huge proportions, and calumnify a woman he had every reason to hate.

John drank his brandy and poured himself another. He felt battered in spirit. After the day's revelations about Peter Ainderby, about Gabriella, and now about Caroline—how was a man to trust anyone? Until he had fallen in love with Gabriella the Ancrofts had in general steered clear of the Ainderbys. The two families had never really felt at ease with each other. In the recent past his own uncle had quarrelled with Martin Ainderby's father and frowned on John's engagement to an Ainderby. Now, it seemed, history had been right all along. Old Peter Ainderby had been a thief, and Gabriella Ainderby had been a faithless hussy, to put it at its best. And what about Caroline? An Ainderby by blood, if not by name. Yes, what about Caroline?

He sat drinking brandy and brooding about the Ainderbys until Betts came to remind him that it was time to go down to dinner.

* * *

Caroline had taken some trouble with her appearance. The occasion was not likely to be one of celebration. On the other hand she wanted to forget her grandfather's misdeeds and remember only his love and care for her—and that he had tried in the end to make reparation. What was far more important for her tonight was to make an effort to raise John's spirits. She could remember the devastating humiliation she had felt at the betrayal of her love for Laurent Duval, at the discovery of his true nature. John had today gone through the same agonising process, not gradually over a period of weeks as she had, but brutally, in as many minutes. Like Maggie, she did not believe he would continue to blame her, once he had calmed down a little, for not passing on to him what she had heard of Gabriella. He had probably already seen for himself that it would have been impossible. Her new task, her new aim, would be to do what her grandfather had done for her—to restore his pride and self-esteem, to show him how highly she regarded him. And, if the occasion arose, how much she loved him.

So she dressed with care in her white silk dress, and Maggie arranged some yellow roses from the garden at its neckline. She wore no other ornament. Maggie had brushed her hair until it shone like silk, several strands of it bleached by the sun to copper. Her eyes were huge, shadowed by the emotions of the day and the lack of sleep of the night before. Looking at her before she went down, Maggie thought that she looked unusually fragile, but more beautiful than she had ever seen her.

John was waiting when Caroline came into the saloon. He had a glass of wine in his hand and fetched another for her as soon as he saw her. They drank.

'Shall we go in to dinner?'

The question was uttered in a cool, formal voice, almost like the one she had first heard in Mr Turner's chambers. Her heart sank. So he was still angry, after all. But Caroline was not a fighter for nothing. She lifted her chin and gave him a smile. 'Of course. It will be strange, will it not, to be quite alone? Not even Harriet and Mrs Abbington for company. The house seems very quiet without them.'

Caroline had secretly been pleased that Harriet and Mrs Abbington were away, thinking that their absence would make it easier to talk more freely to John. But by the end of an hour she was wishing desperately that they had stayed. For the sake of the servants she made conversation, about the ball, about the weather, about Harriet's appearance, all so trivial that she could have screamed with frustration. John responded suitably, but with such an indifferent manner that she began to wonder if he was quite himself. He seemed to be carrying on some inner debate, occasionally staring at her fixedly, then looking away when he caught her eye. She noticed that he was eating little, but drinking fairly heavily, filling his glass from the decanter beside him with disturbing frequency.

The servants cleared the table and brought in the last course. 'That's all,' John said abruptly. 'Leave the rest. We'll call you if we need you.'

Caroline's heart ached for him—he looked so unhappy, as if the black burden of Gabriella's fall from grace was almost too much to bear. She had kept silent about Gabriella out of a wish to spare him, not for any other reason, but if he wished to vent some of his bitter anger on her she would try to be patient. But his first words astonished her, they were so far removed from what she had expected from him.

'Tell me about your time in New Orleans,' he began.

'It must have been hard. I believe you were on your own?'

His tone was hard, judgmental. She replied carefully, 'No, I was married.'

'Ah, yes! To Laurent Duval. So you said.'

Had there been a very slight question in his tone? Surely not! She was imagining things. 'I said I was unprotected. Duval wasn't an ideal husband.'

'I remember. You told me once that your marriage had been unhappy.'

'That's perhaps one way of putting it.'

'Why? What other way is there?'

'It was a nightmare.'

'Oh, come! If it was as bad as that, why didn't you leave him?'

The scepticism in his voice was a shock, but she said calmly enough, 'John, why do you sound so critical? Have you ever been to New Orleans?'

'No, I haven't.'

'Then I must tell you that it is not the sort of place where a penniless seventeen-year-old girl should run away from the only man who might keep away others even worse than he was. It would have been suicidal folly. Curiously enough, I felt some obligation to my marriage vows, too. Whatever Laurent Duval did, however he behaved, I had promised to love, honour and obey him, to stay with him for life. For that I had given up my home in Kingston and deeply hurt my grandfather and everyone who loved me. I couldn't simply abandon my marriage when things got difficult. I had made my bed, as they say, and had to lie on it. I did run away after he was dead, of course. But by then I was a little more experienced.'

'Experienced. Yes. I suppose you were as beautiful then as you are now—and tonight you are quite extraordinarily beautiful! It can't have been difficult for you to find protectors.'

How odd, thought Caroline painfully, that when he eventually pays me a compliment it should have such a sting in the tail! She said, still calm, 'I wanted none of the sort I think you mean. What's going on, John? What are you trying to say?'

'Nothing. We're alone after dinner. Relaxing after a somewhat difficult day. I just want to learn more about you. What's wrong with that?'

'I don't know…'

'Tell me, Caroline. In New Orleans, were you forced to do things you wouldn't normally have wanted to do? Have your portrait painted, for example?'

Her first impulse was to tell him to go to the devil. What had this to do with what had happened today? But then she decided to humour him. His questions were not idle. John was working to an end, but what it was she was not yet sure. She answered with care. 'Yes. We lived in an artistic community. Laurent had friends who wanted to paint me, and he…he made me pose for them.'

'Naked?'

'Why do you ask?' When he didn't reply she went on, 'I see. I suppose that worm, Edmund, told you while he was here of the pictures my grandfather suppressed. I'm surprised that you listened to him.'

'I learned it from Edmund, yes. So, you had a colourful time in New Orleans?'

'Is that what you would call it? Then, yes, I did. A reprehensible past. I told you that myself.' Caroline's anger was growing. These questions arose from something more than John's resentment at her omission to tell him about Gabriella. He was quite deliberately probing old hurts that she thought she had managed to forget. Why

was he doing it? Surely he wouldn't be so cruel as to
soothe his own sense of humiliation by reminding her of
hers! He seemed to be reviving what Edmund had told
him weeks ago with the express aim of wounding her. Of
one thing she was quite, quite sure. Whatever his motive,
John Ancroft was not about to see her crumple. She might
have become foolishly soft about him, but she would not
let *any* man see how much he was hurting her. It was
time to gather her defences together.

'Well,' she said, sitting back and making herself smile,
refusing to give way to the growing apprehension which
was sending icy shivers down her spine. 'This *is* fun!
What other misdeeds can I confess? There's no shortage,
I assure you.'

'The duel?'

'Now that's one I can't remember. I don't think I ever
actually fought a duel—'

'A duel fought *about* you. In New Orleans.'

Cousin Edmund *has* been busy with his lies, she
thought. And, fool that I was, I thought John Ancroft
would never believe them! She pretended to consider.
'No,' she said finally. 'It would have been amusing, but
I'm sorry to say that I've never had a duel fought in my
honour. Isn't it a shame? I can't have been misbehaving
badly enough!'

She threw him a glance to see how he took this, but
his expression gave nothing away. With a mental shrug
she went on, 'I do remember a duel in New Orleans,
you're right there. But that was over some cheating at
cards. Poor man. He left a wife and family behind, too.
But there! If you're going to be caught cheating at cards,
you at least need to be a good shot, and he wasn't very
good at that, either. As my grandfather always said, if
you can't cheat well, you shouldn't cheat at all!' This

wouldn't do, the icy shivers were gaining ground. 'Are you having some more wine? May I have a little?'

He got up and brought his own glass and the decanter over. He filled her glass and, instead of going back to his own place, sat down beside her.

'Let's drink to your misdeeds, then,' he said softly, touching her glass with his. He was too close.

'John, I—'

'Drink!'

She drank and felt the wine warming, giving her courage. The questioning continued.

'What about Kingston? You were older then. And protected.'

'Protected?'

'I mean by your grandfather, of course. What else did you think I meant?'

'I don't know. In this present mood of yours you might mean anything.'

'My present mood has little to do with the facts, Caroline. What happened in Kingston?'

She drank some more wine, then said lightly, 'Those good people of Kingston! How they talked! But the cream of it was that there never were any *facts*.' She gave a little laugh. 'No one could actually prove I had done anything at all!'

'Perhaps not. But surely young Mr Coburn's death was a fact? Didn't you feel anything about that?'

Caroline felt as if she had had a blow to the heart. It took her a moment to conquer the feeling of nausea that nearly overcame her. But she held on to her nerve. John Ancroft was not the man she had thought him. She was *damned* if she would let him see how violently affected she was! She got up, went round to the other side of the table and faced him across it.

'What are you trying to do, John?' she demanded, her deep voice harsh, but holding little trace of the tumult inside. 'Are you punishing me for what Gabriella did to you? Is that it? I hadn't realised how much filth Edmund must have poured into your ears, while he lay on his sick bed. But why bring it up now? You've never so much as hinted at any of it before!'

He made no reply, but drew Edmund Willoughby's letter out of his pocket and threw it across to her. 'I hadn't heard it before. Willoughby wrote to me before he left Falmouth. Betts gave me the letter tonight. Read it.'

She picked the letter up and scanned it. Then she threw it back and said contemptuously, 'It doesn't surprise me. He spread such insinuations about me in Kingston, too. Some were even believed. What I can't understand is why *you* appear to believe them.'

'Defend yourself, then! Be serious for once!'

Caroline shook her head. 'I won't. I can't. But I'm disappointed in you, Lord Coverdale. You aren't the man I thought you. Trying to make your own hurt easier by making mine worse is unworthy. Completely unworthy! But yes! If it makes you feel happier—yes, I made a mistake with Robbie Coburn.' She paused. 'I let my feelings get the better of me, and I'm sorry for it. You can't possibly know how sorry!' She knew she sounded hard. The effort she was making to control her voice allowed no softer tone. And from the look of contempt on his face he thought she sounded hard, too. She said angrily, 'But I refuse to excuse myself to you or to anyone else! Damn you all!'

John finished his wine and strode over to her. 'Look!' he said grasping her arm and pulling her to the large mirror over the side table. He stared at their reflection in the mirror, his eyes glittering with anger, his face flushed with the wine. 'Look at you! In that white dress, roses disguising that superbly enticing bosom, the picture of innocence itself! Do you know how like Gabriella you are? Did you hope that I would think of marrying you, as well? And, fool that I was, blind, wilful idiot that I was, I *did* think of it! What supreme irony that would have been! That I should escape from Gabriella, only to fall into Widow Duval's trap! Look at you! How can anything so beautiful be such an agent of destruction? You and Gabriella—cheats, both of you!'

Caroline wrenched herself free. 'How *dare* you call me a cheat! How *dare* you confuse me with Gabriella! I don't cheat! I never even pretended to be an innocent!'

'You could hardly do that,' he said with a contemptuous laugh. 'It was obvious at Buckden that you were well used to flaunting your body to anyone who cared to look. What stopped you that night? Was I too much of a fool for you? Too far gone? Why didn't you close the trap on me? I'd have thought a sick man would be an easy target for your kind of game!'

Caroline slapped his face hard. 'I was not playing games,' she shouted. 'I thought to comfort you!'

He swore, then snatched her to him and tore the roses from her bosom. 'You don't need these,' he said, his voice thick with desire. 'No games, no pretence, you said. *Now* is the time I need comfort. Damn your past! Damn your empty heart! I want to see you again as I saw you at Buckden! To know you fully this time. To bury this torment in the comfort of your body. Tomorrow you can go your own heartless way, but tonight I need you, I want you, Caroline Duval!' He kissed her cruelly, then, forcing her back over his arm, wrenched her dress off her shoulder and buried his face in her breast.

Caroline's deep sense of hurt was overcome by a wave

of pure fury. She broke free and ran to the table. Snatching up the decanter she smashed it against the fireplace and held its jagged edges in front of her like a weapon.

'Marrick has seen a good deal of drama in its time,' she said fiercely. 'But I don't think you'd like your daughter to see you held on a charge of rape. That's what it would be. What I give, I give freely or not at all. And I don't choose to make love with you, not just to drown your *pathetic* illusions about Gabriella Ainderby! If you come any nearer I will use this decanter, don't think I won't. I've had plenty of practice in *this* sort of *game*, though I never thought I'd have to use it against an English *gentleman*!'

Her swift and deadly reaction seemed to have sobered him. The wildness in his eyes slowly died, and he shook his head in self-disgust. He turned away. 'You can put that thing down,' he said, his voice full of shocked loathing. 'I must have been mad. You shouldn't have struck me.' There was silence in the room, as he sought to regain his calm. Then he faced her again, and said deliberately, 'Don't worry! I don't want anything you can offer. I prefer to buy my pleasures. It's at least an honest transaction. No hidden costs—or none that I'm not prepared to pay.'

Caroline hesitated, suspicious of this change of mood.

'Go!' he said. 'I won't stop you. I've had enough.'

She pulled her dress up and stepped warily round to the other side of the table. He didn't stir. Moving with more confidence, she laid the remains of the decanter down at the other end and went to the door. When she looked back he was still standing motionless, watching her as she left. She went out.

One or two of the servants were gathered in the hall, looking apprehensive.

'Has there been an accident, ma'am?' asked one of the footmen.

'Yes,' she replied calmly. 'Fortunately no one was hurt. A broken decanter, that's all. You'll have to watch out for the pieces. Goodnight!'

She went up the stairs and along to her room, where Maggie was waiting. Caroline shut the door and leaned against it. She was suddenly exhausted. Maggie took her arm and led her to the chair. 'The sooner you're in bed, Miss Caro, the better! Let me just get this dress off you. There! What happened to the roses? It's a pity if you've lost them. They were so pretty.'

'I must have dropped them,' said Caroline wearily. 'Don't bother too much with the dress, Maggie. I shall never wear it again.'

'Was...was the Colonel still angry?'

'You could say that. But not because I hadn't told him about Miss Ainderby. He had a letter from Edmund Willoughby. My cousin had excelled himself in raking up the old scandals. He had even improved on them.'

'The Colonel wouldn't believe them, surely?'

'He seemed to believe every word. I even tested him. He asked me about...about Robbie Coburn.'

'There was nothing wrong in that!'

'There was after Edmund had rewritten the story.'

'And you lost your temper. You let the Colonel carry on thinking the worst! Oh, Miss Caro, why did you?'

Caroline made a gesture of despair. 'It wasn't worth the effort to disabuse him. I said I had let my feelings get the better of me. He didn't ask what I meant, he came, without a single moment's hesitation, to the same conclusion as all the gentlemen of Kingston. Together with their wives. Caroline Duval had shared her bed with Robbie Coburn, and then abandoned him. It was just like Kingston. Instant, unthinking, condemnation. That hurt!' She caught her breath. 'Oh, *how* it hurt! I thought he was different. I trusted him, thought he liked me. I'm such a *fool*, Maggie! Why did I let him get so close to me? Why can't I *learn*?'

'But you should have told him! You didn't do anything of the sort with Mr Coburn! You never did do anything of the sort. Not with any of them!'

Caroline laughed harshly. 'Try telling that to the gossips of Kingston! Or even to the gentlemen of England! No, Maggie, I'd rather let them stew in their own prejudice.' She drew in a long shuddering breath. 'And now we shall forget it.'

Maggie knew when to stop. She went about her work in silence, fetching water and towels, brushing Caroline's hair, dressing her in her nightgown and wrapper. When she had finished she asked, 'Is there anything more, Miss Caro? Can I fetch a warm drink? Or a sleeping draught?'

'No, thank you, Maggie. You go to bed. I'll just sit here for a while. Tomorrow we must think about our journey back to London.'

Maggie went into the small dressing room next door and made herself ready for bed. But she lay for a long time listening to the stifled sobs coming from Miss Caro's room. Miss Caro never cried. Not even when her parents had drowned. Not even for her grandfather. She had gone about the world pale and withdrawn, but she had not cried. Colonel Ancroft, for all his gentlemanly ways, had dealt her mistress a mortal blow.

But there was no sign of this the next morning. It was as if the night before had never been. Caroline was a touch pale, but as she said, the visit to the Ainderbys had been a harrowing experience. She was full of plans for their return to London.

'What about Lady Harriet?' asked Maggie.

'Lady Harriet will be back at midday. We can leave an hour later. I'm sure we can rely on Lord Coverdale's stables to take us as far as the inn at Richmond, and we'll hire a post chaise to take us onward. Joseph can ride ahead to arrange it. We should be able to reach London in four or five days, but it doesn't really matter. We might even try a different route, spend some time on the way, perhaps go through York.'

'I'll see to the packing, then. At least we don't have to worry about that blessed chalice!'

Before Caroline went downstairs she spent some time in the little solar room composing a letter to Mr Turner, intending it to catch the mail in time to reach him well in advance of her own arrival. In it she reported the success of her mission and asked him to look for a suitable lodging for a few weeks until she could make up her mind what she wanted to do. John found her here. He was looking pale and stern, and said stiffly, 'I've been looking for you. I wanted to apologise. My behaviour last night was unworthy. I can only say in extenuation that the experiences of the day, and my efforts to drown them in brandy, had done more damage than I realised. I hope you will forgive me.'

Caroline replied with equally cool formality, 'It was a difficult day for everyone, Lord Coverdale. The events after dinner are best forgotten.'

'You are generous. Thank you. However, I cannot believe that I shall forget, or recover my self-respect, for some time.' He paused. 'I hear that Bellerby has gone to Richmond to reserve a chaise from the King's Head for your journey south. My carriage will convey you there at whatever hour you wish.' He paused a second time. 'Harriet will be glad that you stayed to see her.'

'I don't break promises lightly.'

'Are you planning to be in London next spring?' When Caroline raised an eyebrow in mock surprise, John added even more stiffly, 'Harriet will be eager to know.'

'Ah, yes! Harriet. I'm afraid that's a promise I cannot make to Harriet at the moment. My plans are not yet fixed. Perhaps. But since you're here, Lord Coverdale, I must thank you for your help in delivering the chalice to my grandfather's family. I don't think I could have done it as easily, or even at all, without your support. I am only sorry that the visit was such a personal disaster for you. For us both.'

He nodded and said with no perceptible warmth, 'I owe you thanks, too. I think the barrier that existed between Harriet and me would not so soon have been breached without your encouragement.'

Caroline gave a small, ironic smile. 'How civilized! Obligation acknowledged on both sides. We must both take satisfaction at the small good we have achieved out of our acquaintance.'

The bags and valises were packed and put into Lord Coverdale's carriage. Caroline went off to make the rounds of the servants to thank them and show her appreciation of their efforts on her behalf. Maggie was upstairs collecting the last of Caroline's things from the room. John saw her there and came in.

'I'm sorry, my lord. My mistress isn't here. She's seeing your lordship's servants,' she said, very formally.

'What's this extreme politeness, Maggie? I'm not used

to it from you. You used to call me Colonel, and I rather liked it.'

'His lordship is very kind,' said Maggie woodenly.

He gave a sigh. 'I wanted to give you this…' He held out a small purse. 'And to ask you to take care of your mistress on the road to London. I've already spoken to Bellerby.'

'And I'm sure Mr Bellerby's reply was the same as mine, my lord,' said Maggie, curtsying, but refusing to take the purse. 'Thank you, but we need no rewards for looking after Miss Caroline. She's always been the sweetest-natured creature you could ever want to serve, and except for the time when she was married to that black-hearted villain in New Orleans, who beat her black and blue and starved her till she did what he wanted, we've done it all her life. I don't think Mr Duval made her as unhappy as she is now, though.'

'I'm sure she will recover,' said John coldly, offended at Maggie's forthright manner.

'That she will. She's a lady with courage, my lady. And a heart.' Maggie paused, then made up her mind. 'It isn't my place to say so, my lord, but we shall probably not see you again and I'd like to put something right. I love Miss Caroline, you see.'

'I really don't think—'

'Excuse me, my lord, but that's just it! You *haven't* thought!' she said. 'You *know* Miss Caroline! Do you really believe, with all that pride in her, she would throw herself away on a scrubby young fellow hardly more than a schoolboy? When no one else in Kingston could come *near* her, however hard they tried, and that included her own cousin!'

'Edmund!'

'Yes, Edmund, for all he was married!' Maggie shook

her head. 'Why did you have to believe that good-for-nothing? Did you really think that young Mr Coburn died because of her? She gave him *money*, not anything else! He was too frightened to go to his father for it. He owed *thousands*. He begged Miss Caro to lend him money, and in spite of herself, Miss Caro felt sorry for him and gave him something to pay off the worst of his debts. But he betrayed her...' here Maggie threw him a quick glance '...just like all the other men she's let herself trust. He spent her money on more gambling, more drugs, and killed himself in the process. She still blames herself, says she should have taken more trouble to find out the real problem, persuaded him to talk to his father. But that's what really happened, my lord, and I'll swear to it in a court of law.'

John said nothing. He should have silenced Maggie earlier, she had overstepped the line in talking to him as she had. But her indignation had been genuine, and an innate sense of justice told him that he had deserved it.

'It's a pity your mistress didn't bother to explain,' he said after a while, 'Though it would have made little difference in the end.'

'The pity of it is that you're the one who could have made her happy,' said Maggie bitterly. 'I know you could. But I doubt she'll ever let you or anyone else as near again.'

Caroline entered, but came to a halt when she saw John. She looked from one to the other and gave them a glittering smile. 'Oh, Maggie,' she said. 'Have you been trying to rehabilitate me? What a waste of time! Lord Coverdale knows me for what I am, you see. I think we'd better leave before he hangs me from the battlements, or buries me in the dungeons. Would you take these shawls down to the carriage for me, please?' Maggie went and

Caroline gave John a curtsy. 'Harriet has arrived, and I've been saying my farewells. You would have been touched. I didn't say a word about reprehensible pasts and the like. No, I gave her some excellent advice. I told her again: Never cringe, never apologise. Hold on to the code you carry inside you. And hold your head high—whatever the rest of the world believes.' She looked at him with her familiar air of mockery. 'So, I'll take my leave, Lord Coverdale. Allow me to wish you all happiness and success with Harriet. She's a lovely girl. Make sure you look after her. If we meet in London, don't be afraid that I'll embarrass you by claiming any…intimate acquaintance. In fact, I can *promise* you I won't!'

With that she turned and went out of the solar and down the stairs. John followed her, and waited at the top of the steps outside until she was in the carriage, and it had swept round and started down the drive. Harriet was crying, and Mrs Abbington took her in. John followed them inside and went to his own room. He looked for a while at some crumpled yellow roses lying on the dressing table. He must have brought them up to his room after that dinner, though he couldn't remember doing so. He picked them up and threw them away angrily. He wanted no reminders.

Chapter Twelve

Caroline's only wish when she left was to put Marrick, High Hutton and the whole unhappy story of the past few weeks as far behind her as she could. Except for a determination to avoid the places she had travelled through on her road north, she had no other plans. The weather was still warm, and her original intention of going back to London was an uninviting prospect. When Joseph suggested they should leave the Great North Road soon after York Gate and stay the first night at Ripon, she agreed without argument.

At Ripon she met some travellers who had been touring Derbyshire, and their enthusiastic account of the accommodation and entertainment to be found at the spa resort of Buxton persuaded her to try it. Here she spent some time in the hotel at one end of Buxton's impressive crescent, trying the waters, and making use of the many excursions to be made in the surrounding countryside. Though the season was well advanced, balls and assemblies were still being held in the Assembly rooms, and she made herself attend one or two. It helped to put aside for a time some of the anger and hurt which were still burning beneath the graceful self-possession she showed the world.

From Buxton she travelled on through the Derbyshire Dales, among some of the most beautiful landscapes in England, stopping for two or three nights wherever she found an inn which she liked, and spending a great deal of time walking in the hills. She wanted no companion other than Joseph on these walks. He was exactly the sort of escort she preferred—there to protect her, but otherwise silent and self-effacing. Her sore heart found solace in the sunshine and shade of these hills and dales, so unlike the brightly coloured luxuriance of the scenery in Jamaica, and so different from the spare hillsides of Yorkshire. She sometimes walked for hours, returning exhausted to the inn, with energy only to eat her evening meal, wait till Maggie had undressed her, and then drop into bed. But she still could not sleep.

It was not as if she had not suffered before in her life. But the struggle she was now engaged in was different. In the years since New Orleans she had grown into a mature woman, a woman who had sworn never to be caught again in the trap of love, never to be reduced again to the state she had been in on her return from New Orleans. She had taught herself to despise the weaknesses of men, and her weapons had been cynicism and mocking laughter, which she had used against herself as well as against the world.

But John Ancroft had caught her off guard. He had crept into her heart so insidiously that he was there before she noticed. The man she had first met, the wooden soldier, the rigid authoritarian, the humourless hero, was too easy a target for her laughter to represent any kind of danger. But during the night at Buckden he had been unexpectedly revealed as a vulnerable man, a man who had suffered and was still suffering, and she had been moved by the anguish he had involuntarily shown into an attempt to comfort him.

Pity alone, however, would still not have been enough to capture her. Her whole acquaintance with him had been a voyage of discovery. He had turned out to have a sense of humour as strong as her own, to be capable not only of taking her mockery in his stride, but of turning the tables on her. Unlike other men of her acquaintance, he had not been put off by her more outrageous statements, refusing to accept them at face value, and seeing through, she had thought, to the defensive woman beneath. More than all that, she had found in him someone who had an extraordinary power to re-awaken feelings she thought she had put behind her forever. In his arms she had re-discovered physical desire, but this time it was that of a mature woman, where desire was mixed with compassion, and physical excitement with tenderness.

As their curious friendship progressed she had begun to think that here was a man who could look beyond the mask of the sophisticated woman and see the untouched heart behind. She had begun to believe that here at last was someone she could trust not to hurt her. And she had fallen in love. Not that she had known that, or realised how deep it went, until she had been forced to leave Marrick.

And then had come that disastrous day at High Hutton and the scene in the dining room at Marrick that had followed it. After Gabriella's true character had been revealed, his idol shattered, she had *expected* John to be angry. As indeed he had been. Knowing from her own experience how bitterly humiliated he must feel, she had waited to offer him comfort, as she had offered it once before. No, it was not his anger that had surprised and distressed her. It was his readiness to accept Edmund's calumnies as truth, to believe the worst of *her*, to condemn *her* along with Gabriella. His harsh questions, the ruthless contempt he had shown that evening, had struck her to the heart. But John Ancroft had not cared. He had not cared. His apology the next day had been formal, without feeling. A sop to the god of hospitality.

During her long walks Caroline gradually came to acknowledge that she had made a mistake. Influenced perhaps by Maggie's dire warnings about future loneliness, she had persuaded herself that John Ancroft was someone he was not. She had thought him someone special, whereas in fact he was just another man—no better and no worse than all the rest. She had been a fool, and now she was paying for it in deep unhappiness. But not for long! She would get over him as she had got over Laurent Duval. And sooner! If only she could recover from this sense of loss!

As the days passed the beauty and solitude around her began to make her feel better, and she started to think of what she would do. Marrick was behind her, she must look to the future. That night she announced to her two faithful servants that she had decided to leave Derbyshire the next morning and make for London.

'Mr Turner will be wondering what has happened to us—he hasn't heard from me since Buxton. Maggie, Joseph, what would you say if I decided to spend the winter in England? I should like to see something of London life—we saw very little of it when we were last there. Joseph, what about you? Is the winter over here likely to prove too cold for you? Do you want to return to Jamaica? I shan't stand in your way, if you do.'

'I told the master I would look after you, Miss Caro. I

won't leave you. Not till you pension me off! London would suit me pretty well.'

'Maggie?'

'Well, someone has to keep an eye on you, especially if you'll be mixing with all the nobs, Miss Caro! What would you do without me to dress you up and remind you how to behave? No, I'm not letting you stay in London on your own!'

Caroline smiled in relief. 'Then let's hope Mr Turner has found a house to suit us! I'm quite looking forward to it—we'll have a lot to do to make ourselves comfortable during our stay. I shall find out what other servants we need, and engage them, and if the house is not as well furnished as we like I shall visit the showrooms and buy extras. It will be an adventure!'

Maggie was much relieved at the excited note in Caroline's voice. She had begun to think that John Ancroft's defection had changed her mistress forever.

They arrived in London on a glorious day at the end of October. Mr Turner had reserved rooms at the Pulteney Hotel in Piccadilly for them and asked if he might call on Caroline the day after her arrival. He came armed with details of houses for rent in the fashionable quarter of London.

'However, if I may, I should like to draw something to your attention.'

'What is that, Mr Turner?' she asked, leafing through the papers he had brought. 'This house in Bruton Street might do, perhaps?'

'It may not have occurred to you that it won't be easy to live in London on your own.'

Caroline looked up. 'What do you mean? I have Maggie and Joseph, and will engage a whole houseful of other servants. That could hardly be called living on my own!'

'But it's not what I meant. You are still, if I may say so, a young woman. Now "Mrs Hopkins" could have lived alone in London as long as she liked, with no word of criticism. But you are still of an age where society will look askance at it. I assume you wish to enjoy a social life, to move in the first circles?'

'I have every intention of doing so.'

'Then you will need someone to keep you company. I could, if I wish, look for a respectable lady, someone in need of employment, to live with you.'

'You mean a paid companion?'

'Yes.'

'Must I have someone? For a while my grandfather employed a companion of that sort for me, and I found her a dead bore. She agreed with everything I said! I am sorry for such ladies, of course, but they are always so nervous, so afraid of offending! And that really doesn't suit me. Can't you think of something else, Mr Turner?'

'I'm afraid not. It won't be easy…' He frowned and thought. 'Unless… I wonder… It could be the very thing. Mrs Duval, I need to consult someone else before I say another word. You are happy to stay here at the Pulteney for a little? Could you leave it with me for a day or two?'

Caroline said, 'My dear sir, if it is true that the Tsar of Russia chose to put up at the Pulteney in preference to staying at St James's Palace, it would hardly be becoming in me to complain! But, in fact, I find the hotel extremely comfortable and very well appointed. Of course I can wait!' They went on to talk of other matters.

At the end of a short, but satisfactory discussion about the arrangements for financing Caroline's London stay, Mr Turner exclaimed, 'But I am remiss! We have been so occupied with business, that I have not asked about your journey north! Was it a success?'

'A great success,' said Caroline trying to inject some enthusiasm into her voice. 'My grandfather's...bequest is once again in place—with the Ainderbys in High Hutton.'

'Ah!' said Mr Turner in a satisfied tone. 'Mr Fennybright rather thought it would be there. Am I to understand that your late grandfather was an Ainderby?'

'Yes,' said Caroline abruptly.

'Quite!' Mr Turner's tone gave her the impression that he knew more about past events in Yorkshire than he was prepared to admit, and understood her reluctance to talk about it. 'And Lord Coverdale?' he went on. 'Is he well? Mr Fennybright tells me that his lordship has reached a measure of reconciliation with his daughter.'

'Yes, he has. They are both very happy.'

'And now it will be Lord Coverdale himself who will see to Miss Ancroft's début. A highly satisfactory conclusion. Tell me, what did you think of Yorkshire, ma'am?'

'It is very beautiful. But then so is Derbyshire. Did I tell you I came south through Buxton and Matlock?' To Caroline's relief Mr Turner rhapsodised about the beauties of the Derbyshire countryside for most of the time left, and did not refer again to Yorkshire, or to the families who lived there. He took his leave, promising to let her know more about her possible future home as soon as he had consulted another of his clients. Caroline admired his discretion, but was very doubtful if he would propose anything that would appeal to her. On the whole she would prefer to defy convention and live by herself in spite of society's possible frowns. It would not be the first time she had braved criticism. But she would wait and listen to Mr Turner's suggestion.

* * *

Mr Turner wasted no time. He made an appointment to see a certain Lady Danby who had recently come back to London and taken up residence in her house in Charles Street.

'What can I do for you, Turner?' she said briskly once they were settled. Lady Danby was a favourite of Mr Turner's. She belonged to one of the best families in Somerset, and though she wouldn't stand for any nonsense she was usually ready to listen to any reasonable suggestion or argument. She knew how to treat her visitors, too. On a small table at his side was a glass of first-class Madeira.

'Last week, when I expressed surprise at seeing you so soon in London again, Lady Danby, you said, I think, that you had found life in Somerset somewhat dull.'

'I certainly did! I don't mind telling you, Turner, I couldn't bear it a moment longer. I miss my goddaughter, d'y'see! When she married my nephew this summer I lost the company of both of 'em. Not that I'm complaining about the marriage! I was delighted at that. Perfect match! Jossie will keep Ivo in line, mark my words. There'll be no more scandals about my nephew! He's well and truly caught.'

'The new Lady Trenchard is a delightful young lady. It will surprise no one that Lord Trenchard is in love with her.'

'Absolutely besotted! They both are! And now he's taking her round the battlefields of Europe for a bridal trip!'

'Good heavens! What a very strange sort of thing to do! Lord Trenchard fought under Wellington, of course. I suppose it is natural for him to revisit the scene of the great victory at Waterloo. But what does his new wife think of it?'

'It was she who begged him to take her! I wouldn't be surprised if she knew more about that battle than anyone else, except perhaps the Great Duke himself!'

'Astonishing!'

'Not if you know my goddaughter. But I don't suppose you're here to gossip about my nephew and his wife, Turner. So, what *are* you here to say?'

'During that conversation, Lady Danby, you voiced a doubt that you would feel any better in London.'

'It was the lack of company! It's a strange thing. For years I lived quite happily on my own in Lyne St Michael, then my goddaughter came to live with me for just twelve months and now I find I dislike living alone! I suppose I miss all the bustle and activity of her début, too. What a time we had! Lyne St Michael was deadly dull without her, and I fear London might prove the same, but I have to give it a try. Why don't you tell me what you've come for? I can see you're working your way round to a suggestion that you don't think I'll like.'

'Have you ever thought of engaging a companion?'

'Never! Poor creatures, most of 'em. If that's your suggestion you can take it away again!'

'That isn't it exactly…' Mr Turner took the plunge. 'Among my other clients I have a highly respectable widow, who is alone in London…'

'And you want me to give her a home. No, Turner. Even if you aren't suggesting that I pay her, she would still be too dependent on me to hold her own in an argument. I'd be bored in a month!'

'Mrs Duval is a very wealthy woman.' He gave a dry cough. 'And I think she is not at all averse to expressing her views. I may say, she rejects the idea of a paid companion every bit as energetically as you yourself.'

'So what are you suggesting?'

'Mrs Duval needs somewhere to live. She wishes to experience something of London society.'

'Respectable, you said?'

'She belongs to one of the first families in the Caribbean. Her grandmother was a Willoughby. Her late grandfather was a prominent citizen of Kingston, Jamaica.'

'Jamaica, eh? That sounds interesting... What does she want?'

'Mrs Duval is not familiar with the views of our London *ton*. I have told her that society would not look favourably on a young and attractive woman living alone. If she will not engage a companion, then she ought to look for some congenial person who would be prepared to invite her to stay for a while.'

'Are you suggesting that I start letting out the rooms of this house?' Lady Danby demanded.

Mr Turner permitted himself a small smile. 'I would not dare to suggest anything of the sort, Lady Danby. There would be no question of money between you. Mrs Duval has a groom and a maidservant, and I dare say she would expect to pay for their keep. But for the rest she would be a charming and interesting guest. I really think you would enjoy her company.'

'Where is she staying at the moment?'

'At the Pulteney.'

'Well, that's a good enough address. If she can afford to keep herself, a groom and a maid at the Pulteney she cannot have any shortage of funds! I'll come to see her. Can you arrange a meeting? I'm not promising anything, mind!'

'I'll see to it straight away. Will tomorrow be too soon?'

'No, if I am to consider your mad scheme at all, then the sooner I meet your widow the better!'

* * *

After a little skirmishing on both sides, the two ladies found they had enjoyed their meeting—so much so that Lady Danby invited Mrs Duval for an indefinite stay, with the proviso that either lady could terminate the arrangement at any time. But the outlook was favourable. Lady Danby was soon treating Caroline like a young relative, calling her by her first name, and talking freely to her about the rest of the family. Both ladies had lively, independent minds, but they soon discovered that they liked each other's company. They were not always together, of course. Caroline had a small suite of rooms upstairs, which she could retire to whenever she wished, and Lady Danby kept one of the reception rooms downstairs for her own use. But on the whole the arrangement suited them both more than Mr Turner could have dreamed.

Lady Danby had a wide circle of acquaintances, who never left the capital except in the height of summer, and she took Caroline with her to the various parties, musical evenings and soirées held in their houses. Autumn in London was really quite pleasant. The streets and parks were not as crowded as they were in the season, but there were plenty of theatres, exhibitions, concerts and other amusements to go to, and riding or driving in the Park was very agreeable. Caroline joined in all this whirl of activity with enthusiasm, and managed to forget her strange sense of loss, sometimes for as much as a whole day. She made an impression, of course. Before very long the house in Charles Street had a good few callers looking for this ravishing newcomer to the London scene.

'It's almost like last season, when I had Jossie here!' said Lady Danby, sitting back in relief when the last of the four gentlemen to call that afternoon had just left. 'So many callers! I really cannot claim that life is dull since you've been here, dear Caroline.'

'I'm sorry, ma'am! Do these constant visitors tire you?'

'Not in the slightest! In fact, I think I enjoy them rather more than you. Did you have to be quite so offhand with Mr Powerstock?'

'Unfortunately, yes! I know the type. Young and impressionable. One word of encouragement from me and he will convince himself he is in love.'

'Is that such a bad thing?'

'Since I have no intention of marrying again, yes, I think it is. Mr Powerstock could be hurt. I prefer to flirt with gentlemen who know the rules of the game, Lady Danby. Of the four who were here this afternoon, Sir Anthony is much more to my taste.'

Lady Danby frowned. 'You should be careful, my dear. Sir Anthony Grainger may know the rules of the game, but I'm not at all sure he abides by them. He is not a desirable acquaintance. Ivo never approved of him.'

'From what I have heard, Lady Danby,' said Caroline with a grin at her hostess, 'your nephew was in no position to approve or disapprove of flirts! According to your own friends, he was the worst flirt in London!'

'My dear, you do him an injustice. Before his marriage, he was the worst flirt in *Europe*!' She started to laugh. 'I wish you could have been here when he suddenly discovered that he was in love for the first time in his life! The greatest flirt in Europe trapped by a nineteen-year-old innocent! London was stunned. It upset quite a few ladies, I can tell you! But then, Jossie is someone special.' She smiled reminiscently. Then she went on, 'Ivo may have been something of a rogue, Caroline, but he was always fair. You might say that the ladies he charmed were all well able to take care of themselves. I didn't approve of his antics, mind, but he never flirted with débutantes or indeed anyone else who was vulnerable. Sir

Anthony is quite different. He has no such scruples. Besides which, he's a gazetted fortune hunter.'

Caroline smiled and raised a sceptical eyebrow. 'You think me vulnerable?'

'Neither vulnerable nor even susceptible. What *have* you done with your heart, girl?'

'Oh, I threw that away a long time ago. It was too inconvenient. But since you say I am neither vulnerable nor susceptible, why are you concerned about Sir Anthony?'

'He's not someone you should trifle with. I notice, even if he does not, that under that charming air of attention you adopt towards him you are laughing at him in the same way as you laugh at all of them. He has the pride of the devil, Caroline. Be careful.'

'Well, since your brother has been kind enough to invite me to join you both in Somerset over Christmas, I shan't see very much of any of my beaux for a while. Perhaps Sir Anthony will have forgotten me by the time we return. Now, are you going to take me to this famous dressmaker of yours?'

'Caroline! Never let her hear you calling her a dressmaker! A mantua maker, perhaps, or a modiste… But never a dressmaker! There's no dressmaker born who could afford premises in Bruton Street. But you're right, we should think of going. We dare not be late. I would rather keep the Prince Regent waiting than I would Madame Rosa!'

Meanwhile, up in Yorkshire John had become deeply involved in Marrick's affairs. Mr Fennybright had been right when he had stressed how badly the estate needed a new hand to guide it, and it would take months, if not years, to restore it to its former splendour. But John had no desire to see it a museum piece, its old ways carefully preserved. A new age was beginning, and all the Ancroft possessions would have to respond to the demands of the times. That took study and consultation, visits of inspection and commissioning of designs... John was kept more than busy in the months that followed Caroline's departure.

He took time to cultivate his daughter, too, and was rewarded with an increasingly loving relationship with her. He devoted a great deal of time to her, riding with her, talking of his adventures abroad, about the Great Duke and others he had known, discussing books they had both read, listening to her... He gradually pieced together a picture of a lonely childhood spent in the limited company of his uncle, various nurses and, later, Mrs Abbington. Her mother did not seem to feature greatly in her accounts. Rose had apparently been an invalid for much of Harriet's childhood.

One day at the beginning of winter they had been for a long ride and had ended up looking down at Marrick from the hill above. John suddenly asked her, 'Why did you regard me with such horror the last time I came here?'

Harriet's reply was indirect. 'When I was a child I was terrified of my Uncle Coverdale. He spent all his time in his study, and it was always so gloomy in there. The curtains were never completely opened, even in summer. There was a portrait of his son on the wall beside him with a lamp in front of it, and he used to sit staring at the picture for hours. One day he stood me in front of it, and asked me if I knew who it was. I did, of course, but I wasn't sure what he wanted me to say. So I told him all of it—his son, Lord Philip Ancroft, my papa's cousin.'

'What did he say?'

'He got so angry! He shook me till my head rattled, and told me never to mention you again. That you had killed his son, and I was never to forget it. He threatened to put me in the deepest dungeons Marrick had, and leave me there for the rats to eat me, if I ever spoke to you or let you near me.'

'My poor child!'

'Papa, I used to have nightmares about those rats. I would dream that you came and I couldn't stop you from coming up to me, I couldn't even speak to you to tell you why you mustn't. Then Uncle Coverdale would suddenly appear and drag me away from you... I used to wake up screaming.'

John swore under his breath. 'I knew the loss of Philip had turned his mind. But not that it was as bad as that. I thought you were safe and happy at Marrick. Poor, poor Harriet!' He took Harriet and held her. She spoke from the shelter of his arms. 'Papa, Uncle Coverdale said something else. He said that I was the only bit of Philip he had left. What...what did he mean?'

There was a silence. John let Harriet go, then took her hands in his. 'I'll tell you. But first I want to say something else. Since coming back to Marrick, I've found that I really have a daughter after all, someone I can love and be proud of. It's been a wonderfully powerful consolation in a difficult time. Do you believe me?'

'But I'm Philip's child, aren't I? Not your daughter at all,' she said in a small voice.

'Your mother loved Philip very much, and if he hadn't been killed she would have married him. You were born of that love. But you're *my* daughter, Harriet. In far more than name.'

Harriet gave a contented sigh. 'I'm glad, Papa.' She hesitated, then said shyly, 'I thought at one time you liked

Mrs Duval, Papa. I should have liked it more than anything if you had married her.'

'No! That was impossible!'

'But why? She was always so kind and amusing. And I think she loved us both quite a lot. Think of all the things she did for us!'

'You're young, Harriet. You don't understand. Mrs Duval might have been everything you say, but her past life hardly made her a suitable person to be in charge of you.'

'How can you say that, Papa! She taught me so much about how I should behave.'

'Dancing and curtsies and the like?'

'Not just that! She explained about morals, too.'

'Morals? Caroline Duval?'

'Yes, Papa,' said Harriet gravely. 'Mrs Abbington and the Reverend Smythe have taught me the usual rules, but Mrs Duval explained them better.'

John stared at her. 'You'd better tell me what that woman has said to you!' he said grimly. If Caroline Duval had taught his daughter her own cynical scorn for the conventions...

But when Harriet told him he was amazed. The only part of what he might have called Caroline's own philosophy came in the form she had already told him—he remembered her saying it in the solar on the morning she left. *'Never cringe, never apologise. Hold on to the code you carry inside you...'* The curious thing was that, according to Harriet, the code emphasized honesty, pride in one's own integrity, loyalty, straight dealing—all qualities that he valued himself.

'There doesn't seem to be anything wrong with that,' he said gruffly. 'But I still think we are better off without Mrs Duval. So let me hear no more of her.'

* * *

But through all the work, all the discussions, he was conscious of a gap, a constant feeling that something precious had gone from his life. At first he thought it was his youthful dream of Gabriella, until one day he realised that she no longer meant anything at all to him, good or bad. Though he had clung to her memory for so many years, it was now on the way to being forgotten, simply a part of the dead past. But the gap, the sense of loss, remained. And now, though Harriet obeyed him, and never mentioned her name, Caroline Duval came back to haunt him. The curious thing was that his memory of her, of their whole acquaintance, was still as clear and as vivid in his mind as if it had happened the day before. He lay awake at night going over their time together, always ending with the evening of the day at High Hutton. That evening, the memory of all those years spent mourning Gabriella had eaten into him like a canker. And he realised that he had made Caroline Duval a scapegoat.

Maggie's reproaches the day she left now burned into his memory. Had her defence of Caroline been rooted in the *facts*, not a faithful servant's blind loyalty? In his futile anger at Gabriella's fallen image, had he rejected something much more real? Not a faultless idol, the object of veneration by an infatuated young man, but a woman of warmth and passion, a woman who was not afraid of the truth, who placed a high value on loyalty, keeping faith... Someone who would be a companion for a lifetime, a friend to laugh with... John punched his pillow and tossed restlessly in his bed. Damn Caroline Duval! She remained a tormenting enigma still!

Christmas came and went, and after Harriet's birthday in February they started to make plans for her entry into London society. Kate Calthorpe had already agreed to sponsor Harriet, and now wrote to offer her help in choosing a suitable wardrobe.

Though, from what I hear, Jossie Trenchard would be a better person for you to consult on that. Her come-out dresses are said to have been exquisite. I hope she will be in London when we are there. She and Ivo can't stay in Europe forever—they must run out of battlefields soon! But what do you think? They met Countess Leiken in Brussels, and she and Jossie got on enormously well. Ivo says he felt quite left out! Adam was wishing he could have been there to see it.

He was saying the other day what a splendid thing it would be if we were all to meet in London next year during the Season—you and Harriet, Ivo and Jossie, and Adam and I. Ivo and Jossie might have come down from their honeymoon cloud by then. I shall get Adam to write to Ivo to suggest it.

Baby Tom is robustly healthy and looking forward to showing you how well he can walk, my loving lord and master sends his salutes, and I send my best regards and love to your daughter. Tell her I cannot wait to meet her!

Yes, thought John, folding the letter with a smile. Kate Calthorpe was just as her brother had been, warm-hearted, impulsive and amusing, though with a good deal more sense. What would she have made of Caroline Duval? Or, indeed, what would she *make* of Caroline Duval! They were bound to meet. The world of London society was too small for it not to happen. Fennybright, who was under the impression that Mrs Duval's movements would be of interest to Lord Coverdale, had said in his last letter that Mrs Duval was intending to take part in the Season before returning to Jamaica. So she would be there. He would see Caroline Duval again. Would he find the answer to his enigma then?

Chapter Thirteen

The winter passed and spring came early. The daffodils in London's parks and gardens blew merrily in the winds of early March, inviting the world to come out and enjoy them. Society slowly returned to the capital to prepare for the great excitement of its year—the London Season. Hordes of servants arrived to open up the great houses round Berkeley Square, Grosvenor Square, Brook Street, Mount Street and the rest, and London suddenly grew busy. Caroline was enchanted. Jamaica and all its problems had never seemed less attractive. This England, so different from her Caribbean island, delighted her in all its moods and situations.

The new arrivals to the London scene were equally pleased with Mrs Duval. Charming, was the general verdict. As well as rich, of course. She was invited everywhere, and was frequently seen driving or riding in the park, sometimes with Lady Danby, or more often with an attentive gentleman at her side. The number of callers at Charles Street increased. Even mothers with daughters to marry off liked Mrs Duval—she was seldom seen with any of the young men they considered to be ideal husband material, but seemed to prefer the company of older, more experienced admirers. Soon Mrs Duval was an acknowledged success, and no function was considered complete without her.

Caroline came in from a drive one day to find Lady Danby reading her *Gazette*. She did this faithfully every day, eager to learn the names of the latest arrivals in town.

'Caroline! Come and sit down, my dear! Did you enjoy your drive? Who was it this time?'

'Sir Anthony, ma'am.'

Lady Danby frowned. 'He is still attentive? I hoped he would have forgotten you.'

'He might forget me, but I doubt he'd forget my fortune. You needn't be concerned. I think I have his measure.'

'Then why encourage him?'

'He's amusing. And not at all dangerous, I assure you. Unlike some others, he is most unlikely to break his heart over me. I quite enjoy fencing with him.'

'I don't suppose it's any use warning you again, but I think you may be mistaken. Sir Anthony Grainger is not as harmless as you believe.'

Caroline shrugged her shoulders. 'I can manage him. Who are the latest arrivals, ma'am?'

'A most interesting one!' She read out, 'Lord Coverdale has taken up residence in his house in Mount Street. His lordship is accompanied by his daughter, the Lady Harriet, who is to be presented to society this coming April.' She turned to Caroline. 'There! Do you know who that is? Before he succeeded to the title, Lord Coverdale was Colonel Ancroft, Ivo's commanding officer!' Fortunately Lady Danby was not paying attention to Caroline's reaction to her news. She was frowning down at the newspaper. 'It's strange, Ivo never said anything about a daughter. And there's no mention of a wife here...'

'Lord Coverdale's wife died some time ago. The family lived up north in Yorkshire while he was with the army,' Caroline said, keeping her voice cool. 'It's possible that your nephew wasn't aware of the daughter's existence.'

'You know them?'

'I spent some time in Yorkshire before I came to London,' said Caroline.

Lady Danby glanced at her curiously. Caroline's voice seemed rather constricted. 'I didn't know that. I thought you had come direct from Jamaica?'

'No, before he died my grandfather asked me to visit his family in High Hutton. That is quite near Marrick Castle, the Ancroft family seat. I went there first.'

'I see. So you knew the Ancrofts up in the north,' said Lady Danby, satisfied.

By this time Caroline had got her voice under control. 'Yes,' she said more naturally. 'I liked Harriet. She is a lovely girl, though rather shy.'

'I thought her father was a stiff sort of man. But Ivo liked him, and they became quite friendly after they had both left the army. I should imagine he'll be pleased his Colonel is in London again.' Lady Danby went on to talk once again about her nephew, and Caroline, who had heard some of these stories before, was left to her own thoughts.

She did not know how to feel about Lord Coverdale's arrival. She had known he would come eventually, and in the narrow world of London society their paths were bound to cross. How would he behave towards her? How was she to behave towards him—especially under the critical eye of the *ton*? She had discovered that the polite world in London was much like the polite world anywhere else. Scandal and gossip occupied a great deal of its time. What would the polite world here say if they even suspected what had passed between Lord Coverdale and herself? Even in the middle of her horror at the thought, Caroline could not suppress a grin. That would give the tabbies something to talk about!

Then she sighed. Their parting in Yorkshire had been very final, and their likely meeting in London would not change the situation. The sadness that still waited to pounce and twist her heart at unwary moments was not for this Lord Coverdale. However much she missed John Ancroft, whatever pangs she might suffer when she was reminded of him, the man she had begun to love had not really ever existed. When the Lord Coverdale mentioned in the *Gazette* came to London, she would have no need of him. He would simply be one man among many others, and not by any means the most handsome, or the most charming of them. London was full of attractive men, all eager to please her. And he would mean as much as any of the rest to her—which was nothing at all.

They finally met at a soirée given by Lady Marchant, though John had been observing Caroline for some minutes before they actually spoke to one another. He had seen her as soon as he entered the room. She was over by one of the windows attended by a number of admirers, looking even more lovely and more self-possessed than he remembered her. The ball at Marrick had been the only event during their extraordinary relationship when he had seen her dressed for a formal evening, and on that occasion, in a grey silk dress and a modest amount of jewellery, she had deliberately set out to underplay her appearance. Tonight she looked magnificent. The rich chestnut locks of her hair were dressed on top of her head *à l'antique*, held with a crescent of diamonds and pearls. One or two curls had escaped to frame her face, to fall behind to the nape of her neck. Diamonds sparkled in her ears and at her throat, and the lines of her superb figure were discreetly hinted at under the dull sheen of her ivory silk dress. For the first time John saw her in her proper setting, a beautiful and wealthy woman holding her own in the most demanding society in the world. The sight took his breath away.

His hostess came up and led him away to meet someone on the other side of the room, and during the conversation that followed he needed all the discipline he had learned during interminable social evenings spent with the Duke in Europe to disguise his complete lack of interest in what his companions were saying. As soon as he decently could, he made his excuses and escaped. He needed to be alone, to think, to sort out the rush of feeling he had experienced on seeing Caroline Duval again. His recent depression, the sense of loss, the feeling that something precious had disappeared, were all accounted for in that one vision. He now realised that all his efforts to forget Caroline Duval had been a waste of time. There was no enigma, not about her, nor about his feelings for her. She was everything and more that he wanted. She was *part* of him in a way that Gabriella had never been. The lift of her head, the lazily mocking expression, the deep voice, all so instantly familiar, all newly exciting. Even from such a distance, he could tell with no trouble at all what she was thinking as she stood there, enchanting her companions with her slow smile and wicked green eyes. Caroline was bored. If it was any comfort to him, she was as remote, as securely hidden behind her defences, as ever. No rivals there!

Lady Marchant came up to him again. 'Lord Coverdale! You're alone. What can I do to please you?'

'I should like to talk to the lady by the window, if I may.'

'Ah! You are not alone in wishing to meet her, Lord Coverdale. But I shall do as you ask.' She led the way through the crowded room...

The rooms were crowded, the atmosphere very warm. Caroline had dismissed her entourage and was standing by the open window enjoying a breath of air and a moment of quiet. She heard Lady Marchant's voice behind her.

'And this is our new star from the West Indies, Lord Coverdale,' said Lady Marchant. 'Mrs Duval, may I present Lord Coverdale?' Caroline turned slowly, her heart suddenly pounding. John was looking at her, his expression difficult to read.

'Mrs Duval and I already know each other,' he said calmly.

'Really?' said Lady Marchant, obviously intrigued. 'In Jamaica or England?'

'England,' said John at his most wooden. When neither party seemed inclined to enlighten her further, Lady Marchant said with a significant smile, 'In that case I shall leave you to talk. I see that poor Lady Parker needs a helping hand. Excuse me.' Neither of her guests noticed her going.

'You're looking well,' John said.

Caroline had control of herself. 'Thank you,' she said, in her slow, deep voice. 'London agrees with me, I think. How is Harriet?'

'A little overpowered by the city. I left her at home tonight in the care of Mrs Abbington. You were frowning just then. Was it wrong of me to say that we had already met?'

'Of course not. I wouldn't want you to be less than honest, Lord Coverdale,' she said ironically. 'And even if I was prepared to dissimulate, I couldn't ask it of Harriet. As a matter of fact, I have already told Lady Danby that I know you.'

'What did you say?'

'That I knew the Ancrofts in Yorkshire where I had been to visit my grandfather's family.'

'I see. No more?'

'I don't think there's a need to say more. After all, we're strangers, aren't we?'

'I don't feel like a stranger, Caroline. How can you call me one?'

'Very easily. We discovered that we hardly knew each other, as far as I remember. We certainly parted as strangers, and now we meet again as such. I remember promising you we would.'

'Caroline, I—'

'I really think it better if we're more formal, Lord Coverdale. I should prefer you to call me Mrs Duval. We meet, as I said, as comparative strangers, and I've no desire to cause gossip.'

'This is a different Caroline Duval from the one I knew. She was ready to shock the world.'

'That was a different world. At present I'm happy to be a respectable part of this one. Why the frown? Aren't you relieved to know that I'm now a reformed character?'

'I see,' he said grimly, unamused by the mockery in her voice. 'Well then, *Mrs Duval*, since it's obviously impossible to have a lengthy conversation here, may I call on you tomorrow?'

'I don't think—'

'I should like to bring Harriet to see you. She's feeling a little lost. Lady Calthorpe will take her under her wing when she arrives, but the Calthorpes have been delayed.'

'I see. Well, in that case…'

'Good! May I have your direction?'

'I'm staying with Lady Danby in Charles Street.'

Lord Coverdale looked surprised. 'Ivo's aunt? I know her quite well. There should be no difficulty about my visiting you.'

'Not from Lady Danby, no,' agreed Caroline pleasantly.

He ignored this. 'Is Ivo back yet?'

'Not yet, though he and his wife are expected any time now. Lady Danby talks a great deal about them. I have to say that I can't wait to meet the famous Lord Trenchard.'

He frowned and said disapprovingly, 'Ivo's wife is a lovely girl and he's deeply in love with her. You'll be disappointed if you're expecting to amuse yourself with a rake. He's reformed.'

So his opinion of her had not changed! She gave him a slow look through her lashes, her green eyes full of amusement. 'So am I,' she said solemnly. 'Had you forgotten? Lord Trenchard and I can compare notes.'

'He's a married man! Wouldn't that stop you?'

'Not at all! Married men are much more fun!'

'I refuse to believe you mean what you say, Caro— Mrs Duval!' he said angrily.

In a voice full of mock reproach she replied, 'Really, Lord Coverdale, I can't understand you! The last time we met you were angry because you believed I had seduced Robbie Coburn who, as far as I know, had never married. Now you're angry because I say I want to meet Lord Trenchard, who is! There's no pleasing you!'

'If, as I suspect, you are amusing yourself at my expense, then I warn you—'

'Yes, Lord Coverdale? What will you do?' She shook her head and said with a malicious smile, 'I don't think you had better punish me in your usual manner. That wouldn't do at all, not in Lady Marchant's drawing room. What *would* the *ton* say? Indeed, may I suggest you keep your voice a *tiny* bit lower? I'd hate anyone to overhear this conversation.'

'Dammit, that was not my usual manner!' he said in a low voice. 'I've already apologised for my behaviour that night, or have you forgotten?'

'No, I haven't forgotten exactly. But your apology wasn't exactly handsome. I wasn't sure afterwards whether you had meant it or not. You might try again, perhaps, if we are ever in a more private situation...'

'Caroline—'

'Though that's most unlikely. It wouldn't be proper, you see.' She sighed. 'Being a reformed character is sometimes *most* inconvenient.'

'I can see you don't mean to be serious,' he said, irritation in his voice. 'Let's hope Harriet finds you in a more amenable frame of mind tomorrow.'

'I assure you she will. She at least has a special place in my affection. And now I see Mr Powerstock coming towards us. I think we have talked for long enough. Till tomorrow, Lord Coverdale. At three.'

After he had gone Caroline felt exhausted, and as soon as she had managed to escape from Mr Powerstock she sought out Lady Danby and excused herself.

'I think I'll go back to Charles Street. I have the headache. It's the weather, I expect.'

'My dear child! I'm sorry to hear that. You'll take the

carriage? John Coachman can bring it back for me. Or would you like me to come with you?'

'No, no! I'd rather slip quietly away. But I'd be obliged if you would make my excuses to Lady Marchant. I can't find her at the moment.'

'Of course! Have a good night's rest, my dear.'

Caroline fetched her shawl. To leave Lady Marchant's house discreetly was impossible—no fewer than four footmen were waiting at the door. But once outside she congratulated herself on escaping without being observed by any of her admirers. She could not have borne a journey back to Charles Street in the company of any other person. She needed peace and tranquillity to persuade her unruly heart to settle down. All her brave thoughts had been quite useless. John Ancroft would never be just another one of the crowd to her. The mere sight of him had roused the sharp unhappiness she had tried so hard to forget. It had taken all her strength to keep a smiling mask in place, to treat his words with lighthearted irreverence when what she really wanted was to hurl reproaches at him for having betrayed the trust she had so stupidly placed in him, to berate him for throwing so much away. A useless exercise, if ever there was one!

But peace was to be denied her. The other door of the carriage opened and John Ancroft got in beside her.

'What are you doing here?' she demanded.

'Seeing you safely home,' he said briefly.

'But I don't need you!'

'I think you do. London streets are hardly safe at night. Don't bother trying to dissuade me, Caroline. I shall accompany you to Charles Street.'

She sat back against the squabs and said ungraciously, 'I suppose I can't throw you out, much as I should like to. But I don't have to talk to you.' She turned her head towards the window, and prayed that the darkness hid the sheen of tears in her eyes. Her time for recovery was not yet, it appeared.

His voice came out of the dark. 'Then I'll talk to *you*. You said I had not apologised handsomely enough. I'd like to remedy that. Caroline, I'm truly sorry for the way I behaved. I was driven mad that night with anger and humiliation. I had worshipped at a shrine for seventeen years, and suddenly the illusion had been ripped away and I was left with a very ugly reality. And…and in my madness I linked you and Gabriella together. Edmund's letter was the final straw. I didn't really believe the things I said to you, even while I was saying them, but it's true that I wanted to hurt you. And I did. Believe me, I bitterly regret what I did that night, how I behaved. Can't you forgive me?'

'You mustn't blame yourself too much, Lord Coverdale,' she managed to say coolly. 'Perhaps I was hurt, but that was entirely my own fault. I *let* you hurt me! It won't happen again. I believe I once said to you—I make many mistakes, but I do try not to make the same mistake twice.'

'What does that mean?'

'That for a while up in Yorkshire I was in danger of forgetting a resolve I made many years ago.'

'And that was?'

'That I would never again take *any* man seriously enough to be hurt by anything he did.'

'You haven't forgiven me, then?'

'I'm not sure what you want me to say. I understood at the time how you felt. I still understand. As I said afterwards, it shall be forgotten.'

'Then, can't we go back to the beginning? Start again?'

'You haven't been listening, Lord Coverdale. No!'

'Why not?'

Caroline took a deep breath and turned round. 'Circumstances threw us together on that damned road north. We both behaved uncharacteristically, and it was a mistake. It wasn't my style. When I said a few moments ago that what happened at Marrick should be forgotten, I meant *all* of it. The whole episode. I cannot imagine what I was thinking of to get so involved with you and your concerns.'

There was a short silence. Then he said, 'I won't accept this! I know there's something between us that not even you can ignore.'

'I can and will!'

The carriage was turning into Charles Street. John took her chin in his hand and drew it round. His lips close to hers, he said softly, 'Kiss me, and then tell me you can!'

This man needed a lesson, thought Caroline with a spurt of anger. How dare he think he has only to speak sweetly, cajole me with a kiss, and I'll come running! She looked into his eyes and he bent his head and kissed her. With the best will in the world her response was not quite as controlled as she would have wished. The devil was right, she thought with habitual self-mockery. There was something quite powerful between them. But if it *killed* her she would ignore it!

'You see?' he said in tones of satisfaction. 'Doesn't that prove it?'

Caroline leaned back, her green eyes glowing in the light of the flambeaux as they drew up to the house. 'Oh, John!' she breathed softly. 'That was wonderful! In fact…in fact, it was very nearly the nicest kiss I've had since coming to London.'

John complacent smile was transformed into angry

astonishment. The sight amused her so much that she was laughing as they got out of the carriage.

She was still laughing as they walked up to the door, and he gave her another furious look. But after a moment she pulled herself together to bid him goodnight, and he shook his head and smiled reluctantly in response. 'I'd forgotten your tricks,' he said in a resigned voice. 'No quarter given. But you haven't put me off, Caroline. I promise you I shall win!'

'I wouldn't wager too much on your chances if I were you, Lord Coverdale. That is, if you have marriage in mind. If I *was* looking for a husband, there are more than a few gentlemen in London who could be serious rivals. Even discounting those who are only attracted by my fortune. Goodnight.'

When John called at Charles Street the next afternoon he was once again perfectly self-possessed. Harriet was with him, and responded very affectionately to Caroline's greeting. Lady Danby sat back and listened with interest to Harriet's artless account of what had been happening at Marrick since Caroline's departure, and began to suspect that Caroline had been rather less than frank with her about her activities in Yorkshire. She was intrigued by Lord Coverdale's attitude to her friend, too. There was no doubt that he was interested in her. But he was also clearly on his guard, and after a few minutes Lady Danby came to the conclusion that there was much more between her guest and Lord Coverdale than either would admit. How delightful it would be if Ivo's Colonel had found the woman of his choice in Caroline Duval! She would make a wonderful Marchioness! Lady Danby began to think out ways of promoting the match...

Unfortunately, her happy plotting was interrupted by

the arrival of Sir Anthony Grainger. Sir Anthony had a decided air of fashion, and prided himself on being acquainted with anyone worth knowing in London. His family was an ancient one, and his estate in Kent was large, though somewhat run down. His first wife had brought him a fortune, but rumour had it that his expenditure so outstripped his income that his funds were now beginning to run out. If he was to keep the standard of living he had set for himself, said the gossips, he had an urgent need to find a second wife as well endowed as the first. But if Sir Anthony was worried it did not show in his manner.

'My dear Lady Danby,' he said in his fashionable drawl, bending low over his hostess's hand. 'I have no need to ask after your health—I can see you are flourishing! Your stay in the country obviously agreed with you.'

'Thank you, Sir Anthony,' said Lady Danby with something of a snap.

'And Mrs Duval! Lovely as ever!'

Caroline was conscious of something like a snort from the man standing next to her. She said hastily, 'You are always very kind, sir. May I present you to Lord Coverdale and his daughter, Lady Harriet Ancroft?'

'Grainger,' said John with a curt nod.

'I already have the pleasure of Lord Coverdale's acquaintance, Mrs Duval. But not that of his charming daughter...Lady Harriet?'

Harriet coloured at the admiration in Sir Anthony's light blue eyes, but after a quick glance at Caroline she smiled politely and gave him a perfectly judged curtsy. Caroline glanced at John and they shared a brief moment of pride.

'How may I help you, Sir Anthony?' said Lady Danby briskly.

'I fear my mission is in vain. I was hoping to invite Mrs Duval for a drive, but I see she is occupied this afternoon. May I hope for better luck tomorrow?'

Before Caroline could speak, John said, 'Unfortunately Mrs Duval has just promised to take my daughter to… to…'

'Hampton Court,' said Lady Danby.

'Ah, yes! I knew it was one of the palaces, but couldn't remember which,' said John blandly.

'Did you really, Mrs Duval?' exclaimed Harriet. 'I didn't know. Oh, thank you! I've wanted to go there ever since I heard of the maze. I long to see it!'

Caroline gave first John, then Lady Danby a very straight look, then smiled apologetically at Sir Anthony. 'Perhaps the day after?' she said.

In the face of Lady Danby's support Sir Anthony could hardly say he was undeceived by Lord Coverdale's manoeuvre. He put a good face on it and arranged with Caroline to meet her in two days' time, and shortly afterwards took a somewhat cool leave of his hostess.

'What do you think you're doing?' demanded Caroline as soon as Sir Anthony had gone.

'Trying to save you from yourself!' said John. 'I'm surprised you want to spend your time on that second-rater!'

'When I want your interference I'll ask for it!' she began hotly. She stopped and looked at Lady Danby, who was observing this exchange with interest. Caroline took a breath and after a pause said thoughtfully, 'Why didn't I think of it before? Of course, I could ask Sir Anthony to escort us! To…to…Hampton Court!'

'I shall be your escort,' said John. 'I'm not letting a well-known fortune hunter loose on my daughter! Or anyone else I care for.'

'Was I wrong?' asked Harriet anxiously. 'Do you not wish to go after all, Mrs Duval?'

Caroline went over and took her arm. 'Of course I do!'

'Then I should like Papa to come, too.' She smiled innocently into Caroline's eyes. 'You and I, and Papa.'

Caroline turned somewhat desperately to Lady Danby. 'Wouldn't you like to come, too, ma'am? The drive should be a pleasant one.'

Lady Danby could have laughed aloud at the renewed anxiety on Harriet's face. Lady Harriet Ancroft was not quite the mouse she seemed! The little minx was apparently as eager as she was to promote a match between these two! She would wager a substantial amount that at some point in the expedition the girl would see to it that Caroline and her father were left *à deux*. Of *course* she didn't want anyone else along to play chaperon. So she said obligingly, 'It's kind of you to ask, my dear Caro, but I'm already engaged.' She added innocently, 'I could come on the drive the next afternoon with you and Sir Anthony, if you wish?'

Lady Danby was perfectly correct. Harriet disappeared into the maze at Hampton Court with an airy wave of the hand and, unknown to the two she left behind, armed with a plan of its layout. She had no intention of accidentally finding her way out too soon. The other two sat down to wait on a bench under a large oak tree. The spot was quiet, removed from the busy pathways of the park.

'Did you plan this, Lord Coverdale?' asked Caroline calmly.

John began to chuckle. 'I wish I had! But the credit lies with my daughter alone. With a little help from your hostess.'

'I can't imagine what they hope to gain from it.'

'I'd have thought that was obvious! To leave us to have a talk. It was clearly impossible yesterday.'

Caroline considered him with her habitual expression of secret amusement. 'And what does Lord Coverdale wish to say? I do so hope he is not about to remind me again of what a dissolute creature I am!'

He became serious at once. 'Please, Caroline! I beg you! I've thought hard about what you said the other night. I'd like to talk to you more about it. Don't you think you owe it to me?'

'In what way?'

'Because our acquaintance has been such an extraordinary one! We both know so much about one another, in spite of the barriers we have both put up against the rest of the world. We can't simply deny that knowledge exists.'

'I can and will!'

'I say you cannot. The events of that journey north did away with pretence, you know they did. You say you can't forgive yourself for becoming involved, but you could no more help getting involved than I could. In Buckden you witnessed my most private feelings, feelings I had kept hidden for years. You were there at High Hutton when I discovered that Gabriella, whose memory I had venerated for years, hadn't been worth a single moment's grief. On that terrible evening at Marrick, you experienced the very worst of my nature. You have seen me as no other creature in this world has seen me, the best, and the worst of me. Don't you think you owe me a chance to plead my case? Can't you drop those defences of yours with me in return?'

Her expression changed. She looked down at her hands. 'Very well. I'll be serious. For a while I thought I *could* abandon my defences with you. Up to the moment you showed me how little you really thought of me.'

'When I attacked you?'

'No. When you believed all those things Edmund had written about me. I knew how you must be hurting, how angry you must be about Gabriella. And I had come down that evening ready to comfort you in any way I could. Freely. In *any* way. You wouldn't have had to coerce me, I was prepared to offer you whatever kind of comfort you wanted.' She looked at him then, the green eyes for once dark and unguarded, and he could see through to the truth in them.

'And I threw it away,' he said heavily.

'I saw that you really believed I could have seduced Robbie Coburn. I had thought you different, that you would know that to be impossible. But you believed it, just like all the others. That was the moment I decided I had made a mistake.'

There was a short silence. Then he said, 'Tell me. At one point—before the ball at Marrick—I was almost sure I wanted to marry you. I thought we could even learn to love one another. If I had asked you then, before we went to High Hutton, what would you have said?'

She jumped up and started walking away. 'Why are we talking of this? It's in the past! And best left there!'

He caught up with her. 'Is it really too late, Caroline? If I ask you to marry me now, could you bring yourself to agree?'

She stopped short. 'No! I would not!'

'You don't love me? Not in the slightest?'

'That's not the question! Whether I love you or not doesn't matter. I don't trust you!'

'Would you marry anyone else?'

'No, of course not!'

'So there is some feeling there for me! Caroline, I promise you, if it's the last thing I do, I'll teach you to trust me again.'

She looked at him then, her expression openly derisive. 'And how will you begin to do that, Colonel Ancroft? Even supposing I let you near enough to try!'

In the carriage on the homeward journey Harriet chattered gaily about the people she had met in the maze. But from time to time she looked anxiously at the two people she loved best. To judge by their faces, their afternoon talk didn't seem to have done much good. And her concern increased during the days that followed.

Caroline went out with Sir Anthony the next afternoon, and quite frequently after that. In the evenings, too, she seemed to be encouraging him, allowing him more than the conventional number of dances, and flirting with him outrageously in the interval. Soon odds were being offered in the London clubs that Sir Anthony had at last succeeded in finding his second rich wife.

Lady Danby was seriously worried. Caroline was deaf to pleas and warnings alike, and her assurances that she had no intention of ever marrying Sir Anthony were little consolation. When Lord Coverdale called one afternoon, only to find Caroline out with Sir Anthony yet again, Lady Danby invited him to sit down and talk to her. She wasted no time in coming to the point.

'Lord Coverdale, am I right to suspect that you have an interest in Mrs Duval?'

John stiffened. 'I fail to see—'

'This is not the time for conventional politeness! I have become very fond of her myself, and at the moment am considerably worried about her! She is running a quite extraordinary risk. Sir Anthony Grainger—'

'I know something of his character, ma'am.'

'You need not be afraid she will marry him!'

'I am not. At the moment Mrs Duval is determined to marry no one. When she changes her mind, it will be to marry me.'

'Excellent!'

He smiled and said wryly, 'I am glad you approve, Lady Danby. As you've probably guessed, there's something of a history between Mrs Duval and myself, which makes matters complicated, but in the end I hope to persuade her. Meanwhile, I'm aware of the risks she runs with Grainger, but if she will not listen to you, then she will certainly not listen to me.'

'She has raised Sir Anthony's hopes too high, and indeed, society, too, expects an announcement soon. Caroline hasn't realised what it will do to him when she rejects him—as we know she will. The loss of a rich bride will be nothing compared with the loss of face he will suffer. And that is something Sir Anthony Grainger's pride won't tolerate. He'll seek some sort of revenge, I know he will.'

'I agree. It's also worth remembering that almost the only thing which keeps Sir Anthony's creditors at bay is the prospect of his marriage to a very wealthy woman. For this reason I do try to keep an unobtrusive eye on them both, but for God's sake don't tell Caroline this!'

Lady Danby was happier after this conversation. Lord Coverdale's hopes that Caroline would marry him heartened her. She had already suspected that Caroline was running away from something, and now she knew what it was. Caroline was clearly more attracted to Lord Coverdale than she would admit, and she was afraid. Her stubborn resolve not to marry was being tested to its limits, and her persistent cultivation of Sir Anthony was no more than a desperate attempt to break that attraction. What puzzled Lady Danby was why she should wish to do so!

She decided to tackle her guest one day, and broke one of her house rules and entered Caroline's room without being asked. Caroline was surprised but invited her to sit down.

'My dear, can't you tell me what is behind all this?' Lady Danby asked when they were settled. 'I don't believe you would behave as you are doing without a very good reason.'

Caroline stiffened but said coolly, 'I'm not sure what you mean.'

'Why, your constant appearances in the company of Sir Anthony Grainger.'

'Are you trying to warn me yet again?'

'Against Sir Anthony? I know better than to try. But I am now concerned for *you*. If you carry on encouraging Sir Anthony without eventually becoming engaged to him, you risk being ostracised from Society—not because the *ton* approve of the man himself, but they approve even less of an outright flirt. A jilt. There, I've been frank with you. I hope you appreciate my motive. And now I'll repeat my question. Why are you doing it? Is it because you're running away from a different engagement?'

'What do you mean?' asked Caroline sharply.

'Caroline, I've seen a good few love affairs in my time, including the one between Ivo and Jossie this last year. That had its moments of drama, I assure you! So I am not without experience in these matters. I suspect that you are in love. Not with Anthony Grainger, but with John Ancroft. Now tell me I'm an interfering old woman!'

Caroline was silent for a good few minutes. Then she

said, 'I do love John Ancroft, yes. But I won't marry him!'

'So he *has* asked you?'

'Yes.'

'Then why? Apart from the fact that he must be one of London's most eligible bachelors, he is a fine man! You've said you love him. Why on earth won't you marry him?'

'If I loved him less I should be more likely to consider marrying him! I was hurt quite badly once before by a man I thought I adored, Lady Danby. I won't risk it again.'

'How old were you that first time?'

'Seventeen.'

'Then you are being quite extraordinarily foolish. Seventeen is no age to throw away all the richness that marriage and the love of a decent man can bring. Marry him, Caroline!'

'I won't! I thought he knew me, but he betrayed me!'

'Did he go off with another woman?'

'No! But he believed that I had seduced another man!'

'He was probably wild with jealousy at the time. Caroline, you're too sensible to condemn a good man for one mistake. They're too rare to waste.'

Caroline was silent, and Lady Danby left her alone to think over what she had said.

This conversation had its effect, though the end result was not one which would please Lady Danby. At first Caroline stubbornly dismissed her advice. Lady Danby didn't know the full story. She was wrong in her assumptions. John had not been jealous; his behaviour had been far from that of a decent man... There was no reason to listen to any of it! But she was more influenced by Lady Danby's words than she wanted to admit, and when she found herself wondering whether she *had* judged John too harshly and started to imagine what marriage to him would be like, she panicked. Instead of softening towards John, she pushed the thoughts angrily away, and flirted all the more outrageously with Sir Anthony.

An end had to come. Eventually the time came when Sir Anthony decided he could safely declare himself. During an afternoon drive in his phaeton he offered Mrs Duval his hand, his heart, and his ancient name.

Chapter Fourteen

To do her justice, Caroline had never intended her affair with Sir Anthony to get as far as an actual offer. She thought he had accepted the fact that she was not interested in marriage, and would therefore not risk making one. But she saw now that she had made a mistake. His ardour, or more probably the pressure of his financial commitments, had driven him to disregard her many warnings and she was faced with the embarrassing task of refusing him.

'You do me a great honour, Sir Anthony,' she said slowly. 'I truly hadn't realised that you intended to spring this on me so suddenly...'

'Oh come, my dear!' he said. 'You needn't play feminine games. You're not a blushing débutante. I've had a great deal of encouragement from you in the past few weeks. Don't pretend you're surprised.'

'But I am! I thought I had made it clear that I had no intention of marrying again.'

'I know you said so. But I couldn't possibly take such a ridiculous notion seriously. And I still don't. As my wife, you will have a position in the world that no widow could aspire to. My name is one of the proudest in England.'

'I...I'm sorry if you feel you've been deceived, but I can't accept your very flattering offer. I assure you that, when I told you I would never marry again, I meant every word.'

'But the whole of London expects you to marry me!'

'Then the whole of London will be disappointed!'

He drew in a breath. His face was normally pale, but now it was ashen. For a moment she was frightened, as he gave her a glittering stare, and the fingers holding his whip tightened. But after a moment's visible effort, he smiled ruefully and said, 'I can't deny this is a blow. I've been too hasty, I see. I thought we knew each other well enough for me to hope... No matter. Perhaps I will persuade you to change your mind later.'

'I am quite sure you won't, Sir Anthony. I repeat. I will never marry again.'

'But you—' he began again angrily. Then he stopped short, and smiled again. 'You will have to forgive me. Of course, I must accept what you say. For the moment, at least.' He looked at her and added lightly, 'What an awkward situation! I dare say you would prefer me to take you back to Charles Street?'

'Thank you,' said Caroline, feeling very uncomfortable, and wondering about that first reaction of his. She was sure it had been one not of disappointment, but of fury. The blow to his pride had been immense. But as they drove back he resumed the light-hearted, urbane manner that she had always enjoyed and she was reassured. As they drew to a halt in Charles Street he spoke more seriously again.

'I trust my impulsive actions haven't destroyed our

friendship, Caroline. I've enjoyed your company more than I can say during these past weeks.'

'As I have enjoyed yours. But I think it would be wiser to—'

'Please!'

She looked at him. He seemed quite calm, but his hands were trembling. He saw her glance at them and smiled ruefully. 'You can't blame me for feeling somewhat disappointed that the most beautiful woman in London has turned me down. If you will grant me your occasional company I shall promise not to importune you again. Not till you show me you have changed your mind.'

Somewhat reluctantly she said, 'Very well. As long as you understand, Sir Anthony, that my decision won't change. And, in fairness to both of us, I think we should see rather less of each other.'

'Of course! Good! Good!' He spoke almost disjointedly, and after seeing her down from the phaeton he drove off again without saying anything more.

The gossips soon observed the change in Mrs Duval's behaviour. She seemed to be perfectly friendly with Sir Anthony Grainger, but spent altogether less time with him. The odds on an engagement between them lengthened considerably, and Sir Anthony came in for a fair number of sly digs. He took it all in surprisingly good part. Caroline was impressed and said so to Lady Danby.

'Beware the smile on the face of the tiger,' said that good lady. 'Leopards don't change their spots!'

'I suppose you'll tell me next to watch out for the snake in the grass,' laughed Caroline. 'Well, before you bring out any more of your menagerie, I shall tell you that I shall be as prudent as you could wish. Though I really don't think there's any need. Sir Anthony was surprisingly disappointed, but took my decision very well, and his behaviour since has been exemplary.'

'Ha!' was all Lady Danby could find to say.

The Calthorpes arrived in London and Lady Danby invited them to an evening party. Caroline was introduced to a tall, hazel-eyed man with a most attractive smile. His wife was also tall, dark-haired, and at first sight only moderately good-looking. But when she smiled, which was often, her whole face lit up, the unusual golden-brown eyes glowed and she was suddenly beautiful. It was obvious that they and Lord Coverdale were very good friends, and Caroline remembered that Adam Calthorpe was the man in whom John had confided when they were both wounded in Spain.

John seemed somewhat preoccupied, and spent some time talking quietly to Lady Danby on the other side of the room. At last Caroline couldn't resist going over to ask him if there was anything wrong.

'Wrong? Why should there be?' he asked.

'Don't fob me off, John. I'd like to help if you have a problem. Harriet looks well enough—in fact she gets prettier every time I see her—but is she happy?'

'Perfectly! Especially now that Kate is here to see to her.'

It was unworthy, Caroline told herself, to feel a pang of jealousy. It had always been intended that Lady Calthorpe would sponsor Harriet during the season. In any case she herself was hardly suitable!

John went on, 'Kate has arranged to take Harriet to Lady Danby's dressmaker tomorrow.'

'*Modiste*, John. *Modiste*. Dressmakers don't live in Bruton Street.'

'You know her?'

'Madame Rosa made the dress I'm wearing tonight.'

'In that case, I can have no doubt that Harriet will be well served. You look very lovely in that dress.'

'Good God! Is that a compliment? A genuine, undiluted compliment? This is a rare event.'

He smiled. 'I often think them. I'm not always sure how you'll receive them, so I say nothing.'

Caroline was disarmed. 'A woman is always pleased to hear she is looking her best, sir! But this doesn't put me off. What were you saying to Lady Danby that made you both so serious?'

'I...I was reassuring her. About Harriet's dressmaker. *Modiste!*'

He refused to say any more. Caroline was not satisfied, but when she saw the Calthorpes regarding the two of them with keen interest she had to let the matter drop.

In fact, John had been telling Lady Danby that Sir Anthony's affairs were now in a desperate state. The word in the clubs was that his creditors were closing in on him.

'What happens if he can't pay?' asked Lady Danby.

'If he can't fob them off, and I doubt very much that he can, he will go to prison. Unless he flees the country first.'

'Let's hope he decides to run,' she said. 'We'll be well rid of him.'

'My concern is what he might do before it comes to that. Caroline is a very rich woman.'

'You know he has already asked her and she refused?'

'How on earth should I know that?'

'I'm sure I don't know, Lord Coverdale, but it has happened.'

'So, Grainger now knows she won't marry him, does he?'

'I told you she wouldn't.'

'So you did—and I agreed. Does she realise that she's now at risk? I've told you before, Grainger can be a very dangerous man when cornered.'

'Oh, come! You're being too melodramatic. What can he possibly do?'

'I don't know, but I don't trust him. He still sees Caroline, doesn't he? And she can be a touch foolhardy, wouldn't you say? Scornful of risks?'

She stared at him, then said, 'I'll try to keep an eye on her. It won't be easy.'

'Make sure she keeps Bellerby with her when she goes out.'

'Of course!'

The next afternoon Caroline was walking back along Piccadilly from Hatchard's bookshop when Sir Anthony Grainger drew up beside her.

'Good afternoon!' he called. 'May I take you up?' Caroline hesitated and he added, 'I wish to consult you. Come with me for a short drive in the park and then I promise to deliver you safe and sound to Charles Street in good time to change for dinner.'

She made up her mind. 'Very well!'

It took a minute or two for Sir Anthony to give the reins to his groom and jump down, and Joseph, who had escorted her to the bookshop, took the opportunity to protest. 'It's all right, Joseph!' she said. 'What can anyone do to me in broad daylight, on one of the busiest thoroughfares in London? I really don't think I need you!'

Sir Anthony appeared at her side. 'Ready?' he asked with a smile.

Joseph was still doubtful He stood watching them drive away with a frown on his face.

* * *

'Surly devil, your groom!'

'Joseph is a very faithful servant, Sir Anthony. But I don't think he likes you!'

'The likes or dislikes of a servant are of small consequence!' he said. 'Are you comfortable?'

'Thank you, yes. What was it you wanted to ask me?'

'I've been interested for some time in moving to Jamaica. I understand that life is comparatively cheap there, and, as you've probably heard, it may shortly become necessary for me to leave England. A friend of mine has sent me some views of a certain property on Jamaica. They are very beautiful, but since I have never been there I have no idea whether they are authentic. Could you have a look at them for me?'

'Of course. Where is the property? In Kingston itself?'

'Just outside. Will you come with me now to see these pictures?'

'I…er…I'm not sure… That is—'

'My dear Caroline! I'm asking you out of friendship. I have promised not to ask anything more until you are ready to listen. Surely we can deal sensibly with this?'

'I just wish Joseph was—'

'Shall we return for him? Or, I have a better idea! I could send for him as soon as we arrive. Would that do? Would you come with me if I promised to do that?' He smiled at her so indulgently that she felt she was being too prudish for words.

'Yes,' she said. 'That would do very well. Where are these pictures? In Curzon Street?'

'No, I have them in my other house.'

Caroline hesitated. 'Your other house?'

'It's in Kensington, just a short drive through the park, as I said. The whole excursion shouldn't take long.'

Caroline knew Kensington, which was a pretty little

village not far out of the centre, and a fashionable place to live. She was reassured. 'Where did you say the place in Jamaica is?' she asked as they set off at a good pace through Hyde Park. 'Outside Kingston? Do you have its name?'

'You shall see,' he said. 'I think you will agree that it is extremely beautiful.'

Meanwhile Lady Danby was busy with a houseful of guests. Just after Caroline had left for Hatchard's book-shop, Ivo and Jossie Trenchard had finally arrived in London. A message had been sent to let Lord Coverdale know, and he, Harriet, and the Calthorpes had come round immediately. The reunion between the three veterans of Waterloo was complete, and the house was buzzing with excited questions, exclamations and greetings.

When Joseph arrived on the scene he had difficulty in reaching Lord Coverdale, but as soon as John heard that Mrs Duval's groom was outside he made some hasty excuses and hurried out to see him.

'What is it?'

'He's taken her, Colonel! And I don't trust him to bring her back safe.'

John didn't waste time asking who 'he' was. 'What the devil are you doing here?' he asked angrily. 'Why aren't you with her?'

'She said she didn't need me—he were only taking her for a drive round the park.'

'The fool! I could wring her neck!'

'Best do that after she's safe, Colonel,' Joseph said stolidly. 'I wasted some time going to look for you at Mount Street first. They've been gone half an hour already.'

'Go round to the stables. Get some horses. It might all

be above board, Joseph, in which case we shall meet them in the park. If not... We shall pay a visit to Curzon Street. I'll make my excuses.'

John went back into the room and began to explain why he had to leave so suddenly.

'Hold on, Colonel! Is someone in trouble?'

'I don't know, Ivo.'

'It's Mrs Duval,' said Lady Danby, sounding very worried. 'We think she may be in some danger.'

'It's probably nothing at all, ma'am,' John said encouragingly. 'Grainger could hardly abduct her in broad daylight.'

'Grainger!' exclaimed Ivo. 'That villain! He's capable of anything! I'm coming with you. I'd enjoy a ride in the park, especially if it means I can spike Grainger's guns.'

'I'm coming, too,' said Adam. 'If gossip is to be believed, Grainger's a desperate man at present. I don't think Mrs Duval understands how dangerous he can be.'

John turned to the manservant in the door. 'Get two more horses. Fresh ones. These gentlemen are coming with me.'

A minute or two later the three men left the ladies behind and joined Joseph Bellerby outside.

'Well!' said Jossie Trenchard. 'Will one of you please tell me who this Mrs Duval is? She sounds a complete nitwit to me! Why is everyone so concerned about her?'

Lady Danby exchanged a glance with Kate Calthorpe. 'She comes from Jamaica. A widow. She's staying with me at present.'

'There's something you're not telling me, Godmother! Out with it!'

'We think that the Colonel may be...may be interested in her,' said Kate. 'You'd like her, Jossie. She's certainly not a nitwit.'

'Colonel Ancroft! In *love*? I can't believe it—I've obviously stayed away too long! But wait! Mrs Duval isn't by any chance an *elderly* widow, is she? Did she go north with the Colonel last July?'

'Yes,' said Lady Danby. 'At least, she was in the north. With the Colonel. But she's far from elderly.'

'She's a beauty,' said Kate. 'And Lady Harriet is very fond of her, too. I do hope they find her soon.'

'I wonder...' said Jossie, her sea-green eyes glowing. 'I wonder...' She saw the anxiety on her godmother's face. 'You needn't worry,' she said confidently. 'Those three men dealt with Napoleon. They're not going to let a piece of vermin like Sir Anthony Grainger beat them. But I can't wait to see the Colonel's "elderly widow".'

'She isn't elderly, Jossie. I've just told you.'

'She was when the Colonel first met her.' But when the other two asked her what she meant, Jossie only laughed. 'Don't you remember, Godmama? Ivo told us about her last year.'

The four men found no trace of Sir Anthony's carriage in the park. 'Then it's Curzon Street,' said Ivo.

'Mount Street first. To fetch some pistols. It won't take long.' John led the way to his house, where they armed themselves. Then they went round to Grainger's house in Curzon Street. A band of creditors was waiting outside the front door. John made his way through them and hammered on the door. It was opened by a harassed manservant. 'I've told you,' he said, 'Sir Anthony is not at home!' He made to shut the door, but John put his foot in it.

'In that case, where is he? I'm not one of his creditors. I shan't dun him. Just tell me where I can find him. In fact, I have a guinea or two right here. For you, if you can tell me where to find your master.' The man eyed the gold held in front of him. He drew John into the hall and whispered, 'He went for a drive in the park, but he has a house on the road to Kensington. Grainger Lodge. He might have gone there to avoid this lot.'

'Thank you!' John passed over the money and pushed his way out again.

'He's not there,' he shouted. 'You're wasting your time. Come on, Ivo, Adam. We'll come another day.'

As soon as they were out of sight of the horde, John said tersely, 'Kensington. Grainger Lodge. Come *on*!'

They galloped off again in the direction of the park.

Grainger Lodge lay on the Bath Road some way out of Kensington Village itself. It was quite a substantial house, set in a small park, but somewhat isolated. Remembering the picturesque village street and the pretty houses crowded together, which she had seen before, it was not quite what Caroline had imagined. There was also a remarkable lack of staff, a surly-looking fellow keeping the door the only visible servant. Caroline stopped at the door and turned to her companion. 'Who will fetch Joseph Bellerby?' she demanded.

'I promise to send my groom as soon as you give me the word. He could be back with your servant in half an hour or so.' Sir Anthony laughed. 'Surely you can trust me to restrain myself for such a short time?'

'I'll make sure you do! I'll be frank with you, Sir Anthony. This is not at all what I expected. I don't like the absence of other people around. And I think I've been unwise to accompany you to this house when my friends have no idea where I am. I think I should like you to take me back!'

Sir Anthony looked at her with surprised reproach. 'My

dear girl, don't be so foolish! What have I done to give you such distrust of me? I thought we were still friends, Caroline. And I was so looking forward to having your opinion.'

Caroline eyed him thoughtfully. It was true, he had behaved very well over the last few weeks. It couldn't have been easy for him. She had hurt him once. Perhaps, after all, she owed him something. 'Very well. But I want you to send for Joseph immediately!'

'It shall be done.' He went back to his groom and said a few words. The man nodded and led the horses away. 'Now, let me show you this picture.'

'I thought you said they were views.'

'There is only one that matters. You will be astonished how lovely it is! Come this way! It's in the saloon. The light is better there.' He led the way through to a large, airy room that overlooked the back of the house. At any other time Caroline would have been full of admiration for its outlook. But her eyes were fixed on an easel that stood by one of the windows, placed to get maximum light. The picture on it was draped in a cloth.

'Would you like to draw aside the cloth, Caroline?' The anticipation in his smile made her uneasy.

'No, you do it,' she said. He stepped up and removed the drapery. Caroline caught her breath. The painting on the easel was not a landscape. It was a nude portrait of her, one of a number of such pictures painted in New Orleans, most of which her grandfather had bought up and burnt. After a moment's silence she asked curtly, 'Where did you get this?'

'Beautiful, isn't it? As a view of Jamaica it could hardly be surpassed.'

'Where did you get it?'

'My cousin Edmund sent it. You realise, of course, that

it's a copy, a copy of the one in a certain house in Kingston. I understand men over there pay large sums of money to see the original. Do you think they might do the same here for this copy? Or shall I keep it for my own delectation?'

'*Your* cousin Edmund?'

'And yours. Edmund Willoughby's father married a Grainger—my father's sister.'

Caroline turned to him, the picture forgotten for the moment. '*You* were the one who helped him in his attempts to steal the chalice!'

'Poor Edmund! He didn't do very well in spite of all my efforts. Still, he did send me this after he got back. However, I'm not yet sure what I should do with it. What do you suggest?'

Caroline was herself again. 'You can do what you damned well like with it, Sir Anthony! As a piece of art it isn't worth the canvas it's painted on. A very poor copy!'

'So you wouldn't mind if I displayed it? Not even if it proved embarrassing to your friends?'

Caroline hesitated. Then she said, 'What do you want?'

'That's better! I want what I've always wanted from you. Marriage.'

'I can't believe you love me.'

The mask dropped for a moment from Sir Anthony's face. 'Please!' he exclaimed with contempt. 'Let's not deal in fantasy. If I weren't in the direst necessity I wouldn't for one moment consider marrying the whore who posed for that picture, or was guilty of some of the other antics Edmund told me about. Till now I have been proud of my family name. But alas! I need your fortune. Necessity forces undesirable bedfellows on us all!'

'How right you are! Let me be quite clear on this. You

are threatening to publish this picture unless I marry you. Your…honourable name doesn't object to blackmail?'

'I tried to persuade you first, remember.'

'And I gave you my answer. It is still the same.'

'You deceived me,' he said with sudden passion. 'You led me to believe you would marry me!'

'I did not!'

'You made me a laughing-stock! And you're going to pay for that! One way or another, you'll pay! And I promise you! Unless you agree to marry me—immediately— the world will see that picture!'

'You may be prepared to marry a whore for her money. But I refuse to marry a liar and a cheat, a fraud, and a loser! You haven't the nerve to show that painting, Sir Anthony! My friends would soon have you despatched and you know it!'

Her words stung him. He snarled, 'I doubt your friends will be so anxious to defend you when they see that picture and hear of the tricks you got up to before you came to England. As soon as those stories get out—and they will—there isn't a soul in London who would have anything to do with you!'

'You're wrong! There's one who knows everything you know about me, and more, too, and he would marry me tomorrow if I agreed. No, you can do your worst! I'm not afraid of a cockroach such as you!'

He went white. A new, more vicious, tone entered his voice as he said, 'Are you too stupid to understand? You haven't a choice. If neither persuasion nor blackmail will work, there are other ways of convincing you, not all of them as pleasant! You said yourself that your friends don't know where you are. We are quite alone here, except for my men at the doors, and they won't interfere.

There's no way for you to escape. Oh no, Caroline, I assure you, you'll be happy in the end to marry me!'

'I'd rather kill you first!' Even as Caroline hurled this defiance at him she was cursing her stupidity in coming here so unprotected. She didn't even have her pistol...

The blow from his fist on the side of her head was so completely unexpected that she staggered and almost fell.

'How?' he asked softly, advancing towards her. 'How will you kill me, Caroline?' He aimed another blow, but she managed to dodge it and ran round the other side of the table in the centre of the room. His whip lay where he had left it on the table. Snatching it up, she let fly with it. It caught him full in the face. He gave a shout of pain, but quickly recovered and grabbed the end of the whip, jerking it out of her hand.

'Something else to add to the score,' he said thickly, wiping a trickle of blood from his cheek. 'It will be a pleasure to teach you a lesson.'

Caroline picked up a heavy candlestick that stood on the console nearby. 'You'll have to catch me first,' she said.

'I will, my dear, I will,' Sir Anthony said, coming slowly round the end of the table. 'Eventually.'

Keeping her eye on him, Caroline edged away towards a side table. On it was a favourite weapon. She picked up the decanter in her free hand and smashed it against the wall. A stream of red wine splashed over her dress like blood. 'You won't find it easy,' she said fiercely, holding the jagged edges towards him.

'No?' With a sudden flick of his wrist he sent the whip snaking across to wind itself round her wrist. He gave it a vicious tug and the decanter dropped from a hand that was suddenly nerveless. Beside herself with pain and fury, she threw the candlestick at him. It caught him on his shoulder, but didn't stop him. With a shout of triumph he rushed towards her and threw her against the table.

'Now who's master?' he gloated, pinning her beneath him and forcing cruel kisses on her.

The feel of his body pressed hard against hers made her feel sick, his hot breath was stifling her... Caroline fought like a demon, using all the tricks she knew, but he was stronger than she was and he knew it. He pressed her back over the table, till she thought her spine would snap. She thought briefly of John. How she wished she could have told him what she really felt about him, how much she loved him! Too late now. Her strength was failing, but she would kill herself before she gave in to this madman. Though, she thought with a last touch of irony, it looked as if Sir Anthony was crazed enough to do that for her. In his fury he appeared to have forgotten that he needed her alive! He was staring wildly, his hands round her throat, squeezing the breath out of her lungs. She felt herself growing dizzy...

John burst through the door and what he saw brought a mist of rage to his eyes. With a roar of anger he leapt through the room, took Sir Anthony by the collar and flung him away to the floor, uncaring that his quarry landed with his head hard against the leg of the side table. He pulled Caroline up and cradled her. 'Are you all right?' he asked, his voice hoarse with anxiety.

'John!' she said faintly. 'John, it's you! Oh, thank God! Thank God!'

Still holding her, John turned to face Sir Anthony, who was struggling to his feet, trying to pull a gun out of his pocket at the same time.

John drew his own pistol. 'I'm a better shot than you, Grainger,' he said levelly. 'Though there's nothing I'd like better, don't tempt me to shoot you. Put the gun down. Put it down, I say!'

Sir Anthony had little fight left in him. His sundry hurts got the better of him, and he threw the gun away and collapsed to the floor again.

John's two friends came in, looking remarkably cool for two men who had just dealt, very roughly, with Sir Anthony's henchmen. 'Pity!' said Ivo, dusting his hands. 'I see we're too late. I'd have enjoyed dealing with this one, too.'

'You can take him away,' said John. 'Where are the others?'

'Tied up in the cellar with Bellerby in charge. He might now consent to march them to the watch house. There's one just down the road. Till now he's refused to leave the house before he knew Mrs Duval was safe. What shall we do with this fellow?' Adam asked.

'I don't want him taken with the others. Take him to the cellar and leave him there for the moment. I need to think.' He turned to Caroline, who had been held close to him throughout this. 'Caroline?'

'John, I...I thought I...' Caroline burst into tears.

'Oh, my love, my darling!' John said shakily, folding her close in his arms and kissing her. 'Don't cry, I can't bear it. Caroline, my love...'

Ivo and Adam looked on with amazement at the scene before them. Was this Colonel Ancroft, the stiffest, most coldly reserved of all Wellington's officers, passionately comforting a woman, who, in spite of her distraught state, her tumbled hair, her dishevelled clothes, was one of the most attractive women they had ever seen? They could hardly believe it. But then, as the kiss showed no signs of coming to an end, the two friends recalled their manners, went over to Sir Anthony and hauled him to his feet.

Their Colonel didn't even notice them leaving, as they removed their captive, and took him to join the others in the cellar.

When they returned after a suitable interval, they were relieved to find the atmosphere slightly less intense, though Caroline was still held close to the Colonel's side.

'What's this?' asked Adam as he picked up a picture that had fallen to the floor. 'Good God!' he exclaimed, as he put it back on the easel. He threw a quick glance at Caroline, then stammered, 'Excuse me, ma'am! I didn't realise…'

John said, 'What is it?' and went to look, closely followed by Ivo.

'Good God!' they said, practically in unison. Ivo looked back at Caroline with renewed interest.

John cleared his throat. 'You'll forget you ever saw this,' he said sternly to the other two.

Lords Calthorpe and Trenchard both hastened to assure him they would, indeed they would, on their honour!

'It's a very poor forgery,' said John. 'Nothing like the original.'

'But, John, how did you know that?' asked Caroline in amazement. 'You've never seen the original!'

'Oh, yes, I have,' said John. 'Twice.'

Adam and Ivo watched with interest as Mrs Duval, who had so far not turned a hair, even while they examined her portrait, was suddenly scarlet with embarrassment. 'John!' she exclaimed. 'How could you! What will your friends think?'

'That you'll *have* to marry me now,' he said with satisfaction.

Caroline looked at him and started to laugh. She turned to Adam. 'Lord Calthorpe, I am more obliged than I can say for your help in rescuing me. If you can forget every second of the last five minutes, I should be even more obliged.'

'Readily, ma'am. On one condition.'

'Really?' said Caroline raising an eyebrow.

'That you'll put my commanding officer out of his misery. I haven't yet heard you say yes.'

Caroline's lovely smile flashed out. 'I'll do that with all my heart!' She turned to John. 'Can you forget the stupid things I've said?'

'If you'll forgive the stupid things I've done.'

'It's a bargain. I'll marry you, John.' He took her hand and kissed it, then drew her to him again. Ivo cleared his throat apologetically.

'Er... Strange as it may seem, I haven't yet been introduced to the lady at present in your arms, Colonel.' With a wicked twinkle in his eye he added, 'Though I feel I already know her quite well.'

Caroline burst out laughing again. 'I've waited so long to meet you, Lord Trenchard. I've heard so much about you and your wife. But I never thought the meeting would be quite as unconventional as this!'

'I'm honoured to make your acquaintance, Mrs Duval. May I wish you and John all happiness?'

'And I,' said Adam. 'But we still haven't settled the problem of Sir Anthony.'

'May I make a suggestion?' said Caroline.

'About Sir Anthony?'

'He said he was thinking of going to Jamaica to escape his creditors. I think it might be wise to help him on his way.'

'He certainly can't stay in England without being sent to a debtors' prison,' John said thoughtfully. 'He won't want to risk that. I think it's a good idea.'

'But that means he gets away with attacking Mrs Duval!' exclaimed Ivo.

'A court case might be...a touch embarrassing?' suggested Adam. 'Evidence, and so on... Not that I'm remembering anything, mind!'

'Quite! I think we should adopt Caroline's suggestion. I've already sent one man off to Jamaica. Sir Anthony can follow him. Betts will deal with it.'

'He can join his cousin,' said Caroline. 'Two villains together.'

They returned to Charles Street, and while Caroline escaped to her room to make herself respectable, the gentlemen gave their version of the events in Grainger Lodge. By the time she came downstairs they were waiting for her, glasses at the ready and several bottles of champagne in a cooler on the side. John handed her a glass, and smiled deep into her eyes, giving her his own private toast. Lady Danby dismissed the servants who had been busy laying refreshments out on the table, then raised her glass.

'There are so many toasts that I don't know where to begin! To Caroline and Lord Coverdale. Happiness and long life! I can't say how relieved I am that you've finally come to your senses, Caroline! And I hope Lord Coverdale realizes what a lucky man he is!'

They laughed and drank and she went on, 'Next, to Jossie and Ivo. Welcome back to England. We've missed you! And...' she paused, and gave a mischievous glance first at Kate and then at Jossie '...to the future generation! To the first young Trenchard, and the second young Calthorpe!' New exclamations and congratulations ensued, as Kate and Jossie laughed and shook their heads at Lady Danby.

Then Caroline stepped forward. 'I am so glad you are all here. And I'd like to propose a toast to our own future generation. To the first young Ancroft. To Harriet!' She held out her arms and Harriet ran to her and was roundly hugged.

Finally, John held up his hand.

'A last toast,' he said. 'To Wellington and the men of Waterloo. To all those who, like Kate's brother, our friend Tom Payne, didn't survive. And to those of us who did.'

It was a solemn moment. They stood round in a circle and raised their glasses. Lady Danby stood beside Captain Lord Trenchard and his Jossie. Major Lord Calthorpe had a comforting arm round Kate. And Colonel Ancroft, now Lord Coverdale, stood with Harriet, his daughter, on one side—and Caroline, his love, on the other.

'The Duke!' they said. 'And the men of Waterloo!'

* * * * *

Watch out for more in Miranda Jarrett's
Sparhawk series!
The Sparhawk Bride
by Miranda Jarrett
is available next month in
Regency High-Society Affairs, Volume 7

Regency

HIGH-SOCIETY AFFAIRS

BOOK SEVEN

These dangerous gentlemen are bent on seduction

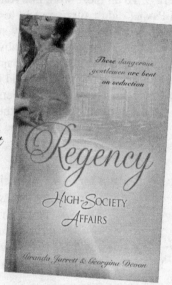

The Sparhawk Bride by Miranda Jarrett
The Rogue's Seduction by Georgina Devon

On sale 4th September 2009